This boo

THE KING'S AGENT

THE

King's Agent

BY

J. Kent Clark

New York

CHARLES SCRIBNER'S SONS

THE KING'S AGENT

CHAPTER

One

IT OCCURRED to Sir Ralph Barnard, as he waited for Lord Stair's secretary to announce him, that he had spent all his life waiting. He had waited for generals, for ministers, for women, for servants, for informers, and for kings. He had waited for orders, remittances, dispatches, decisions, and letters. Now, he reflected with a wry smile, he must wait to see whether Lord Stair would pardon him for his past life, for having awaited the wrong people and the wrong events.

Outside, he noticed idly, a soggy French rain was drenching the embassy garden. The garden was a poor one at best, even by Paris standards; in the March rain it appeared particularly depressing. He often wondered how the French endured their weather, the wet cobblestones, the limp trees, and the sloshing gutters. In twenty-seven years, he had not grown used to it. There was a good deal of rain in England, of course; but in England, rain meant something entirely different. It meant wet gorse, washed tiles, and snug fires. England was cleansed by rain, not turned into a quagmire.

Sir Ralph looked away from the window and began once again to study the other people waiting in Lord Stair's antechamber. When he had first come in, he had been relieved that he knew no one. The news of his decision was sure to get abroad eventually, but he hoped he could keep it secret until Lord Stair gave his verdict. It was good to know that he was not recognized. He could regard his companions in waiting with almost complete detachment.

Two of the eight were evidently Lord Stair's countrymen. From their lank frames, their severe wigs, and their sober black coats, one could be reasonably sure they were Scottish merchants; one could hear the cadences and burring of their talk, even though the softly spoken words were indistinguishable.

Another man, lounging half-asleep in a high-backed chair, was easy to identify. The comfortable paunch, the rich green coat, the broad shoebuckles, and the slightly ill-fitting breeches marked him as the travelling English gentleman. The papers sticking out from his pocket were probably letters of reference and credit. He had undoubtedly come to get information, advice, and further letters of reference from Lord Stair. One saw many such gentlemen these days, now that the wars were over and the continent completely open to English travellers.

The other five people, four men and a woman, appeared to be debris from the Jacobite cause. Although no two were dressed alike, or resembled each other in general appearance, there was an unmistakable similarity about their manner. The faces wore a look of restrained anxiety and frustrated hope as if their owners had abandoned their dreams and feared nothing could be salvaged from reality. Sir Ralph had seen the look so often he had become hardened to it. Still, it gave him a vague uneasiness. If he were not careful, his old feeling of personal responsibility would come back.

Sir Ralph hoped that his own face showed no such signs. After all, his case was entirely different—perhaps worse but certainly different. These people were the hangers-on of the cause. They were someone's servants, or relatives, or agents. Now that the money and prospects of their principals had vanished, they could no longer be supported. They could follow their inclinations and sue to return to England. Their very obscurity would make pardon easy, unless by ill chance they had offended someone with power. Obviously, these applicants had convinced themselves that they had good prospects; otherwise, they would have tried to slip back without official sanction, to endure the perpetual fear of discovery. Even so, the nervous strain written on their faces showed the fear with which they put their chances to the touch. Most of them must have lived for years on what they thought were good prospects. One could hardly blame them for distrusting good prospects.

No, Sir Ralph told himself, he had never been deceived about the chances. He must always have known that some day, unless he was killed, he would be waiting in the antechamber of an English ambassador. What he had not foreseen were the particular events that would lead him there. They still seemed strange, even though he had experienced them. They appeared now to be a long series of accidents leading to a foregone conclusion.

The return of Lord Stair's secretary seemed almost an impertinence, an interruption of an interesting line of thought. Sir Ralph straightened himself, endeavoring, he supposed, to look more impressive to the bustling, officious young Scotsman coming toward him.

"His lordship will see you now, Sir," the man said. "Will it please you to follow me?"

As Sir Ralph rose from his chair and followed the secretary, his meditative detachment vanished. A buzz of excitement seemed to rise inside him. The engagement was beginning; the forces were committed. He hoped, briefly, that his self-control would not desert him, that his hands and voice would be steady. Beyond this he refused to think.

"Your lordship, allow me to present Sir Ralph Barnard," he heard the secretary saying. "Sir Ralph, His Excellency the Earl of Stair."

Sir Ralph concentrated upon the precision of his bow. "Your servant, Sir," he said.

"I am greatly honored," said Lord Stair bowing. "You will forgive me if I look at you closely. We have almost met many times."

"Not at all, your lordship."

Lord Stair, he observed, did not correspond with his description. He was much taller than he had been pictured, standing well over six feet, even without the addition of the full, powdered wig. He also appeared very young for a man who had fought at Steinkirk—not over thirty-five, although he must be at least forty.

"And now," said Lord Stair, "may I ask how I can be of use to you? From your note I assume you have some matter of importance you wish to discuss."

Sir Ralph took a deep breath, and looked at Lord Stair carefully. "Yes, your lordship. I want to return to England."

Now that he had said the words, he felt relieved and calm. He watched Lord Stair move to his desk without speaking, motioning him to a chair.

"I suppose," he went on, "that since receiving my note you have had time to examine my dossier and to reach some tentative conclusions."

"I fear you flatter me," Lord Stair said. "I did, indeed, refresh my memory on your career, but since I had no notion that you were contemplating a return to England, I did not attempt to reach any decisions on the subject. Even now I find your statement hard to believe. I could hardly be more astonished if the Pretender himself applied for a passport."

"Believe me, my lord, I am in earnest. I am ready to put my case before you as openly as possible and rely on your judgment and that of your government to arrive at a just decision."

Lord Stair was silent for a moment. His face remained pleasantly bland and noncommittal, but his fingers began to tap reflectively. He hitched himself forward in his chair until the brocade on his red coat touched the desk.

"I am to understand, then," he said slowly, "that you will renounce the Stuarts and swear allegiance to His Majesty King George."

Sir Ralph was surprised to find how easily his words came now they were started. "Yes, your lordship," he said. "That is what I mean."

"You must forgive me for appearing dull and incredulous," said Lord Stair; "you can realize how unbelievable this seems. Our party has seen many Jacobites come and go during the past twenty-five years; we have seen Jacobites created and uncreated by each turn of events. But we have never had cause to doubt your complete fidelity to your misguided, unlucky masters."

Sir Ralph felt his color begin to rise. "I accept your rebuke, my lord. No doubt I am a traitor."

The expression on Lord Stair's face did not change. "Not at all, Sir Ralph," he said. "I implied no such thing. I should be a traitor myself if I considered desertion of the Pretender treason. Please understand that I applaud your action, if it is sincere. My duty is to be sure that it is. You know, of course, that His Majesty's government cannot risk bringing you home without being certain of your complete change of heart. England has enough Jacobites already."

"I understand perfectly," Sir Ralph said. "I hope to convince you."

"And there is another consideration also, perhaps a more difficult one. It must be proved that you have committed no unpardonable crime against the state. Otherwise you could be brought home only for punishment."

"As the Jacobite rebels in Scotland are to be punished, I assume."

"Exactly. You must realize that the government is anxious to heal old wounds and to extend clemency wherever possible; but it is compelled to regard armed insurrection as treason. My foolish Jacobite countrymen knew this when they took up arms. No one regrets the necessity more than I."

Sir Ralph heard himself sigh. "Perhaps I do, my lord," he said, "but I do not intend to argue the point. For the present we are concerned only with my political crimes. I see you have my dossier on your desk. If your agents have been industrious, you should have all the information you need to make a decision."

"You are very observant, Sir Ralph," said Lord Stair, picking up the sheaf of papers and leafing through them negligently. "Yes, I

think we have a great deal of information about you. I am sure you
would be flattered if you knew the time, labor, and money expended
to get it. Our informants, I might add, were the best available. We
know, for instance, that you were at Boyne, Limerick, Steinkirk,
Landen, Blenheim, Ramillies, Almanza, and Malplaquet. We know
that you were in England three times after the Revolution, once at
the time of the Fenwick plot; also twice in Amsterdam and once
in Vienna. We know many other things about you—enough, in short,
to corroborate or disprove whatever you may say. I will not pretend,
however, that we have all the facts about you, or even the most
interesting facts. As you know, the really vital information has a way
of escaping from documents, however carefully prepared."

For a moment Sir Ralph allowed himself to stare at the papers.
There it was, his life as seen through the eyes of miscellaneous informers. It would be interesting to know who they were, which
soldiers, servants, chance acquaintances, innkeepers, women, politicians, and friends had been in the pay of the English government.

"You may ask me what questions you like," he said. "I am at your
disposal."

Lord Stair smiled. "There will be time later to examine you on
your record—after you have written me a complete report of your
actions. For the present I am interested in knowing what prompted
your decision to return to England."

"Many things, my lord," Sir Ralph said slowly. "One of them was
my age. I am now fifty-five, as you know—much too old to be wandering on the Continent, or even settled in France. It is time I went
home. Another is my sons. Now, at twelve and fourteen, they are
more French than English. Unless I go quickly they will never be
anything but Frenchmen. You understand my feelings, I suppose?"

"I think I do," said Lord Stair.

"And then there is the fact that the Jacobite cause is irrevocably
lost. The rising in Scotland, undertaken against my advice, was the
final demonstration that everything is finished. Oh, there are still
madmen who will carry on. There will undoubtedly be more bloodshed sooner or later. But I am a reasonable man, your lordship. Nothing can help the Stuarts now, and I see no reason for wearing out the
rest of my life trying."

"I am glad you realize the futility of resistance," said Lord Stair.
"I could wish that more of your party had your sanity. My work
would be considerably easier. Unfortunately, conspiracy still goes
on. The madmen, as you call them, are hard to convince."

"That is true, my lord," said Sir Ralph, "but they are madmen nevertheless."

Lord Stair put down the papers and leaned back in his chair, letting his gaze wander about the room and then back again to Sir Ralph. "I take it then," he said, "you feel you have done your duty; you may now resign honorably."

"Frankly your lordship, I don't know." Sir Ralph could feel himself struggling for words. "It has been my misfortune never to be sure what my duty was. Very probably my duty was something entirely different from what I have done. You see, my lord, I once had a chance to change the entire course of events. By performing one single, simple crime I might have saved two hundred thousand lives, perhaps more. Since then I have been expiating my failure, if it was a failure. I don't know that I have been successful. I only know I am through trying. As far as young James is concerned—the Pretender, if you will—I shall never lift another finger for him. I have done enough."

Although the expression on Lord Stair's face did not change, Sir Ralph could see a subtle change in his manner. His muscles seemed to have tightened imperceptibly. He looked as if he were about ready to rise from his chair. Then he seemed consciously to relax.

"You must pardon me again, Sir Ralph," he said. "The morning has been full of surprises. I don't seem to grasp what you are talking about. What is this about a crime you fancy might have changed the fate of England?"

"My lord," said Sir Ralph, carefully choosing his words, "on June 13, 1688, I had a perfect opportunity to assassinate King James II."

Now that he had spoken, the words seemed to hang in the air. The room was so still he could hear Lord Stair breathing. The man had lowered his head so that his chin was almost buried in his cravat. His breath, coming at slow, regular intervals, stirred the ruffles. Finally, after what seemed a long time, he looked up. The bland impassivity had disappeared from his long Scots face.

"Will you please say that again?" he said.

Sir Ralph nodded. "I said that shortly after the birth of young James and shortly before the Revolution, I had a perfect opportunity to kill the King. I failed to do it."

Lord Stair stood up. Without a word he began to walk around the room, past the tall windows, past the long table with the candelabra, past the door, and back past the desk. He seemed to have forgotten that anyone else was in the room. Then he turned abruptly.

"You can't be serious."

"But I am, my lord," Sir Ralph said, keeping his voice as steady and even as possible. "Until you know that fact, you know nothing about me. The record in my dossier will never make sense to you. You will not be able to understand how I became a Jacobite in the first place, or why it is safe now to let me return to England."

Lord Stair sat down again as suddenly as he had got up. Now that he was excited, a faint Scottish accent began to appear in his carefully studied English. "Let me see if I follow you, man," he said. "If you are not trying some obscure trick, and if you have not gone mad, you must seriously believe that you might have prevented the Revolution by killing King James?"

"I am sure of it, my lord," Sir Ralph said calmly. "When you have had time to think of the possibilities, I believe you will agree with me."

"At the moment," said Lord Stair, "I am not interested in the possibilities. You may very well be right about them. Right now I am trying to make out your position in the matter. If what you say is true, you are personally responsible for the bloodshed that followed."

"That is true, my lord," Sir Ralph said. "That is what I said. I hope, however, that you will not blame me too severely for not committing a murder. God knows I have repented often enough."

Lord Stair appeared to be engrossed in a perplexing tangle of thought. "But that means you have had all those deaths on your conscience."

"That is true too, my lord; and I would not be thought to deprecate the effects of a bad conscience. But you must remember, my lord, that I am not a Presbyterian like you. Among us Anglicans, I find, conscience operates only in the young. By the time a man reaches my age, he has nothing but a set of habits and a way of calculating probabilities. Perhaps this is one of the few advantages of age and Anglicanism."

"And also it is your fault," Lord Stair seemed not to have heard the interruption, "that the Pretender is not king of England."

"Yes, my lord."

"But at the time you made your decision you had no way of knowing what would happen; so you can hardly be responsible." Lord Stair shook his head stubbornly.

"Oh yes, my lord. The results were easy to foresee." The conversation began to remind Sir Ralph of the debates he had once carried on in his insomnia. "You must not forget that I was the King's agent. I had all the information possible. But even if I had not been, I think I could have predicted the approximate results. As soon as the young prince was born, a child could have foreseen that revolution was inevitable unless James were put out of the way; and a reasonably bright child could have seen how this would affect the posture of affairs in Europe. No, your lordship, if I am to be exculpated, it cannot be on the grounds of ignorance. In some ways the results were not as bloody as I had anticipated, at least not in England."

Lord Stair stroked his long chin and gazed absently at the rainstreaked windows. "There was always hope, however, that something unforeseen would change the course of events. You could hardly commit a murder on mere probability."

"Yes, my lord, there was always hope. James might have had apoplexy; the child might have died; James might have apostatized. But the hopes were unreasonable, and I knew it. No one has tried to delude himself with false hopes more than I, but I have never been very successful."

"You feel then," said Lord Stair, "that you should have committed the murder?"

Sir Ralph let his thoughts run over the question again, knowing in advance that no new insight would result. "I have often thought so, your lordship," he said, "but I don't know how I feel now. I am determined to quit thinking about the subject."

"One more question," said Lord Stair. "Why didn't you do the deed when you had the opportunity?"

"I don't know," Sir Ralph said. "I really don't know."

Lord Stair sat up straight. His face had resumed its normal expression. There was no evidence now that he had ever been disconcerted. "What you have said is extremely interesting, Sir Ralph," he said briskly. "I confess, it gives your case a different, not to say strange, aspect. You can readily understand that I will need time to consider all the implications. Meantime, I would be grateful if you would prepare a detailed statement of your activities, together with their motives, from the time you entered King James's service in 1685 to the first of March of this year, 1716. As I told you, this will allow me to compare your statement with our records."

"And to acquire additional information about Jacobite activities," Sir Ralph added.

"Exactly," said Lord Stair. "When you make your report I should be grateful if you would give particular attention to the Fenwick plot, the intended invasion of 1707, and the transactions at the time of Queen Anne's death."

Sir Ralph allowed himself a bleak smile.

"I shall do my best for you, my lord; but I must tell you frankly that I will never write down what I have told you. That information is for your ears alone, to help you in judging my case. If you report it, I shall be obliged to deny it. I must say further that I shall write down only what concerns my own particular activities. You must not expect me to turn informer."

"I can understand your feelings," said Lord Stair. "I merely ask you to remember that your return depends upon the complete honesty of your account."

"I shall remember, your lordship," Sir Ralph said. "When would you like to have my report?"

"I shall await your convenience," said Lord Stair. "Please let me know when you are ready to see me again."

Sir Ralph nodded. "Certainly, my lord," he said. "Is there anything else you would like to know now?"

"Only one small detail," said Lord Stair. "Did you ever talk to anyone else about what you have told me? Is there someone who could corroborate the allegation that you actually considered assassinating the King? Someone you knew at the time."

"Yes, my lord." Sir Ralph took a deep breath. "I discussed the possibility with one person. Aside from that person I have told no one."

"And that person?" Lord Stair leaned forward again.

"Esther Hemphill, my lord."

"Ah yes, Lady Sheldon," said Lord Stair.

"I suppose you know her."

"I have met her a few times. I cannot honestly say that I know her."

"I thought, my lord, that as a good Whig you would know her very well."

"I have not been so fortunate," Lord Stair said, rising. "Perhaps I shall be soon."

Sir Ralph rose. "If there is nothing else, your lordship, I will not impose further on your time. You have several other clients waiting."

"It has been a pleasure," said Lord Stair, with a slight bow. "I shall expect to see you soon. Perhaps Monday."

As Sir Ralph started toward the door, the secretary reappeared.

"Will you please show Sir Ralph out and send in Mr. Andrew Herbert," said Lord Stair.

Following the secretary through the antechamber, Sir Ralph noticed that two more men had come in, obviously Frenchmen. The others were still sitting in the same places, as if they were rooted there. To see them made Sir Ralph uncomfortable; he was glad when he got out into the hall. With a perfunctory goodbye to the secretary, he picked up his hat and great coat, and stepped outside. It was still raining.

CHAPTER

TWO

"YOU LIKE the rain, Monsieur?"

The harsh French voice, sudden as a blow, halted Sir Ralph in mid stride. He had whirled half way round, his back against the dripping wall, before he recognized the sound.

"D'Argenson," he said. "What are you doing here?"

The man gave a grating chuckle as he stepped out from the doorway which had concealed him. He seemed to be enjoying the shock he had produced.

"It is the rain," he said. "I like walking in it. You like the rain too, I see."

God's fish, but the man is hideous, Sir Ralph thought. Small wonder he terrifies the Parisians.

"No, Monsieur," he said aloud, "I do not like the rain. I want to get out of it as soon as I can."

D'Argenson's smile distorted the long scar that ran across his cheek. "That is the trouble with you English, Monsieur Barnard; you are too melancholy. Three days of Paris rain would drive your whole nation to suicide. I should have to triple the watch on the Seine bridges. As it is, every month or so one of your Jacobite compatriots tries to drown himself. You were not trying to drown yourself, were you?"

"No," Sir Ralph said, "I was not thinking of drowning myself."

"Very good." The contorted smile had not left d'Argenson's face, but his voice was serious. "One can never be certain about you English."

"You can be easy about me," Sir Ralph said, "unless, of course, we both drown while we are standing here."

"Ah yes, the rain. You must pardon me for delaying you. Perhaps you will permit me to accompany you for a short distance."

"I shall be flattered." Sir Ralph tried to keep the suspicion out of his voice. "It is not often that I am escorted by the lieutenant general of police."

Could this be coincidence, he asked himself, or had d'Argenson been waiting for him?

"I should suppose," he continued, "that on a day like this you police would be too busy to walk around in the rain."

"On the contrary, Monsieur." D'Argenson evaded a large puddle. "On a day like this Paris can be trusted to mind itself. What Frenchman would go out on such a day to pick pockets or burglarize houses?"

"I understand," Sir Ralph said.

"No, Monsieur, on such days one has only to deal with crimes of brooding and passion. Among the French, rape and murder; among the English, suicide."

D'Argenson looked up along the row of drizzling roof tiles as if he were calculating the amount of violence that might be expected from this particular rain. For the moment, he reminded Sir Ralph of a thoughtful gargoyle.

"I suppose then, Monsieur d'Argenson, that you are strolling about trying to prevent rape and murder."

"Not at all, Monsieur. Who can prevent rape and murder? One is fortunate to catch the criminals afterwards. Ah, but I see you were laughing at me."

"Laughing?" Sir Ralph said. "I assure you, I was not. I thought you had found some method of your own—something we English have not discovered."

"You are too generous, Monsieur Barnard." D'Argenson's voice had become almost pleasant. "But alas, there is no such method. If a man wants to commit rape or murder, there is no one who can stop him."

"Except himself," Sir Ralph said softly.

"Yes, Monsieur, except himself. I see you understand these matters very well."

Sir Ralph could feel d'Argenson studying him, but he kept his own eyes fixed upon the wet cobblestones ahead of him.

"It is different with a conspiracy," d'Argenson said. "Conspirators, you know, frequently talk too much, and they often act like conspirators."

"Yes, I know."

"But one man determined to commit murder cannot be prevented, unless he is extraordinarily stupid or unlucky."

"I have already agreed, Monsieur."

"So you have."

Was it possible, Sir Ralph asked himself, that d'Argenson suspected him of some criminal plot? Was this a circuitous cross-examination?

"No, Monsieur," the man was saying. "If someone wanted to assassinate the Regent himself, I doubt that I could stop him."

"I doubt it too," Sir Ralph said. "But don't you think we have discussed murder long enough? It is a depressing subject for such a day."

"A thousand pardons, Monsieur. I keep forgetting that you are an Englishman. You prefer to discuss rape, I suppose."

"Not particularly."

"What a pity." A trace of the rasping chuckle returned. "It is a fascinating study. A terrible problem in the provinces. In Paris, fortunately, the ladies are more complaisant. One is seldom troubled—except, as I said, on days like this."

"I am happy to hear it," Sir Ralph said.

Ahead, through the rain, he could see where the street joined the road which ran along the bank of the river. The water itself was not visible yet, but he could easily picture it in his imagination. It would be seething now as the rain poured into it.

"That brings us back to suicide," d'Argenson said. "Tell me, Monsieur, did you ever contemplate it?"

Sir Ralph, glancing quickly, could not tell from the expression on the ugly face how seriously the question was intended.

"I am not sure," he said reflectively. "Once a long time ago, I thought about suicide; but now I can hardly believe that I actually considered going through with it."

"Very good, Monsieur. Now tell me something else, if you please. Are you in any sort of financial distress?"

"No, Monsieur. Do I look as if I were?"

"Certainly not, but one must be sure. You should not be offended."

"I am not in the habit of discussing my finances, Monsieur d'Argenson, but if it will relieve your mind I will tell you this much: besides the income from a small estate in England and my wife's property near Arras, I have some investments in Paris and my half pay from the French Army."

"Thank you, Monsieur. That is what I wanted to know. Now, one more question, if you don't mind. You have a charming French wife and two fine sons, is that right?"

"That is right, Monsieur."

"Then you would not kill yourself no matter what Milord Stair might say?"

Sir Ralph stopped in his tracks. D'Argenson plodded on two or three steps before he turned around.

"You were watching Lord Stair's house."

"Yes, Monsieur." D'Argenson removed his hat and shook the water out of the broad brim. "When one goes out on days like this to look for trouble, he must look where trouble already exists."

"And you think I might kill myself."

"It is possible, Monsieur. As I said, I have fished too many of your countrymen out of the river."

"Let me assure you again, Monsieur, I shall not kill myself, no matter what happens."

"Ah, good. I take it, then, that Milord Stair has not refused to let you go back to England."

"Not yet, Monsieur. There is a chance."

"Truly? Then, Monsieur Barnard, I can relax—for a time."

D'Argenson was still holding his hat in his hand, gazing at the bedraggled feather, apparently oblivious of the rain pelting down on his wig.

"Yes, you may relax," Sir Ralph said. "And I should be grateful for a favor."

"What is it, Monsieur?"

"I should like your promise that you will tell no one you saw me at Lord Stair's."

"You have my word."

"Thank you, Monsieur d'Argenson. Now if you don't object, I must hurry along. Henriette, my wife, will be expecting me."

"Of course," d'Argenson said. "There is just one thing more."

"Name it."

"I hope you will not be offended if I accompany you until you have crossed the bridge over the Seine."

Sir Ralph managed a smile. "Not at all, Monsieur," he said.

The rain had almost stopped by the time he reached his own street. It was easier now, he found, to be amused at d'Argenson's notions, to be a little less depressed by the probability of a lifetime in Paris. True the little suburban gardens were pathetic, true the eternal walls and cobblestones were monotonous, but one could endure them. One might even be able to extend to them some of the affection he felt for his own house and garden, although it would be difficult to do, especially if there were no hope of leaving. Impatiently he brushed the thought from his mind. For the present he

would think only of getting away. There would be time for practicing
endurance if all else failed.

Henriette met him at the door.

"Where have you been?" she asked quickly, giving him a hasty,
preoccupied kiss. "I have been worried about you."

"There was no need to worry," he said reassuringly. "I was in no
danger."

"But there was a man here."

"A man?"

"Yes, one of your Jacobites. I think he must have come from young
James himself. He said it was very urgent."

Henriette's concern was clearly registered in her face and in her
rapid volleys of French. In moments of stress the English she
prided herself upon proved totally inadequate. In spite of his own
concern at her news, Sir Ralph had the impulse to kiss her. Instead he slowly and deliberately removed his wet coat.

"Did you ask him what he wanted?" he said calmly.

"He would only say that he wished to see you. But I know he
wants you to go on some mission."

"How do you know?"

"From the way he acted, of course." Henriette pulled a wry face.
"When there is nothing in the wind, those people come in as casually
as anyone else, but as soon as they get some commission, they become important and mysterious. This one was only about twenty
years old. But he had a mission. I am sure of it."

"When is he coming back?"

"This evening—or so he said. But remember, you promised you
would never accept another mission. You said you had resigned."

"I have resigned," he said, struggling with his sword belt. "There
will be no more missions."

"Are you sure?" Henriette's voice was deeply troubled. "You said
the same thing after Malplaquet, remember?"

"Yes, I remember," he said slowly. "But things were different then.
The war was still going on, and the Duke of Berwick needed me."

"But certainly he needed you. Someone will always need you. The
Jacobites need you now."

"Very likely." He sat down and began to remove his wet shoes
and stockings. "But this time I am through. I have already taken
steps."

"Please listen to me, Ralph. The Jacobites don't need you as much
as the boys and I do. You have done enough. We have done enough.
You don't know what it means to be always waiting for you."

Sir Ralph reached out and took her hand. It was trembling, he noticed. She seemed to be on the verge of tears.

"Please, Henriette. I said I had taken steps."

"It is not fair," she said, as if she had not heard. "You have never had to answer the door when the messenger came. You have never suffered that sick moment wondering whether the message is a note from you or the regrets of the war minister. You can be calm because you have never waited for gazettes and casualty lists, and you have never gone for months without knowing whether you were alive or dead."

"I know it has been difficult," he heard himself say. "I promise you all of that is over."

"You do not know what you are doing to me. You say to yourself, Henriette is a little French kitten; she can adapt herself to anything. You keep thinking I am eighteen instead of thirty-four. You think I can endure anything without getting old and ugly. But I can't stand things as I used to. There have been too many missions and too many battles and too much waiting."

Yes, he admitted to himself, Henriette was right. It had all been unfair. This outburst, so unnatural to her, was itself a proof of the torment he had put her through. Ten years ago—even five years ago —such a scene would have been impossible.

"Believe me, Henriette," he said, "you can't be as anxious to get away from all this as I am."

Henriette changed her tone abruptly and began speaking in English.

"Ah, but you will think I am frightful. You will think I am a complaining shrew. You will wish you had married one of those cold Englishwomen who would not shed a tear if you were hanged."

"I shall think nothing of the kind," he said. "I shall only be sorry that I gave you such just ground for complaint."

"You will say to yourself, she knew what to expect when she married me. She should be accustomed to the life by now. She is a miserable, ungrateful French minx who should be soundly beaten— another woman who wants to meddle in her husband's affairs."

"No," he said, "I shall say that I am fortunate to have an affectionate, understanding wife. It is you who will have regrets. You will wish you had stayed in Arras and married a comfortable French aristocrat instead of a selfish English heretic."

"You are an English idiot," she said. "You must forgive me for the tantrum. I shall try to do better."

"If we are lucky," he said, "you will have no more reason to worry."

"Ah yes." Henriette leaned over and began picking up the wet clothes. "You were saying something about steps. What was it?"

"It was about—" He stopped himself in the middle of the sentence. Was this all a horrible mistake, this attempt to return to England? Was it all a crude, sentimental fancy—the sort of greensickness that sooner or later affected all exiles, the cancer which gnawed on those wretches in Lord Stair's anteroom and devoured those self-pitying simpletons who jumped into the Seine. Could d'Argenson have been right in watching him after all?

And even if the notion were sound, did he have any right to uproot Henriette and the boys? Yes, they had always talked about going to England, but none of them knew what the change entailed. They had been content to see England through his eyes—the eyes of an exile. To them, England was a complicated fairy tale.

"Yes, yes, go on." Henriette had stopped gathering up the clothes. She was looking at him.

"I have changed my mind about telling you now," he said. "I will tell you later, when the boys come in for tea."

And possibly it was too late now. Henriette had left her family and friends in Arras as easily as she would have changed coats. But that was fifteen years ago. Perhaps, as she had said, she was no longer an adaptable French kitten.

"Did you go to see the English ambassador?" Henriette was saying.

"Yes," he said, "but I will tell you about it later."

"I understand," she said. "I will get you some dry shoes and stockings and see if I can speed Lisette. From the sound of things, Henry and Richard are in the kitchen now."

No, Sir Ralph thought as he watched her move across the room, the change would not be easy. Henriette was much too lively to become an English lady. Undoubtedly she would charm everyone, but even while they adored her they would patronize her, as if she were a pretty child who could not learn deportment. It was his own fault, he supposed. If he had begun when she was nineteen or twenty he might have instilled something like a proper sense of decorum; but somehow he had never wanted to. Now it was too late. Although she might pick up a few English mannerisms, she would never really conform. Perhaps it was just as well. Very likely he would find it difficult to get back into the old patterns himself.

And what of Richard and Henry? Listening to their voices now, as they carried on one of their interminable arguments in the kitchen, he could not help wondering whether they were not already hopelessly Frenchified. The sounds, certainly, were British—no French voice could reproduce Henry's squeaking reproaches and Richard's pained, half-baritone expostulations. But there was something not quite right, something French, about the rhythms. Transforming the two into Englishmen would take months.

He hoped Henriette would hurry with his shoes and stockings. Richard was getting to the age of requiring that his father always act the part of the great soldier. He was sure to look vaguely injured and disappointed if he found his general bare legged. What was the use of having a father who had commanded a brigade at Malplaquet if he were going to behave like an elderly shopkeeper?

By the time Lisette had brought in the tea service and grudgingly lit two more candles, Sir Ralph was beginning to feel better. The warmth of the fire had driven most of the damp depression from his thoughts. All this self-examination, he told himself, was futile nonsense. He had been through it all before; he had made his decision. Now he would carry it out as if he were conducting another military operation. Could it be, he asked himself, that hearing Lord Stair talk of Esther Hemphill had provoked this sudden burst of apprehension? He did not think so.

From the solemn look on the boys' faces, as the two of them followed Henriette into the room, he could tell that she had prepared them for some sort of announcement. Where normally they might have come into the room like a pair of awkward puppies, they were now making a passable attempt at a dignified formality. Richard, half a head taller than his brother, held the chair for Henriette, while Henry brought over the dry shoes and stockings. Henriette, Sir Ralph noticed, had changed her dress and done something to her hair.

"Here we are," Henriette said when they were all seated. "Now what was it you were going to tell us?"

"Simply this." He looked from one face to another. "Today I went to see Lord Stair, the English ambassador, and asked him if I might return to England. If he agrees—and the English government consents—we will all go to England soon, possibly within a month."

For a few moments there was almost complete silence. He could hear Henry's spoon clinking in his cup. Richard was gulping a mouthful of tea, and Henriette was brushing at a stray wisp of hair.

Richard spoke first. "Does that mean, Sir, that you will become an officer for the Duke of Marlborough?"

"No, Richard," Henriette said gently. "It means that your father will retire from the service. Perhaps someday, if you have talent that way, you may serve under the Duke."

Henry laughed. "It means that we shall be rich, stupid. Everyone in England is rich, aren't they, Sir?"

"I am afraid not, Henry." Sir Ralph picked up his cup. "We will not be rich until you two gentlemen become large and clever. Then you can make our fortune."

"But we shall be very happy in England," Henriette said quickly. "England is your father's country."

Again there was a disquieting silence. The two boys contemplated the designs on their cups. Henry was swinging one foot back and forth, an odd half-smile on his face; Richard was fingering his spoon.

"But Sir," Richard said finally, "what about King James?"

King James, Sir Ralph thought. So that was it. They were not concerned about leaving France, as he feared; they were only concerned that their father might be a deserter. He wondered if he would ever be able to explain things to their satisfaction.

He bent down and began putting on his shoes and stockings. Being busy, he found, made talking easier.

"Gentlemen," he said slowly, "I have served young James and his father for thirty years. During that time they have done many foolish things and few wise ones. They have thrown away the lives of thousands of brave men. It is clear now that young James will never be king of England. Any further fighting for him would be murder. You must not suppose that I have betrayed him. I can do nothing more for him, and so I am going back to England. Do you understand that?"

"But Sir," Richard said doggedly, "isn't he the true king?"

"He might have been if his father had not been foolish, just as many young men would have large estates if their father had not been foolish. You see, Richard, a true king cannot make fatal mistakes."

The sight of Richard grappling with this new information made Sir Ralph sorry that the boy was too big to kiss. His brow was wrinkled up in a puzzled frown; his right foot rubbed meditatively against his left ankle.

"You must not worry about it now, gentlemen," Sir Ralph said. "You must take your father's word that he is behaving honorably. When you get a bit older, you will be able to understand the whole thing."

He wondered if he were telling the truth. One could never tell.

When they grew up they might understand even less than they did now. Certainly he could never tell them the whole story.

Henry came to his older brother's aid. "But Sir, what about the Duke of Berwick?"

"The Duke of Berwick is now a French subject. He has always been a Frenchman at heart. You must not worry about him. He can get on very well without me."

"I think that will be enough for the present," Henriette said. "You have heard your father, and you know that he would do nothing dishonorable. Now you must prepare yourselves to go to England in case the ambassador gives his permission."

Sir Ralph watched the two boys scramble awkwardly to their feet. They were standing at attention now after the manner of French recruits.

"I take it," he said solemnly, "that my council of war concurs in this action. You will preserve the utmost secrecy, since any breach of silence might jeopardize my position. Are you with me, gentlemen?"

"Yes Sir," they said, almost in unison. Richard gave a low bow, Henry gave a clumsy nod, and the two retreated to the kitchen.

"Do you think they will accept the change?" Sir Ralph asked. "They seem very much disturbed."

"I think so," Henriette said. "You see, they adore their father. He could hardly do anything wrong in their eyes."

"And what about you?"

"Oh I adore their father too." Henriette laughed.

"No, no, I mean, can you stand the change." He wished she would be serious. "You have always said you wanted to go to England, but now the chance is here, you may feel differently. If you do, tell me. I am not so set on going back that I cannot change my mind."

She laughed again. "Would you love me if I kept you from going back? Would you forget all about England and never talk about the place? Would you be content to see your sons remain in Paris?"

"I am sure I should love you," he said quickly.

"Ah yes." She had suddenly become solemn. "But I am not going to take the chance. We must go to England if we can. Please don't worry about me and the boys. We shall all be happy in your England."

"I wish I could be sure of that," he said.

"I don't see why you should doubt it. Is there someone or something in England that you don't want me to know about?"

"You know there isn't," he said.

"I am not so sure." Henriette began to smile again. "I have always felt that you were hiding something from me—some woman, some crime."

"You have?"

"But certainly I have. Was she pretty?"

Sir Ralph thought his laugh sounded hollow. "The idea is charmingly ridiculous," he said. "You should not tease me when I am trying to discuss a serious problem."

"I am not teasing, but we won't talk about it if it embarrasses you." She put down the dish she was holding and came over and kissed him. "You will have enough trouble with Lord Stair and the Chevalier's messenger."

"You will be glad to go then?"

"I will be glad to go anywhere, as long as there are no more missions, no more battles, and no more waiting. Please, don't let anything stop you from returning to England."

CHAPTER

Three

"SIR RALPH BARNARD?" the man said, not waiting to be greeted.

"Yes, please come in." Sir Ralph stepped back from the door.

"I am Robert Randall." He moved briskly past Sir Ralph into the full light. "Emissary of His Majesty King James."

Sir Ralph closed the door and turned to look at the man more closely. "Please sit down," he said.

"No thank you," the man said quickly. "When I deliver an order I prefer to stand."

There was something faintly ridiculous about Robert Randall, Sir Ralph thought. It was difficult not to laugh at him, and yet it was impossible to tell just what was funny. Perhaps it was the disproportion between the man's size and his bearing. He could not have been more than four inches above five feet, but he carried himself as proudly as a French cavalry officer. Again, perhaps it was something about the way he dressed. His breeches, his stockings, his shoes, and his coat were of the best quality, but somehow they did not look right. The coat seemed a trifle long for the rest of the ensemble; the sword almost dragged on the ground. Most likely, Sir Ralph decided, the real trouble was the man's mustache. Although it was obviously intended to make its owner look older than he was, and although it bristled with assurance, it was still the mustache of a twenty-year-old. It succeeded only in making him look callow.

Sir Ralph repressed a smile. "If it will not offend you," he said, "I will sit down. When I receive an order, I like to be seated."

"Very well," said Randall, pausing until Sir Ralph had taken a chair. "Now, here is my message. His Majesty is at Avignon, along with some of the other members of the expedition to Scotland. He commands you to come to him at once. He has an important mission for you."

"You may tell His Majesty that I cannot obey his command." Sir

Ralph watched Randall steadily. "You may remind him that when he allowed himself to be persuaded to sanction the Scottish rising, I resigned. I told him then that I could no longer serve him. I have not changed my mind."

Randall appeared too stunned by the answer to give an immediate reply. Instead of talking he began to rock back and forth on his heels. His face pulled down into a frown. Finally, when Sir Ralph had almost become convinced that he had forgotten where he was, he spoke.

"You refuse to obey a direct command from His Majesty. Perhaps you are unaware that you are committing treason."

It was amazing, Sir Ralph thought, how seriously these men kept up the elaborate pretence of royal power and sovereignty. Technically, of course, to refuse to obey young James's command was a serious offense, and under certain conditions, treason. Actually, it was no such thing. It merely meant that the man involved had recalculated the chances and decided the risks were disproportionate to any possible benefits. To pretend that the Jacobite cause was anything but a voluntary organization bordered on the farcical. Still the game had to be kept up, and many men seemed able to deceive themselves completely—especially the young ones. Sir Ralph's impulse was to tell the young fool to quit joking, but he did not yield to it.

"I am perfectly aware of the legal aspects of my refusal," he said, as kindly as possible, "and I do not intend to argue them. If you will just relay my message to His Majesty, you will have performed your duty."

The young man bristled visibly. "You must not suppose, Sir, that you are dealing with a fool. I was sent to get you, not to bring your regrets. I shall not leave without you, or without a full and satisfactory explanation."

"In that case," said Sir Ralph, "you should make yourself comfortable. I refuse either to go or to explain."

Randall began to rock back and forth again.

"So my information was correct," he said. "When our agent told me that Sir Ralph Barnard went sneaking to Lord Stair this morning, I did not believe him. I told him he must be mistaken. Now I see he was telling the truth. Do you deny it?"

Sir Ralph observed Randall carefully. The man was not quite so ridiculous as he appeared. He had at least taken the precaution of checking with the Paris informers while he was waiting to deliver his message. It was idle now to speculate which of the people waiting in the anteroom had carried the information, or to regret being observed. Still, the situation was awkward. Complications were almost sure to follow.

"Your information was correct," he said coolly, "except for the word 'sneaked.' You may report to your master that I have had an interview with Lord Stair."

"If I report to my master that you refuse his command and that you have been with Lord Stair, you will have cause to regret it. His Majesty will not sit idly by and allow you to make peace with the usurpers, you may be sure of that. You cannot be allowed to return to England, even if the English consent. You know too much." Randall was pacing up and down now, speaking rapidly.

"Please don't excite yourself," Sir Ralph said, trying not to get annoyed with this loud-mouthed child. "Believe me, Mr. Randall, threats do not move me. If His Majesty wishes to prevent me from going to England, he is at perfect liberty to try. If, on the other hand, he wishes to remember my long services to his family and to trust my discretion in the matter of keeping secrets, he can save himself a good deal of trouble. Meantime, you and I should remain perfectly calm. We have nothing to gain by shouting at each other."

"It is not too late," Randall said, lowering his voice and speaking with quiet intensity. "You can still change your mind and keep from becoming a traitor. I am obliged to report your interview, of course; but I am sure His Majesty will pardon the slip in view of your record."

Sir Ralph was careful to keep the irony out of his voice. "You are very kind," he said, "but you must consider that once my indiscretion is known, His Majesty will feel impelled to hire two men to watch me. We must not put him to that trouble."

"So you are determined to be a traitor." Randall drew himself up to his full five feet four inches. "You will be sorry, I assure you. When the King learns of this, he can let the information leak out that he is conniving at your return. This would convince Lord Stair that you cannot be trusted. You will never profit from your treachery."

Sir Ralph smiled. "I have no doubt His Majesty can find many ways of making my return difficult if he wishes, but that would hardly be one of them. Lord Stair would scarcely believe that His Majesty would send a man as well known as I am to help direct Jacobite activities in England. The notion is absurd."

"It might seem so to you," said Randall, "but it might not to the *de facto* government, especially if the information leaked out that you were being sent for the specific purpose of organizing the defense or the escape of the gentlemen captured in Scotland."

So that was the mission, Sir Ralph thought. The Chevalier intended to send him to England in an attempt to extricate the poor devils left stranded by the rising. Several of them were certain to be hanged for treason, the exact number depending upon the government's estimate of political necessities. It was very unlikely that much could be done to save them; but no doubt James felt strongly that everything should be tried. James must be desperate, Sir Ralph thought, to risk sending him to England. Still, to James, the gesture would be the important thing. He would sacrifice one man for the advantage of demonstrating that he had left no stone unturned in trying to save his followers. In this way, he could hearten the English and Scots Jacobites and silence some of the criticism which had followed his flight from Scotland.

"Yes," he said, "the English might easily believe such a story. It sounds plausible enough. But you should not have told me about it. You have inadvertently told me what the King wants of me and I did not wish to know. You have also given me an opportunity to prepare counter measures. If I were to tell His Majesty of your blunder, he would be highly displeased."

For an instant Randall's face showed alarm. Stripped momentarily of its customary look of insolence and self-confidence, it appeared almost pathetically young, like the face of a bewildered, worried child. Although the expression disappeared immediately, it affected Sir Ralph. He felt vaguely ashamed of himself for having been needlessly difficult with the boy.

"Please don't worry," he added. "I will keep everything secret."

"I am not worried," Randall said sharply, obviously eager to reestablish himself in his own estimation. "You may tell whatever you choose. The King will know that the information came from a man who refused to risk his neck to save his old comrades. He will pay no attention to it. Besides, I was authorized to tell you about the mission if you balked at obeying the order. The King was sure you would change your mind about resigning if you knew the nature of the mission. I would have told you immediately if I had not learned about Lord Stair."

Yes, Sir Ralph thought wearily, James knew his man. How could he refuse to aid those stupid, blundering wretches now they were facing the hangman? Even though the chances of success were small and the only probable result a slight increase in the dwindling prestige of James, perhaps he was morally obligated to take the risk.

Damn James anyway. He bungled everything he touched, and yet he knew enough to recognize the feeling of responsibility in a man. Well, he wouldn't get away with it this time. There would always be crises in the cause, at least for years; and if a man did not draw a line somewhere, he could never escape.

"In that case," he said, "you may tell your master I am sorry. This mission would tempt me if anything could, but I must refuse to be involved. Say that I advise him to send someone not so well known to the English government, preferably someone who cannot see too clearly the odds against the venture."

The outrage in young Randall's voice became more intense. "Very well, Sir. I will take the message. But remember, the blood of those gentlemen will be upon your head, and I assure you, Sir, it will not go unrevenged."

Sir Ralph paused. "What you say," he said gently, "may very well be true. It is entirely possible that I am to blame for the misfortunes of our friends, but not in the way you think, certainly not because I refuse to be sent on another fool's-errand. I shall attempt to bear my responsibility with patience. Meantime, I shall await whatever revenge may be taken without undue alarm."

"You are a traitor and a coward, Sir." Randall began to tremble with excitement and rage. It was obvious that he expected to be challenged immediately, and that he was nervous at the prospect. No doubt he had felt honor bound to offer the affront. He had been working up to it for some time. Now, finally, he had reached the proper state of righteous indignation.

Sir Ralph allowed himself a flash of anger. It would be a pleasure, he told himself, to take this pompous young snipe across his knee and spank him with his own sword. But that would never do. The boy, after all, was more pathetic than insulting. Silly and callow as he was, he seemed passionately determined to risk his life.

"I said that you are a traitor and a coward," Randall repeated.

"I know you did," Sir Ralph said, rising to his feet and folding his arms across his chest, "and you were a very brave lad to say it. Please don't suppose that I am treating your insult with contempt. But you see, Mr. Randall, although you have just given a fine example of courage, you are still too young to know what treason and cowardice are. While I respect your feelings, I cannot trust your judgment in these matters."

Randall turned a shade redder. It appeared that he might begin to jump up and down. "So you refuse to fight me? I might have known it. You miserable coward." His voice was louder than ever, but Sir Ralph thought he noticed a tone of relief in it.

"I am afraid I must," Sir Ralph said. "Otherwise none of the valuable information you have gained today might reach the King."

"Damned traitor," Randall yelled.

Sir Ralph reached out suddenly and seized Randall by the collar, pulling the coat down so that it pinioned the boy's arms.

"Come now, Son, enough is enough."

Ignoring the kicks and curses, he picked the boy up bodily, carried him out the door, and threw him as far as he could. Before the clatter had died away, he closed the door. In a few moments he heard footsteps leaving the garden.

The fat was in the fire now, Sir Ralph thought. Within three days James would know what was going on. He and his advisers would be forced to make a decision. They might decide to do nothing about it. They must have other pressing problems. On the other hand, they might take action. If they did, they had so many possible lines of attack that one could hardly guard against them all. All one could do, Sir Ralph told himself, was wait until they committed themselves to some move and then try to counter it. This was a very unsatisfactory way of conducting a campaign, but there was no use worrying about something that could not be helped.

Meantime, he could not help feeling sorry for Randall. Some obscure north country squire had been willing to gamble a son, probably a younger son, on the remote but exciting possibility that James might ultimately be restored. If the gamble paid off, the fortunes of the family would be made—or so the father must hope. And now the son, full of wide-eyed enthusiasm and utterly ignorant of what his commitment entailed, was beginning the long, dreary futility of exile. The father should be whipped, even if he were a loyal, doctrinaire Jacobite. Common sense should have told him that a cause which was rapidly being reduced to recruiting the sons of obscure squires to fill responsible positions was doomed to failure.

Sir Ralph shook himself out of his reverie and looked around. It was ten o'clock, he noticed. The house was completely quiet. Henriette had taken the boys off to bed before Randall arrived. She had probably gone to bed herself by now. Perhaps she was lying there waiting for him. But he must allow himself no luxuries. While his mind was still busy with the events of the day, he must begin writing his report. If he hurried, he might get it into Lord Stair's hands before the Jacobites could take any action. With luck, he might have his return practically assured by the time young James deployed his forces.

He sat down resolutely at his desk and cut a fresh pen. Then he got up to put some coal on the fire and bring the candelabra from the table to the desk. After he was seated again, he selected a large sheet of paper and wrote across the top of it, "Account of the Activities of Ralph Barnard from the Year 1685 to the Year 1716." Then he stopped. Writing his report, he saw, would be more difficult than he had supposed. The memories refused to come back in proper order, or in anything resembling proper proportion. Like a hastily levied band of Spanish partisans, they crowded around without regard for rank or place, each one with its own demands for attention. Sir Ralph chewed the end of the quill in vexation. He could not afford to waste his time sorting and maundering over irrelevancies. There should be a way of writing a simple, straightforward account, of bringing thirty-one years under discipline. At least, he should be able to make a logical beginning. It would have to be something about his employment by James II—but what? The whole thing was too complicated to write down in detail, even if he could remember it all. Well, he must try. He must make a start.

In April of 1685 [he wrote] Ralph Barnard, then twenty-four years of age and recently admitted to the bar, entered the service of King James II through the offices of his uncle Sir Lawrence Barnard, then a judge on the King's bench. He was brought before His Majesty and given a private audience. In the course of that audience, the King conveyed to Ralph Barnard his desire for what he was pleased to call 'special legal counsel.' He said that being newly ascended to the throne and aware of the mistrust occasioned by his religion, he was fearful of sedition and treason and that he needed a young man who was trained in law and perfectly trustworthy to aid him in ferreting out and preventing the same. He said, further, that this work should be carried out secretly, without the knowledge of his official counsellors. All information, he said, should be brought directly to him, and the connection between the two of them disclosed to no one. He represented this work to be of great value to the kingdom, whose fundamental laws, he declared, he would in no wise alter, in spite of the allegations of his detractors. Ralph Barnard assented to His Majesty's request for his services and undertook to furnish the King with information.

Shortly thereafter, Monmouth's rebellion broke out, and Mr. Barnard was sent in the train of Lord Feversham's army to carry out investigations.

Sir Ralph raised his head and chewed reflectively at his pen. Now that he was started, his thoughts were beginning to move more easily. Still, there was an air of strangeness about some of them, as if the events had happened to someone else, as if, for instance, some-one else had been at the battle of Sedgemoor.

CHAPTER

Four

WHEN THE SOUND of musket-fire awakened Ralph Barnard, he could not tell where he was. Everything around him was pitch black. Somewhere outside, someone was shooting. The shots had come first like explosive raindrops, the scattered beginning of a storm. Now, within a few seconds, they were coming in violent irregular gusts. Almost in his ear, a drum began to beat, and not far away someone was yelling at the top of his lungs. Young Ralph rolled over on his side. He was in bed, that much was clear, but he seemed to be buried in a hole or shut up in a box. Not even the faintest outline of a window shone through the blackness. He could get no thread to unravel this tumultuous nightmare. With an effort, he began to shake his head to clear out the sleep, but the movement did not seem to help. With each shake the noise increased astoundingly. The shots had become a shattering roar, almost drowning out the sound of the drum and what sounded like running, shouting men. Something hideous was happening, and he was trapped.

He heard himself yell as he jumped out of bed. His head hit something, he stumbled and the next moment he was on the ground and a smothering weight had fallen on him. Then he remembered where he was. He was in a tent, and he had knocked it down on top of him. He began to struggle with the canvas, more terrified than ever. Out there, the Duke of Monmouth was attacking the army. In a moment his infantry or cavalry would sweep through the camp. Someone would thrust a saber or a pike through the canvas; and that would be the end of Ralph Barnard. The army had been surprised in its beds. Now all was lost. He must get out at once.

The canvas seemed endless. The more he squirmed and pulled, the tighter it pinned him down. Someone very near him was weeping in racking sobs. He must make his way to the edge of the tent. If he kept squirming in a straight line, he could get out; but he knew he would never get out in time. The crash of the firing was getting louder than ever. In a few seconds, it would be upon him. He might as well give up. If he lay still maybe no one would notice him. There was no use yelling any more; he could not hear himself.

Then, abruptly, his hand hit a familiar object, his trunk. For a moment his terror subsided. The trunk, he knew, had been placed against the rear wall of the tent, the direction from which the firing was coming. It was protecting him now from musket balls; he had only to crawl around it to be outside. Did he dare? The panic threatened to return as he lay there balancing his fears. If he did not get out soon, the enemy would come and cut his throat; but if he crawled out he would be shot through the head. As he listened, he thought he could hear the bullets whistling through the air. Certainly it was better to lie still and hope to be passed by than to get up only to be shot down.

Just as he made his decision, it was unmade for him. Something hit him in the side and fell across him. In a moment it was gone, and in another moment he had scrambled out of the tent. Before he could get to his feet, he was hit again and stepped on. Through the din, he could hear someone curse, and then dark figures disappeared toward the firing. The next thing he knew, he was running.

He could not see where he was going. He could dimly make out the forms of the tents as he ran down the row. Twice he stumbled, and once he ran squarely into a soldier, knocking them both down. He got up immediately and ran on, realizing as he did so that he had on nothing but a nightshirt. After what seemed years of running, he found himself free of the camp. The musketfire still sounded as loud as ever, but at least he was beyond the tents. A little farther and he would be out of musket range. He glanced back over his shoulder. The misty night was full of fire. There seemed to be thousands of small flashes. They silhouetted the tents and, vaguely, the half-formed lines of infantry, which were alarmingly close.

Suddenly he fell in a ditch. For a second or two he tried frantically to get up out of the water and the slick mud. Then he thought better of it. Momentarily, at least, he was safe here. The ditch, although not a huge drain like the one that protected the front of the camp, was more than three feet deep. Lying in the bottom of it, half-immersed in water and mud, he was perfectly protected from the musket balls. He could catch his breath and decide what to do next. Cautiously he raised his head a little.

The night, he decided, was not quite so black as he had thought. Probably there was a moon somewhere, although it could never be

seen because of the mist which seemed to cover everything. Straight
ahead of him, away from the battle, lay the open moor. If he could
get out of the ditch without being shot, he could pick his way across
it to safety. The journey would be terrible in bare feet, but better
than being killed. He must hurry though. If dawn caught him still
on the moor, the cavalry would ride him down. Somewhere, about a
mile ahead and to his right, lay the little village where Feversham,
Churchill, and the royal cavalry were camped. Perhaps he should
try for that. But what was the use? When the infantry was broken,
the rebels would go through the town like Cromwell through Preston. Unless he could find a horse, he would be hanged in the square.
Besides, he might be ridden down by his own troopers. By now they
must have heard the firing; eventually they would ride up, too late
to save the battle but early enough to ride over him. No he must
try the moor.

Still, something seemed to be holding him in the ditch. His body
refused to leave. Fifty yards at most would put him beyond the
wildest musket shot. He raised himself to his hands and knees,
tensed his muscles, muttered a little prayer, and remained where he
was. Try as he would, he could not make himself lift his head above
the ditch bank, much less jump out of the ditch. He felt himself begin to tremble all over. Unless he did something quickly he would
be screaming.

Then he heard a sound which froze him. Beneath the frenzied
violence of the musketry, he could hear low, earth-shaking thumps.
These, he realized with horror, could mean only one thing—cavalry.
Although he was so ignorant of warfare that he hardly knew a pike
from a pistol, even his intestines knew what cavalry meant at a time
like this. If it were the royal cavalry, possibly the situation could be
saved. The royal infantry, though confused and surprised, was apparently still unbroken. With help it might continue to stand firm.
If the cavalry were Monmouth's, it would crash through the camp
and fall upon the rear of the royal troops. In a few seconds the battle
would be over and the slaughter begun.

But these horsemen must be rebels. The King's horse, except for
the few who were stationed northeast of the camp, could not have
had time to get saddled up and organized since the firing began.
The enemy had planned the attack. They had been in motion when
the first shot was fired. Now they were ready to deliver the coup de
grâce. Ralph sank back into the slime and listened. If the hoofbeats
came from his left, he was lost; if they came from his right, he had a
chance. Behind him, some cannon began to boom. The musketry was

crashing furiously. The more he strained to hear, the less he could
tell about the direction. For an instant, he considered running out
into the moor, but he knew he was too late. Even if the squadrons
were friendly, he would be trampled. He could only wait. In a few
moments he would know the worst.

Suddenly he found himself kneeling, peering over the bank out
into the mist. Straight ahead of him he could not see fifty feet, but
slightly to his left there seemed to be an open patch. In this direction,
he thought he could see thirty or forty yards. He fixed his eyes on the
spot where the rebels must emerge. As he did so, a horse passed
within ten feet of his nose. It was moving from his right to his left.
The man on top of it was yelling something unintelligible to someone behind him. Almost before Ralph could cry out in surprise, the
mist in front of him was full of shadowy horsemen, passing in a slow
regular trot. They were the King's squadrons, he knew immediately.
The direction of their movement made this certain, even if he had
not noticed the outline of their hats. Their leader, somehow warned
in time, was bringing them across to protect the right flank of the
army. Maybe they could hold off the enemy. Ralph watched them
move by until the last horseman disappeared into the mist. Then he
put his head down against the ditch bank and began to sob with
relief.

How long he remained kneeling there, he had no way of knowing.
From time to time he told himself that he should get up and run
while he had the chance, but his body felt limp and tired. He could
scarcely have moved if he had been prodded with a pike. Wearily
he berated himself for his foolishness. Why had he been stupid
enough to lodge with the infantry in the first place? The King's order
to keep a sharp eye on the loyalty and behavior of the officers certainly did not require him to dispense with the comparative comforts
of Weston Zoyland for the discomforts and, now, deadly peril of the
infantry camp. He had been absurdly overzealous about his duty.
Instead of observing and sounding out the generals and colonels, he
had taken it upon himself to examine all officers, from general to
ensign. He was determined to be thorough and to impress the King
with his report. Now the report might never be written. He might
be killed in a ditch for his silly pains, and it would serve him right.

In the midst of these vacant reflections, he gradually began to
notice a change in the sounds. The musketry, which had been coming in wild spasms or continuous concussions, was now beginning to
take on a pattern, a series of almost regular crashes. Although Ralph
had no clear idea of what the change meant, it made him feel a little

better. Something about the regularity was reassuring. For the first
time the thought struck him forcibly that the royal army might hold.
He raised his head and listened. The sounds seemed not to have
moved. There was, however, one alarming note which he had not
taken account of; all the cannon fire was coming from the enemy.
The roar was too far away to be produced by friendly guns. Apparently, the rebels had been able to bring three or four cannon into
action, while as yet not a sound could be heard from the royal
artillery.

When Ralph attempted to turn around in the ditch, he found his
feet and legs so cold and paralyzed that he could hardly move.
Twice he slipped down sideways and buried his hands in the slime
before he was able to make the awkward transition. Finally he
found himself facing the battle, cautiously peering over the ditch-
bank toward the camp. His first impression was comforting. He
could see a little better now; the mist seemed to have dispersed
somewhat. The tents were clearly visible, and although they hid the
battle line from his view as he lay there, their obvious vacancy
seemed to show that the troops had not been pushed back from
their position at the edge of the big drain. The tent-tops were being
lighted by large, intermittent flashes instead of by constant small
flickers of light. The battalions, he suddenly realized, were firing in
volleys.

Ralph could feel his breathing becoming more regular. Heartbeat
by heartbeat his courage seemed to be returning. Momentarily, he
was tempted to stand up to get a full view, but he thought better of it.
It would be foolish, he told himself, to get shot merely out of curiosity. He could not change the outcome of the battle by looking. He
must be wise and keep out of harm's way as much as possible. Here,
he realized, he was in a good position. If the enemy retreated, he
could get up and return to the tents. If the royal army began to fall
back, he would have two hundred yards head start. But what if the
army held and dawn found him skulking in a ditch dressed in a
soaking nightshirt? He would be hooted out of camp. And what
would the King say when he found that his agent had run terror-
stricken from a victorious battle? The thought was too distressing to
contemplate. On the other hand, what did people expect? After all,
he was a civilian with the army, not a soldier. Although he had
learned a little about fencing, he had never fired a musket in his
life. Even if he blundered up to the lines, he could only get in the
way. No one but a fool would rush into the middle of a battle merely
to show his courage. Yet a wise man would never be given a chance

to explain this obvious truth if he were found in a ditch without breeches. One thing was certain, Ralph thought; he must get some clothes.

Ralph stood up. For a moment he stood watching the flashes from the volleys light up the battle line; then he started to climb out of the ditch. He must run for the tents quickly before he lost his nerve. Just as he stepped to the top of the bank he heard a loud noise. Something brushed against his right hand and someone yelled hoarsely. He was almost knocked down by a stumbling horse. The next thing he knew, he was back in the ditch, this time with two horses and a cannon. Voices were swearing horribly in his ear.

"You god-damn fool," a man shrieked, "why didn't you look where you were going?"

Ralph began to answer, but a voice behind him drowned out his reply. "How could I see the dirty bastard," it roared. "No one told me there was a ditch."

"Now you've torn it," a third figure yelled. "The god-damn gun is stuck up to the hubs."

"Well, don't stand there," the first voice shrieked. "Untangle the traces and let's pull her out."

"Gentlemen, gentlemen," another voice said in a heavy, injured tone. "Let us have no foul language please. Cursing will not mend matters."

When Ralph looked up to see who was speaking, he could have sworn that he recognized the shovel hat of a clergyman, but he knew he must be mistaken.

"Here you," one of the men shouted, "help me with this tug."

Ralph was not sure that he was being addressed but he hurriedly bent over the harness of the near horse. When the horse had stumbled in the ditch, it had stepped over the outside trace with its hind foot. Now it was struggling spasmodically to get free, with its forefeet up on the bank and its hind feet down in the slime next to the cannon. After an exasperating effort, Ralph got the trace unhooked. Meanwhile someone else had grasped the horse's head and straightened him out. Ralph hooked the trace up again.

All the while the man with the odd hat was shouting encouragement and advice at the top of his lungs. "Steady now lads," he said. "Easy does it. Run back to the ammunition wagon, Jack, and see if you can get another team of horses. Tell them to look out for the ditch. It's a bad one. Steady with that off horse. See if the traces are long enough to let him get up on the bank. Hurry men. You there, you with the long shirt, look to that inside line; it's fouled up in the wheel. Don't worry, Lord Churchill will hold them until we get there."

The man right next to Ralph was cursing in a low, steady, incomprehensible stream. Suddenly he straightened up, apparently satisfied with the condition of the traces. "I'll lead the sons of bitches," he yelled. "You men get hold of those wheels."

Ralph seized two spokes and heaved against the wheel with all his might. Nothing happened. In spite of the slithering lunges of the horses and the straining of the men, the cannon did not budge. Finally, the man holding the horses called a halt.

"She won't go," he yelled. "We'll have to wait till Jack gets back with more horses. Damn the luck."

"Patience, men," the man in the hat said. "Unhook the horses and get them up on the bank. Maybe we can put together a harness that will do the business from up there."

Once more Ralph bent over the traces. This time, he found the task easier. Within a minute, he had the near horse atop the ditch-bank. A few seconds later, the other horse was there also. Ralph held his horse with difficulty. The beast appeared to be frightened now and threatened momentarily to break away. In the intervals between calming the horse and trying to see what the others were doing with the harness, Ralph glanced toward the battle. He could not tell what was happening in spite of the fact that the sky did not appear quite so dark. Volleys were still crashing, the cannon were still firing. It seemed to Ralph that the armies had been shooting at each other for years. He wondered momentarily how the group on the ditchbank had escaped being shot. They had been exposed for a long time.

"The fanatics are giving the boys hot work," he shouted to the man holding the other horse.

"Don't worry, Son," the man shouted back. "They can't beat the regulars. When we get up there with this gun, we'll make things lively."

"Look alive up there," a voice shouted from the ditch. "One of you come down and grab a wheel."

Ralph slid back into the ditch and took his position at the wheel. This time the cannon moved. With much slipping and sloshing it inched forward up the bank. Once it stopped and threatened to roll backwards, but the horses braced, the men dug their feet into the mud, and the gun steadied. One final shove brought it safely to dry ground.

"There we are, men," yelled the man in the hat. "Now, bear off to the right up past that line of tents. The ammunition must be there by now. John, you lead the team."

As Ralph followed the cannon up toward the battle, the thought occurred to him that he could stay behind, but he dismissed it immediately. The men might need him. Besides, now that he was sweating and excited, he was no longer afraid. He almost hoped the enemy would not run until he got there. He was within fifty yards of the line before he realized that he was under fire. This time there could be no mistake. A musket ball whizzed so close to his ear that for a moment he thought he was hit. Another glanced off the barrel of the cannon with a terrifying whine. His new courage ebbed suddenly, but since the other men seemed to take no notice, he plodded on after them. In the gradually thinning darkness, he could occasionally make out a man staggering to the rear, and once he stepped on a body.

Soon the cannon halted behind a dark row of men. A moment later an officer came running back.

"Thank God you got here, Bishop," he said. "I thought you were lost. You may retire now, Sir. Your men and mine will serve the cannon."

"Thank you, Colonel," the man in the shovel hat said. "Unhitch the horses, men."

Ralph sprang toward the traces, but another man was already cutting the makeshift harness with a knife. Several soldiers immediately gathered round, and soon, after much shoving and bumping, Ralph found himself and the cannon at the edge of a huge drainage ditch. On both sides of him, lines of infantrymen were firing into the gloom.

"Here you," the man who seemed to be chief gunner shouted. "You carry the cannon balls until Jack gets back. Look alive."

About ten feet from the gun was a pile of cannon balls. Ralph hurried over to it. As he bent over to pick up a ball, a flight of bullets hummed overhead. A man close to him fell to the ground and began screaming. Another man slumped down almost at his feet. When he got back to the cannon, he saw the gunner holding his arm. The man was cursing furiously.

"Don't hand me the god-damn thing," he screamed. "Put it in the gun. The bloody bastards nicked me."

Ralph placed the ball in the muzzle of the cannon. Immediately the man with the ramrod shoved it home. In contrast to the gunner, he seemed remarkably cheerful.

"Ready, Sir," he yelled. "Here's a present for the fanatics."

Straining his eyes, Ralph peered across the drain. In spite of the smoke and the pre-dawn darkness, he could make out the lines of the enemy. They seemed to be no more than fifty yards away. Even as he looked, a ragged flash of fire burst across their ranks and another flight of bullets came whizzing and thudding past. Ralph ducked instinctively and scrambled back toward the pile of cannon balls.

When he returned with another ball, the gunner had aimed the gun to his satisfaction and was applying the fire to the touchhole. A huge blast of flame shot from the muzzle; there was a roar; and in an instant everything was enveloped in smoke. Ralph could not see whether or not the shot took effect, but a cheer went up immediately from the surrounding soldiers.

"That will give them something to think about," the man with the ramrod shouted. "A little lower this time."

Ralph half expected that when the smoke cleared, the enemy would be gone. He was dismayed to find, as the cloud rolled away, that nothing seemed to have changed. He could see no gap in the line. The enemy front rank appeared to be leveling its muskets for another volley.

"Hurry up with that powder and shot," the gunner yelled.

Ralph tried not to think of the musket balls. He waited a moment for the man to ram the powder in tight; then he placed the ball in the muzzle and went back to get another one. Meantime the infantry ranks on his left and his right each fired a volley.

By the time the gun had fired four rounds, Ralph took no further notice of the enemy. He was too intent on serving the gun to be frightened. Even when his partner with the ramrod suddenly fell dead across the cannon barrel, his first thought was not of the danger but of the blow to the operation of the gun. He almost wept with relief when the missing cannoneer appeared out of the smoke and seized the ramrod.

Shortly after this an officer came running down the line. "Hold your fire," he shouted. "Our cavalry is going to charge."

Ralph straightened up. The noise of the volleys and the cannon ceased abruptly. The smoke gradually drifted back across the ranks, and Ralph saw clearly for the first time exactly what was happening. Across the big ditch, about sixty-five or seventy yards away, stood a ragged mass of men. In the first light of dawn they looked more like a large knot of peasants than an army. Few of them had uniforms, and many of them had no muskets or pikes, only crude lances fashioned from poles and scythes. On the ground were a great

number of bodies. Now Ralph could see where the cannon balls
had swept through their ranks; smashed corpses marked out the
shots. Still, the remaining men were reloading methodically and preparing to deliver a volley.

Away on the right about three or four hundred yards, Ralph
could see a mass of horsemen formed up on the other side of the
drain. They were beginning to move toward the enemy. It appeared
that in a few moments they would ride over the motley infantry
that opposed them; but as the gap between them narrowed Ralph
saw three lines of musketeers deliver successive volleys; then the
pikemen stepped forward to receive the charge. For about four or
five minutes, there was a furious melee all along the right side of
the line, front and rear. Then, suddenly, the horsemen disengaged
and galloped away out of musket range.

Meantime, about a hundred yards to the left, a battalion of royal
infantry was filing rapidly across the drain over what appeared to
be a bridge and forming ranks on the other side. Just as the horsemen retreated, the battalion delivered a volley and began to advance on the enemy. A moment later, at a command from the colonel, the soldiers around Ralph scrambled down into the ditch,
waded through the knee-deep mud and water, and climbed up the
opposite bank. Before the assault battalion had reached the enemy,
Ralph's regiment was ready to charge.

Ralph could not see precisely what happened then; the men
blocked his vision. Besides, the gunner was shouting at him.

"Look alive there, nightshirt. Here come the other guns, and here
is some grapeshot."

When Ralph looked around, he saw four or five more cannon
being wheeled up to the ditch at intervals of about twenty-five
yards. An ammunition cart was making its way toward them,
through and over the bodies lying on the ground. Ralph tried not
to look at the corpses as he ran to unload the cart. He was afraid
that if he did, he would be sick. Soon he was busy unloading kegs
of powder and shot, intent upon getting the gun ready for action.
He did not look around again until he suddenly realized that the
soldiers were scrambling back through the ditch. The charge, apparently, had failed. The rebel ranks were still there, more ragged
than ever but still unbroken.

As Ralph placed the shot in the cannon mouth, an unaccountable
feeling of revulsion came over him. The tattered army across the
ditch was helpless now. Sometime during the night it had lost its
cannons—at least Ralph could not see or hear them; its cavalry, if it

had ever had any, had disappeared. Its volleys were scattering and feeble now. Very likely the ammunition had run low. If the men broke ranks to charge or retreat, the royal cavalry was sure to cut them to pieces. They could only stand there and await another onslaught, or wait to be cut down at a distance.

In spite of the sickness in the pit of his stomach, Ralph could not take his eyes off the enemy ranks. After all, he told himself, they were fanatics and rebels. They deserved whatever they got. Their incredible courage in a bad cause merely showed how dangerous and depraved they were. They would have shown no mercy themselves. Raising rebellions and starting civil wars were horrible crimes—more horrible than he had ever realized. Still, to be obliged to slaughter the poor devils was sickening.

Then, one after another, the cannon went off. Ralph's view was obscured by smoke. Mechanically, he reached for another charge of shot and waited to reload. Through a rift in the smoke, he thought he could see a change in the rebel line. More men, he was sure, were lying on the ground like bundles of rags. He stepped back from the gun and it fired again. This time, he did not try to look.

When the guns fired a third time, a yell went up from the regulars, and the gunner began to dance up and down. "That broke them," he yelled.

Through the rapidly clearing smoke, Ralph could see the moor in front of him filled with running men. Already the rows of dead and wounded were yards behind the runners. As he looked, Ralph saw the cavalry on the right break into pursuit, and a moment later the infantry was scrambling back across the ditch to join the chase.

Ralph leaned against the cannon and put his head in his hands. Through the confused shouts of the pursuit and the occasional shots, he could hear someone talking in a calm, matter-of-fact voice.

"A brisk action, Sir. I would say we have lost three or four hundred men. The enemy must have lost about a thousand, and the cavalry will ride down two or three hundred more. We can safely say the rebellion is finished."

Through his nausea, Ralph wanted to protest. Thousands of men must have been killed on both sides. This must have been the bloodiest battle in all history.

"Yes, Colonel," a voice replied, "the rebels stood to it very well. If their cavalry had done its duty we should have had even hotter work. The attack was bold and well planned. When your men have finished chasing the stragglers, reform them in Bridgwater. We will camp there tonight."

Ralph raised his head. He immediately recognized the speakers, Colonel Kirke and Lord Churchill. Lord Churchill looked at him and smiled.

"I am pleased to see you, Mr. Barnard," he said. "I hardly expected to find a lawyer serving one of our guns. If I had been aware of your talents, I should have found you a more convenient uniform."

Ordinarily Ralph would have blushed and stammered. Now he felt too tired and ill to care whether Lord Churchill was praising him or laughing at him.

"I am afraid, Sir," he said, "that I am not very presentable. The rebels gave me no time to dress."

"Mr. Barnard," Lord Churchill said, "you are the most eminently presentable lawyer I have ever seen. The mud and powder give your nightgown an undeniable air of gallantry. I shall see that your devotion is mentioned in the dispatches. And now, gentlemen, if you will excuse me, I must return to Lord Feversham. Remember, Colonel, no pillaging, no unnecessary cruelty."

When Lord Churchill and Colonel Kirke had left, Ralph surveyed the scene once more. Far across the moor, the pursuit was continuing. He could still hear the yells echoing faintly. Close at hand, a few soldiers were beginning to pick up the wounded. The gunner had disappeared, probably to find his horses. The dead cannoneer was still lying beside the gun, with one hand thrust limply between two wheel spokes. Along the bank of the drainage ditch lay the untidy rows of red-coated bodies. Already, Ralph could see, the flies were beginning to collect on the three men lying next to the cannon. Ralph sat down suddenly on the ditchbank, and after glancing around to see that no one was looking, he began to retch quietly.

CHAPTER

Five

"MISTRESS HEMPHILL!" Lord Jeffreys' face turned a shade redder. "You lie like a fanatic preacher. Damn me, I have never heard such nonsense. Don't perjure yourself in this court, young lady, or I'll pack you off to the Barbadoes with your friends."

Ralph looked around the crowded hall. The spectators were leaning forward as if they had frozen in an attitude of anxiety. Even Pollexfen, the chief prosecutor for the crown, who ordinarily affected an air of business-like boredom, sat up straight and stared at the witness.

The expression on the girl's face did not change. "I have told the truth, my lord," she said calmly. "George was in London with me throughout the insurrection. We did not come back to Hemphill House until July thirteenth, a week after the battle. He was never in arms against the King."

Ralph was amazed. There could be no doubt the girl was lying; he had prepared the evidence against George Hemphill himself. Yet she gave her testimony with such poise and assurance, with such serene confidence, that even Lord Jeffreys appeared to be taken aback.

Jeffreys recovered himself quickly. A contemptuous smile came over his florid face. "No, no, my pretty young perjurer. This won't do. You will never save your brother with monstrous lies. You should try pleading and whining like your friends. You should claim extenuating circumstances. You should say he was misled by evil companions, that he was forced into Monmouth's army against his will. You should say he is too young to know what he is doing. You should shuffle and hedge and evade questions. Outright lies are too easy to disprove." The smile disappeared from his face. "Why you impudent slut," he shouted suddenly, "here is the proof right in my hand. Do you see what this says?"

Ralph knew what the paper contained. It was part of the muster roll for Lord Grey's cavalry. Someone had tried to burn it after the flight, but enough remained to incriminate two hundred men—among them George Hemphill.

The girl examined the paper with cool detachment. "Yes, I see, my lord. It is a list of names."

"A list of names," said Jeffreys with heavy sarcasm, "a list of names. Indeed it is a list of names—a list of the traitors enrolled in Colonel Holmes' squadron. And on that list you will see the name of that double-dyed rebel your brother. Speak up, young lady, do you see it?"

Again the girl glanced at the paper. "Perfectly well," she said, "and I can hardly blame your lordship for being suspicious. But you must remember, Sir, that my brother and I cannot be responsible for what the fanatics chose to write on their lists. Surely your lordship does not contend that the list is in my brother's handwriting."

It was a shrewd stroke, Ralph admitted. In a few words the girl had cast doubt upon the accuracy of the rebel records, put the crown on the defensive, and perhaps most important, identified her social and religious prejudices with those of the jury. He could tell by looking at the jurors that they were impressed. They must be thinking that after all she was a lady. Nominally, at least, she was a member of the Church of England, not a Presbyterian, an Anabaptist, a Quaker, or an Independent—not, in short, a fanatic. Like themselves, her family were gentry; they were not plowmen, tinkers, miners, or small shopkeepers. They might be tainted with vile Whig principles, but that did not necessarily mean they were stupid enough to join Monmouth. Perhaps this case would bear looking into.

Jeffreys hastened to retrieve the situation. "I might have known," he said, "that the Hemphills would hire some Whig pettifogger to help them cavil at the evidence. What sneaking lawyer inspired you to try that trick?"

"I have no lawyer, my lord," the girl said quietly. "The reflection was obvious. The gentlemen of this county have often complained of false muster, even among the royal troops. I cannot suppose the rebels were faultless in this respect. Nor can I suppose that they would stick at putting down any name which would lend their odious cause respectability. But, however that may be, my brother was not with Lord Grey or the Duke of Monmouth; he was with me."

Again, Ralph thought, the answer was perfect. The girl had not shown the slightest trace of confusion or embarrassment. She seemed studiously to avoid trying to impress the jury with her beauty. Her only aim apparently was to convince them of her ingenuousness and candor. The large brown eyes, framed by the black wavy hair, seemed to reflect conscious innocence. Certainly, they said, no English gentleman could doubt the statements of their owner.

Pollexfen half rose from his chair as if he were about to come to the rescue of Lord Jeffreys, but the judge rallied quickly.

"Ah Esther, Esther," he said, "how it pains me to see a girl so young such an accomplished liar. I am sure that the jury admires your courage and your address in attempting to save your brother's life; but when they consider that you are damning your soul to perdition, when they realize that you have enmeshed yourself in a hopeless labyrinth of falsehood, then they will have cause to pity your brazenness and to prosecute without mercy the vile rebels who have brought you to this useless perjury. Believe me, Esther, I can bring forth witnesses who saw your brother at the battle. I shall do so presently. Before I do, however, I should like to hear your explanation for your brother's wound. What cock-and-bull story have you composed to amuse the court with?"

A suppressed sigh ran through the hall. The audience, Ralph thought, had realized the girl's predicament. For a moment her skill and audacity had given them a wild, improbable hope. Now they knew it was too good to last. George Hemphill would never get away from Lord Jeffreys. Ralph's impression was reinforced when he looked again at the prisoner. The man had been too weak and sick to interrogate. In the two months since the battle he had been more dead than alive. Now, propped up on a litter between two soldiers, he could barely talk above a whisper. When he had been brought in at the beginning of the trial, he had almost fainted, or pretended to faint, before he could identify himself, plead not guilty, and call his sister to defend him. To defend a man half-dead from a gunshot wound on the grounds that he had been in London one hundred fifty miles away when he was shot was clearly impossible.

Esther Hemphill looked serenely around the courtroom and then back to Lord Jeffreys. "I am sure your lordship does not mean to prejudice the minds of the jury against the truth. I know you are carried away merely by your concern for justice and your desire to serve the King faithfully. The story I must tell does have an air of improbability about it. If it were not the truth, I would not dare to tell it. I shall need the sympathetic attention of the whole court to make the facts appear."

"She means," Lord Jeffreys interrupted, "that the jury must loosen its gullets to swallow a fantastic lie."

The girl's look was mildly reproachful, as if she were pained at the manners of a boor. "Luckily," she went on, "I have an unimpeachable witness who can prove what I say. When I have finished giving you the truth of the matter, I shall call on him to corroborate my testimony."

The statement brought a stir in the courtroom. Ralph found himself looking around like the others to see who the witness might be. He half expected to see some notorious professional swearer, some depraved wretch out of the London gutter willing to risk his ears and back for a hundred pounds; but he could not pick anyone out from the crowd.

"My brother had the misfortune of being shot by a highwayman," the girl said. "We were set upon by two robbers as we came across Turnham Green. When my brother drew his sword they discharged their pistols. One of the bullets pierced my brother's shoulder."

Lord Jeffreys snorted and nodded to Pollexfen with a look which indicated clearly that the Lord Chief Justice would not waste his time examining such trash. The prosecutor took up the questioning.

"And when did this convenient robbery take place?" he asked.

"It took place on the third of July, Sir." Esther Hemphill paused briefly. "But it can hardly be called a robbery. The robbers fled as soon as they fired. We lost nothing."

Pollexfen smiled indulgently. "You immediately reported the matter to a magistrate, I suppose?"

"I did nothing of the kind." The girl seemed to pity his stupidity. "I reported the matter to a surgeon."

"I see," said Pollexfen. "How unfortunate you did not report it to the magistrate. Then you could have been vouched for by an official, or by the official records. You two were alone on the heath, no doubt?"

"Fortunately we were not, Sir. If we had been, my brother would have bled to death before I could get him to the doctor. As it was, I was obliged to stuff my handkerchief into the wound, and even that did not entirely stop the bleeding. No Sir, we were accompanied by the driver of a hackney coach. It was he who helped me bind up the wound and showed me where I could find a physician."

"What was the name of this helpful gentleman?" Pollexfen asked. He was still trying to appear bored and contemptuous, but Ralph could see that he was becoming annoyed.

"He was no gentleman, Sir. He was just an ordinary hackney coachman." The girl gently corrected Pollexfen's obvious social ignorance. "He told me his name, but I have forgotten it. It began with *M* I think. But he has no reason to complain. I gave him a whole guinea for his services."

"Again we have an unfortunate circumstance," Pollexfen said. "If you had remembered his name you might have brought him down from London as a witness. His testimony, added to that of the unimpeachable witness you have promised to produce, might win your brother an acquittal."

The girl looked almost scornful. "Surely, Sir, you would not expect the gentlemen of this county to take seriously the word of a hackney coachman. Why, they would as soon take the word of a servant or a tenant or a tradesman. Even if I were sure I could find the man, I would not bring him all the way out here for nothing."

Once more Ralph admired the girl's shrewdness. Besides appealing to the class-consciousness of the jurors and accounting for her lack of witnesses, she was discounting in advance the testimony of the men who were to be produced against her brother. Somehow, Ralph thought, she must have found out who they were. Possibly she had bribed one of the crown clerks, or again, possibly she had found out from the witnesses themselves.

Pollexfen was visibly annoyed. Ralph could see that he was faced with a decision. If he continued to cross-examine the witness he might trip her up on some detail of what appeared to be a clumsy and complicated lie. Once he had done so, the case would be finished. But this course of action entailed considerable risk. The witness was cool and clever. Undoubtedly she had rehearsed every detail of her improbable story. If he failed to shake her testimony, he would only succeed in giving it an exaggerated importance to the jury. Already, Ralph thought, Pollexfen must have realized that the girl had aroused considerable sympathy and admiration among the jurors. To bully her and worry her after the manner of Jeffreys might antagonize them against the crown witnesses.

"Mistress Hemphill," Pollexfen said, "I shall waste little of the court's time with this fiction. Produce your witness and we will see whether or not he can lie with such brazen self-assurance as you do."

"Sir," she said with injured dignity, "I have always considered you a gentleman—not perhaps as steady in your principles as one could wish, but a gentleman. Please do not force me to lower my opinion of you by telling a lady that she lies. You will soon have proof of my statements. With the court's permission I will call upon Mr. Richard Keith."

Again the spectators buzzed expectantly. Ralph could see them craning their necks, looking around the hall. After what seemed to be a half minute, a man rose from a seat near the back of the room and began to make his way slowly toward the front. Ralph observed him curiously. Everything about the man seemed to denote the affluent Londoner. His dark red velvet coat, although quietly conservative by aristocratic standards, contrasted sharply with the coarse black broadcloth of the countrymen who filled the courtroom. It even made the finery of the country gentlemen who served on the jury look a trifle tawdry. A gold watch chain reached from the third button to the right pocket of the coat, but this odd manner of wearing a watch and chain seemed somehow practical instead of ostentatious. Even more impressive was the way the man wore his hair. It hung down below his shoulders in rich brown curls, as if to proclaim that its owner was neither a crop-haired fanatic nor a bewigged would-be courtier, but a gentleman who could afford to follow his own tastes.

As the man came closer, Ralph saw that he was not so young as he appeared from a distance. Although his hair showed no trace of gray, it was evident from his features that he was at least forty-five. He was a large man, somewhat inclined to corpulence, but managing to look well fed and healthy rather than fat. Compared with Lord Jeffreys, he did not appear florid, only a trifle ruddy and inclined toward jowls.

The Lord Chief Justice favored the man with a scowl.

"Let us have a good look at this unimpeachable witness," he said. "Damn me, Mr. Keith, or whatever your real name is, the Hemphills went to great expense to dress you up. Hold up your hair, Mr. Keith. Let us see if you have any ears."

"Any ears?" said Keith.

"Yes, ears," said Jeffreys. "Men in your trade often lose their ears. Surely you have noticed your friend Titus Oates. Hold up your hair."

"As you say, my lord." Keith appeared puzzled. "Here are my ears."

He pulled two locks of hair above his head, exposing two large, well-shaped ears.

"That is good," said Lord Jeffreys. "Now listen to me. If you are caught in the smallest falsehood during this examination, you will have those ears cut off at the root. Furthermore, I can promise you that you will be lashed at the tail of a cart from Taunton to Bridgwater. Consider a moment. Is the money the Hemphills are paying you worth being permanently maimed? If it is, step up and give your evidence. If it is not, you can leave now without being prosecuted. What will it be?"

"My lord," Keith said, "I have had little experience in courts. I did not realize that it was the duty of the judge to begin by intimidating the witness. Members of my profession are not accustomed to being threatened, nor, for that matter are they accustomed to lying—although perhaps I could name a profession whose members are not so scrupulous. Please bring forth the Bible and let me be sworn."

"I ask the jury to pay careful heed to this man's bravado," Lord Jeffreys said. "He wishes to bandy words with the court. Notice also the artful way in which he pretends that he knows nothing about treason trials—asking to be sworn, when he knows that witnesses for the accused are never sworn." Jeffreys turned to the witness. "No, your Whigship, you will not be sworn, but you will suffer the penalties of perjury nevertheless. Stand closer there, and we will begin."

Ralph watched Keith move a step or two closer to the justices. If the man was frightened he did not show it. He rubbed his large, well-kept hands together, apparently from force of habit rather than agitation.

Pollexfen began the questioning. He had reassumed his air of nonchalance.

"What is your name?" he said.

"Richard Whitstone Keith, Sir."

"Where do you live?"

"On Lytton Street, London."

"What is your occupation?"

"I am a physician, Sir."

So that was it. Ralph felt his pulses quicken. Esther Hemphill's unimpeachable witness was the man who could do her cause the most good—or the most harm. He could do the most good if he really was a physician and also a dexterous liar, and the most harm if he was only one or the other, or neither. As to the possibility of the man's actually telling the truth, it was so remote that it was not worth considering. Ralph remembered well his examination of the witnesses against George Hemphill. They could not have been mistaken.

Pollexfen paused. "Do you know the accused?" he asked.

"Yes Sir," Keith said promptly, looking at the pale young man on the litter. "It was I who removed the pistol bullet from his shoulder and dressed his wound."

"Tell the court when and where this took place." Pollexfen smiled drily.

"It took place at my house on Lytton Street sometime around ten o'clock at night on July third." Mechanically, Keith took the watch from his coat pocket, opened the case, glanced at the dial, then closed the watch and replaced it, as if he were about to tell Pollexfen that he was late for an appointment.

"Perhaps you can tell the court how you happen to remember so clearly the time of an event which took place over two months ago," Pollexfen said.

"Very readily, Sir," Keith said. "I keep an appointment book. When Mistress Hemphill asked me if I would come down and clear up the false accusations against her brother, I looked up the entry."

"I suppose you have the book with you," Pollexfen asked.

"Yes Sir." Keith looked toward the door. "If you would like to see it, I will have my man bring it in."

Pollexfen hesitated a moment. "That will not be necessary," he said. "Anyone can make entries in a book. Later I might want to talk to your man, however. If he escapes from the courtroom I shall assume he has not been thoroughly schooled in his part."

"I will be happy to have him testify, Sir," Keith said.

"Now let us get on with the business," said Pollexfen. "Tell the court about this wound and your treatment."

Keith's face brightened visibly. To Ralph he looked like an enthusiast who has just been asked to explain the lodestone or an old soldier asked to refight a campaign.

"Ah yes," he said. "Well, it happened thus. That evening just as I was thinking about retiring, my man brought in a hackney coachman who said that a young gentleman was outside in his coach severely wounded. We went out to the coach, and there I saw this young lady and this young man, whom I later found to be Mistress and Mr. Hemphill. Together we got the young man onto one of my beds. When I removed his coat and the clumsy dressing that had been used to stop the bleeding, I perceived a strange thing. The bullet, Sir, apparently fired from above the young man, had pierced his left shoulder just below the clavicle, passed through his upper thorax and between two ribs, and was lodged against his left scapula. Now then, Sir, you will ask, what was strange about that? Well Sir, the strange thing was that it did not touch a lung. You are undoubtedly familiar with gunshot wounds." For a moment Keith seemed to have forgotten that Pollexfen was a lawyer. "Ah, perhaps you are not. Fortunately, I am. When I was younger, I was for a

time a surgeon with Colonel Churchill's regiment in the French
service on the Rhine. There, I can assure you, we had many gunshot wounds. It would have amazed you, Sir, to see the number of
soldiers shot in the thorax. My point is that fourteen out of fifteen
were hit in the lungs. Well, you may say, put on a plaster to keep
the wound from sucking. Plug up the hole in time and you may
win the day. But I tell you gentlemen, it is not so simple as that.
How is one to stop the internal hemorrhage? How does one repair
the damage to the lung? I hear gentlemen say they can save fifty
percent of such cases; but I tell you frankly that after the battle of
Enzheim the most experienced surgeons in the French Army did not
save two cases in ten."

Keith paused and looked about triumphantly as if he had scored
a telling point against his opponents. Either he was the best actor
in England, Ralph thought, or else he had actually forgotten where
he was.

"Get on with it," Lord Jeffreys broke in shortly.

"Ah yes," Keith said affably. "It was strange, as I say, that the
ball did not touch the young man's lungs. At first I could hardly
believe it, even though it was obvious from the nature of the bleeding and from the way the young man inhaled. My next surprise was
finding the bullet against the scapula. Here was a piece of luck indeed. If I had been obliged to probe for the ball through the wound
itself, I could not have answered for the young man's life. Still I
had a problem, how to get the bullet from under the scapula. I
solved it by making a small incision on the left side of the bone,
cutting inward, and finally removing the ball with an invention of
my own—these specially bent forceps."

Keith calmly reached in the left pocket of his coat and brought
out a pair of forceps, bent at right angles about two inches from
the end. He also brought out a small round pellet.

"Here, if it interests you," he added, "is the bullet."

For a few moments Ralph found himself as completely carried
away as the spectators. He did not, like them, give an audible sigh
of surprise and relief; but he gave an involuntary stunned assent to
the man's testimony. Keith's enthusiastic assurance, his pedantic in-
sistence on details, carried almost irresistible conviction. It was not
until Lord Jeffreys scowled down the audience and prepared to
counter-attack that Ralph recovered himself. No, it was impossible.
The man was lying. The forceps and the pistol ball were only clever
theatrics.

"Damn me," Jeffreys' voice boomed out, "the gentlemen of this

county are lucky. Instead of getting to hear only one skilled Whig
perjurer, they are privileged to hear two. Upon my word, gentlemen, I have not heard such damned impudence since the trials for
the Rye House plot. Now then, Mr. Keith, perhaps you will answer
a few questions."

Keith put the forceps and the bullet back in his pocket and turned
to face Jeffreys squarely.

"How can you prove you got that ball out of the back of the accused rebel?" Jeffreys glowered.

Again Keith reached in his pocket and pulled out the ball. "You
will observe, your lordship," he said, "that the ball is covered with
dried blood. Now you will say, it is easy to cover a pistol ball with
dried blood, and you are right; but Sir, you must also observe that
the ball is slightly flattened, and flattened in a way that occurs only
when a bullet goes through flesh and lodges against bone, as any
military surgeon can attest. Now then, your lordship may say, but it
is impossible to prove that this identical ball was drawn from underneath the scapula of this falsely accused gentleman. This I freely
own. Indeed if one were to examine four or five hundred gunshot
wounds, one might find three or four balls with a configuration which
matched the circumstances of this particular wound."

"Enough of this," Lord Jeffreys broke in again. "The court is willing
to assume that the manufactured evidence fits the circumstances of
the case. We will not hear another harangue on gunshot wounds.
We are content with your admission that you have no proof for your
identification. Now let us hear an exact description of the scar on
the rebel's back."

"Gladly, your lordship," Keith said. "If you will remove the young
gentleman's shirt, you will find the scar of a vertical incision, beginning about an inch from the bottom of the left scapula and about half
an inch from the left edge of the bone. The incision runs upward for
precisely an inch and a quarter. I was curious enough to measure it
when I sewed it up. Taking as I do a modest pride in my surgery,
I should be pleased to show the scar to the court."

Ralph saw Lord Jeffreys hesitate. Jeffreys, Ralph knew, had never
examined the wound. It was possible, perhaps probable, that Keith
was merely guessing from a general description given to him by Esther Hemphill. But if Jeffreys stripped the prisoner and Keith were
proven right in a living demonstration, the jury was sure to be convinced.

"That will not be necessary," Lord Jeffreys snapped, declining the
challenge. "Even if your description is correct, it only proves that

someone has taken the trouble to prepare your testimony thoroughly. We have more important things to talk about. How long did the young traitor stay at your house?"

"He left the morning of the second day, your lordship. That would be July fifth."

"Did you attend him to his house?"

"Yes Sir."

Lord Jeffreys leaned forward. "Where is the Hemphill house in London?"

"On Lincoln Street, your lordship, just off the Strand."

"Why did you keep him for two nights and a day?" Lord Jeffreys seemed to have relaxed his careful attention.

"Because of the severity of his wound, your lordship."

"How long did you attend him after he left your house?"

"Until he quitted London, the morning of the tenth."

Jeffreys suddenly stood up, walked around the table, and thrust his face almost into Keith's. "Now you sniveling Whig dog, tell the court why you let a severely wounded man travel from London to Somersetshire. Did you advise a hundred and fifty mile coach trip for his health? Speak up, man. Don't stand there inventing a lie."

"I advise the journey, my lord?" Keith drew back with an air of outrage. "The imputation is monstrous. The journey was undertaken against my specific admonition and advice. It was little short of criminal folly. Had my advice been followed, the young gentleman would have been perfectly well within three weeks, or a month at the worst. When the wound started healing splendidly, the young man began to entertain the vulgar delusion that he was almost cured. On the eighth, he heard the news of Sedgemoor; he learned that some of his own tenants had foolishly and criminally taken part on the rebel side. He was determined to return home at once. I urged the suicidal character of the journey and strictly forbade him to go. I thought I had convinced him, but when I arrived on the morning of the tenth, he and his sister had already started out upon the west road. The results were exactly as I foretold—except that I had no way of knowing he would be taken up on the fourteenth of July and clapped into a damp noisome gaol. I wonder that he is still alive."

Jeffreys turned in obvious disgust and resumed his seat. "You see, gentlemen," he said, "how diabolically cunning these Whigs can be and how important it is that the smooth traitors be signally punished. They have rehearsed every detail of this intricate fiction, hoping to wear out the crown lawyers and unseat the common sense of the jury. But gentlemen, they will not succeed. No amount of ingenious testimony will ever convince the court that the young rebel was almost mortally wounded by robbers in London and then carried down here just in time to be taken up by the officers of the crown. Soon you will hear a true relation of the facts. Before this man goes, however, I shall ask him one more question. Turn around, Sir, and tell the jury who commanded the British troops when you were with my lord Churchill's regiment."

"Certainly your lordship," said Keith. "It was the Duke of Monmouth."

"Precisely," said Jeffreys. "That will be all."

The man looked as if he were about to say something else, but instead of speaking, he gave a slight bow to the justices and carefully made his way to his seat at the back of the hall.

CHAPTER

Six

RALPH COMPELLED HIMSELF to relax while the first crown witness was being sworn. The tension of watching Esther Hemphill and Richard Keith battle for the boy's life had been almost unendurable—like watching two tightrope walkers make their way across a deep chasm. The spectators, Ralph could see, were exhausted by the strain. It was almost criminal, he thought, to put them through more agony. Almost to a man they were praying for George Hemphill. When their friends and relatives—their social equals—had been condemned, they had watched with groans and tears, but with resignation. Nothing, they knew, could save a poor man. But perhaps a gentleman had a chance. To them, George Hemphill would be a symbol of the good cause; if he escaped, all was not lost.

"Tell the court your name." Pollexfen's voice brought Ralph's attention back to the action.

"Roger Hicks, your honor."

Ralph looked at the witness as if he were seeing him for the first time. The man seemed to have shrunk since the interrogation. Compared with Keith, he appeared small and disreputable.

"Do you know the accused?" Pollexfen was wasting no time.

"Yes, your honor." Hicks brushed a straggling lock of straight brown hair from his eye. "I am his father's tenant."

"Good," said Pollexfen. "Now tell us what you know of his association with Lord Grey and the Duke of Monmouth."

Hicks shuffled back and forth on his feet for a moment. He began to look toward the spectators, but quickly turned his head.

"When the Duke's army came to Taunton, Mr. Hemphill sent for me. He said he was going to join the Protestant Duke; those were his words, your honor. He said he had a commission in the cavalry and if I would bring my horse I could be a sergeant. I told him I didn't know soldiery. He said nobody else did neither, but I could learn. Then I asked him was it right. He said it was right. He said that King James was a papist. He said that if the Duke didn't drive him out he would bring in popery. Then everyone who stood by his religion would have his throat cut by the King's troopers and if they couldn't do it, the King would bring in the French and Irish. I said I'd enlist, so I got my horse and we joined the army at Taunton."

Pollexfen smiled encouragingly. "Just so," he said. "Now tell us, did the accused leave the army at any time before the battle at Sedgemoor?"

"No, your honor." Hicks was warming to his work now. As long as he kept his eyes fixed on Pollexfen, he was apparently able to ignore the contempt and hostility of the spectators. "We went up to Bristol together and finally back to Bridgwater."

"Did you see the accused on the night of the battle?"

"Yes, your honor, he rode out at the head of our troop."

"What happened then?" Again Pollexfen nodded encouragement.

"We were fired upon; my horse ran away with the others. I didn't see Mr. Hemphill again, but I heard he was wounded."

"I see," said Pollexfen, turning toward the jury. "The last time you saw the accused was on the field of battle."

"Yes, your honor." The witness took a deep breath. The ordeal, he seemed to think, was almost over.

Lord Jeffreys smiled broadly. "You see, gentlemen, how simple the truth is? Why damn me, these people lied until they made us dizzy with their talk about robbers, coaches, gunshot wounds and pistol balls; but like all liars, they made their story too complicated. Now the truth comes out, and what do we find? A plain case, plainly made out."

Jeffreys turned suddenly toward George Hemphill. "What do you say to this man's evidence?"

The injured man raised himself slightly. "It is a lie."

"With the court's permission, I will examine the witness," Esther Hemphill said firmly.

"Please do," Jeffreys sneered.

"Now Roger," she said. "Look at me. Don't look at Mr. Pollexfen now. He can't help you. Look at me and at the people in the court, and prepare yourself to tell the truth."

The witness hung his head and looked at the floor about a foot in front of Esther Hemphill. Ralph pitied the man. To face his old friends and neighbors while he was in effect killing one of them took more courage than he had. For the moment his fear of his friends had replaced his fear of his enemies.

"Tell me, Roger," the girl went on, "did these gentlemen promise you a pardon if you would swear away my brother's life?"

Hicks muttered something undistinguishable.

"Speak up, Roger," she said. "Don't be afraid."

"I said yes they did." He looked toward Pollexfen appealingly.

"What you mean is," Pollexfen interrupted, "that you were offered a recommendation for clemency if you would tell the truth. Is that right?"

"Yes Sir," said Hicks, much relieved.

"That is to say," the girl added, "if you would tell what these gentlemen wanted to hear. Am I right?"

"Yes."

Jeffreys cleared his throat, but Esther Hemphill hurried on.

"Now, Roger, tell us, did you see the remains of Jemmy Slade after Colonel Kirke's men got through with him?"

Hicks swallowed. "Yes," he said faintly.

"You saw the remains, then, after Jemmy had been hanged, disembowelled and chopped into four pieces? You saw his head on a pike?"

Hicks nodded miserably.

"You also saw the remains of Dick Hill, John Friars, and John Waters?"

"Enough of this recital." Jeffreys came to the rescue of the witness. "Get on with the examination."

"I am getting on with it, your lordship," the girl said. "I am now coming to a very important question. Roger, you did not want to die for treason, did you? You did not want your head on a pike?"

Hicks shook his head miserably and wiped his nose on his sleeve.

"You could not bear the thought of having your entrails burned and your quarters boiled in pitch, could you?"

Hicks shook his head again.

Esther Hemphill lowered her voice sympathetically. "You must not feel like a criminal, Roger," she said. "Not everyone can be brave. You did not want to swear away my brother's life, did you?"

Tears began to run down Roger Hicks' face. He shook his head violently.

"You told the story you told just now only to save your own life, didn't you?"

Hicks nodded. His "yes" was almost inaudible.

Lord Jeffreys cleared his throat. Ralph wondered now why he had not interrupted the girl sooner.

"Hicks," he thundered.

The witness wiped his eyes and straightened up abruptly. One could almost see the idea cross the poor fellow's mind that perhaps he had forfeited his right to clemency by answering the girl's questions.

"Hicks," Jeffreys roared. "The story you told is true, is it not?"

Hicks shivered visibly and looked at Jeffreys like a bird at a snake. "Yes, your lordship," he said in a hoarse whisper.

"You did not invent it."

"No Sir." Ralph thought the man was going to faint.

"George Hemphill was with Lord Grey's cavalry both before and during the battle at Sedgemoor."

Hicks began to sway back and forth. "Yes, your lordship."

"That will be all," said Jeffreys. "Take him away."

Ralph spared himself a glance at the spectators. There was something depressing and indecent about seeing a man tortured into revealing his innermost fears. The sight made people avoid each other's eyes. Ralph wondered if the spectators and jury were asking themselves whether they would have saved their own lives at the expense of someone else. And if they were asking the question, how they were answering it. He was not sure about himself. One thing he was sure of: the whole experience with the Assizes, from start to finish, had been hideous. It was even worse than the battle. When he had begun collecting evidence against the rebels, he had known that some of them would be executed. Treason, after all, was a capital offense, and traitors deserved to be punished. He remembered agreeing with King James's statement in their last interview: the safety of the throne and the state demands that examples should be made. He still agreed in principle. But he had not been prepared for what now seemed like wholesale slaughter. He had long since lost count of the exact number of executions. There must have been more than two hundred, not counting today's batch, with three towns still to be visited.

Perhaps, he thought, the Inns of Court should train their men better. They should require each student to attend at least four state executions. Ordinary hangings would not serve. But then again, maybe such training would do no good. As far as he was concerned personally, the two hundredth execution was as sickening as the first.

"Do you know the accused?" he heard Pollexfen say. He looked up.

Ralph had no trouble recognizing Obadiah Marsh. The long spare frame, the gaunt harsh features were unforgettable. Marsh, Ralph realized suddenly, looked like the caricature of a fanatic—like a true blue Presbyterian out of *Hudibras.*

"I do," said Marsh in a loud rasping voice.

"Did you see the accused immediately before the battle at Sedgemoor?"

"I did."

Pollexfen waited for the echoes of Marsh's voice to die away. "Please tell the court the circumstances," he said.

Marsh looked carefully around the hall, as if to make sure that everyone was listening to his testimony.

"As your honor knows," he said, "I am the chemist at Bridgwater. When Monmouth's army passed through on their way to Bristol, Mr. Hemphill stopped in to get a preparation for his horse's galled forefoot. I was astonished, your honor, to see the young gentleman with the rebels and I told him so. He said the Duke of Monmouth had come to save England from popery. I asked him if he thought the Duke had a title to the crown. He said 'title be damned. When your house is on fire you don't question the title of the man with the water.' Well, your honor, when the rebel army came back, I saw him again. On the day before the battle, the rebels were camped in Bridgwater, and I was curious enough to walk through their camp. There I saw Mr. Hemphill. I asked him what he thought of the Duke's fortunes now. He said things looked bad, but the Duke still had a chance. They would make a fight for it."

"Did you see the accused after that?" Pollexfen asked.

"No, your honor," said Marsh, "but the day after the battle his servant Mathers came to me to get bandages and ointments for a wound."

"I see," said Pollexfen. "Does your lordship wish to question the witness further?" He turned to Jeffreys.

"Not at all." Jeffreys laughed good-naturedly. "I will leave the caviling to Mistress Hemphill. No doubt she has prepared another harangue on the fear of death."

Esther Hemphill stepped forward again, apparently undismayed. "I have two questions, your lordship. They will not take long."

She turned to Obadiah Marsh. "Think carefully now," she said. "When the government hired you as an informer against the rebels, did they pay you a lump sum or did they pay you by the victim?"

Marsh hesitated. "They paid me fifty pounds," he rasped defiantly.

"Not a bad sum for a fanatic tradesman," Esther said. "Now one final question, and remember that you are under oath. Remember also that I have a slip of paper with your name on it. How much money do you owe my brother?"

Obadiah Marsh shot a quick glance at Pollexfen, but the prosecutor was even more stunned than he. Marsh licked his lips and opened his mouth. No sound came out.

"I said, how much money do you owe my brother?"

Lord Jeffreys banged his hand on the table. "That will be enough of your tricks. By God, this court has been patient with you, young lady. It has come dangerously near treason itself in protecting your brother's rights and avoiding any implication of unfairness. Now this nonsense will stop. You have produced your last irrelevancy."

"Mr. Marsh." Jeffreys turned suddenly. "The evidence you gave is true, is it not?"

"Yes, your lordship." Marsh had recovered his composure.

"No moneys you might have received from the crown and no personal financial interests affected the truth of your testimony."

"No, your lordship."

"You actually saw the accused in Bridgwater at the stated times."

"Yes, your lordship."

"You are under no threats nor coercion from the crown."

"No, your lordship."

"Very well, then. You may go."

As the witness made his way back to his seat, Ralph watched Lord Jeffreys begin to gather up his papers. Quite obviously he was preparing to close the case. Evidently he was confident of a conviction. Otherwise, he would continue his proceedings until the next day. In the meantime, Ralph knew, three or four more witnesses like Hicks could be produced. If the crown had dreamed that the case would be contested in such a fashion it could have filled the room with testifiers. Certainly, Ralph told himself, no one could accuse him of dereliction. He had produced the two witnesses required. Their testimony had been adequate. The fact that their characters had been assailed was not his fault. At any rate, Lord Jeffreys seemed satisfied. He would not hold the court over another day at Taunton on the remote chance that a loyal jury might let a criminal escape.

When Jeffreys had gathered the papers into a neat pile, he turned back toward Esther Hemphill. "Does the accused or his counsel have anything further to say before the court instructs the jury? If so, make the remarks short. It is already late."

"Your lordship." The girl drew herself up gracefully. "I have several things to say, but I will be as brief as I can. First let me express my firm belief that the gentlemen of this county will never be party to a judicial murder. No hope of favors or fear of reprisal will make them take the life of an innocent man. You gentlemen have heard me testify that my brother was with me in London at the time of the battle. You have also heard the testimony of an eminent physician giving a detailed account of his injury. This testimony was not impeached, except by the innuendo that Mr. Keith had served with the army when it was commanded by the traitor Monmouth, a charge which could be made against my Lord Churchill, my Lord Feversham, half the regulars in the royal army, and two of the members of the jury. Then you saw the witnesses the crown produced."

Esther Hemphill paused. "As for poor Roger Hicks, I am sure he did not wish to do my brother any harm. But he is a fearful coward. No gentleman of this county could be simple enough to doubt that Roger Hicks would swear that the moon is made of green cheese if he thought he could save his life by doing so. Nor could anyone doubt that the renegade fanatic Obadiah Marsh would perjure himself a thousand times to earn fifty pounds from the King and to cancel the debt he owes my brother. Yes, a hundred pounds is the sum he owes, the sum for which he was willing to swear away the life of his creditor.

"And now, gentlemen," the girl moved two steps closer to the jurors and lowered her voice confidentially, "let me tell you the reason for this conspiracy against my brother's life. Three days ago a man came down from London to see my father. He let it be known that if my brother would plead guilty to the charges against him, my father could buy his release for fifteen thousand pounds. You realize what this means. It means that a few scheming, influential courtiers hope to make a fortune out of the accusation against my brother. They also hope to ruin my family in the process. I hardly need tell you gentlemen that we refused the offer. We would not plead guilty to a false accusation and place my brother's life in the hands of court politicians for the chance of bankrupting ourselves to buy it back. We chose to trust the wisdom and justice of the gentlemen of this county. I am sure our confidence was not misplaced.

"One final word, gentlemen. The false charges against my brother touch every gentleman here. If a gentleman's life and property are to be held at the mercy of every smooth politician who can worm his way into favor and influence, who can consider himself safe? Someday you gentlemen may be offered the chance to buy your sons and brothers for fifteen thousand pounds. Consider it well, gentlemen, and consider also that your wisdom and honor are all that stand between my brother and an unjust, horrible death. It is upon brave, honest gentlemen like you that the property and lives of the King's loyal subjects depend."

Ralph watched the girl go back to the chair near her brother. As far as he could make out there was not the slightest trace of fear or anxiety on her face. She seemed as calm and confident as she had when she delivered her first audacious lie. Compared to her the judges, the lawyers and the spectators appeared to be consumed with emotion. Jeffreys' face was a study in anger; Pollexfen was twisting a coat button in nervous agitation; the other judges and lawyers frowned ominously. A look of timorous hope had come over the faces of the spectators. Ralph was surprised, as he looked at the poor devils, that none of them had said "amen" when Esther Hemphill finished her speech. They must have feared Jeffreys, or feared that their approval of the argument would antagonize the jury. Only the jury remained noncommittal; the members looked as impassive as card sharpers. Each one, Ralph thought, was determined to give no sign of approval or disapproval.

It occurred to Ralph that perhaps his own face was registering emotion. He hoped not. The emotion he felt was not suitable to a young crown lawyer and a private agent of King James. In spite of his firm conviction of George Hemphill's guilt, he could not repress the hope that the boy would be acquitted. It was not, he told himself, that he was fascinated by Esther Hemphill, although there was no denying her beauty and her dexterity. It was not even a particular sympathy with the boy. Compared with the dozens of poor, ignorant fanatics who had been executed, George Hemphill was a seditious monster. He, at least, had known something about politics, something about what he was getting into. No, Ralph told himself, it was not the girl or her brother who had influenced him; it was only his disgust with bloodletting. There had been more than enough already. He was beginning to see tarred quarters, impaled heads, and burning entrails in his sleep. If through the skill and courage of Esther Hemphill her brother could be saved, there would be one dismembered corpse the less. The throne, Ralph was convinced, would not be endangered.

While Jeffreys was preparing to give his instructions to the jury, two attendants lighted the candles in the great hall. The gathering crepuscular gloom was not so much dispelled by the candlelight as agitated. The room was suddenly filled with grotesque moving shadows. Jeffreys' florid face was framed in the light of two candles placed on his table.

"It is now my duty," he began slowly, "to instruct this jury in the law. I shall not waste the jury's time with a long explanation. A jury which has already today convicted sixteen rebels obviously understands its duty. If the jury feels—as it must feel from the evidence presented—that the accused was in arms against the crown, it must convict him of treason. Conspiracy against the King and harboring traitors are in themselves treasonable acts, but armed rebellion is the quintessence of treachery. No loyal subject of the King can fail to realize the foulness, the depravity, and the sacrilege of such a crime, or fail to convict the traitor.

"Now then, since this jury has been subjected to such a cannonade of foul Whig lies and insinuations, I am forced to say something about the evidence. Mistress Hemphill, in her artful, caviling, fanatic argument, has attempted to impugn the testimony of the crown witnesses. One of the witnesses, she alleged, is not to be trusted because he fears for his life; the other because he owes the accused money. No gentleman with an understanding fit for even the meanest crown employment should be misled. In the first case, you must remember that treason is most often uncovered by traitors. The villains must be identified by their friends and acquaintances, by people who have knowledge of their plots and acts. The crown must get its evidence from men implicated in the crimes. To get this evidence it must often promise leniency to criminals—throw back a small fish to get a number of big ones. All the men you have convicted today have been convicted on such evidence.

"In the second case, the allegation that the witness was acting as a paid informer for the crown is easily answered. All officers of the crown are paid. Must we reject their testimony because His Majesty's government pays them to get information? The notion is absurd. As for the insinuation that a debtor cannot testify against his creditor, this is even more absurd. If it were true, no gentleman on this jury could testify against a rascally London scrivener or goldsmith to whom he owes money, even if he saw him commit murder or treason.

"But what can you expect from the arguments of people raised on treason, taught from their cradle every sleight and subterfuge with which to escape the consequences of their crimes." Jeffreys leaned toward the jurors. His voice was rising now from its tone of calm, contemptuous argument to a tone of angry declamation. "They imbibe doctrines of resistance and rebellion with their mothers' milk! They are brought up on sedition and impiety. Look at the record of the Hemphill family. This young traitor's grandfather was Richard

Hemphill, a colonel in the parliamentary army, in arms against the blessed martyr, Charles First. His father James Hemphill was a friend of the traitors Sidney and Russell. If justice had been done, he would have been executed himself, before he infected his son and daughter with treason.

"You see the results. Why damn me, gentlemen, the daughter had the infernal impudence to attack the King in your very presence. She accuses His Majesty of selecting corrupt servants, and implies that his clemency can be bought with money. Not content with that, she accuses this court of suborning witnesses and plotting judicial murder. You saw how smoothly these lies came to the tongue of a young woman who has been trained all her life to attack the King's justice, the King's servants, and the King himself, God's vicegerent on earth."

Jeffreys checked the wrathful flow of words and allowed himself a sarcastic laugh. "Of all Mistress Hemphill's inventions, the most fanciful is the story about the fifteen thousand pounds. No courtier is stupid enough to attempt extortion from James Hemphill. The old fox would not give fifteen pounds to save his son's life, let alone fifteen thousand. A loyal gentleman might indeed believe the ruin of the Hemphills to be a public service but he would never believe it could be compassed by holding one of the Hemphill children for ransom.

"But enough of this." Jeffreys' face suddenly became solemn and judicial. "You understand the evidence. You have heard the young traitor's guilt established by two competent witnesses and by the rebels' own record. You understand your duty as loyal subjects of the King, as the gentlemen on whom His Majesty depends to uphold his justice, fill his places of honor and profit, and suppress his enemies. The court expects, therefore, that you will return a quick and satisfactory verdict. You may now retire."

When the jurors had filed out, Ralph noticed a peculiar silence in the courtroom. Pollexfen was whispering with one of his assistants, but aside from that no one said a word. Esther Hemphill held her brother's hand. Jeffreys stared truculently about the hall. The crown clerks made notes. Ralph could hear the scratching of the quills. Among the spectators, there was scarcely a movement. In the uncertain candlelight, they looked uncomfortably like corpses.

Ralph picked up the pen that lay on the table in front of him, dipped it and began to draw designs on a piece of foolscap. He felt utterly exhausted. If he were not careful he would begin running the whole case over again in his mind, and he was much too tired. It was idle now, he told himself, to wonder how the jury had responded to Jeffreys' final speech. Very probably they had been convinced. Still, there might be a chance. The girl understood the feelings of the jurors uncommonly well. It was odd, he thought, that Jeffreys should heap such scorn on the story about the solicitation to bribery. That was the only part of the girl's story which was undoubtedly true. If he had been Jeffreys, he would have passed over the story completely. But then, Jeffreys knew best. Certainly he had played his part uncommonly well.

As he looked at Esther Hemphill again, he found it hard to believe that her brother's life was at stake. The expression of serenity and composure had not left her face. It was almost inhuman, he thought, that she should stay so calm now that her calmness could not affect the jury's decision. He would have felt better if she had burst into tears, but the more he looked at her the more he became convinced that she was as unlikely to weep as Lord Jeffreys.

The heavy silence, broken only by an occasional cough, lasted for about ten minutes. Then the jury filed in, led by their foreman, Sir Peter Bascourt. While the other gentlemen found their seats, Sir Peter stood surveying the court and the spectators. His beefy face showed no sign of animation, only its habitual sullen discontent.

Lord Jeffreys waited for the confusion to subside. "Gentlemen," he said finally, "have you reached a verdict?"

An audible sigh arose from among the spectators.

"We have, my lord." Sir Peter's voice was flat and toneless.

"How say you, do you find the accused guilty or not guilty?"

Sir Peter gave a final expressionless stare at his audience.

"We find the accused not guilty, my lord."

A long moan of relief and joy filled the hall. It seemed to Ralph as if all the spectators had begun weeping at once. A woman leaped up suddenly and shouted "praise God!"; her cry was answered by a low chorus of *amens*. Several of the spectators fell to their knees and began to pray. Even Esther Hemphill seemed moved. As Ralph watched her, he saw a relieved smile come over her face. She leaned over and kissed her brother's hand. Then she took her handkerchief and mopped off his forehead. This done, she straightened up to observe Lord Jeffreys. Only a trace of her smile remained.

Lord Jeffreys, Ralph could see, was engaged in a fierce internal conflict. His natural impulse was to flay the jurors with his tongue and send them out again. Ralph knew he would have done so if this had been a London jury. He could have harangued them, bullied them, and sent them out all night. But to use these tactics on a jury of independent, loyal country gentlemen was quite another matter. These men were stubborn on principle. They would never submit to brow-beating. Such methods would only make him enemies among the politically powerful western squirearchy, the King's most devoted subjects.

"Gentlemen," he said finally in a surprisingly calm tone, "you see that your verdict has brought joy to the fanatics. No doubt they will mention you in their copious prayers. I question, however, that it will bring such joy to our master, King James. The escape of a traitor will hardly delight him. You may consider this as you go to your homes. I have nothing further to say to you. The court is now adjourned."

Ralph sat quietly as the courtroom emptied. Jeffreys and his entourage left immediately without even looking back. Behind them the spectators crowded toward the rear door, buzzing feverishly. Four men, probably servants, took George Hemphill from the two soldiers and began to carry him out. As they did so, several of the jurors, who had lingered behind, shook the boy's hand. As far as Ralph could see, the lad was barely conscious. His sister walked behind him, talking to him and patting him on the head. Just as they reached the door, Ralph heard her give a clear, delighted laugh. In another moment they were gone.

Wearily, Ralph stood up. Now, he thought, for a hot bath and a hot dinner. The only good thing about Taunton was the service at the inn. As he reached down to crumple the foolscap he had been drawing on, he whistled with surprise. There, underneath several words of law Latin and a drawing of a scaffold, were the words, "Esther Hemphill, Lincoln Street, off the Strand, London."

CHAPTER

Seven

A DROP OF SWEAT rolled off King James's forehead and down his long nose. Ralph watched it, fascinated, and waited for the King to continue. James reached up with his handkerchief and brushed it off.

"You understand what this means, Mr. Barnard," he said. "It means that someone is trying to kill me."

Ralph chose his words carefully. How did one go about suggesting to the King that it was perfectly natural for drunken Londoners to shout "Down with the Papists" whenever they recognized a Roman Catholic, and to brandish bottles, swords, or whatever they had in their hands? How could one hint discreetly that the incident was more likely ridiculous than dangerous?

"We must proceed very carefully in this, Your Majesty," he said finally; "the affair may turn out to be some sort of coincidence."

"Not at all." Apparently James was offended at the suggestion. "The man was sent there, I assure you. It is true he gave the appearance of being drunk, but when my guards tried to apprehend him, he outran them easily. No ordinary drunken troublemaker could have done that."

Ralph was unimpressed by the argument. Half the citizens of London, he thought, drunk or sober, could escape from the King's guards in a race through the alleys of the city. In some respects the royal cavalry made excellent guards, but speed afoot was not one of their virtues. Still, he could hardly contradict the King.

"I see," he said. "You think the man was feigning drunkenness, and that he intended to lurch against you and stab you before the guards could interfere."

"I am sure of it," James said sharply, "and you must find out who the man is, and who is behind the plot."

"Very well, Your Majesty," Ralph said. He knew he might as well pretend to be cheerful. If the King was determined to order an investigation, there was no help for it. And after all, there was always a bare possibility that James was right. In a way, Ralph hoped he was.

"Before I can start my investigation," he went on, "I must ask a few questions. Can you tell me exactly where in London the incident took place?"

The King was visibly annoyed. "I see no reason for telling you that, Mr. Barnard," he said.

For a moment, Ralph was so surprised by the answer that he could think of nothing to say. "I am sorry, Your Majesty," he heard himself mumble when he was able to find his voice. "I had no notion that the question was offensive. My only thought in asking it was to locate the place so I would know where to start looking. Your Majesty understands that if I am to find the man, I must have information."

The King's face showed obvious confusion and embarrassment. James, Ralph thought, was unfortunate in having such a mobile countenance. It registered emotion, especially unpleasant emotion, with disconcerting accuracy. No wonder James had the reputation of being a poor dissembler. Every movement of his long, thin face gave him away.

"I understand," the King said finally. "The incident took place in Lincoln Street, just off the Strand—in front of a small house belonging to the Countess of Dorchester, if you must know."

Now it was Ralph's turn to be confused. He hoped his confusion did not show. How could he have been so stupid? James had been visiting his mistress, Catherine Sedley. That accounted for his embarrassment.

"I see, Your Majesty," he said as noncommittally as possible. "Now then, did anyone know that you were going to be at that place at that time?"

"No one," James said firmly. "That is what makes the incident so suspicious. I have kept my visits to that area absolutely secret. Only a diabolically clever cabal of plotters could have ferreted out the information."

In spite of the King's earnestness, it was all Ralph could do to keep from laughing. How was it possible that a man could be so thoroughly deceived? Everyone in London, from the greatest lord down to the humblest cobbler, knew of the King's meetings with the Countess. The coffee houses were all buzzing with speculation whether the Queen would put an end to the visits or whether Catherine would succeed in keeping her grip on the King. Some people even affected to hope that the "Protestant Mistress" might reconvert James to Anglicanism.

"I see," Ralph said again. "Do you know of any possible way that the information could have leaked out?"

"None at all," James said. "I do not tell my guards in advance where I am going. I tell no one about the court, not even my confessor Father Mansuete. I merely send a message, carefully sealed, to the Countess, telling her when to meet me in Lincoln Street. Then with a few of my guards I get into an ordinary coach and travel to Lincoln Street by an indirect route."

"You don't suppose that the Countess's servants can be at fault, do you?" Ralph found himself asking questions out of curiosity about the King's way of thinking. "After all, they would be involved in the preparations for your visit. They could easily pass on information if they were so inclined."

Evidently, James had never considered the possibility. It had not occurred to him that knowledge shared by so many people could not be kept secret. Apparently, he had convinced himself that his absurd precautions were perfectly adequate.

"I refuse to believe that," James said, irritated again. "The Countess and her servants are perfectly trustworthy. They have been cautioned repeatedly, and I am sure none of them would breathe a word."

"I suppose not," said Ralph. "Still, I hope Your Majesty does not mind if I question them. Possibly one of them might be able to identify the offender. He might very well turn out to be someone from the neighborhood."

"I don't mind," the King said, "but you are wasting time. This is a well-laid plot, and the man is undoubtedly a professional assassin. You must find out who he is and who hired him."

"I intend to, Your Majesty," Ralph said. "Now, if you will please describe the man again to fix his image in my mind, I shall be greatly obliged."

The King rubbed his long hands together. "The scoundrel was almost six feet tall, with long, black hair. I should say he was forty-five years old—perhaps a little younger. He was dressed in a black velvet suit trimmed with white lace, and armed with a short, silver-handled sword. If I saw him again, I should know him immediately."

"Good." Ralph made a note of the description. "One final question, Your Majesty. Do you suspect anyone or any group in particular?"

The drooping corners of James's mouth straightened to help form a firm, stubborn line. "The only people capable of such monstrous wickedness," he said, "are the fanatics, and a few of their abettors, like the Russells and the Hemphills. You were at the Assizes. You know the kind of people I mean. We must find the villains and extirpate them."

There were still several things Ralph wanted to ask. With a few more questions, he thought, he could clarify the affair in his own mind and estimate its seriousness. But it was impossible to cross-examine the King. Unless James wanted to volunteer additional information, there was no politic way of getting it. One had to be very careful not to offend him by seeming to pry too closely into his affairs or by contradicting his opinions. Already, Ralph feared, he had gone too far. From now on he must rely on his own resources. He would begin with the Countess.

"You will hear from me soon, Your Majesty," he said, as Father Mansuete appeared to conduct him from the chamber. "Until you do, I suggest that you take no unnecessary chances."

The King returned Ralph's bow with what appeared to be a nod of approval.

There was something infuriating about this, Ralph thought as he made his way across Saint James's Park. He had been half way home to Lincolnshire when the King's messenger had overtaken him and summoned him back to London. The King's life was in danger, the messenger had said. Without a second's hesitation, he had turned around and ridden back to London, foundering two horses on the way. And now it appeared he might as well have saved his trouble. The King was perfectly safe. From all appearances he had never been in any danger.

Ralph swore softly to himself. Ever since the Assizes, the King had been promising him that he could go home for a week or two; but something always happened. First there was that miserable trip to Edinburgh, the trouble about the mad Covenanters; then there was the investigation at Portsmouth, the affair of the Whig naval officers; and now this. At this rate he would never get to Lincolnshire. He wished now that he had at least taken the time to send Walter and Rachel a note before he had headed back to London. There was no telling how many dinners would be spoiled waiting for him. Well, he would get a message off today with one of the couriers.

Meantime, he supposed, he might as well make the best of a bad situation. There was always a chance, of course, that the King actually had been threatened—that there was some sort of conspiracy afoot. And even if there was no conspiracy, things could be worse. It was not every day that one got the chance to meet Catherine Sedley, the new Countess of Dorchester.

"Please stop gaping and sit down, Mr. Barnard," Catherine Sedley laughed by way of greeting. "Have you never seen a woman before? I suppose you've come about that silly business over in Lincoln Street last Thursday. Now then, if you will just stop staring at me, we will discuss it. I have been expecting you, you know."

"You have?" Ralph was surprised and dismayed.

"Oh, you mustn't worry because the King told me about you. I was sure to find out about you sooner or later, and I won't tell anyone. I think you can trust the King too. He is not very bright, but he is close-mouthed. You would never believe what I went through to find out who does his spying for him. What's the matter, don't you like being called a spy? I am sorry. I forgot how long it takes to get used to hearing things called by their right names. I'll never forget the first time someone called me a whore. Now, you know, I rather like the term. And by the way, now that you have had a little time to look at me, are you disappointed?"

"On the contrary." Ralph was pleased at how smoothly the words came out. "I am delighted. You have been maligned."

Catherine Sedley laughed. "Oh yes, it is a great advantage to be described as a hag. After those fearful descriptions, I seem almost beautiful. I wouldn't be a countess today if it were not for my detractors. But then, on the other hand, if I were just a thought prettier I would be queen and Mary Beatrice would be packed off to a convent; so you see detraction is not enough after all."

Ralph heard himself chuckle. He had expected to find a blowzy, hard-faced harridan of thirty-five or forty. He saw, instead, a charming, almost beautiful woman, only a year or two older than himself. Perhaps she would have been beautiful, he thought, if it had not been for her eyes, which were too small, busy, and intelligent to fit with beauty. They were watching him now as if their owner might break into laughter at any minute.

"I believe," he said, "that you pay your detractors. Surely they would never tell such incredible lies without being bribed."

Catherine laughed. "You are very kind to say so, Mr. Barnard; but let me assure you that no one around the King's court will ever want for detractors, or need to buy calumny. And perhaps, after all, detractors are not nearly so dangerous as flatterers, like you."

"You see what an age we live in," he said, "when simple truth is called flattery. From now on, I shall never say another word about you."

"What an irritating man you are," she said, "to seize on such a flimsy excuse for changing the subject. Very well, then, since you don't like to talk about me, we shall talk about you. How did a bright young lawyer like you become an agent for the King? Were you blackmailed?"

"Well, I suppose you might say so." Ralph smiled. "You see, I was poor."

"No, no, Mr. Barnard. I am serious. You will never convince me that you were bought. You are not the type. You must have been blackmailed."

"Not at all," Ralph said. "You are trying to make the matter complex when it is really quite simple. The truth is, I became the King's agent because someone must guard the King and the kingdom. It is my duty."

After Ralph had said the words, he was sorry. Somehow the statement sounded fatuous. Catherine Sedley looked as if she were going to laugh again.

"This is worse than I thought," she said. "Here I was just beginning to like you, and you turn out to be a fanatic. I shall tell the King to keep a wary eye upon you. Men who have a sense of duty are capable of anything. The next thing I know you will be cutting the King's throat. Now, I suppose, you want to track down the poor fellow who shouted at the King and torture him into a confession of treason."

She carried off her raillery so well that Ralph could not be entirely sure whether she was joking or serious.

"Then you believe the man to be innocent," he said.

"Of course I do," she said. "I never saw anything funnier. The man was weaving down my street, as drunk as three tinkers, when suddenly he saw the King leaving my house. He stopped, staggered back two paces, dropped the bottle he was carrying, and stared at the King for a moment. Then he pulled out his sword and waved it round his head, made an obscene noise with his tongue, and shouted 'Down with the Papists.' The King and the guards out by the coach were so stunned that no one moved a muscle. All at once, the man seemed to realize what he had done. You would have died laughing to see the look of shock and horror come over the poor fellow's face. For a moment, I thought he was going to collapse on the spot. But then the guards made a dash for him, and the next thing I knew he was off like a rabbit. When I last saw him he was rounding the corner about twenty yards ahead of two bow-legged guardsmen, and gaining steadily."

Ralph could not help smiling at the description in spite of his irritation. Just as he had suspected, he was being asked to track down
an obnoxious drunk, some poor devil who at this moment must be
hiding somewhere, expecting the King's officers.

"You are sure, then," he said, conscious that Catherine Sedley was
studying him carefully, "that the man was perfectly harmless."

"I am certain," she said. "And I am surprised that you could have
a moment's doubt. Only an idiot, or the King, could take the matter
seriously for five minutes."

She began to laugh again. "Now please don't misunderstand me,
the King is a perfectly fine gentleman. I am very fond of him, and
I would not malign him for the world. He has been more than generous to me and my predecessors in office. But you know as well as
I do that if he were not king of England, he would be arrested for
sheer stupidity. No brewer in London would trust him to operate a
bungstarter."

Catherine Sedley paused and looked at him, apparently waiting
for him to nod in agreement or to join in her laughter. Ralph managed a smile, but he was sure that it looked insincere. Somehow,
frank discussion of James's stupidity made him feel uncomfortable.
For months now he had been trying to convince himself that his
master was at least normally intelligent—not brilliant, perhaps, but
a frank, open English gentleman.

"You exaggerate," he managed to say.

"Of course I exaggerate." Catherine Sedley was laughing at him
now. "I could never maintain my reputation as a wit if I did not
exaggerate. But you know what I mean. His Majesty does not have
enough brains to know anything. He has just enough to suspect everything. The poor dear has lived all his life among people who
were brighter than he, and they have used him shamefully. It is no
wonder he is stubborn and suspicious. He knows that he has been
continuously pelted with rotten eggs, but he has no idea where they
have been coming from."

"Don't worry about the King," he said. "I shall protect him from
the rotten eggs."

Catherine Sedley suddenly grew serious. "I am afraid you can't,
Mr. Barnard. When his brother King Charles was alive, James had
a protector who could save him from the worst consequences of his
folly; now there is no one. As long as he was only Duke of York,
there was hope; but now he has the power to ruin himself, and
there is nothing you can do about it."

"Come now, Countess," Ralph said, "you must quit teasing me.

You know the King's situation is not nearly so dangerous as you pretend. He has friends and advisers to keep him from making any fatal mistakes, and to keep his enemies from harming him."

The Countess looked at him sharply. "You are joking, of course. His advisers are a collection of fools and knaves. Half of them are as silly and bigoted as he is, and the rest are merely anxious to profit from serving him. You don't think that men like Father Petre and the Earl of Sunderland could save His Majesty from anything, do you?"

Again Ralph felt vaguely embarrassed. Yes, the Countess had put her finger on something. She exaggerated, perhaps, but there was enough truth in her statement to make it bite. After all, what could one expect from a popish zealot and an unprincipled opportunist?

He shook his head. "I suppose not, but you must remember that there are honest men around."

"I am willing to believe so, although I can't think of one myself. But no honest man will be around long. Imagine what would happen if someone were to tell His Majesty what a fool he is?" Catherine Sedley laughed slyly. "If you would like to find out what happens to honest men, why don't you go to him and tell him that he is entirely mistaken about the plot? Why don't you tell him that the culprit was just an honest London citizen who hates papists—a man who probably got besotted drinking the King's health and then remembered inopportunely, on seeing the King, his religious prejudices? Why don't you tell him that?"

"Well," Ralph said slowly, "for one thing, he wouldn't believe me."

"Exactly, and that is only half of it. He would discharge you for incompetence and find someone who would tell him what he wants to hear. He might even suspect you of being in league with the plotters."

Ralph was becoming annoyed with Catherine Sedley. In spite of her good humor, she had a way of making him uncomfortable.

"It is not quite so bad as you say." He tried to keep his tone light. "Undoubtedly, he would discharge me for incompetence if I contradicted him without further evidence than I now have. But when I catch the culprit and examination shows he was not implicated in a plot, I can report that fact to the King. I will have shown my competence by catching the man, even though the King does not approve of my report."

"I see." Catherine Sedley nodded understandingly. "And what do you think will happen to the—what was the word you used?—culprit?"

"Oh," Ralph said quickly, "he will be turned over to the courts for further examination and trial."

"You are evading my question, Mr. Barnard. You know what I mean. What will happen to him?"

"That is not my responsibility; that depends upon the courts." Ralph could hear the irritation rising in his voice.

"You have a pleasant way of putting it," she said, "but I am a little ashamed of you for being so squeamish. What you mean is, the man will be killed or maimed. At worst, he will have his head chopped off for brandishing a sword at the King. At best, he will only lose his ears and be flogged from Aldgate to Tyburn. You must not suppose that the judges are any more anxious to be discharged for incompetence than you are."

Ralph was silent. Catherine Sedley's statement, he knew, was unanswerable. The woman was as remorseless as a bad conscience.

She laughed slyly. "I suppose you want to ask me why I don't try to save the man myself, since I am so scrupulous, and since the King can hardly discharge me for incompetence. Well, the fact is I am no better than you. Why should I anger the King, when I can't possibly convince him? Why should I endanger my pension? God knows, I have enemies enough already. Milord Sunderland and Father Petre are trying to have me packed off to Ireland. I suppose they will succeed, but I will not help them for the sake of a drunken sword waver. If the man is saved, it must be by the spy and not by the whore."

Ralph felt better. Somehow it helped to know that he and Catherine Sedley were in the same position. "Are you suggesting, then, that I fail to find our comical friend—that I lie to the King?"

Catherine laughed again, this time with no trace of maliciousness. "I suggest nothing," she said finally, "although I can't see why you should be the only man in England who tells my poor stupid James the truth. No, seriously, I suppose you must do your duty. You know, I rather like you. I would sooner have you around the King than any man who could be hired to replace you."

Ralph made a mock bow. "I am honored."

"You can do better than that, Mr. Barnard." Catherine Sedley made a face. "You should say that you would sooner have me around the King than any woman who could be hired to replace me."

"But that goes without saying, Your Grace." Ralph bowed again.

"No compliment goes without saying, Mr. Barnard, but your amends are prettily expressed. If you are not careful you will become a courtier and a fop. Please watch yourself closely. Now then, can I give you any further advice or information? Please don't hesitate to ask. I love giving advice and information."

"Thank you, Your Grace," Ralph said, "there are a few things you can tell me. First, do you think any of the neighbors on Lincoln Street observed the incident? Perhaps one of them might be able to identify the man."

"If I were given to gambling, I should bet that everyone on Lincoln Street saw what happened. Every time the King and I have a secret meeting there, all the windows in the neighborhood are filled with faces. It would not surprise me if the Hemphills sold tickets."

"The Hemphills?" Ralph tried to make his voice sound casual.

"Yes. I see you know them."

"Slightly," Ralph said. "I was at the Assizes."

"Ah yes, I remember, and George escaped you. That was just as well. It would have been a shame to hang George and leave his father and sister alive. Perhaps you will have better luck next time."

"Oh, I have nothing against them. I have no intention of hunting down all the Whigs in England. But if they are enemies of yours, that is another matter; I shall have them hanged immediately." Ralph paused. "What are the charges?"

"There are no charges," Catherine said. "That is just the trouble. They are much too sly and slippery to be charged with anything concrete. But I have a feeling about them. The old man hated King Charles; he hates James even more. That sleek, smooth-talking daughter of his could deceive the devil himself, and she would stick at nothing. The two of them together are the most dangerous pair in England. Besides, I hate her for being pretty."

"I see," said Ralph. "This is serious indeed. Perhaps you would like an inch or so cut off Mistress Hemphill's nose."

"Believe me, Mr. Barnard, an inch or so cut from that nose might save His Majesty's throne, and maybe his life." Catherine appeared to pout. "But I can see you don't believe a word I am saying. The girl has bewitched you too. Very well, then, ignore my advice. Let her keep her nose. You will be sorry."

"I am sorry already," Ralph said, "if you think I slight your warning. You forget that I have seen the girl in action. I too believe she could get away with anything. The question is, what is she trying to get away with? Do you think she could have had anything to do with our fleet-footed sot?"

"Impossible." Catherine Sedley shook her head. "The Hemphills would never be stupid enough to murder the King on their own front door step. They would be hanged without a trial, and the whole

Whig party would be hunted down like dogs. No, Mr. Barnard, if the Hemphills ever try to assassinate the King, it will appear that the attempt was made by a loyal Tory gentleman."

Yes, Ralph thought, the Countess was undoubtedly right. For just a moment, a suspicion had crossed his mind. Now he dismissed it. Even if the Hemphills were depraved enough to assassinate the King —and this was by no means certain—they would not sacrifice themselves, their friends, and their cause to the project.

"No," Catherine Sedley went on. "The King is in no immediate danger of being murdered. His enemies are too bright to commit murder, and his friends are too stupid to think of it."

"Think of murdering the King?" Ralph could hardly believe he had understood her.

"Why certainly, Mr. Barnard." Catherine laughed at him. "If the Tories had any brains they would murder him tomorrow. Some faithful, loyal gentleman would run a sword through him. You must not suppose that the King is doing his followers any good. On the contrary, he is ruining them as fast as he can. Of course, everyone in the kingdom would be better off if he were dead—everyone, that is, except you, me, five politicians, and six or seven priests. But the ones who would profit most would be the jolly gentlemen who cried up the divine right of kings and nonresistance."

Ralph stared at her. Probably she expected him to laugh. But if this was some sort of joke, he did not think it very funny.

"I am afraid I don't understand you," he said.

"I know you don't. That is what I just got through saying. Loyal gentlemen don't see anything. They don't see that my poor, foolish James is fatal to them and all their beliefs. They think they can control him and use him against the Whigs and fanatics. But one of these days the country will be forced to make a choice between resisting James and becoming Papists. Believe me, Mr. Barnard, they won't choose to become Papists; and the party which supported James and talked nonsense about nonresistance will be ruined. That is why I say that if the Tories had any brains they would have him killed. Murdering James would save their doctrines, their party, and maybe the country."

Ralph felt his muscles relax. For a minute or two he had actually believed she was serious with her absurd talk, but now he saw she was being ridiculous.

"I see," he said with exaggerated gravity. "And I suppose you think it would be easy to find a loyal gentleman who would save his party, his church and his country at the price of his life and of certain damnation."

"Oh no," Catherine shook her head. "I think it would be very difficult to find such a man, and yet there must be a few men who would go to hell themselves to keep their friends and countrymen from going there. But you and I have no need to worry. Men with principles and courage seldom have brains. None of the King's friends will ever dream of killing him."

Ralph pretended to sigh with relief. "I am glad to hear you say so, Your Grace. Now I won't be obliged to watch the King's friends. I have trouble enough with his enemies. If, as you say, the King is determined to force England into popery, I am sure to have my hands full."

Catherine sighed too. "Alas, Mr. Barnard. No one believes me when I am serious. It is my wretched fate. You think I am joking about James. Well, I am; but not about his plans for England. I know him, I tell you. I know what is in that twopenny mind of his better than he does. Ever since he crushed his enemies at Sedgemoor and the Assizes, he has thought himself strong enough to bring in popery. He pretends, of course, to be anxious for toleration; but once he can remodel the army and pack the Parliament, you will see what he means by toleration. Just give him two or three more years."

Ralph laughed tolerantly; at least he hoped he was laughing tolerantly. "Could it be possible, Your Grace, that you are testing my loyalty to the King? Are you by any chance repeating Whig insinuations to see whether I agree with them? It is no use. Whatever your motives, I will never believe that King James intends to harm England."

He watched Catherine smile and shrug her pretty shoulders. "Very well, then, Mr. Barnard. Believe what you like. In a way, it is rather sweet of you to be so trusting. As I said before, the King is lucky to have such a faithful servant. Still, you might do me the courtesy of pretending to believe me, especially since I am telling the truth. But what can one expect of men? All the good ones have absurd loyalties. They see only what they want to. Maybe that is what makes them so helpless and appealing."

Ralph stood up. "Thank you for the compliments," he said, "but I must not wait to hear more. I must attend to my duties. Don't allow our differences of opinion to lower your opinion of me or obscure my gratitude. Our interview has been most instructive."

"Please come again, Mr. Barnard." Catherine Sedley rose and put out her hand for him to kiss. "The morning has been delightful. If

His Majesty does not have me transported to Ireland I shall look forward to many pleasant conversations with you. If he does, it will only help to prove my contention that he is not to be trusted. Any man who would banish me for the sake of his religion and his wife would not hesitate to subvert the laws of the nation. Even you should see that."

"I agree perfectly," Ralph said. "The man would be mad."

"Your perception is so acute that you make me wonder how we ever disagreed on anything," Catherine said. "I forgive you for doubting me, and I even wish you luck with your fugitive and with the Hemphills. Goodbye, Mr. Barnard."

Ralph was smiling to himself as he left the house. Although Catherine Sedley liked to talk nonsense, she was perfectly charming. With an effort, Ralph shook his head. He must get the Countess and the conversation out of his mind and concentrate on his task. Whatever the moral problems involved, he must find the drunkard.

Eight

As SIR RALPH put down his pen and looked about the room, he was mildly surprised to find that the fire was almost burned out. Mechanically, he rose and added a few lumps of coal. Somewhere, a few streets away, a watchman was bawling out the hour, one o'clock. Just outside the window, a few loitering drops of water were falling off the eaves. Their irregular rhythm, beating faintly against the ticking of the clock, had a soothing effect.

Sir Ralph looked down at what he had written. The few carefully phrased paragraphs which he had managed to get down on paper seemed ridiculously cold and strained. At this rate, he thought, the history would take three days, and Lord Stair would refuse to accept it. Still, it was better to say too little than too much. He could be sure of one thing: practically all of his life was irrelevant. In a way, even Esther was irrelevant. Except for the influence she had almost exercised in the matter of the assassination—and he would never write of that—she did not deserve more than two paragraphs. Yes, a paragraph or two, or maybe a long marginal note, would easily dispose of the thousands of hours he had devoted to Esther. It was idle now to wish he had the hours back or to wish he had spent them differently. It was vainer still to speculate on what might have happened if the Countess of Dorchester had not told him who her neighbors were. Perhaps there might have been another two-paragraph parenthesis even more foolish and more agonizing, if such a thing were possible.

He remembered now waiting in the antechamber for the servant to announce him. He remembered thinking that for a man reputed to be one of the richest in the kingdom old James Hemphill kept a very austere and unprepossessing town house. Nowhere in the halls or in the antechamber was anything resembling an ornament. Every item of furniture looked ugly, solid, and serviceable. People said, of course, that the old man was a miser; but Ralph, on seeing the furnishings, could not help thinking them wrong. More likely, old James was a determined, secular puritan—a little more suave than his father before him, but just as opposed to the blandishments of finery and waste, and just as stubborn.

Ralph waited patiently. After all, he was not likely to learn anything from the Hemphills. Even if they knew something they would probably take great pleasure in keeping it secret. He would be better advised to begin his search in the regular way with the tavern keepers in the neighborhood. If his man were merely a wandering sot, he could hardly have wandered far from the source of his supply. And then again, one never made a mistake in making the rounds of the tavern keepers. Many of them were sure to have interesting bits of political gossip and information. An occasional visit helped keep them alert. It was almost laughable, Ralph thought, the way conspirators of every kind insisted on meeting in public houses. If it were not for taverns, he told himself, criminal investigation would be impossible.

Ralph's first sight of Esther, when he was finally ushered into the dingy study, was a vague disappointment. It was not that she was less beautiful than he remembered her, he told himself. No, her hair and eyes were just as dark, and they contrasted just as sharply with the pallor of her skin and the vivid color of her lips. She was dressed with something of the same rich simplicity she had affected when she faced Lord Jeffreys at Taunton, a way of dressing which seemed both to conceal and to suggest the slim fullness of her figure. Still, Ralph thought, there was something slightly wrong about the total effect. Perhaps it was the absence of the gallows and the axe in the background. Who would now believe that the young lady waiting quietly to receive him was the dexterous liar and consummate actress of the bloody circuit?

Esther fixed her large brown eyes on his face and smiled pleasantly. "Ah, Mr. Barnard," she said. "If I am not mistaken we have seen each other before, and under less happy circumstances."

"Yes, Mistress Hemphill, we have." He bowed politely. "I am flattered at being recognized. When I saw you at Taunton you were so busy defending your brother, I hardly imagined that you had any opportunity to notice subordinate crown lawyers."

Esther's smile, Ralph thought, became a little less pleasant. "When I was defending my brother's life, it was my occupation to study everyone and everything that might have a bearing on the outcome. Let me hasten to add, however, that I should have noticed

you anyway." Her smile brightened perceptibly. "You formed a remarkable contrast to those hardened old butchers who managed the
prosecution."

"Thank you," Ralph heard himself say. "But you must not judge
the crown officials too severely. They were merely doing their duty."

"And loving it, Mr. Barnard," Esther said quickly. "No, Mr. Barnard, you must not excuse them to me. They are villains. You must
be aware of that. But pardon me, there I go talking about unpleasant
subjects. I am afraid you will think of me as a female politician, not
as a lady."

Ralph bowed again, noticing as he did so the slim grace of her
hands and arms. "On the contrary," he said. "I should have great
difficulty in thinking of you as anything but a lady."

"You are gallant to say so, but you may be wrong. Unhappily,
my family has always been involved in politics. You must beware
of me, Mr. Barnard, or I shall corrupt you with my Whig principles."

Ralph smiled. "I shall be on my guard constantly. A man who
hopes to rise in the service of the crown cannot be too careful."

"Now that we understand each other," Esther said, "please sit
down and we will discuss the business that brought you here to
brighten a dull afternoon. I hope it is nothing further concerning
my brother."

Ralph seated himself in the high uncomfortable chair across the
table from Esther. "No," he said. "It is nothing so serious as that;
in fact, I may be wasting your time with nothing at all. It is about
the incident which took place the other day in your neighborhood."

"Incident?" Esther looked puzzled. "Oh, you must mean the affair
in front of the Countess's house. Well?"

"You see," Ralph hurried on, "although the affair seems much
more odd than sinister the government cannot take any unnecessary
chances; so I am obliged to investigate it. I hope you will help me."

"I see," Esther said slowly. "And does the government habitually
send lawyers to get information of this kind? I was under the impression that peace officers did this sort of duty."

"I suppose they do, ordinarily," Ralph said, endeavoring to sound
as casual as possible. "But I did not feel that I should question the
motives of my superiors. If they wish to send a novice to dispatch
their business, I can scarcely object. I hope you will not refuse to
aid me merely because I am not a justice of the peace."

Ralph could not tell whether she was satisfied with the explanation or not. The expression on her face seemed pleasantly noncommittal.

"I suppose they did not consider the case very important," he went on, "or they would have taken more pains. As I say the situation was probably much more comical than dangerous."

Esther leaned forward, resting her elbows on the table. "If I am going to help you, Mr. Barnard," she said, "I must tell you my opinion frankly. I did not think the affair comical in the least—only disgusting."

"Disgusting? You mean disgusting that a citizen should threaten the King?"

"Not at all," and Ralph could hear indignation begin to rise in her voice. "Disgusting that the King of England should be an elderly lecher. If he had stayed where his honor and duty required him to be, no incident would have occurred."

"You don't like the King, then?" Ralph said.

"Like the King? Of course I don't like the King. Does anyone? He is a disgrace to the kingdom. Even if he were not a papist, he would be intolerable. His tawdry little love affairs would be inexcusable in a man of twenty-five; in an old goat of fifty they are grotesque." Esther paused, letting the indignation fade out of her voice and replacing her look of scorn with one of exaggerated repentance. "Ah, but I see I have gone too far. Now you will denounce me to the government and I shall be pilloried for insulting His Majesty."

"I could hardly do that," Ralph said, trying to imitate her serious tone of voice. "Putting you in the stocks would be sure to cause a riot, if not a revolution. When the government wishes to make martyrs, it takes every precaution to make sure they are ugly. Be easy, Mistress Hemphill. Your opinion of the King does not concern me."

The expression on Esther's face did not change. "But perhaps it should, Mr. Barnard. You must have heard from a dozen people that my father and I are the most dangerous traitors in the kingdom. If you tell me that you don't fear me and that you haven't been sent to implicate me in some plot or other, I will be offended."

"I am sorry to disappoint you," Ralph said. "I have no charges to bring against you. Please forgive me."

"Surely you are trifling with me, Mr. Barnard." Esther raised her eyebrows roguishly. "The thought must have occurred to you that the Hemphills might have had something to do with the incident which took place almost on their doorstep."

"Oh, I won't disappoint you utterly, Mistress Hemphill. Certainly the thought occurred to me. Still, I blush to admit that I dismissed it in less than a minute. I considered, you see, that the Hemphills were neither depraved nor insane."

"You are very kind." Esther favored him with an enchanting smile. "Possibly you are too kind. For all you know, we counted on just such a conclusion."

"You will be glad to know," Ralph said, "that I also let that thought cross my mind, but I rejected it."

Again the tone of Esther's voice changed abruptly.

"And you did well to reject it," she said icily. "The notion is monstrous. The Hemphills are not assassins. Nothing could induce us to connive at the murder of the King."

Ralph felt as if he were squirming under the direct penetration of her gaze, but he had no difficulty in keeping his voice calm and even. "Please don't feel that you must convince me of your innocence," he said. "I am convinced of it already, as I told you."

"I apologize, Mr. Barnard. As you can imagine, being constantly under suspicion and surveillance gets a bit wearing at times. Really now, do I appear to be some kind of monster?" She looked at him as if she expected an answer.

"On the contrary," he said, "you look like some kind of angel."

Ralph thought he could detect a trace of a blush, but he was not sure.

"Please don't be absurd, Mr. Barnard. I am trying to explain my position to you. I don't want you to misunderstand me. First, as I told you before, I want it clearly understood that I consider the King a miserable specimen of humanity. I think him wretched both as a king and as a man. But believe me, Mr. Barnard, I would not have him harmed for the world. He is much too valuable to me and to my party."

Ralph could not refrain from smiling. "This is news, indeed, Mistress Hemphill. If I had not heard you say so, I would never have believed that the party which tried to exclude the King from the throne, and who have opposed all his policies, had such a tender regard for his safety."

Esther made a gesture of annoyance. "I grant you that the notion sounds strange, and I also grant you that most of our party do not yet see the point themselves; but you and I can see farther than the vulgar. We can see that King James will make arbitrary power odious and divine right ridiculous. These are the enemies we are fighting, not the miserable papist James II. We are trying to break up the obscene coalition between priestcraft and tyranny. The King will be our most valuable ally."

"You must be a friend of the Countess of Dorchester," Ralph said, watching Esther carefully. "She told me the same thing this morning, although with somewhat different emphasis."

"I hate to agree with that bad, immoral woman on anything," Esther said coolly, "but this time I must admit she is right. By the way, Mr. Barnard, is it your custom to converse with the Countess?"

The question seemed innocent enough, but Ralph had the momentary impression that he was being cross-examined. It was just possible, he told himself, that Esther was trying to find out how close his connection with the court was. On the other hand, he told himself, the girl might have some curiosity about the Countess. It was too much to hope that she was personally interested in him.

"I am afraid I must disappoint you again," he said. "I met the Countess for the first time this morning."

Esther arched her eyebrows. "If I were given to interfering in other people's affairs, I should warn you to stay away from that woman. She is cunning and dangerous."

"You will be flattered to know," Ralph said, "that she said the same thing about you. Personally, I am inclined to think you are both mistaken."

"You are much too trusting to be an investigator, Mr. Barnard. Obviously you know nothing about women."

Ralph laughed. "I shall be glad to learn, Mistress Hemphill, if you will take the trouble to teach me. Perhaps you can instruct me as we conduct our enquiries."

"You must forgive me again," Esther smiled in return. "Somehow we became so involved with talking politics that I forgot all about the investigation. I told you I was a determined politician."

"And you must forgive me," Ralph said, "for forgetting why I came. Before I leave politics, however, I am curious about your opinion on one point: your friends affect to fear that the King will bring in popery. What do you think?"

"I am sure he is trying to the best of his ability. And, of course there is always the possibility that he will succeed. I think the chances are against him. You must remember, Mr. Barnard, that the subversion of a kingdom takes time. The King is over fifty, with no popish heir. Time, I think, would surely run out on him, even if he were as bright as his brother was, instead of being stupid, stubborn, and probably poxed."

"I see," Ralph said reflectively. "You don't fear, like your friends, that he will remodel the army and bring in the French and the Irish."

"Certainly I fear it, Mr. Barnard. He is sure to make the attempt. But again, you must consider his difficulties. He cannot bring in the French without provoking a full scale revolution. England would rise up, almost to a man. Besides, even if the project were successful, James would no longer be king of England, only a retainer of Louis. To bring in the Irish unless he had first remodelled his army completely and disarmed all England would be even more disastrous. Remodelling his army here is sure to be opposed at every step. It will take a long time, and time, as I told you, is what James does not have."

Esther leaned toward him and put her chin on her left hand. "There, Mr. Barnard," she added. "I have been perfectly open with you. You can see that the Countess is wrong. You have nothing to fear from me."

Ralph wished he could think of something clever and gallant to say in reply, something that would somehow hint at the little tremor of excitement she caused when she looked at him. He must be careful, he told himself, or he would find himself believing every word she said.

"I am glad to hear you say so," he said. "And now we have established that point, let us return to the episode of the other day. What can you tell me about it?"

"Well, Mr. Barnard, for one thing, I saw it happen, if that interests you."

"It interests me a great deal," Ralph said. "What did you see?"

Esther rose from her chair. "Give me your sword, Mr. Barnard," she said, "and I will show you what I saw. You stand over there by the door and play the part of the King. All you must do is look surprised and stupid; but you may also look like an ancient debauchee if you think you can manage it."

Ralph drew his sword and handed it to her. She tested it expertly, saluted him with it after the manner of fencers, and then walked across the room, picking up a book in her left hand as she reached the bookcase.

"Now then," she said, "watch. The book is a bottle."

Almost instantaneously, Esther transformed herself into a dignified drunk. As she picked her way cautiously toward him, Ralph could see her studious concentration, her look of triumph when she successfully avoided the gutter, and her bewilderment on observing the coach and four blocking her path. When she saw him, her eyes came slowly into focus. She cocked her head on one side and stared, letting the book fall from her hand. Then, with a long, sweeping gesture she drew the sword from its imaginary scabbard, staggered back a step or two as if she were rallying herself for the charge, waved the sword over her head, and shouted "Down with the Papists." This action seemed to sap her energy. Her attempt to make an obscene noise with her tongue ended in a weak hiccough; the sword sank abruptly until its point almost touched the ground. For a moment she looked as if she might fall on her face. Then she straightened up, gave a little yell of fright, and began to run away, upsetting a small table as she did.

"There you are, Mr. Barnard," she said, handing him the sword. "That is what happened."

"I congratulate you on the performance," Ralph said. "You are a very acute observer, Mistress Hemphill. I suppose you could dramatize all the visits which the King has paid to the Countess."

"That was unkind, Mr. Barnard, and I should resent the implication that I am constantly spying on the King. Unfortunately, it is almost the truth. You see how dull my life is when I have nothing better to do than to watch the assignations of a man and woman whom I despise. But then, you must remember, Mr. Barnard, that one can never tell when information will become useful. If the King is not ashamed of his actions, I suppose I should not be ashamed of mine."

"You misunderstand me," Ralph said in what he thought was a smooth, bland tone. "My hope in asking the question was that you might have seen the man with the sword before, possibly lurking around during former visits of the King."

"You are much too devious, Mr. Barnard." Esther sat down again and motioned him to his chair. "If you want help in identifying the culprit, you should merely ask me. I am not sure that you really want to know who he is, but if you do I will be glad to tell you."

Ralph was sure he looked an utter fool. His mouth was not actually hanging open, but it might as well have been, he knew.

"If I tell you," she went on, smiling at him, "you will be obliged to arrest him. He will be tried and perhaps executed, certainly punished severely. As you must know, the result will be to make the King more unpopular than he is already, and to give people who might otherwise behave themselves the notion that assassinating the King would be an easy and commendable undertaking. If you want to make a great scandal from this trifling incident, I would not wish to stop you."

"I see," said Ralph, still a trifle stupefied, but rallying. "You would be willing to risk a man's life to damage the King's cause."

"Most certainly," Esther said, "especially the life of a Tory, as this gentleman happens to be. You have an unfortunate way of phrasing it, however. Let us say that I am willing to let the King's justice take its course—if you are."

"Very well, Mistress Hemphill," he said slowly, "I am willing to let the King's justice take its course. What is the man's name?"

"The gentleman is Thomas Gerrard." She had not hesitated a moment. "He lives on Trinity Lane, in the house next to the Hall Inn."

Esther observed him quizzically. "What is the matter, Mr. Barnard? You don't seem happy to get the information? Is it possible that you did not want the information after all? Or," she added softly, "do you think me cruel and cold-blooded for telling you what you wanted to know?"

That was it, of course, Ralph told himself. Unreasonable as it was to blame her for helping him, he could not repress a feeling of dismay. Apparently she had been deadly serious when she said she would sacrifice lives to damage the King's cause. And yet, when he looked at her, this seemed impossible to believe. He was simply unable to picture her as a political zealot. Zealots, after all, were intense and passionate. They never sounded like cynics, and they did not radiate a subtle friendly warmth.

"I am sorry, Mistress Hemphill, for seeming ungrateful," he said, "and I do thank you for your help. I suppose I was making plans for catching the gentleman. Please forgive me."

Esther smiled. "Set your mind at ease, Mr. Barnard. I was sure you would catch the man anyway; otherwise I would not have informed on him. But I am glad I did. Now you will be worried about me, and you will be forced to come see me occasionally, if only to find out how I got my information. You can see how shrewd and Macchiavellian I am, Mr. Barnard."

Ralph felt his pulses give an absurd leap. Yes, he did have an excuse to see her again—maybe even a reason. Certainly she would bear watching. An agent of the crown could hardly do better than to keep an eye on the Hemphills; and what a delightful duty. There was little chance that Esther would ever be seriously interested in him; but at least he must have amused her or she would not have invited him back.

"I should have worried about you anyway," he said, almost gaily. "And I won't miss an opportunity of cross-examining you. You may expect to see me often."

"Good," she said. "I shall be waiting to hear the outcome of our little episode."

As Ralph got to his feet, Esther rose and held out her hand. He kissed it hurriedly, afraid that if he paused she might detect some of his excitement. Then he cursed himself for not making more of the little ceremony. Esther too, he thought, looked a little disappointed. For a moment they stood there looking at each other, smiling. Then the servant Esther had rung for arrived to conduct him out.

CHAPTER

Nine

THE BODY was hanging from an oaken beam in the very center of the room, the feet dangling about six inches from the floor. Beside it was an overturned table.

Ralph's first impulse was to close the door again and leave, but he overcame it quickly.

"Please wait below," he called over his shoulder to the landlady, who had followed him upstairs. "Your lodger has hanged himself."

As he stepped inside the room and closed the door behind him, the thought suddenly occurred to him that the man might not be dead. Perhaps there was still time to revive him. He had barely got over to the body, however, when he realized he was wrong. One look at the face, which was turned away from the door, convinced him. The fixed bulging eyes and the frozen contortion of the mouth left no room for doubt. Ralph reached out cautiously and touched the man's right hand. It felt cold, just how cold he couldn't say, but cold enough. The man had probably been dead for several hours.

Now that the first shock of discovery was over, Ralph could feel his self-command returning. He stepped back a couple of paces from the body, noticing as he did so that the man had kicked off one of his shoes. It lay a few feet away from the body, toward the window, as if to testify that one cannot hang himself peaceably. The corpse, Ralph saw immediately, fitted the King's description perfectly. Yes, the man was about six feet tall. In spite of the contortion of the face one could see he was somewhere in his forties. The black hair, a little disheveled from the violence of the struggle, hung down almost to the shoulders. Even the suit was the same as the one described by the King, except that the man had taken off the coat and hung it neatly over the back of a chair. The black velvet breeches fitted the long muscular legs tightly. It was easy to see how the man had been able to outrun the guards.

Ralph fingered the hilt of his sword reflectively. It was just as well, he told himself, that he had not been obliged to take the man by force. No matter what the man's age, he would have been a formidable antagonist, if he had chosen to fight. Unfortunately, Ralph thought, the gentleman had done most of his recent fighting with the bottle. Over on the desk were two wine bottles, one empty, the other half full; near them stood a single glass. Turning his back on the corpse, Ralph walked over to examine them. It was then that he saw the suicide note.

Although the writing wavered and was disfigured by frequent blots, Ralph had no trouble making it out:

> I have insulted the King. In a fit of swinish drunkenness, I aspersed his religion and showed contempt for his person. I think I could bear any punishment he might think fit to give me, but I could never bear public disgrace and shame. I beg his forgiveness. God save the King!
>
> THOMAS GERRARD

Ralph glanced from the note to the body, then back to the note again. Somehow the silent figure on the end of the rope gave a pathetic dignity to the tritely expressed sentiments on the paper. As he reread the note, Ralph shivered a little. He could almost feel the conflict that had gone into the writing of it.

The few letters and papers in the desk told a simple story. One letter, from a business agent in Cornwall, informed Mr. Gerrard that he would soon receive ninety-six pounds, the quarterly income from his land there. Another, signed "your loving niece," thanked him for a gift and informed him that her mother was well. A third, from a Mr. Sidney Lucas, told him that his hundred-pound investment in the cargo of the *Primrose* had returned him two hundred nine pounds, seven shillings. An ornately written letter from his parish priest in Cornwall asked him if he could make another contribution towards the repair of the church. A note from the admiralty office said that his application for a position was being considered.

Thomas Gerrard, the documents showed, was clearly a Cornwall squire with some business interests in London—the sort of man who might hope to improve his status by a few wise investments and a small political sinecure. He would be a Tory, of course; otherwise he would never have applied to the admiralty. No doubt he had pretensions to merit in some Cornwall election or in the Monmouth affair.

Ralph carefully avoided looking at the body as he examined the room and the bedroom which adjoined it. At some time, Ralph could see, Thomas Gerrard had decided to run for it. He had taken all of his clothes except his nightgown out of the wardrobe and packed them in his large trunk. But somewhere in the operation his heart had failed him. His pipes, two formal wigs, and a Book of Common Prayer were still on the table beside his bed, along with another half-empty bottle of wine. Two pairs of shoes were still under the bed. Again Ralph could sense the horror and confusion in the man's mind. After all, where could he run? He could never feel himself safe in England, even if he got away. A poverty-stricken exile on the continent would be worse than death itself, the end of all the man's prosaic and pitiful little ambitions. An ordinary criminal or a political plotter would have fled without thinking twice, but a man like Gerrard was helpless. He had not even thought to change or destroy the suit that might incriminate him. He had been able only to wait, drink, shudder, and pray until he could stand the pressure no longer. Then he had hanged himself.

Ralph sat down on the bed to collect his thoughts. He should be thankful, he told himself, that the man was dead. The suicide solved many problems. Now there would be no trial, no scandal, no imputation of cruelty against the King, merely a quiet announcement that a despondent Cornish squire had committed suicide. As far as he was concerned personally, the hanging relieved him of all responsibility. No one could say he had helped hound an innocent man to mutilation or death. The man would be just as dead if no one had set out to find him, if the King had treated the whole matter as a great joke. Yes, Ralph thought, he should be thankful. But there was no use trying to deceive himself; he felt sick, disgusted, and ashamed.

Catherine Sedley was right after all. He was nothing but a dirty spy for a stupid and brutal autocrat. All the nonsense he had talked about duty to his King and country—all his high-flown mental rhetoric about moral obligation—was nothing but a cloak to hide personal ambition. For a few smiles from the King and a few hundred sovereigns he had helped to send some ignorant misguided peasants to banishment or death; he had been willing to track down a man who he knew to be innocent. The fact that the poor devil had hanged himself did not really exonerate him; it convicted him. He had been willfully blind. The suicide showed the King's reputation among his most loyal subjects for clemency and mercy. Such a thing would have been impossible if Charles had still been King.

Well, enough was enough; he would resign. Somebody else could

do the King's dirty work. Doubtless the King should be protected.
England could not be left at the mercy of the Whigs and the fanatics. But this did not mean a gentleman of honor needed to become
a bloodhound. The safety of the state also demanded a certain number of outhouses and brothels, but that did not mean anyone was
obligated to be a sewer digger or a prostitute.

The more he thought about it, the more agitated he became. He
got up from the bed and began to pace up and down the bedroom.
And what about Esther Hemphill? he asked himself. She was at
least as bad as he. She had betrayed an innocent man without turning a hair. Her excuse that the man was sure to be caught was
just an excuse. She had not been self-deluded as he had been by
any silly notions about duty. She would probably betray her own
father if she thought she could gain any political advantage by doing
it. The only worthwhile aspect of the suicide was the frustration of
her plans. Well, someone else could take over the business of watching the Hemphills too. He would be damned if he'd go back there
again. She could use her brown eyes on some other credulous oaf.
He was glad now he had not been further involved with her.

A knock on the parlor door roused him from his thoughts. He
had almost forgotten the existence of the landlady; but when he
opened the door there she was, trying to peer past him to get a
look at the body. Evidently she had restrained her curiosity as long
as she could.

"I'm sorry, Sir," she said. "I thought I could help you."

Ralph wanted to kick her downstairs, but instead he stepped
aside politely. He might as well satisfy her curiosity. Maybe she
could tell him a few things.

She was glad to tell him anything, it turned out. Mr. Gerrard
had been her lodger every winter for five years, she informed him,
as she stared fascinated at the corpse and moved around to get a
good look at the face. In the summers he went back to Cornwall
where he had his estate. You wouldn't know to look at him now,
with his face all purple, what a handsome gentleman he was for
his years or how little trouble he caused. It was true he touched a
drop now and then. No harm in that; he was always a perfect gentleman. He used to drink, she believed, with some of his friends
from Cornwall and some of his acquaintances from the City over
at the Cock and Lock, about a mile from his lodgings. He was a
very religious gentleman; it would do your heart good to see how
often he went to church. Too bad that now he'd go to hell, but
maybe he was out of his mind when he killed himself. She should

have known something was wrong when he kept staying in his room
and having his meals sent up and ordering wine. He hadn't seen a
soul since Thursday, except her when she went in to bring things
and to clean his room. You never knew what went on in gentlemen's
minds. This morning he'd looked a little paler than usual, but he
didn't say he was ill. Now when her Aunt Laetitia took poison anyone could tell she'd been out of her mind for days. People had tried
to restrain her, but she was too sly for them.

Finally Ralph was able to cut off her ramblings. He was also able
to keep her from touching anything, although this was difficult. She
wanted to climb up on a chair and remove Gerrard's lace collar
so she could see the rope better, but Ralph prevented her. When
he told her to run and fetch the justice of the peace, she was eager
to obey.

Yes, she said, she would bring the Justice of the Peace and the
coroner too. She knew them well; they lived only two streets away.
And she wouldn't stop to tell a soul on the way, although if he didn't
mind, she would stop on the way home and tell her neighbor, Mrs.
Jenkins, but she would only stop a moment because maybe she
could help the Justice and the coroner just like she'd helped Ralph.
Ralph told her he didn't mind. She could tell as many people as
she liked on the way home.

The Justice of the Peace was a quiet, sensible man. After he had
looked at the evidence and heard Ralph's explanation, he agreed
perfectly with Ralph that there was no reason for mentioning the
suicide note in the reports. If, as Ralph assured him, it would please
the King to hush up the incident, he would certainly be willing to
abide by the King's wishes. He would not even mention the note
to the coroner. The fewer people who knew about it the better.
The suicide was clearly established without the note, and no purpose could be served by inflicting additional pain on the Gerrard
family. Ralph could rely on him to see that all the details were taken
care of in proper order. Gerrard's death, the Justice agreed, was a
sad occurrence, but then when you were a justice of the peace in
London you had to get used to such things. Only yesterday, the
mother of seven children had cut her throat. There was blood all
over the floor and the children screaming so you could hear them for
miles. Things like that could drive a man insane if he let them.

Ralph thanked the Justice for his help, took the note, and left,
before the coroner or the landlady arrived. He was surprised, on
getting outside, to notice that nothing had changed. It seemed to
him he had been in the house a lifetime, yet the whole episode

could not have lasted an hour. If he hurried, he might be able to get to Whitehall before dark.

The farther he got from the house, the more he could feel his normal state of mind returning. The horror of Gerrard's death was beginning to pass away like a bad dream. Why, he asked himself, should he let the death of the perfect stranger upset him so much? Was there something wrong with his nerve, or with his temperament? For a man who had seen the slaughter of Sedgemoor and the Assizes wasn't he being childish? Why should he revolt against everything he believed because some irresponsible, unworldly Cornish farmer decided to hang himself? And who could say for sure that the man would have been convicted if he had been caught? The judges would certainly have taken into account the man's pure Tory background. They might have let him off scot free, with only some sort of reprimand. They were not ogres, as their enemies would have people believe, merely officials trying to uphold the King's justice. He knew them all.

Ralph dodged against a wall to avoid a wagon full of barrels. The driver shouted at him. No, he told himself, nothing was really changed. He had nothing to apologize for. When one stopped to think logically and clearly, one had to admit that Gerrard had, after all, threatened the King. The situation had demanded investigation, and it was certainly not the investigator's fault that the man had possessed the courage of a rabbit. To be sure the case was pitiful, but one should be able to feel pity without losing his nerve or his reason. A man of the world, and especially a man with an important duty to perform, should at least have as much detachment as an ordinary justice of the peace.

By the time Ralph had come within a mile of Whitehall, he had brought himself out of his mental haze and begun to notice the things around him. Just ahead of him two cobblers were walking along carrying on some kind of good-natured argument. Just behind him, three or four voices were discussing the wages paid for stonemasonry. Coming toward him and passing him was a miscellaneous assortment of watermen, butchers, carpenters, and chandlers, also a number of plain citizens whose trade could not be identified from their dress, and occasionally a gentleman. All London was on its way home in the twilight.

Watching and listening to the people as they passed was reassuring, Ralph found. What was Thomas Gerrard to them? Nothing. They had their own worries. Oh, they might have been mildly interested if they had seen the body—the event might have furnished them with a few minutes of conversation. But then, what did the death of any single man mean? Again nothing.

When Ralph reached Whitehall, the darkness was almost complete. He made his way unobtrusively around to the rear of the palace, to the small door which opened on Father Mansuete's apartment. He let himself in, as usual, and walked into the study, where he found Mansuete sitting by the fire. Ralph liked Father Mansuete. Big, sympathetic, and soft-spoken, the man seemed to be a natural repository for confidences, a perfect confessor. Now that he had become used to seeing the Capuchin cowl and robes, Ralph often found himself forgetting that Mansuete was a clergyman. He seemed to care nothing about the things most clergymen cared for, theology and politics. He did not even seem to be worried about sin, except perhaps in a professional, legalistic way. Father Mansuete, Ralph thought, would find it easy to forgive anyone for anything.

Father Mansuete looked up at him. "Ah, good evening, Mr. Barnard," he said, in his soft foreign accent. "I suppose you wish me to find His Majesty."

"Yes, Father," Ralph said, "if it is not too much trouble. You look so comfortable that I hate to disturb you."

"Not at all, Mr. Barnard." Mansuete was graciousness itself. "While I am gone, have a glass of claret. You look tired and disturbed. I think His Majesty is expecting you. He has asked after you several times this afternoon."

"Thank you, I will," Ralph said, watching the friar fill the glass and move a chair close to the hearth for him.

"Put yourself at ease," Father Mansuete said. "I shall be back presently."

Sitting back in the comfortable chair and sipping on the really excellent wine, Ralph felt his muscles relax. Once again he was pleased by the convenience and simplicity of his arrangements for seeing the King. The King could visit his confessor any time of the day or night without arousing suspicion, and Ralph's own access to Mansuete was easy too. A pass authorizing him to visit the friar was sufficient to get him by the guards outside the palace if he should be challenged. Yes, the arrangement was ideal.

"Well, Mr. Barnard, what have you discovered?"

King James was almost breathless with haste. He had come through the door and addressed Ralph before Ralph could get to his feet and bow.

"I have found the man, Your Majesty," he said.

"Very good, Mr. Barnard. I knew I could count on you." The firelight made the King's face look longer than ever. "Well, what is his name and where is he?"

Ralph took a deep breath. There was no use mincing matters. The King must be told as quickly and simply as possible that there was no assassination plot. "The man is dead, Your Majesty," he said. "He hanged himself this morning."

James cut him off. "Good," he said, "that saves us the trouble of trying him. Who were his accomplices?"

"There were no accomplices, Your Majesty." Ralph felt himself warming to his work. "The man was a simple Cornish squire, a gentleman named Thomas Gerrard. From examining his papers and questioning his landlady, I found him to be a loyalist and a Church of England man. Apparently he insulted Your Majesty only because he was drunk. When he became sober he realized what he had done and hanged himself. Here is his suicide note."

Ralph watched the King take the note and read it. The stubborn expression on his long face did not soften, as Ralph hoped it might. He merely wrinkled his forehead and stroked his chin. When he had finished reading the note he threw it down on the table.

"Just as I thought," he said, "the remorse of an unsuccessful assassin. Monmouth could have said as much."

For a moment Ralph felt disgust and anger boil up again inside him. It was irrational, he knew, to blame the King for his stubbornness. The King, after all, had not seen Gerrard's body or the pitiful evidences of his dismay and horror. Still, a man who could read Gerrard's note without responding in some degree to the feeling it expressed was either obtuse or pitiless.

"Allow me to disagree with Your Majesty," Ralph said as calmly as he could. "There was no evidence of a plot. On the other hand, there was every evidence that the man was a loyal, religious, law-abiding subject. It was his misfortune to be drunk at an inopportune time."

Ralph could see that James was deeply displeased, but he stood his ground.

"I grant you," he hurried on, "that Mr. Gerrard had a lamentable prejudice against Your Majesty's religion, and that he expressed it in a shocking and disrespectful way. But this, as I told Your Majesty, was merely the effect of drink."

"Mr. Barnard," the King said, "you may save yourself the trouble of defending the man in my presence. I am willing to believe there was no plot, that he had no accomplices. But I will never believe he did not intend to kill me. Remember, Mr. Barnard, I saw his face.

That he was drunk does not excuse him. Are assassins to be exonerated because they get drunk? Am I and my religion to be insulted and threatened by every drunkard in London? Is this what you mean by a loyal, law-abiding subject—a man who pretends to respect me when he is sober but reverts to his true feelings when he is drunk? I am only sorry the man hanged himself. If he had not, I should have made an example of him that London would not soon forget."

Yes, Ralph said to himself, I am sure you would, you stupid bigot. You would have killed a harmless man and strengthened your enemies because you had been insulted by a drunk.

"You misunderstand me, Your Majesty," he said aloud. "I am not defending the act. I am merely accounting for it, explaining how it came about. I must confess, however, I do not share Your Majesty's views on public punishment. It would seem to me that the less public excitement on the score of assassinations and religious prejudice the better."

James stared at him as if he were going to make a sharp retort, then apparently changed his mind. "You are welcome to your opinion, Mr. Barnard," he said. "You would think differently if your life were being threatened and your religion insulted. You would think that a few public examples of sufficient severity might help affairs. They might teach a proper respect for the King of England and his religion. They might impress people who think they can thwart and oppose the King at every turn as long as they pretend a sublime loyalty."

I suppose I would think differently, Ralph told himself, but I hope I would have the good sense not to let personal resentment cloud my judgement.

"Yes, Your Majesty, I see what you mean," he said. "But Your Majesty must consider that Englishmen are easy to arouse and hard to intimidate. The headsman's axe is a very dangerous instrument."

"There are times when it is dangerous not to use it, Mr. Barnard." James paused and frowned. "The opportunity is lost in this case, however, so we need not discuss it further."

"Very well, Your Majesty. I shall say no more on the subject."

No, Ralph told himself, there was no use being angry with the King. One might as well be angry with a stupid and stubborn child. The important thing was to keep the silly old ass from ruining himself and ruining England. There was no use arguing with him of course; he was impervious to argument. What he needed was not advisers, but a guardian.

"You have done a good day's work," the King was saying. "In one day you have done what Milord Sunderland's agents failed to do in four. You will be suitably rewarded."

"Thank you, Your Majesty," he said. "If there is nothing further, perhaps Your Majesty will permit me to continue my journey to Lincolnshire. My brother is expecting me."

James began to move toward the door. "I am sorry about the visit to Lincolnshire, Mr. Barnard, but I fear it must be postponed again. Today I received a dispatch from Holland. My envoy tells me that the exiles there are busy with plots against me. Please prepare yourself for the journey. I shall send you within the week."

"As you wish, Your Majesty," Ralph said, bowing.

"I must employ someone I can trust to keep an eye on those people, Mr. Barnard, and also to keep watch on my son-in-law the Prince of Orange."

The King opened the door. "And now good night, Mr. Barnard."

"Good night, Your Majesty." Ralph bowed again. "You may rely on me."

And you may rely on me to keep an eye on you too, he added under his breath.

CHAPTER

Ten

SIR RALPH'S ENERGY ran out abruptly. Although the memories swarmed as thickly as before, suddenly he found himself unable to get anything down on paper. He could visualize clearly the scenes from Amsterdam and The Hague. He could see Ferguson's crafty fanatical face; he could see Prince William, cool and saturnine; and he could hear Esther's voice, low and excited, saying, "Please, Ralph, we must be careful." He could even recall the whole first page from the book he had used to learn Dutch. Still the task was impossible. He could not write another word. Like a broken squadron, the experiences refused to rally. With a little shrug of disgust, he put down the pen, blew out the candles, and made his way to the bedroom in the dark.

As he lay down beside Henriette, listening to her quiet breathing and waiting for her to respond to his presence by snuggling against him, he began to relax. It was impossible, after all, to write the whole report in one night. He would do much better to get some sleep and start fresh tomorrow. One hard day's work would finish the thing, then he could take it to Lord Stair. Meantime it was soothing to lie here in the warmth of the bed waiting for the thoughts to disperse into dreams. He must be careful, of course, not to think of certain things or he would never go to sleep. It was all right to think of things that were merely horrible—things like the wounded horses screaming at Landen, like old Leroux getting his head shot off, or like the drownings at Blenheim. These things were now like pictures in a book, vivid and grim but unreal. The things to avoid were arguments, insults, and decisions. He must not begin debating the past or justifying himself. No, it was better to let his mind wander over random scenes and events. He might think of the way the North Sea looked when he set out for Holland on his first sea voyage, and how he tried to look unruffled when he was almost dead with

seasickness. Or he might think of Arras as it had appeared the day
he rode in from Lille, just before he met Henriette for the first time.
Meeting Henriette, he supposed, had fixed the scene in his mind.
He could remember vividly a spotted cow standing insolently in
front of the door of the Lion d'Or.

Unbidden, another picture floated across his mind, of Dublin the
night after the battle of Boyne. A crowd of soldiers and civilians
were milling about in the streets; women were trying to find their
husbands, officers trying to find their men, a few dragoons trying
to establish order, and mounted messengers trying to get through
the crowd—all this in the wavering light of torches and lanterns,
and accompanied by a frenzied moaning and wailing. In the midst
of all this, one huge fat woman was seizing every man within reach
and kissing him. Ralph could still recall his revulsion as she tried to
pull him off his horse. He had held her off with his foot and she had
grabbed a grenadier instead. It seemed funny now. All Ireland was
collapsing, and she was salvaging something out of the wreckage,
with her own method of looting.

It seemed to Ralph that he was still trying to go to sleep when
Henriette woke him.

"Get up," she was saying. "You have a visitor."

"What time is it?" He rolled over, trying to get the sleep out of
his eyes. The curtains were still drawn.

"It is almost nine," she said. "I held the lady off as long as I could.
I knew you needed the sleep. She came at eight o'clock."

"Lady?" He sat up quickly, putting his feet solidly on the floor.
"What lady?"

Henriette laughed. "Please try not to appear so anxious, Love,"
she said. "The lady is pretty, yes, but she is not English and I don't
think you will like her. She is a Scots lady, named Maclé I believe."

Sir Ralph laughed too. "You must mean Mackay or Maclean, and
you are too observant. Now, hand me a clean shirt and my newest
breeches so that I can impress this pretty Scots lady. Did she say
what she wants?"

Henriette burrowed in the drawer that contained his linens. "She
will not say. All she will do is drink coffee and cry. She has drunk
three cupfuls and cried three cupfuls. It is very distressing."

"I am sure it is," he said, struggling into the shirt she handed
him, "but she must have said something through her tears and sips."

"Well, yes." Henriette examined his breeches critically before she
gave them to him. "She did say something about Prêton and Nougat,
or some such names; but I could not understand whether she was

talking about people or places, and I don't think she knew either. I hope you have better luck with her."

Sir Ralph smiled. As well as Henriette spoke English, names often had a way of coming out slightly wrong. Her version of a Scots version of English place names was even more exotic than usual. He stood up, seized her by the shoulders, and kissed her.

"There," he said. "That is for Prêton and Nougat."

"You are an idiot," she said, lapsing into French. "I will never learn English if you reward me for getting it wrong. Do I laugh at you when you pronounce Ramillies?"

"Only secretly," he said, kissing her again. "Now then, hand me my wig and my waistcoat. We must not keep the lady waiting. Possibly she was crying about Preston and Newgate. My guess is that her husband or lover was one of the Scots Jacobites taken at Preston and lodged at Newgate prison. Does that sound reasonable?"

Henriette adjusted his wig. "Possibly," she said. "Hold still. I told you I couldn't understand her. But I am sure you can. Now your waistcoat."

When Henriette had arranged his waistcoat and coat to her satisfaction, she turned him toward the mirror. "Very handsome," she said. "Don't you think so?"

"I have always thought so," he said.

Henriette began pushing him toward the door. "Don't forget," she added, "I shall be listening to everything that sobbing Scotswoman says."

The girl stood up when she saw him enter the room and advanced toward him. Without giving him a chance to say a word she threw herself down and embraced his knees, almost tripping him.

"Please, Sir Ralph," she said, "say you will help him."

Sir Ralph steadied himself by grasping the end of the mantle-piece. He had never felt more ridiculous and uncomfortable in his life. Suddenly he seemed to be taking a part in a very bad play.

"Please, Sir Ralph," she said again. "You must save him."

Sir Ralph bent over awkwardly and tried to disengage her arms. "Now, now, my lass, you must stand up and tell me what you are talking about. I will help you if I can."

Apparently he had said the right thing, because she relaxed her hold on his knees and allowed him to help her to her feet. She did not quit sobbing, however. Her face was puckered into an undignified, tear-stained expression of woe. Ralph expected that at any second she would begin to howl like a baby. At any rate, he told

himself, she could not be playing a part, as he had half suspected
from her theatrical gesture. No actress would look so unappealing if
she could help it.

He waited for the girl to get control of herself and begin her
story, but she showed no signs of ceasing her snivels.

"Who is it you want me to save?" he said finally.

The girl looked at him in astonishment and almost quit crying.
It was incredible, her look said, that anyone should be ignorant of
the cause of her grief. Certainly the whole world must know her
tragedy.

"It's Jamie," she wailed. "It's Jamie."

Evidently, Sir Ralph told himself, he was supposed to know Jamie.
But what Jamie? Half the Scotsmen he knew were named Jamie.

The girl seemed to sense his confusion. "It's my Jamie, Jamie
Maclean. You must remember Jamie."

There was no use pretending to know who she was talking about.
He hadn't the faintest idea. "I am afraid I don't," he said. "You
must refresh my memory."

"But Jamie served under you," she said. "He was at Denain. Don't
you remember?" She began to cry louder than ever.

Sir Ralph hastened to soften the blow. Jamie Maclean, whoever
he was, had evidently given his wife the impression that he was
hand in glove with his general.

"Oh yes," he said, "of course. Jamie Maclean. How stupid of me.
Go on, please. Where is he, and what is the trouble?"

Denain, he said to himself. What Scotsman did I know in that
campaign?

Again she gave him that look of astonishment. How could he be
so stupid, it said, as not to know where Jamie was. Jamie's old general must be a doddering imbecile.

She took out her handkerchief and blew her nose violently.
"Jamie is in Newgate. Where else would he be? Ooh—" and she began to wail again.

His translation of Henriette's garbled language had been correct,
then. Jamie Maclean was one of the prisoners taken at Preston. Not
a very important prisoner either. Ralph knew Old Borlum, Thomas
Forster, Lord Widdrington, Colonel Oxburgh, and the rest of the
leaders, English and Scots. Except for Old Borlum, a more inept
set of military men never tried to lead a rising against a government. But he knew no Jamie Maclean.

He tried again. "Ah yes, Newgate, of course. Forgive me. I

thought Jamie had been with the Earl of Mar up in Scotland. I hoped he had got away."

The girl's face brightened a little, as if perhaps he was not so stupid after all.

"He was for a while," she said, "but General Mackintosh could not get on without him, so he went south with the General's party. And now they will hang him."

"I am surprised that the Earl let him go," Sir Ralph said soothingly. "If he had kept Jamie with him, he would have beaten Argyle at Sheriffmuir and saved the cause in Scotland."

"Oh there's no doubt of that," the girl said, wiping her eyes. "Jamie would have chased Red John right into the Firth."

And at the mention of Red John, Sir Ralph suddenly knew who Jamie was, a redheaded ensign in one of his companies of foot during the campaign of 1712. Only no one had called him Jamie—or even Sandy. He had been called Spot. That was it—Spot, Spot Maclean. He could see the boy now, a tall, raw-boned freckled lad of about nineteen—one of the least likely officers he could remember. How such a gangling, disorganized lout had ever inspired the confidence and devotion of this girl was a mystery, but there it was.

"He would have beaten General Carpenter and General Wills too," she was saying, "if it had not been for the cowardice of General Forster. The traitor surrendered without allowing Jamie to strike a blow."

"Yes, Jamie would have beaten them," Sir Ralph agreed.

"But now they are sure to hang him. They won't let a dangerous man like my Jamie go free. The Elector of Hanover will never be safe on the throne of England as long as Jamie can draw a sword." She drew herself up proudly, as if she were queen of Scotland, and her husband captain-general of the forces rather than a lowly lieutenant, or at most captain, of infantry.

This mood lasted only a few seconds. Suddenly she broke down again.

"But they are going to hang him," she wailed. "And we've only been married a year."

"Now, now, my lass," Sir Ralph said quietly, leading her to a chair. "No more of that. Crying won't help. Calm yourself, and we will see what can be done."

Sir Ralph watched the girl try to control her crying. She was doing a miserable job of it. The tears kept running down her face, collecting on her chin, and then splashing on her dress. Occasionally, she dabbed at them with her handkerchief, but only enough to disturb the lines of flow.

His own feelings were almost too complicated to sort out. In a way, he supposed, he was amused—amused at her wonderful and gullible belief in Jamie's importance, amused at the contrast between the devotion and its object, and amused, finally, just to hear her pronounce "general" and "Elector of Hanover" in her Scots manner. In another way, he was angry. What business did an unfledged, red-haired, self-important clod like Jamie Maclean have in politics? Why did men like him get mixed up in these things in the first place? What, in God's name, did the Pretender mean to them? They did not have sense enough to make a rational decision of any kind, let alone a decision on state policy; yet at the first sign of disturbance, they picked up their muskets and their claymores and went out to kill each other. Sometimes Ralph wondered whether there were any brains at all north of the Tweed, or whether the whole Scottish nation, Whig and Jacobite, Presbyterian and Episcopalian, lived only to quarrel, conspire, and fight—with the women egging on the men.

Maybe, Ralph told himself, he was angry because he was being forced to a decision. It had been relatively easy to refuse to help the prisoners when asked by a snipe like Randall and ordered by a bungler like Young James. But how could he refuse this heartbroken child? His impulse was to tell her that her husband was a fool who deserved hanging for sheer stupidity; but of course he would never say it.

Or maybe—and he could feel himself grimace—he was angry because he was responsible for the whole bloody affair. If he had done what he should have done, there would have been no Jacobite party, no Jacobite risings, no Jacobite hangings. Factious knaves like the Erskines, the Gordons, the Campbells, and the Macleans might have killed each other anyway; but at least they would have had to find some other excuse, and they would have been no concern of his.

"I should have killed him," he said aloud, and was startled at the sound of his own voice.

The girl was startled too. She broke off crying abruptly, in the middle of a sob. "Killed who?" she said. "Killed who, Sir?"

"Nobody," Sir Ralph shook his head, clearing it. "Nobody. An old dog I used to know, who is now dead anyway."

"Oh," she said. "Oh, I see. For a moment I thought you meant Jamie."

"Forgive me, Mrs. Maclean, for startling you. Men of my age sometimes talk to themselves. It does not mean anything, really."

It only means, he added to himself, that I am getting senile.

"I see," she said doubtfully. "I see."

"Now that you are through crying," he said, hurrying on to hide his embarrassment, "perhaps you can answer a few questions about your husband. First, what was his rank in this campaign?"

"Lieutenant," she said proudly.

"Very good," Sir Ralph said. "Is he related to any of the leaders —I mean to any of the generals and colonels?"

"Yes indeed," she said, "he is a second cousin on his mother's side to General Mackintosh."

"I see. Are you sure he is not more closely related to some of the others?"

"Perfectly sure, Sir." He wondered how she managed to enunciate so many r's without choking. "But why should he be related to those gentlemen? The Maclean blood is as honorable as any in Scotland."

"I am sure it is," he said. "I was afraid he might be closely related to the leaders. It would injure his chances. Now, what about money? Does he have any?"

The girl blushed defiantly. "We get along. Jamie has his commission in the French foot, and I am in the service of Madame la Comtesse d'Iberville."

"That is not what I mean, Mrs. Maclean," he said gently. "I know that a good Scots lad and lassie like yourself and Jamie would not live off anyone's charity. I know that you can support yourselves and that you will get on in the world. Jamie would never have brought you from Scotland without prospects. I am speaking now of larger sums of money, the kind people use to buy justice—say a thousand pounds or so."

The look of defiance vanished from the girl's face; it was replaced by one of despair. "Oh no," she said miserably, "we have nothing like that. Jamie used his inheritance and his savings to buy his commission."

"I see," Sir Ralph said, "and I suppose no one else in your families could raise such a sum."

He saw her make an attempt at calculation. "No," she said, "no one."

He was sorry now he had mentioned the subject of money. He might have guessed their situation. She had been discouraged and embarrassed to no purpose.

"I have it," she said. "I will go to His Majesty King James. He will not let Jamie die for want of a thousand pounds. Jamie was fighting in his cause."

"I am afraid you can't do that," he said. "You see, King James has been obliged to spend most of his money to support the rising and his followers. He cannot afford to buy favors for all the gentlemen imprisoned, and he cannot show favoritism by helping your husband when he cannot help others."

He congratulated himself on his phrasing. He had conveyed the notion, he thought, without saying directly that Jamie's life was not worth a thousand pounds to the Stuart cause.

"No," he said. "We must think of something else. Could you make a journey to London?"

"I will go anywhere," she said, "if it will help."

"I think it will help," he said. "Yes, I am sure it will help."

The idea had come so suddenly that he had had no time to examine it. He had only a half-excited feeling in the pit of his stomach to tell him it was good. Well, why not? Why not write to Esther? What if he had promised himself that he would be damned eternally in hell before he would ever see her again or write her a line? She could save an obscure Scots lieutenant without spending a penny or even raising her voice. Her merest whisper to Townshend, Stanhope, or Cowper—or any of the other Whig leaders—would suffice. It was not as if he were asking a favor for himself. He would still be damned before he would do that.

"Yes," he said again, "I am sure it will help. How soon can you leave?"

For the first time, the girl actually smiled. No doubt she could sense his relief and confidence. Henriette was right. She was very pretty.

"I can leave tonight, as soon as I see the Comtesse and get my clothes," she said quickly.

"Good," he said. "You will need about thirty pounds. If you don't have the money, I will lend it to you. I would consider it an honor to invest in your future—yours and Jamie's."

"No thank you," she said firmly, with a trace of her former defiance, "I can manage very well."

"I am sure you can," he said. "Now listen carefully. Jamie is very lucky. Since he is young—"

"He is twenty-three," she corrected him.

"And since," he went on, "his merits have not been sufficiently recognized—otherwise he would be at least a major—there is a good chance that he will be acquitted without our help. Still, we must take no chances. I shall give you a letter to a very powerful lady in England. She can have Jamie set free, and I am confident that she will use her influence. If you will pardon me, I shall write the letter for you."

He turned hastily toward the writing table, afraid the girl would throw herself at his knees again. Her gratitude, he was sure, would be as violent as her despair.

"Jamie said you would help," he heard her say. "He said you would help. His letter said you would help."

She began to cry again.

Writing the note was surprisingly easy. It was not like composing those long tortured letters he had written her from Holland and Ireland, or like those he had constructed in his imagination after he quit writing her. He was pleased at his dispassion and brevity.

"My dear Lady Sheldon," he wrote,

> The bearer of this letter, a Mrs. James Maclean, is the wife of a young and silly lieutenant of foot now in Newgate charged with treason for his part in the late insurrection. The life of Lieutenant Maclean is of great importance to this woman, as you will no doubt see, and of no importance to the government. Neither his parts nor his family connections are such as to endanger any regime—certainly not the English monarchy. Knowing as I do your scorn of senseless cruelty and your interest in establishing the government's reputation for moderation and clemency, I have felt free to solicit your interest in the young man's behalf. If I have any credit with you, please take him under your protection. In doing so you will perform a great service for the unhappy couple and oblige
>
> Your humble and obedient servant, ever,
> RALPH BARNARD

He folded the letter quickly, before he should be tempted to add anything, applied the wax, and sealed it firmly. Now that it was written, he was anxious to get rid of it.

"Here it is," he said to the girl. "You must take it to Lady Esther Sheldon at Hemphill House in London."

"Lady Esther Sheldon?" The girl dried her eyes again. Now she looked puzzled.

"Yes, Lady Esther Sheldon. You will have no difficulty in finding her. Anyone in London can tell you where her house is."

The girl looked at him uncertainly. "But Sir, isn't that the lady who is coming to see the French Regent?"

Ralph was stunned. "Coming to see the Regent? Who said she was coming to see the Regent?"

"It was in the *Gazette* yesterday," she said.

"Are you sure?" he asked.

"Almost positive. Since Jamie went to Scotland, I have read the *Gazette* faithfully, and yesterday it told about a lady being sent to the Regent—something about a place called Mardique, I think."

Yes, Ralph thought, it sounded plausible. The British government might send someone to help Lord Stair in the Mardyke negotiations. And who more skillful than Esther? No wonder Stair had said he might soon know her better.

"You must pardon my ignorance," he said, recovering quickly. "I was so busy with my own affairs yesterday that I did not read the *Gazette*. Did it say when she is expected at Versailles?"

"Within the week, I believe."

"I see. This is very fortunate for your business. You can give her my letter when she arrives. You will not be obliged to go to London after all."

The girl looked surprised. "Won't you see the lady yourself?"

"No," he said shortly. "The letter will suffice. She will have ample time to write to London before your husband comes to trial."

Now that Esther had been mentioned, the girl and her problems seemed suddenly remote. He found it an effort to finish the interview.

"Please let me know if you have any further difficulty," he said. "If you wish, you may come back when you have talked to Lady Sheldon and tell me what happened. Oh, and one thing more. If you have a few pounds, you should send them to Jamie. They will make his stay in Newgate much more pleasant—perhaps even jolly."

The girl rose from her chair, holding her letter carefully.

"Thank you," she said simply. "We will not forget this."

At the door, she seized his hand and kissed it; then she was gone, hurrying down the path and disappearing behind the high hedge.

When he turned around, Henriette was standing in the center of the room.

"Who is Lady Sheldon?" she asked.

"Lady Sheldon," he said casually, "is an important Whig politician, a lady I used to know. And someone has been eavesdropping."

"I told you I should eavesdrop," she said. "I must protect my interests. But go on, and tell me more about Lady Sheldon."

"There is little to tell," he said, maintaining his calm disinterested

tone. "She is a lady I knew years ago in England, before the Revolution. When King James II was in power and the Whig party was
low, I was able to do favors for her. Now, I hope, she will feel
obligated to do a small favor for me."

"What kind of favors did you do for her? Personal or political?"
Henriette would not let the subject go.

"Political, of course," he said. "With Lady Sheldon, all favors are
political."

Henriette frowned. "I suppose she is very pretty."

"She was at one time, I guess," he said, as if he were trying to
remember. "She is fifty years old now—very likely a perfect witch."

"Was she as pretty as I am?"

"No, not pretty as you. No one is as pretty as you. Come here
and give me a kiss."

"Not until you stop evading my questions. You are being artful
with me. Was her maiden name Esther Hemphill by any chance?"

He hoped he did not look surprised. "Why yes it was. Esther
Hemphill. Have you heard of her?"

"Yes," she said slowly, "I have heard of her. Why don't you want
to see her while she is in Paris?"

"Why should I?" he asked. "The letter will do the business if it
can be done, and I have my own affairs to worry about."

"I see, and you don't wish to ask her help for yourself."

"No, I can do without it."

"I am not sure whether I like this or not." Henriette wrinkled her
forehead. "If she were simply an old friend, you would go see her
without thinking twice; and yet, if you did want to see her, I would
go scratch her eyes out."

"I don't think you would scratch her eyes out," he said. "If you
knew her, you would not bother."

"Perhaps not," she said. "Do you think about her often?"

Sir Ralph laughed, easily and naturally, he was sure.

"You are the most charming and romantic woman in the world,
Henriette, and I am flattered at the picture you have of your husband—a man with a deep, incurable wound. Unfortunately, it is not
true. Even if I had loved the lady, I should have forgotten her long
ago."

"I see," she said. "Then how does it happen you remembered her
so readily this afternoon?"

"Very simple," he said. "I have been writing my report for Lord
Stair. I am obliged to think of people I have known."

Suddenly Henriette was in good humor again. "All right," she said,

"I accept your explanation. But I warn you, if I catch you lingering over your reports, I shall stick pins in you."

"You are full of impossible nonsense," he said.

"You are too," she said. "Now come have your breakfast and get back to your report."

Eleven

SIR RALPH found it easy to begin writing again. Perhaps the night's rest had sharpened his memory, or perhaps—and this he considered more likely—the events themselves were more consistent, more easily arranged into a pattern. They had been surprising at the time, of course; but seen in retrospect they seemed to have a certain inevitability. A more experienced man, he felt, might have predicted them. Even the young Ralph Barnard could have foreseen many of them if he had not been misled by loyalties, love and prejudice.

In February of 1686 [he wrote] Ralph Barnard was sent to the United Provinces of the Netherlands by King James II. Ostensibly his duty was to press the claims of the English merchants in the Dutch maritime courts; actually his mission was to observe the motions of English exiles and to forestall any conspiracies against King James; likewise to collect such information on Dutch opinion and policy as might be useful to His Majesty. This last became of utmost importance because Sir Bevil Skelton, the King's ambassador, had been forced to retire from the Netherlands when one of his agents was discovered spying on the Prince of Orange. Sir Bevil's retirement damaged the King's cause, since it left the regular channels of information wonderfully clogged—a condition which was not corrected until some months later when the Marquis d'Albeville was appointed in his place.

Mr. Barnard found his stay in the Netherlands most instructive. Although the plots he uncovered were trifling, and although he found little to condemn in the conduct of the Prince of Orange, who at that time was trying to maintain good correspondence with his father-in-law King James, Mr. Barnard learned much about the posture of affairs in Europe and much about the chief actors on the political scene.

Sir Ralph smiled to himself when he reread what he had written. Yes, he had learned a great deal in Holland, and a great deal that had nothing to do with exiles and espionage. In a way, he supposed, his stay in the Netherlands marked a stage in his development. It seemed now as if his real education had begun one April afternoon while he was sitting in a tavern, the Prins Marits, in The Hague, and listening to a conversation between two Frenchmen.

"The Dutch are pigs," the foppish one in blue was saying. "One wonders why our king bothers with them."

The man in the snuff-colored coat surveyed the tavern with its spotless tables, polished glass, and gleaming copperware as if to verify his companion's remark. "Ah yes," he said, "one cannot find a decent wine in the seven provinces. Still, one must admit that they are rich pigs."

"But of what use is wealth to a pig?" The man in blue looked aggrieved. "Observe that man there." He pointed out the window at a somberly clad Dutch shopkeeper giving directions to two men loading a cart. "That barbarian probably owns more gold than half the gentlemen at Versailles, and yet regard him. He lives in a cramped house in a swamp, feeds on bad cheese and black bread, and dresses as you see. It is monstrous."

"But certainly." The man in the snuff-colored coat shrugged. "Still one must admit that even pigs have their uses, especially fat, rich pigs. What would you say if I told you that these pigs will someday soon be our pigs?"

"I should say you were making pleasant conversation," the man in blue said disdainfully, adjusting the lace on his left sleeve, "although I do not deny the thing is possible."

"Very well, scoff if you wish," Snuff-color said with a touch of hauteur. "But I had this from Monsieur le Comte d'Avaux himself."

"Ah, that is different." The man in blue stopped toying with his sleeve and drew his chair closer. "Someday soon, you say?"

The man in the snuff-colored coat looked around the tavern again. He looked directly at Ralph, two tables away, and at the four or five other men scattered around the room. He did not lower his voice, however. Apparently he thought, like most other foreigners in Holland, that no one understood his language.

"When I say *soon*," he said, "I do not mean tomorrow, of course."

"Certainly not."

"I mean within the next four or five years."

"I understand perfectly."

"You think, perhaps, that the enterprise will be difficult?"

The gentleman in blue hesitated. "Difficult, possibly," he said, "but not unreasonable. It is well understood that our army is the best in the world."

"Not even difficult," Snuff-color said triumphantly. "Evidently there are things of which you are not aware."

The blue gentleman was insulted. Obviously he too prided himself upon his knowledge of affairs. "I am aware, certainly, that the Prince of Orange is forming a league against us, and that he hopes to stop our king from expanding further; but I hardly see how that promotes our aspirations."

Snuff-color looked out the window with a self-satisfied air, as if he were about to take possession of the country in the name of Louis XIV. "Ah yes, there is a league; but consider to yourself the materials of which the thing is formed: a number of paltry German principalities whose only aim is to earn a few Dutch guilders; an Austrian emperor, who is already up to his ears in battles with the Turks; and a moribund Spain, whose king is literally idiotic. Can the Prince of Orange and his two or three million boors and burghers resist our king with allies of such a sort? It is impossible. Mark my words, inside of five years our king will dominate all Europe."

"And a good thing too," the gentleman in blue said, mollified, it seemed, by contemplation of the glories of France. "A little civilization in the French style would improve a place like this marvelously. Still, one must not forget about the English. Does Monsieur le Comte d'Avaux believe they will sit by peaceably and watch our master swallow up the Low Countries, absorb the Dutch fleet, and crush Protestantism? It does not seem likely."

Snuff-color laughed triumphantly. "But it will happen, nevertheless. Let me tell you something in strictest confidence—something I had from the Count himself. The English king, James, is in the pay of our king."

The blue gentleman almost leaped out of his chair. "Truly? Is this certain?"

"As certain as it is that I am sitting here." Snuff-color was enjoying the sensation he had created. "And what is surprising about the fact? Figure to yourself the English king's situation. He is first of all a Catholic and anxious to establish the blessed religion in England. Can he do so by fighting the French and strengthening Dutch heretics? Clearly not. And even if he were inclined to defend the Low Countries against us, he could not do so. Wars are devilishly expensive, and he could not raise the money without summoning a Parliament. Then, as the English say, there would be the devil to pay. A Parliament would impeach his officers, chase the priests out of the country, and bring him under Protestant control. No, my friend, he will find it much better to dispense altogether with parliaments and get any additional money he needs from King Louis. Do you see?"

"It is transparent," the man in blue said. "But might not the English revolt against him?"

"Impossible. The English king's army is sufficient to put down anything of the sort. A civil war in England would be very agreeable to our king, however. It would keep the English engaged for years. Meantime, our business in Europe would be done."

The gentleman in blue sat back in his chair, obviously satisfied by his friend's explanation. He adjusted his wig a trifle and then wiped the powder off his hands with an elegant lace handkerchief. "One cannot praise too highly the abilities of our king," he said. "He foresees everything. I hope however that when he conquers these Dutch bogs he does not send us here to administer them. I would rather have an acre of ground anywhere in France than all the Dutch provinces together."

Snuff-color nodded and sighed. "But certainly. One must expect inconveniences, nevertheless, and especially when one is as unlucky as I. If I had any luck, I should be back in Paris now instead of drinking inferior wine in Holland."

"It is no wonder the Dutch are pigs," the man in blue said solemnly. "How can one build a civilization on German wine and Dutch beer?"

Ralph watched the two rise, put on their plumed hats, and leave the tavern. When they were safely gone, he called the tavern keeper, a pale unobtrusive little man with a slight limp.

"Who are those men, Mynheer van Norden?" he asked.

The little Dutchman looked after his departed guests as if he might spit. "The thin one in blue is Monsieur Claude de la Roche, a bit of fungus from the French court, with a sinecure in the customs. The one in brown is Monsieur Paul Corot, a gentleman in the retinue of the French Ambassador, le Comte d'Avaux."

Van Norden smiled thinly. "You heard their conversation, I suppose."

"Yes, I heard it," Ralph said. "I suppose everyone in The Hague heard it. Tell me, what did you think of it?"

Again the thin smile crossed van Norden's lips. "Well," he said, forming his precise but slightly accented English carefully, "there was little new in it. We in Holland have known for many years that the French consider us pigs and that they intend to overrun our country and dominate Europe. We remember all too well when they were at the gates of Amsterdam not so long ago and how we were saved only by the grace of God. We also know that our alliances are weak. Monsieur Corot's estimate is only too accurate. Still they are much better than nothing, and you may be sure the Prince of Orange will do everything possible to strengthen them. He was able to beat back the French before with an alliance almost as feeble. I, for one, do not despair. I still have one good leg, you see."

"I see," Ralph said. He could not help admiring the quiet little Dutchman, whose limp, he suspected, had been acquired in the defense of some dike or ravelin during the French invasion. "But what about the rest of Monsieur Corot's statements? Do you believe that King James is in the pay of King Louis?"

Van Norden looked a trifle embarrassed, as if he would gladly have avoided the subject. "I am afraid he is right about that too," he said. "His master, the Comte d'Avaux, is in a position to learn the facts. He is in constant correspondence with Monsieur Barrillon, the French Ambassador to England. I have heard the subject rumored for several months now."

The answer disturbed Ralph. It was one thing to hear a wild allegation from a self-important Frenchman; it was quite another to have the allegation believed by a man as sane and well informed as van Norden. Many spies, agents, plotters, diplomats, and politicians passed under the surveillance of this colorless little Dutchman. He was seldom wrong about anything, as far as Ralph had been able to find out.

"Nevertheless," Ralph said, "I think the rumor is untrue. King James, I am confident, is an Englishman first and a Catholic second. I do not think he will sacrifice England, or Holland, to the French."

Van Norden did not reply at once. Instead he rubbed attentively at a spot on the tankard he was carrying. Ralph could not tell whether the tiny grimace that crossed his face was directed at his work or at the stupidity of the statement. "Perhaps you are right," he said, politely, in a voice which seemed trained to cover only one table at a time. "I hope so. And yet I have the feeling that King James will never join the Prince's league. We shall soon see. When King Louis finishes dragooning the Huguenots at home, he will be ready to move abroad."

Ralph smiled with more confidence than he felt. "Yes, we shall see. You must not forget, Mynheer van Norden, that the Princess of Orange, the next heir to the English throne, is our King's daughter.

King James would never allow his daughter and his son-in-law to be crushed by the French."

"Let us hope not." Van Norden's tone lacked conviction. Suddenly he raised his voice and spoke in Dutch. "Will that be all, Mynheer?"

The abrupt shift of language and tone put Ralph on his guard. A man was passing the table on his way to a seat in the corner. Ralph glanced up casually. There was something familiar about him.

"It will be all for the moment," he said in the best Dutch he could command. "I will take another pot of beer later."

"Very good, Mynheer." Van Norden nodded and moved quietly away toward the barrels.

Ralph picked up his copy of the Haarlem *Courant* and shifted in his chair to a position which allowed him to observe the man, who was now seated about ten or twelve feet away with his face toward the window. Yes, Ralph thought, that profile was assuredly familiar. The slight jowl, the ruddy complexion, the handsome nose—he had seen them all before. But where? Clearly the man was English. The cut of his coat and the shape of his large periwig made this evident. As Ralph studied him, the man made a familiar gesture. He reached into his coat pocket, pulled out a watch, opened it, glanced at it, closed it, and put it back. A scene from the Assizes flashed across Ralph's mind. This was the doctor, whatever his name was, who had testified for the Hemphills. Keith—that was it. What was he doing here?

Ralph continued to study the man. It was the wig, he thought, which had changed Keith's appearance, changed him from the impressive actor of the Assizes into a nondescript Englishman who could be taken for a tobacco merchant, a cloth dealer, or a minor functionary in the government service. His complete ease as he gave his order to the waiter and lounged back in his chair seemed to suggest that whatever his business was it was going well. While talking to the waiter he had glanced briefly at Ralph, but there was no sign of recognition.

As Keith turned back toward the window, a man stopped outside, peered in, and stood for a moment looking at him. Framed in the window, the stranger had the appearance of a bewigged hawk. His long hooked nose completely dominated his sharp features and separated a pair of beady, unblinking brown eyes. His mouth, under the long beak, was merely a thin horizontal slit. These features were set above a wiry neck craned forward out of a dingy, ruffed collar. The impression was completed by a black coat with wide sleeves, which looked almost like wings. Ralph half expected the man to flap them.

As Ralph watched, Keith gave a slight inclination of his head, and the man disappeared from the window to reappear shortly at the door. Once inside, he shuffled quickly over to the corner in an odd, stoop-shouldered gait, while Keith waited nonchalantly to receive him. As far as Ralph could tell, there was no word of greeting. The newcomer crumbled his tall, bent frame into a chair and then leaned forward until his nose almost touched Keith's ear. From the cadence of the harsh whispers, Ralph knew the man was excited, but he could not make out a word of the monologue.

"I have brought your drink, Mynheer."

Van Norden's voice came so unexpectedly that Ralph jumped. He covered his confusion by shifting around in his chair.

"Who are those men?" he asked softly.

"The big man, I do not know. I have never seen him before." Van Norden mopped a few drops of beer from the table. "The tall one I thought you knew—I thought everyone knew. It is the famous Doctor Ferguson. You know, Robert Ferguson, the plotter."

Ralph felt his flesh creep as if he had suddenly stepped on a large snake. So this was Ferguson. This was the villain who had conspired to kill James when he was Duke of York, the man who had tried to kill King Charles—the sneaking fanatic clergyman who had helped lead Monmouth to his doom. No wonder he looked capable of anything. The descriptions Ralph had seen did not do the man justice.

"What is he doing here?"

Van Norden gave his thin smile. "One can never be sure," he said. "One only knows it is nothing good. Most certainly he is not drinking your king's health."

"Have you heard any rumors?"

"One always hears rumors. Exiles live on rumors. Two months ago the rumor was that an attempt would be made on your king's life; but that rumor is dead. Evidently the plan was unmarketable. Now there are half a dozen little rumors: that agents are to be sent out to seduce the army from its allegiance to the king, that a secret press is to be set up in London, that Petre and the priests are to be intimidated, that anti-popish riots will be raised all over England, that the English navy will be brought over to the Dutch—things of that sort. Nothing that should cause immediate alarm, and nothing that could not be better organized from England than from here."

Ralph glanced toward Keith and Ferguson. Ferguson was still talking intently.

"You think, then," Ralph said, "that Ferguson is without a plan at present."

Van Norden shook his head. "Ferguson is never without a plan. He cannot support himself without a plan. The only question is, what kind of plan does he have and who is he trying to sell it to. Perhaps if I leave you, we shall be able to find out."

"Thank you, Mynheer van Norden. If I find out anything of interest I shall let you know. I hope you will do the same kindness for me."

He watched van Norden make his way toward Keith and Ferguson, beckoning his waiter as he went. The move was casually and naturally made—the host taking care of his guests—yet so quietly and expertly that he was sure to overhear a few words of the conversation.

Ralph picked up his paper and shifted again so that his back was toward the two men. He must not appear to be interested in them. As soon as van Norden had left them, they resumed their conversation, Ferguson in his excited harsh whisper and Keith in a flat, colorless monotone. He could hear only an occasional word. Once Ferguson said something that sounded like "from Rotterdam"; once something like "brisk boys"; and once something like "Tory swine." From Keith, at long intervals, Ralph heard the words "stupid," "thousand pounds," "Leyden," "Orange," and "ass." At one point Keith gave a short, sarcastic laugh—at least it seemed sarcastic.

Although it was impossible to make sense out of this disconnected gibberish, Ralph did not feel that his time was wasted. He received the distinct impression—he could not say how—that Ferguson was proposing something that Keith did not like; more important, Keith seemed to be the one with authority, the one giving the orders. The longer the conversation went on the more Keith talked and the less Ferguson talked. Toward the end of the interview, Ferguson quit talking altogether, except for an occasional short whisper, probably a word or two of agreement.

While one part of his mind was busy with the conversation, another part was worrying the problem of Keith—his connections with the Hemphills and his connection with the exiled Whigs. Was the man really a physician as he had appeared to be at the Assizes? Ralph was ashamed of himself now for not having taken the trouble to investigate him. Elementary precaution should have suggested that a man who could lie so fluently and convincingly was no ordinary London surgeon hired especially for the occasion, and that a man so useful in one crisis would certainly be used again. At bottom, Ralph supposed, his reason for neglecting such an obvious duty had been his interest in Esther Hemphill. Well, he had been stupid once, but he would not be stupid again—at least not in the same way. He would follow Mr. Richard Keith, or whatever the man's real name was, and see what he could find out.

In some ways, he thought, being in Holland made spying much easier. Foreigners in this country were easy to identify and trace. When they first arrived, their clothes gave them away. They stood out like robins among a flock of crows. And even the people who consciously tried to blend with their background, or who had been in the Netherlands long enough to acquire Dutch wardrobes, were betrayed by their refusal to learn Dutch, which most of them considered barbarous, and by their sublime confidence that no Dutchman could understand them if they talked in their own language, or in bad French. It was amazing what one could hear simply by sitting in the taverns of Amsterdam, Rotterdam, Leyden, or The Hague. It was even more amazing what could be learned by distributing a few guilders among waiters, servants, bargemen, innkeepers, and port officials. In another month, Ralph was sure, he could finish constructing a complete system for getting information, at a cost which King James would think entirely reasonable.

The conversation between Keith and Ferguson ended as abruptly as it had begun. Keith's monotone suddenly stopped. There was a scraping of chairs, and a moment later Ferguson shuffled past Ralph's table on the way to the door. Keith stayed long enough to summon the waiter and to pay him. Then he too made his way out of the tavern. Ralph, leaving his money on the table, followed quickly.

Ralph had little difficulty in keeping Keith in sight. In spite of the number of people on the narrow, cobblestoned streets, and in spite of the carts and wagons, which often clogged the ways, Keith's broad back and the high-crowned hat perched upon his periwig were easy for Ralph to follow. They soon led him out of the crowded area of shops and high gabled houses and brought him to the Binnenhof, the walled and moated inner court of the town. Keith did not cross the bridge, however; he continued across the town. Soon he was passing through the less crowded districts, the suburbs where each house had its own neatly arranged garden and its carefully clipped hedges. Here, Ralph was forced to lag far behind for fear Keith would notice that he was being followed. Finally, Keith left the town altogether and struck out on a small but well-travelled road leading into the woods.

Ralph waited until his man had crossed the two hundred yards of open country between the last house and the forest; then he followed briskly, afraid that the man might leave the road and disappear into the underbrush. Inside the woods, he slowed his pace again. Keith's footprints were clearly marked in the sandy soil of the road; there was nothing to be gained by keeping the man in sight, and one might suddenly overtake him around a sharp bend.

After twenty-five or thirty minutes of steady plodding, Ralph came to a junction, where a straight lane led away from the winding road toward some kind of lodge or villa dimly visible through the trees. Looking down the lane, he saw Keith about a hundred yards ahead, walking steadily. Once again Ralph was forced to wait, or to risk being seen. Perhaps, he thought, it would be better to turn back and return later, after he had found out something about the place and manufactured some pretext for visiting it. On the other hand, not to look around while he was here seemed a waste of time and effort. When Keith had disappeared, Ralph began to move cautiously up the lane.

He had negotiated about half the length of the lane, keeping close to the edge, near the trees and bushes, when he heard hoofbeats. He glanced back over his shoulder. Someone on horseback had turned the corner behind him and was riding down the lane. Already it was too late to leap for the bushes; he had certainly been seen. He must brazen it out. The chances were it was only some servant anyway. Ralph took a deep breath and squared his shoulders as he marched on, waiting to be overtaken. About ten yards before it reached him, the horse slowed its gallop. Now was the time, Ralph told himself that he must look around casually.

"Well, Mr. Barnard," a voice said, "are you going to ignore me all afternoon?"

He found himself suddenly looking directly into the face of Esther Hemphill.

CHAPTER

Twelve

IF ESTHER was surprised to see him, she did not show it. She had
reined her horse up beside him and was now sitting within arm's
length smiling down at him as if their meeting were the most natural thing in the world.

"Well," she said, "are you determined not to speak at all?"

Ralph recovered quickly. "Pardon me, I had not expected to meet
you until I reached the house."

He took off his hat and made a formal bow.

"You expected to meet me?" She sounded incredulous.

He watched her maneuver her horse back into position. The movement of his hat had frightened it.

"Of course I expected to meet you," he said, lying boldly and, he
hoped, plausibly. "You must not suppose I would walk this far to
meet anyone else."

It was the first time he had seen Esther at a loss, even for a second.
She was studying him carefully, trying to find out, he thought,
whether or not he was serious.

"I hoped you would be pleased and flattered," he added.

"I am," she said thoughtfully.

"As soon as I knew you were in Holland, I set out to find you,
and here I am."

"How very kind of you, Mr. Barnard. And how very prompt—
even before the servants had finished unpacking."

"If I have been too hasty with my visit, I apologize. My zeal outran
my manners. I shall go back to The Hague."

"Not at all," she said. "I was merely curious to find out how you
knew I was here."

Ralph assumed what he hoped was an expression of bland innocence. "Your visit is being talked about all over the city. I heard
about it from a tavern waiter. Was it supposed to be secret?"

"Not secret, precisely," she said, "but not a matter of common knowledge either. Well, there is no help for it now."

"I suppose not," Ralph said cheerfully. "I am sorry."

"You needn't be," she said. "Help me dismount and we will walk to the lodge together."

Almost before Ralph could reach out for the stirrup, she had slid expertly from the horse. For an instant they were standing close together; then she was pulling the reins over the horse's head and handing them to Ralph.

"If you wish to be my groom," she smiled, "you must be very quick."

For the second time in his acquaintance with Esther, he felt he had missed an opportunity.

"You are much too slippery," he said. "I shall never be able to move fast enough."

Esther looked up at him. "You must practice, Mr. Barnard—constantly."

He straightened the horse's bridle, conscious that he was being studied, aware too of a little buzz of excitement.

"You know of course," Esther said, as he began leading the horse, "that I am disappointed in you."

"Disappointed?"

"Yes, disappointed. You promised to come back to see me after that Gerrard affair, but you never did—not even to thank me for the information."

"I intended to," he said, "but there was no time. Shortly after that, I was sent here to the Netherlands. Perhaps I should have written you, but I feared being presumptuous."

"What business could have been so important as to make you break a solemn promise?"

The question was asked in a light tone, but Ralph had the feeling that he was being cross-examined. He chose his words carefully, attempting to match her manner.

"A business so important that it could not suffer an instant's delay —some fifteen-year-old English claims against the Dutch."

"How versatile you are, Mr. Barnard. First I find you prosecuting rebels; next, pursuing malefactors; and now prying money out of Dutchmen. Is there no end to your talent?"

"You are laughing at me," he said. "But it is not my fault that I am given cases no one else will touch. I can't afford to be particular. This time I may be in luck. The Dutch seem to be anxious to curry English favor. I may make my fortune."

"I am afraid I cannot allow the excuse," Esther said. "You have put business and profit before your promise to me. To show you how suspicious you have made me, I think that even this visit has something to do with business."

Ralph took a deep breath. He had thought his explanations had sounded convincing, but it was obvious that Esther suspected something.

"You do?" he said. "What business?"

"That is something you must tell me. If I were not so well acquainted with the sorry band of informers and agents the secretary of state employs, I should say you were some sort of spy."

He managed an easy laugh. "And if I were not so sure of your integrity, I should say that you were engaged in something that makes you fear government agents. Now I suppose it is my duty as a loyal subject to find out what it is. Do you suppose the Secretary will pay me for the information?"

Esther kicked at a small pebble. "You are much too glib, Mr. Barnard, to be entirely honest. You may be sure I shall have you followed constantly."

"You disappoint me," Ralph said quickly. "I was sure you had already studied my life's history. Please don't tell me you have taken no interest in me."

"No, I will not tell you that. I have been interested enough to make some preliminary inquiries. I have found, for instance, that you come from Lincolnshire. Your father, I am told, was an unlucky gentleman who wasted his health and most of his fortune at King Charles' court. Your older brother, Walter, now holds what remains of the family estate. After your father died, you were brought up by your uncle John Barnard, a clergyman who stuffed you with a nauseous amount of Tory doctrine and then sent you off to Cambridge where you were stuffed with even more. Your education—or your ruin, as I prefer to call it—was completed at the Inns of Court. As you see, I have learned a few things about you, but nothing essential."

"You set about your task in the wrong way," he said. "You should have asked me what you wanted to know."

"How could I? You refused to come see me. I have been obliged to chase you all the way to Holland."

"You knew that I was in Holland, then?"

Esther laughed. "Of course I knew you were in Holland."

Something in the way she talked gave him an irrational hope that she had been asking about him for her own satisfaction, but the calculating part of his mind told him that this was nonsense. She had suspected him of being an agent and had set about prying into his affairs.

I must be careful, he repeated to himself as they walked on toward the lodge. From now on she will be doubly suspicious.

Of the four men seated in an irregular semi-circle by the fireplace, Ralph recognized two immediately, George Hemphill and Richard Keith. Young George, recovered from his wound, lounged across the arm of his high backed chair, intent upon what the others were saying. Keith was leaning forward, with his legs spread and his elbows on his knees. The other two men were sitting with their backs toward Ralph. All he could make out for certain was that the little man was English and the large man Dutch.

"Here are some gentlemen you must meet," Esther said in a tone which halted the conversation before he could make out any of it. The men got to their feet.

"My brother George and Mr. Keith you have seen before. The other gentlemen are my father, Mr. James Hemphill, and Mynheer Willem Bentinck. Gentlemen, this is Mr. Ralph Barnard."

"Your servant," he said bowing.

The others were slow in their response. James Hemphill and Bentinck had swung around to face him, awkwardly displacing their chairs. Now all four men stood in a line. There was a pause before they bowed, almost in unison.

James Hemphill's face showed no expression. "We are happy to make your acquaintance, Sir."

"Mr. Barnard is a friend of mine." Esther ignored the constraint. "He is a lawyer and a Tory, to be sure; but he is an honest gentleman for all that. You will find him charming."

James Hemphill looked at him impassively. "I am sure we shall," he said.

Ralph glanced from one face to another. "Please don't allow me to interrupt you, gentlemen. Mistress Hemphill and I can continue our conversation elsewhere."

For the space of six or seven seconds everyone waited for James Hemphill to say something. George looked sullenly at his father, and Keith watched them both, his face studiously indifferent. Only the Dutchman, Bentinck, seemed friendly—in a stolid, apathetic way. Esther seemed to be slyly amused by it all.

"You are interrupting nothing important," James Hemphill said finally. "We have just finished arranging a hunting party. Won't you join these gentlemen in a glass of hock while I speak with my daughter a few moments?"

Hunting party? Ralph tried to keep the incredulity from showing on his face and appearing in his voice. Austere little James Hemphill with his cold Puritan face and his ramrod back seemed as likely to take part in a Spanish fandango as in anything so frivolous as a hunt.

"I would enjoy a glass," he said. "Perhaps I can persuade these gentlemen to invite me along. We did a bit of hunting in Lincolnshire."

"You would not enjoy this sort of hunt," Esther said, shooting a glance at her father. "After Father has given me my lecture we can plan something more exciting."

As he settled into the chair offered him, Ralph attempted to sort out some of his impressions. Clearly he had interrupted some kind of conference between the Hemphills and Bentinck. The conference must have been short and unexpected, since Esther had been out riding and Keith had been in The Hague. Whatever its subject matter, the talk must have been important to James Hemphill, judging by his coldness at being interrupted. Bentinck must be no ordinary Dutchman. Bentinck. He was sure he had heard the name.

"So you are a hunter too, Mr. Barnard," Bentinck's heavily accented voice cut off Ralph's speculations. "You will like the Haagsche Bosch. Only last week the Prince took three stags."

The Prince, Ralph said to himself. Now the affair was beginning to make sense.

"I have heard that the Prince is an excellent huntsman," he said.

"Excellent indeed," Bentinck said. "I have seldom seen him fail in the chase. But then you will see for yourself if you accept the Hemphill's invitation to join the hunt."

Ralph saw George Hemphill give a little convulsive start as if he wanted to check Bentinck, but the Dutchman showed no sign of having said anything wrong.

"The Prince," he continued, "will be glad of your company."

So that was it. The Hemphills had arranged a hunt for the purpose of meeting with the Prince of Orange.

"I would not wish to intrude on a private hunt, Mynheer," Ralph said politely, watching George out of the corner of his eye. "I was not fully aware that Mr. Hemphill had issued me an invitation."

George gave another little start. This time he spoke. "We must not press Mr. Barnard. Perhaps he has other business. Of course he is welcome if he wishes to come."

"You see," Bentinck said, "you are perfectly welcome. Mr. Hemphill would not dream of denying a guest and fellow Englishman the opportunity of hunting with the Prince. As for the Prince and myself, we are always anxious to meet English gentlemen."

Ralph observed the Dutchman carefully. No, he decided, Bentinck could not be so stupid as he appeared—so oblivious to George Hemphill's displeasure. He must have some motive of his own for inviting a stranger along. Still, one could not be sure. Perhaps he had not heard Esther's warning that her guest was a Tory. Perhaps he did not know what the term meant. It was hard to believe that a face so heavy and earnest could mask any duplicity.

"You gentlemen are extremely kind," he said. "I would be a monster if I refused such an invitation. Every Englishman is anxious to meet His Highness the Prince—not only because of his many illustrious accomplishments but also because the future of England rests with him and the Princess. It is an honor that I was as far from expecting as deserving."

He congratulated himself on his rhetoric. George Hemphill would never be able to rescind the invitation after an acceptance like that. This heaven-sent opportunity to meet the Prince and frustrate the Hemphills must not be missed.

George Hemphill looked as if he had taken a gulp of vinegar. He threw an appealing glance at Keith, but Keith ignored it, tacitly refusing to join in a losing battle. Ralph could almost feel George's frustration. The boy had suddenly found himself tangled in a net of social etiquette. Without knowing quite how it happened, he had been forced into making a monstrous invitation. Now he could do nothing but fume and wait for reinforcements.

"You must be an intimate friend of His Highness, Mynheer," Ralph said.

Bentinck's heavy face showed a spark of animation. "Yes," he said. "I am his friend since we were children. I even had the honor to catch smallpox from him."

"Mynheer Bentinck is much too modest." Keith spoke for the first time. "He is more than a friend; he is also the Prince's strong right arm."

"Mr. Keith is excessively kind," Bentinck said. "The Prince is his own right arm. I am merely his servant."

Keith seemed eager to erase the bad impression George had made. "Nevertheless, whenever the Prince has an important diplomatic mission, he sends—or brings—Mynheer Bentinck."

"You must have been to England then," Ralph said.

"Ah yes, several times." Bentinck nodded gravely. "It is a beautiful country."

"He was there only last summer, Mr. Barnard," Keith said. "No doubt you were out of London at the time."

Keith had spoken in a polite, matter-of-fact voice, yet Ralph had the impression he was being teased. Keith was letting him know that he was recognized for his part in the Assizes.

"Yes," Ralph said casually. "Last year I was prosecuting rebels— in a small way."

"Mynheer Bentinck was engaged against the rebels in a large way," Keith said. "It was he who brought over the English regiments from the Dutch service."

"Of course," Ralph said. "I knew I had heard your name, Mynheer. I had forgotten where. You must forgive my poor memory."

Bentinck spoke with a trace of a smile. "There is no reason why you should remember my name, Mr. Barnard. Few people do."

"You may be sure I will not forget it again. What loyal Englishman would forget the man who helped King James defeat the rebels?"

Ralph gazed innocently at George and Keith, hoping they would squirm; but he was disappointed.

"You must not flatter me, Mr. Barnard. I was merely serving the Prince. The Prince could not allow the Duke of Monmouth to depose the father of the Princess. Besides his own interest in the succession, he had the peace of Europe to consider. Nothing could be more fatal to us over here than an England torn by a long civil war. With England's fleet and army engaged, or thrown into the arms of the French, King Louis would find his task immeasurably easier." Bentinck paused suddenly. "But I fear I bore you with this talk."

Ralph shook his head and pursued his advantage. "You think, then, that Monmouth's expedition was criminal."

"Not criminal precisely." The trace of animation in the Dutchman's face had disappeared. "No, not criminal precisely. Let us say rash and foolish. Yes, that would be it—rash and foolish."

Ralph felt vaguely foiled. Bentinck had censured Monmouth, certainly—and by implication George and all others involved in the rebellion; but he had refused to go all the way. He had not stated unequivocally that rebellion against James, or against any other legitimate king, was a crime in itself. He had not shut the door against Whig conspirators.

"Don't get up, gentlemen." Esther's voice cut off the conversation and, as it was probably intended to do, brought everyone to his feet.

Esther and her father had returned and were now standing in

the center of the room, looking as if they had never disagreed on anything. The irritation on the old man's face had vanished; it had been replaced by an expression of cold courtesy.

"Please sit down gentlemen," he said.

"We were just discussing the hunting party," George began abruptly. "Mynheer Bentinck thought Mr. Barnard should meet the Prince of Orange, so I have invited him along. I hope I have not exceeded my authority."

Both Esther and James Hemphill received the information without the least sign of dismay. James Hemphill nodded politely, as if inviting strange Tories to private meetings were an everyday occurrence with him.

"Not at all," he said. "Naturally Mr. Barnard is welcome if he wishes to come."

"We are always delighted with Mr. Barnard's company," Esther said. "If he wishes to hunt, he must hunt. I am sure we can furnish him with a horse and all the necessary equipment."

"Thank you," Ralph said. "What time and where does the hunt begin?"

"The Prince and his party will be here at six o'clock tomorrow morning," Bentinck said. "If everyone is ready at that time, a half hour ride will bring us to our positions. The Prince will furnish his own hounds and huntsmen."

James Hemphill nodded. "Does that suit your convenience, Mr. Barnard?"

"Admirably," Ralph said. "I shall be here."

Now that the meeting was arranged, Ralph found himself able to relax and observe more closely the group in which he found himself. James Hemphill in particular fascinated him. Reputed to be one of the most factious and dangerous knaves in England, he was, in appearance, one of the most ordinary. Not more than five and a half feet tall, from the soles of his plain silver-buckled shoes to the top of his small white wig, he looked as if he had been born to sit at a high stool in a counting house or to teach Latin in the lower forms. Even his face was undistinguished, with no irregular or striking features, except perhaps for a pair of eyebrows that seemed too light for his complexion.

And yet there was something formidable about him. It was not merely his ramrod carriage, his direct unwavering stare—the obvious determination in his manner. These things were impressive, but they could have been the mannerisms of a little man trying to avoid insignificance. No, there was something else. That something, Ralph decided, was an almost inhuman coldness. Apparently the man was immune to pleasure and pain. It was impossible to believe that he had ever laughed or cried, loved or hated. His emotions—if one could call them emotions—seemed to range from indifference to contempt.

In the presence of James Hemphill's coldness the others seemed to lose stature, as if his lack of feeling somehow reduced them to triviality. The smooth and competent Esther seemed almost frivolous compared with her father; Keith seemed like a well-meaning blunderer; and George appeared to be an adolescent idiot. Even the phlegmatic Dutchman was affected. From a dignitary of state he dwindled insensibly into a minor functionary.

Yes, Ralph told himself as he half listened to the polite conversation about Dutch customs, people were right in fearing James Hemphill. Perhaps they did not fear him enough. The name they called him, "The Old Fox," suggested a wily unprincipled opportunist, a man like Sunderland, instead of an impersonal driving force. James Hemphill, Ralph suddenly saw, was worth any ten of his opponents. Tory gentlemen, even the politicians, scattered their energies; they drank, gambled, chased women, schemed to raise their personal fortunes, ornamented their estates, tangled themselves in family obligations; some of them even had pretensions to literature and learning. James Hemphill, on the other hand, concentrated all his forces on the destruction of his enemies. He had neither virtues nor vices to distract him. Watching him, Ralph almost pitied Sunderland, Petre, and the sorry little band of Jesuits surrounding the King.

Ralph stayed as long as he dared. He fought down the temptation to maneuver the Hemphills into inviting him for supper. Every minute he could spend observing them was valuable and every minute with Esther exciting, but he could not risk making himself obnoxious. He had pressed his fortunes to the limit in accepting Bentinck's invitation. Now it was time to retreat.

"If you must go," Esther said when he rose to leave, "I insist upon driving you to your lodging. No guest of the Hemphills can be permitted to walk so long as we have a carriage. Am I not right, Father?"

"Most certainly," James Hemphill said in his cold, polite voice. "And we also insist on sending a coach for you in the morning. Five o'clock is too early to begin a long walk."

Ralph bowed his thanks, smiling to himself. The Hemphills were evidently glad to be rid of him. James Hemphill was covering his relief with something like graciousness.

"Well, what do you think of them?" Esther asked when they were seated in the carriage.

"To be frank," Ralph said, "I find your father a bit formidable."

"Formidable?" Esther seemed genuinely amazed. "I am surprised at you, Mr. Barnard. You will never find anyone more truly warmhearted than my father. And I think he liked you immediately."

Ralph found himself staring at her. Was it possible that she actually believed this? Warmhearted? He had seen more warmth in spiders.

"I am glad to know that I have misjudged him," he managed to say.

"I see you don't believe me," she said. "But you will."

The conversation dropped. Ralph was acutely conscious of being alone in the coach with her. He hoped the coach would lurch and throw her against him, but it moved steadily along the smooth Dutch road. To reach over and take one of her hands was too dangerous. If she resented his importunity, he was lost. His chance to spy on the Hemphills and meet the Prince would disappear. Yet, as he looked at her, he had the feeling that she expected him to do something.

"I have often wondered," he said finally, "how you happened to know Thomas Gerrard."

"Oh, Thomas Gerrard. I met him in church, at St. Andrews where I always go."

"I see," he said, trying to keep the disbelief out of his voice.

"Does that surprise you?" Esther laughed. "You must think I am some sort of monster."

"No, I am not surprised you go to church. It is only . . ."

"I know, you thought God was a Tory. You have been badly misinformed. God is a violent Whig. He cares nothing for conservatives. He is interested only in change."

Esther laughed again. "Above all, God is a wag. Otherwise he could never have allowed James to become King of England. But I see you are shocked, Mr. Barnard."

"Not at all," Ralph said. "I could expect a Whig to hold such views."

Suddenly Esther became serious. "Ralph, you distress me. I don't know why you continue to harbor such a vile opinion of my principles —why you suspect me and my family of something monstrous. You are wrong. When you come to know us better you will see. Why don't you give us a chance to become friends?"

For a few moments Ralph forgot to suspect some ulterior motive behind her charming concern. The excitement of being called by his first name and of having his hand pressed drove all other thoughts away.

"I am sure we shall become great friends," he said in a voice he hardly recognized.

"Good," she said. "I shall look forward to tomorrow."

The carriage had drawn up in front of his lodgings. Ralph alighted and kissed the hand she held out.

"Until tomorrow, then," he said.

It was not until she had driven away that he collected himself. "I wonder what she is planning?" he said aloud.

CHAPTER

Thirteen

RALPH WAS NOT particularly surprised when his horse pulled up lame. From the first, the animal had seemed tender footed and balky. Only by relentless spurring had Ralph been able to keep within a hundred yards of the leaders. Now the baying of the hounds was growing fainter and the sound of the hoofbeats was muffled by distance. He could barely hear the shouts of the huntsmen. He listened several seconds, thinking that perhaps someone would return to see what had happened to him; but no one came.

He smiled wryly to himself as he dismounted. Somehow he had feared that the Hemphills would find a way to be rid of him. He had not suspected any device so simple as a lame horse. Now he was almost relieved. Other accidents could have been easily arranged. The horse stood patiently while he picked up the right forefoot and examined it. The horseshoe, loosely fastened by only three nails, was neatly broken in two about an inch from the center nail; the shorter segment now slanted diagonally across the hoof, galling it cruelly. The neatness of the break showed clearly that the iron had been partially sawed through. Apparently the Hemphills were taking no chances. They had made sure the shoe would either come off or break, or both. Ralph had no trouble pulling off the offending segment with his bare hand and prying off the other segment with the tip of his sword.

When he had removed the shoe, Ralph inspected the girth of the saddle, but he could find no evidence that it was defective in any way. At least his hosts had not tried to throw him off on his head—a good sign they thought him a nuisance, not a spy.

He picked up the two pieces of horseshoe and put them in his pocket; then he unsaddled the horse, removed the bit from its mouth and tethered it where it could get plenty of grass. His situation, he decided, was almost comical. Here he was, four or five miles from the hunting lodge, wearing large riding boots in which it would be difficult to walk five hundred yards without getting blisters. He could not walk back in his stocking feet; the terrain was too rough and bushy. He was marooned as effectively here in the woods as he would have been on an island ten leagues from shore. The Hemphills could finish their hunt, hold their conference with the Prince of Orange, and then come rescue their unwelcome guest at their leisure. A pretty situation, Ralph told himself, for a man who had set out to overreach his enemies.

Still, things could be worse. His brief meeting with the Prince before the hunt had been reassuring. The Prince, he was confident, would never be a catspaw for a Whig conspiracy. Tall, thin, and unprepossessing, William of Orange, with his dark hair and eagle beak, looked as impervious to influence as a bar of iron. There was something else too. In his large brown eyes, there was an expression of lively intelligence which contrasted strangely with the saturnine expression on his face and the reserve in his manner. Here was a man, Ralph thought, who said little and understood everything—a different class of man entirely from his father-in-law King James. Perhaps, Ralph admitted, his impression of the Prince was colored by William's reputation as a statesman and a soldier; but certainly the impression was essentially correct. Let the Hemphills have their little triumph. They would never push the Prince beyond the point he had already decided to go.

Perhaps more important in making the Hemphill's victory bearable was last night's news from van Norden. The little Dutchman had been able to find out the substance of Keith's conversation with Ferguson. The Whigs were calling off their dogs. They were not interested in any of Ferguson's projects. In the immediate future, at least, there would be no insurrections, riots, or assassinations. For the present the party would remain quiet and wait for King James to infuriate the nation. As compensation for his political inactivity, Ferguson was to be allowed to have three of his accomplices in England waylay the Holland mail coach and carry off a five thousand pound gold shipment from the Bank of Amsterdam.

Yes, Ralph told himself, things could be much worse. There would be plenty of time to combat the long range strategy of the Hemphills and their allies. The robbery could easily be prevented, or better yet, allowed to happen, so that three scoundrels could be caught and hanged. On the other hand, what could be more annoying than to be trapped neatly in a Dutch bosch while one's enemies carried on a political intrigue, however unpromising. And what if no one bothered with him until late in the evening? They might not find him until the next day. Perhaps he would be wise to walk back after all, blisters or no blisters. But the decision could wait until midafternoon. If no one came by that time, he could still reach the lodge before dark.

It was about two hours later, Ralph judged, when he heard a horse whinny. For a time, he had tried to amuse himself by sharpening his sword on a stone and by throwing his hunting spear at a tree, but he had long since given up these activities. He had also given up the notion of finding anything to eat. The surrounding woods had not yielded so much as a berry. For the last half hour, at least, he had been sitting disconsolately on his saddle blanket trying to convince himself that he might as well begin the long walk back to the lodge. Now the sound of the whinny brought him to his feet, all attention.

"This way," he shouted at the top of his lungs. "Over here."

A few seconds later, after he had almost given up hearing anything more, his own horse pricked up its ears and whinnied. It was answered almost immediately from what seemed to be a very short distance, and now Ralph could hear distinctly the sound of approaching hoofbeats.

"Over here," he yelled again.

He had barely got the words out of his mouth when a horse and rider appeared through the trees. At the first glimpse, he recognized Esther. Within seconds she had ridden up beside him.

"Here you are," she said. "I was afraid I might not be able to find you."

"You were?" he said wryly. "I am surprised that you bothered to look."

"What kind of nonsense is this?" she said. "You must have known that I would come look for you as soon as I missed you."

Ralph laughed shortly. "I must say, it took you a long time to miss me."

"This is the thanks I get for giving up the hunt to rescue you. I couldn't just turn around and disappear, you know. I had to catch up with Father and tell him where I was going. Otherwise, there would have been gossip."

"I see. And was your father surprised to find I was missing?"

Esther looked at him sharply. "I suppose so. What do you mean?"

He was tempted to produce the broken horseshoe and confront her with it.

"Nothing," he said. "It occurred to me that I was not entirely wel-

come on this hunt and that your father might have been surprised
and glad to be so easily rid of me."

"Mr. Barnard—Ralph," she said slowly, "I can't imagine where you
got the notion that you were not welcome. I was the only person
who objected to letting you go on the hunt, and only because I
thought we could find something better to do."

Was it possible, Ralph asked himself, that Esther herself had cut
the horseshoe? He felt himself give a little start. Was it possible
that she wanted to be alone with him? He must be careful, or the
pulse beginning to buzz in his ears would interfere with his clear
judgment. He took a deep breath.

"I apologize, Mistress Hemphill—Esther." His voice, he assured
himself, sounded calm. "Being left alone in the woods may have
affected my brain."

No. He must not let himself be misled. It was a family plot. Esther
had been sent back only after the hunt was so far away that he
could not possibly catch up. Now she was slyly taking the blame in
case he had noticed the broken shoe.

"I hope it has affected your appetite too," she said. "I brought
some food along in my saddlebags."

"Your foresight is incredible," he said. "Let me help you down
from your horse."

This time, he promised himself, there would be no awkward fumbling. Since she had decided to pretend an interest in him, he would
make the most of his opportunity. Stepping quickly to her side, he
grasped the stirrup with his left hand. As she dismounted he reached
up with his right arm, caught her around the waist, and helped her
firmly to the ground beside him.

"I am down now," she said with a smile. "You may let me go."

"Must I?"

"Yes, I suppose you must." She disengaged herself neatly. "Put
on your coat like a gentleman while I get out the food."

The meal was excellent, but Ralph found that he had little appetite after all. The partridge seemed to lodge in the pit of his stomach
and the wine seemed not to go all the way down. Watching Esther,
seated across the saddle blanket from him, he hoped she was having
the same trouble, but he could not tell. As far as he could observe,
neither her color nor her manner had changed.

One thing encouraged him. Esther seemed anxious to talk about
herself. Although her voice remained self-possessed and cool, its cadences unaltered, Ralph thought he could detect an urgency in it,
as if she too were compelled, almost against her will, to exhibit her

past for his inspection and approval. There was a chance, he admitted to himself, that her talk was designed to draw him out, to probe into his motives, but he did not think so; she seemed genuinely anxious to talk about herself.

"My father," she was saying, "has always been disappointed with George. You can see for yourself that he will never accomplish much, beyond getting us into trouble. Besides, my mother died when George was born, and I believe Father has always held him responsible."

"I see," Ralph said. "And you, I suppose, have taken the place of an older son."

"More or less. You must have noticed that he depends upon me. It has been the same ever since I was a child."

"I can well believe it." Ralph had an alarming vision of a small, pigtailed Esther being ordered about by James Hemphill.

"I confess that at times the role has not been pleasant," she said, as if she had read his thoughts from the tone of his voice, "but at other times it has been very exciting. At an age when many girls were still playing with dolls, I was carrying important messages between my father and the Earl of Shaftesbury. I even visited Lord Russell in the tower before the villains cut off his head."

Ralph felt a twinge of jealousy. "You seem to have spent all your time with men."

"I suppose I have. Yes, I suppose I have." Esther spoke reflectively. "But then, to be frank with you, women have always bored me. Love affairs, clothes, and children have never interested me as topics of conversation."

He wanted to ask her whether love affairs interested her as something besides topics of conversation, but he did not dare.

Again she seemed to read his thoughts. "You must not suppose that I am entirely unfeminine. On odd occasions I have even envied some of my acquaintances whose only aim in life is to get a husband. Although, ordinarily, they seem very dull and very ignorant, sometimes they seem happier than I am. Luckily these moods are fleeting. I have never been tempted by any of the men who wanted to marry me."

"There must have been many." Ralph struggled to keep the irritation out of his voice.

"Oh yes. You can imagine how it has been. Some have wished to improve their fortunes; some have wished to make a political alliance with my father; and some, I believe, have actually been attracted by me."

"I am sure of it," Ralph said.

"Then, of course, there are always the hopeful gentlemen, married or single, who consider themselves lovers. You know the type; London is full of them."

"Yes, I know the type." Ralph wondered if he were being warned.

"One has always to contend with a certain number of them, although they are more ridiculous than dangerous."

"I suppose so."

"And then again, there is Father." Esther seemed to be summing up an argument. "For the last five years his affairs have gone through one crisis after another. He could not have parted with me, even had he been so inclined. Nor can I see how he will be able to let me go in the future, until the King dies or is brought under strong control. As long as that madman is loose, my father will need all his lieutenants."

"And I suppose," Ralph said, ignoring the thrust against the King, "that when your father does permit you to marry, he will insist that you marry some Whig nobleman."

Esther laughed. "Not necessarily a nobleman, but certainly a Whig. I would no more think of marrying a worshipper of kings than I would a Papist or a Moslem."

"But if you married a Tory, you might convert him."

"I could never take the chance." She sounded perfectly serious now. "The man I marry must prove himself a thorough-paced Whig."

Ralph was silent for a time, digesting the information. The thought of marrying Esther had never really occurred to him before. The differences in training, wealth, and politics made the notion ridiculous. And yet, he felt dismayed at finding himself so clearly dismissed as a possible candidate.

"What would you consider proof of orthodoxy?" he said finally.

"No one who asks the question could possibly understand the answer," Esther said abruptly. Then her tone softened. "You were not thinking of becoming a Whig, were you?"

"Oh no." He forced a smile. "I asked the question from curiosity. I could never become a Whig."

"You mean nothing could tempt you?"

He looked at her sharply, but he could see no sign that she was being intentionally provocative.

"I am not rash enough to say that nothing could tempt me; I merely say that I could never become a Whig."

"One never knows," Esther said. "You may be surprised."

Ralph pretended to busy himself with a partridge leg. The con-

versation, he felt, had taken an unfortunate turn. Esther had placed
—deliberately, he was convinced—an impossible barrier between
them. Although she pretended to think that he might change his
views, she could not seriously suppose so. Or could she? Did she
really think she might bring him over? And if she did think so, what
effort was she willing to devote to the enterprise?

"But what about you, Ralph?" Esther was saying. "What are your
views on the subject of marriage?"

"Very indefinite. I have never had enough money to be able to
consider the subject. I can say, however, that I have none of your
bigotry on the matter. When I marry, the last thing I shall consider
is my wife's politics."

"I see," she said, "but certainly in your unbigoted way you must
have had moments when you looked at ladies—Tory ladies, I suppose
—as possible wives."

Ralph thought of lying. The truth was so hopelessly dull. Until
now he had never realized the monotonous triviality of his past. He
almost blushed to think of his few blundering, tentative gestures toward women—his furtive yearnings for Lucy Jennings when he was
in Cambridge, his inconsequential fumblings and fondlings with
Jeannie Drake in Lincolnshire, and his adolescent passion for Sarah
Warrington. Poverty and hard study had spoiled a fine gentleman.
Compared with Esther, who had been raised in the middle of a
conspiracy, he had been brought up in a monastery.

"No," he said. "I realize that you will think me backward, but
you may as well know the worst. No ladies—not even Tory ladies—
have tempted me to think of marriage. Few have tempted me to
think of love at all; and of that few, the most dangerous is a violent
Whig."

"Good," she said. "I despise people who are too susceptible. You
can never trust them with anything important."

"Perhaps you are right," Ralph said. "Yet I worry more about people who have no feelings at all."

"You don't include me as one of those, do you, Ralph?" The question sounded faintly mocking.

"I don't know," he said, half to himself. "I shall give the matter
further study."

"Please do," she said, "and let me know what you decide."

Almost without volition, Ralph moved to her side. "If I am to study
your feelings, I must get closer."

Esther showed no surprise or embarrassment. "I am not sure it is

absolutely necessary," she said. "You might have been more objective
at a greater distance."

Ignoring a warning which beat somewhere in the back of his mind,
a warning that this was foolish and dangerous, he reached out to
put his arm around her waist. Now he had committed himself, there
was no retreat. Better to be damned for rashness than for cowardice.

The movement was quick and easy, but Esther was quicker. She
caught his hand in midair, bringing it back to his side firmly and
smoothly, with a motion so natural that he could make no resistance.
Perhaps, Ralph told himself, she had thought he was reaching for
her hand. At any rate, he was content to let her think so. As long
as she continued to hold his hand, he could make no complaint.

"Before we go too far in examining my feelings," she said, "perhaps
we should examine some of yours."

"I should think that mine are fairly evident," Ralph heard himself
say.

"Not at all," she said softly. "I find them very obscure."

"Obscure?" Ralph pressed her hand and tried, without appearing
too obvious, to draw her closer.

"Yes, obscure." Esther seemed not to resist, but she did not move.
"You have told me almost nothing about yourself, except that you
have no intention of marrying and that few women attract you. How
should I know your feelings?"

Ralph increased the pressure. "Perhaps you would like to feel my
heartbeat."

"I am sure that would be interesting," she said, "but right now I
am much more concerned with what is going on in your head."

"I can hardly tell you. I don't know myself." He now began to
caress Esther's arm with his free hand.

"One thing you might tell me is how you like your work?"

"My work? You mean my legal position? I'm not thinking about
my work."

"Well, Ralph, think about it then." She threatened to withdraw
her hand and arm. "If we are to become good friends, I must know
all about you. What your prospects are."

"Just now I should say my prospects are very bright," he said, foil-
ing her threatened retreat by grasping her wrist. "For the first time,
my whole career looks exciting. I had no idea of the possibilities."

"This won't do, Ralph," she said. "You are not being serious."

"On the contrary," he said, releasing his grip on her wrist and
sliding his hand up to her elbow. "I was never so serious in my life."

With a motion so adroit that Ralph could not tell how the thing happened, Esther disengaged her hand and arm. "Very well," she said. "Since I seem to be confusing you. Let us try this conversation from a safer distance. Now then, suppose you tell me something about yourself."

Ralph tried to conceal the surge of disappointment and annoyance at being rebuffed. "As you please," he said shortly. "What do you want to know?"

"Nothing in particular." She seemed eager to repair the damage. "I want to know anything you care to tell me. For example you might tell me how you happened to take up the law as a career, and how you were able to get a crown employment."

Crown employment. Abruptly his pulses ceased to pound; his head became icily clear. It was almost as if he had awakened from a dream. So that was it. All her pretended interest had been designed to get information. He had suspected it from the first. How could he have allowed himself to forget the danger? Well, for all her artfulness, she had made a fatal mistake. She had withdrawn the bait too soon. Another minute or two close to her and he might have said anything. He restrained an impulse to draw back. He would not let her sense his new awareness.

"I am surprised to find you curious about such dull subjects. There is really no mystery about them. I became a lawyer because it was the only profession within reach of an impoverished gentleman. My family never could have afforded an army commission. Then again, studies always came easy to me, and law easiest of all—a mere memory exercise. Have I bored you enough, or shall I go on?"

"Go on, by all means," she said. "Whatever makes you think that this is dull?"

"As for the crown employment, I was fortunate enough to have an uncle with influence—a judge, perhaps you know him. He secured the appointment about a year ago. Is there anything else I can tell you?"

"Oh yes," Esther smiled disarmingly, "there are a thousand things. You might tell me something about your family and friends."

"There is little to add to what you already know. My mother died soon after I was born, and my father when I was six years old. My brother Walter and I were brought up by my Uncle John, a very charming old clergyman, who would have apoplexy if he could see me now. All my childhood friends still live in Lincolnshire; most of them are now squires of some sort. Of my close school friends, one died two years ago of smallpox, one is a factor for the East India

Company, one is a curate in Derbyshire, and one is very much married in London. Is that what you wanted to know?"

Esther laughed. "You must not answer my questions as if you were being cross-examined. I promise not to use the information against you."

I am sure you won't, he said to himself. You won't get any information to use.

"I am merely trying to be calm and objective," he said aloud.

"It is odd," she went on, "your being brought up by a clergyman. I was too—Father's chaplain, an odious old busybody named Roger Martin. He followed me around like my shadow until I was twelve. Then he died, thank heaven, and I got another tutor. I have never liked clergymen since."

"You would like Uncle John," he said.

"I am sure I shall."

Ralph ignored the implication. On his guard now, with the fever gone, he felt more like a spectator at the scene than a participant in it. Once more he was conscious of his surroundings—the bushy undergrowth, the scattered oaks, the patch of grass with the horses grazing on it. There was a sense of power and exhilaration too in being able to watch Esther with detachment. Her hand, he noticed, was carelessly and gradually moving back toward his hand. He smiled to himself at the maneuver and countered it by casually scratching his ear.

"I had no notion," Esther was saying, "that we had so much in common. I feel I know you very well."

"You do?" He made his voice noncommittal. "I am glad. I feel as if I know you very well too."

"I should hope so. I have tried to be entirely open and honest. You see, Ralph, if we are to be friends, you must trust me. I have told you that before."

This time she reached forth very frankly and put her hand on his. He ignored the gesture, congratulating himself upon remaining perfectly calm. He was more apt, he told himself, to laugh at the silliness involved in the elaborate game of hands, than to respond again.

"I see no reason why I should not trust you," he said.

"Good," Esther smiled. "Now there is just one thing that bothers me."

"And what is that?"

"You," she said abruptly. "Can I trust you? You seem so wary and evasive that you must be hiding something. As I told you yesterday,

I almost suspected you of being an agent of the King. You are not, are you?"

"Certainly not." Ralph put as much scorn as possible into his voice.

"If you were, I should not think any the less of you. I should merely try to outbid the King for your services. My father and I can use political information too."

"You are very flattering," Ralph said, "but I fear I am not devious enough to be an agent."

"I suppose not. Still, you might be trained. A charming, innocent-looking gentleman like you, strategically placed in the law courts and not suspected of Whig sympathies, could pick up many valuable facts."

"No doubt," Ralph said. "But I don't think I would care for the occupation."

The pressure on his hand increased perceptibly. "You might," she said. "You might find working with us very exciting."

"I am sure I should. But I am also sure I should not like spying."

"Not spying," Esther corrected him. "You must not talk as if we were conspirators for a foreign power. We are not plotting anything. We are merely defending the rights of Englishmen against arbitrary power and popery."

"Very well, call it what you wish." He evaded her eyes. "I don't think I would like it."

"We will not argue the point. It was merely a sudden thought. Dismiss it from your mind. Perhaps later we can talk about it again." Esther shifted her position until she was almost leaning against him.

"I understand," Ralph said, trying to draw back without being obvious. "I am sorry I give the impression of being evasive. You see, I am not used to people like you. I feel as if I must be constantly on my guard to keep from getting hopelessly entangled."

Esther sighed and drew back a little. "You are right I suppose. We are not being very intelligent. I was about to kiss you."

"That would never do."

His new-found objectivity and dispassion were vanishing as abruptly as they had come. He was overwhelmingly aware of the pressure of her hand, the nearness of her body, the sharpness of her glance. He must be careful.

"And yet it seems a pity that for a few paltry differences in politics and fortune, we should be debarred from a harmless kiss."

"I can hardly imagine a kiss of yours being harmless."

"If you were not so stubborn about your silly Tory principles, we could chance the dangers. If, for instance, you gave any sign of wishing to help us or to abandon your naïve prejudices about furnishing information, we might be able to forget about the fortune, at least for the time being."

"Those are odd conditions," he said. "Suppose I offer to kiss you if you can convince me that you are not engaged in some sort of plot—that you are not trying to make a secret engagement with the Prince of Orange. I might be willing to run a few risks if you showed any sign of abandoning Whiggery."

Esther drew back. "You have an absurd notion of the value of your kisses."

Ralph laughed. Once more he felt his control and confidence surge back. "No doubt. I got the notion from you."

She acknowledged the reproach with an embarrassed shrug. "Forgive me, Ralph. I did not mean to sound offensive."

"You were charming," he said. "And now don't you think we should be getting back to the lodge? You can ride behind me on your horse and lead mine. The hunt may be over now."

Esther made a face. "I suppose we could go if you are discontented here."

"Far from it," he said soothingly. "I am merely anxious to save appearances. I would not wish the Prince and his party to draw any false inferences."

"This concern for my reputation seems a trifle sudden," she said. "Why don't you have some more wine and let me worry about my reputation?"

Ralph was determined not to be outmaneuvered. If, by any chance, the hunting party was returning to the lodge to hold its conference, he would be there—even if it meant dragging Esther bodily.

"You are very flattering," he said, "to take so much interest in me, but I can't allow you to get yourself into trouble. Come now, let me help you up."

Before she could object, he seized her by both arms and pulled her to her feet. For a moment they stood close together half struggling. The next thing he knew he was kissing her.

The kiss was long, violent, and unsatisfactory. At first he was completely engulfed, conscious only of the pressure of her lips, the warmth of her body, and the eagerness of her response. Then he felt himself begin to tremble all over. As they clung swaying together, he was almost afraid they would fall down. Gradually he became aware that Esther had ceased to respond. She was still pressed tightly against him, her breath was still coming in long, audible gasps, and her hand still caressed the back of his neck; but something had changed. A subtle break in the rhythm of the swaying, an almost imperceptible resistance to the compulsion of his hands, told him that now Esther was merely allowing herself to be kissed.

He straightened up abruptly and, without letting go of her, looked intently into her face. Only the heightened color and a pulse beating visibly at the base of her neck gave any sign that her ordinary calm had ever been disturbed. Her eyes and mouth appeared as cool as ever.

"Do you hear hoofbeats?" she said, in a steady, unruffled tone.

Ralph tried to control his voice. "That is your pulse pounding in your ears."

"It might be," she said, "but I don't think so. Listen."

For a few moments Ralph could hear only the sound of their breathing—Esther's he noticed, was irregular as his own. Then he heard the unmistakable sound of a horse trotting.

"You are right," he said, half relieved to find this explanation for her sudden coolness and half angry that she had not been too deeply engrossed to notice the hoofbeats.

"Don't you think we should let go of each other?" she said.

"I suppose so." He was tempted to kiss her again before releasing her, but he thought better of it. He could be as cool as she. Dropping his hands, he stepped back a pace or two.

They were still standing there silently looking at each other when the horseman arrived. It was George Hemphill, his flushed, sweating face reflecting an undisguised fury. For a few seconds after he pulled his lathered horse to a halt he sat there looking at them without saying a word. Ralph expected to be attacked at once, although he could not imagine what he had done to cause such wrath. Instinctively he set himself to face an assault.

"Well, what is it now?" Esther said, as if talking to a misbehaving child.

"You and your god-damned Tories," George said in a strangled tone. "Do you know what has happened? The Prince sent me to find you both."

"That was most thoughtful of the Prince," Esther said.

"Thoughtful?" George was almost screaming now. "It's a damned outrage. And it's all your fault. You and your damned schemes. If you were not always so damned superior and clever we might thrive. Well, you have botched this business. Let me see you squirm your way out of it."

"Please lower your voice, George, and tell me what you are talking about." Esther stared at her brother steadily. "Do you wish Mr. Barnard and me to believe that you resent having to come find us? Certainly you can't be that childish about not getting in on the kill."

"You know damned well what I'm talking about, Mistress know-all. The hunt is over, but the Prince insists that I find you and your Tory consort before we proceed."

"I still see no reason for the excitement. You may ride back to the Prince now and tell him you have found us—that we are perfectly well and safe and will find our own way to the lodge at our leisure."

"Ride back, my arse. I must bring you back, don't you understand?" The veins were standing out on his neck. "He wants to see you both."

"I see," Esther said coolly, never taking her eyes off her brother. "But I see no reason for vulgarity and anger. Mr. Barnard and I are both very flattered, I am sure, at the Prince's concern. If the Prince wishes to see us, we shall be glad to come."

"You see no reason—well, damn me." George turned suddenly on Ralph. "Mr. Barnard, if you know what is good for you, you will get on Esther's horse this moment and ride to The Hague. Furthermore you will stay there and quit bothering my sister."

"Oh, I could never do that." Ralph made his voice sound as polite and reasonable as possible. "If the Prince wishes to see me, I must certainly comply with his request—unless, of course, you have some great and compelling reason for not wanting me to see the Prince."

George's flush grew even deeper. "My reason is in my scabbard, damn you; and if you are not gone within the minute I will show it to you."

"I don't consider that a very good reason. Even if you were lucky enough to beat me in a fight, you would be obliged to explain to the Prince why you attacked me. I think you are being unreasonable."

George began to climb off his horse, but Esther checked him. "That is enough, George. If I hear another word of this nonsense, I will see what Father can do about it. I can't imagine why you don't want Mr. Barnard to see the Prince, but whatever it is, you are not helping matters by behaving like a child."

"You can't imagine?" George threw his right leg back over the saddle and regained his seat. "Well, I'm damned."

"Not another word, George. Do you hear me?"

"I hear you, Mistress Bungler."

As Ralph saddled the two horses, he could hardly keep from laughing aloud. All the wiles and ingenuity of the Hemphills had been frustrated by a simple whim of the Prince. Why the Prince should wish to see him, he could not imagine. Perhaps it was merely an act of courtesy. But whatever the reason, the results were splendid. Esther's planning—evidently it was she who had planned the day's tactics—had gone for nothing. He would see the Prince after all.

And what of the lovemaking? Watching Esther now as she gathered up the napkins and the unfinished bottle of wine, he could hardly believe that it had ever happened. Was all that part of the day's campaign? Or had she actually been carried away as he had been? The response had been so complete and instantaneous. Or had it been? He was almost sure it had. He must not let his suspicions blur his strong, immediate impressions. No, he thought, with a little shiver of remembrance, she had not been pretending. She had been shaken out of her poise and detachment.

He hoped, unreasonably he knew, that she would ride with him— the two of them on the sound horse. Instead, she climbed up behind her brother, leaving Ralph to ride her horse and lead the lame one. On the way back to the lodge, she spoke occasionally, but nothing in her speech or in her looks betrayed any unusual emotion. To look at her, Ralph told himself, one would suppose that kissing Tories and having complex plans miscarry were not sufficiently unusual to warrant a second thought.

"Oh, here you are," Bentinck said heartily as they entered the lodge. "The Prince was worried about you."

"It is very kind of the Prince to be concerned," Esther said. "Mr. Barnard's horse went lame and I returned to help him. We were just having lunch when my brother arrived. Were you worried too, Father?"

"Not at all. As I told His Highness, I am concerned about many things, but not about my daughter's ability to take care of herself and our friends." James Hemphill made a facial contortion, obviously intended to be a smile.

"Perhaps I did not make the nature of my concern clear." The Prince spoke English with a trace of Dutch accent, but he spoke slowly and drily like a man who prefers to remain silent. "I was not worried unduly about their safety. I should not insult their horsemanship by implying that any but the most extraordinary accident could injure them. I was anxious that they should both be here for our discussion of English politics—particularly Mr. Barnard."

Ralph glanced quickly about the room. He was surprised himself; but not half so surprised, he could tell, as the Hemphills and Keith.

Esther and her father, in spite of their habitual dissimulation, started visibly; Keith sucked in his breath; and George let his jaw drop open.

Esther was the first to recover. "I am grateful, Your Highness, that you considered Mr. Barnard and me so important to your discussion. My father and I, of course, are always glad to have Mr. Barnard with us."

"Good." Prince William's expression became a little less somber, but the tone of his voice did not change. "I feared I might be forcing Mr. Barnard's presence upon you. You see, it is essential at this time to have a Tory gentleman with us. If Mr. Barnard had not happened along so luckily, I should have been obliged to find another such man."

"I am afraid I do not understand, Your Highness," James Hemphill said coldly.

"Let me explain. As you know, a good understanding between the Dutch Republic and England is vital to the peace of Europe. If the two countries do not stand solidly together, France will overrun everything. For this reason, I must do everything in my power to gain the good will and support of King James; and I must not give the impression that I am conspiring with his domestic political opponents. Again, consider the fact that the Princess is the heir to the English throne. I should be very impolitic indeed if I identified myself and her with one party. I wish to make the Princess queen of England, not merely queen of the Whigs. You see, then, that Mr. Barnard's presence is valuable to me—and to you too, since you have nothing to hide."

"We understand perfectly, Your Highness," Esther said, in a tone so sincere that Ralph caught himself almost believing that she meant what she said.

"Very well then. Now I have made my position clear, let me add that I consider myself a warm friend of the Whig gentlemen. I too believe in toleration for dissenters, in constitutional government, and in impartial justice. I look upon the Whigs as the inveterate foes of the French and of universal monarchy. I expect them to stand shoulder to shoulder with me in combating the designs of King Louis."

William paused as if exhausted by so much unaccustomed speech. His eyes regarded each of his listeners in turn, with an unhurried authority. The Prince, his eyes seemed to say, was sure of his position, and sure that no reasonable Englishman could disagree.

"We are in complete accord, Your Highness." James Hemphill's cold tone contrasted strangely with the Prince's dry matter-of-fact-ness. "There are, however, some questions we should like to ask. First, what are we to do—and what will you do—if the King tries to force popery upon England? And second, what will you do if the King refuses to ally himself with you against the French—if, in fact, he allies himself with the French against you?"

Ralph found himself leaning forward awaiting William's answer. Here were the crucial questions.

The Prince spoke with studied care. "If the King attempts to bring in popery, you must oppose the attempt by all legal methods. You may be sure that I will support such opposition to the best of my ability and bring all possible pressure to bear in making him see his folly. You may be sure also—and the King must be brought to realize this—that any illegal privileges given to papists during his reign will certainly be taken away by the Princess and me when we come to the throne.

"The answer to the second question is more difficult. For the King to remain neutral when the French make their next attack would almost certainly be fatal to the liberties of Europe and to Protestantism. Still it is difficult to see any pretext upon which I could directly intervene in English affairs, unless, of course, I were invited to do so by an overwhelming public sentiment and by the leaders of both parties. As for the English-French alliance, if the King joins with the French, I shall be obliged to make war upon him, as upon any other enemy, and I should expect every Englishman who loves liberty to join with me."

"When you speak of 'intervening directly,' Your Highness, do you mean that you would invade England with an army?" Esther's voice was so silky and smooth that it almost concealed the importance of the question.

"I mean that I would take whatever steps are possible and necessary to save the religion and liberty of England and the Dutch Republic." William's voice was drier than ever. "What the steps would be would depend upon the situation."

It was an adroit answer, Ralph thought. While it did not specifically commit William to military intervention, it did not rule out the possibility. It could serve at once as a warning to the King and as encouragement to his opponents. It made the Prince the natural rallying point for anti-Catholic, anti-French action.

"Of course, I do not expect any such dire eventualities." William's saturnine countenance became almost bland, and his large dark eyes fixed themselves upon Ralph. "I expect the King's friends, as well as his opponents, to caution him against foolish and fatal policies. And I expect his honor and his wisdom to keep him to the promises he has made to his subjects."

Whether or not the Prince believed what he was saying Ralph could not tell. There was every reason to hope so. One thing was certain, however: He, Ralph, was being made personally responsible for seeing that his Tory friends were advised of the Prince's position.

It was even possible, he told himself, that the Prince expected him to warn the King directly, although this was hardly likely. The Prince could not know that he was a spy, nor could he reasonably suppose that a mere lawyer would have access to the King of England.

"I am glad Your Highness has so much confidence in our King," he said, looking at William steadily. "We Tories believe that it is not misplaced, in spite of insinuations to the contrary. We know that His Majesty is anxious to give some relief to his coreligionists; but we do not believe he will try to Catholicize England or that he will abandon the Netherlands to the French. We are grateful, nevertheless, for your assurance that you will support the liberties of England and its Church against any threats. You may be sure that I will inform all my friends of your intentions. I think I can also assure Your Excellency that when the Princess and you come to the throne you will find your firmest friends among the men who support royal power and authority, not among those who would turn England into a virtual republic."

From the sour expression on the faces of Richard Keith and George Hemphill, Ralph could tell that his little speech had been effective. His statement of the Tory position had reminded them that the Tories still held the high cards.

"His Highness is grateful for the support of all well-intentioned gentlemen." Bentinck took up the burden of talking, the perfect aide relieving his master. "He has ever considered the Tories as his friends."

"I am sure that all the gentlemen of England will find it easy to unite behind Your Highness," Esther said smoothly, "as soon as Tory gentlemen recognize their folly in trusting the King, and abate some of their prejudice against tolerating dissent."

William put his handkerchief to his mouth and coughed, effectively putting an end to the argument. "Since we understand each other," he said finally, "and since we are in substantial agreement, let us leave this subject and speak of more pleasant things. Long discussions of politics, I find, affect my asthma. Hunting, on the other

hand, is an entirely different matter. Even discussing it improves
my health."

William actually smiled, the first time Ralph had seen his dour
face relax. "Speaking of hunting, I must congratulate you, Mr.
Hemphill, on your son's horsemanship. He made Mynheer Bentinck
and me look like statues. . . ."

As the rest of the party enthusiastically reconstructed the hunt
from the starting of the stag to its death at the hands of the Prince,
Ralph tried to review the day's events and marshal his impressions.
He had been amazingly successful, he tried to tell himself. In spite
of the bizarre efforts of the Hemphills to circumvent him, he had
met with the Prince and obtained an important statement of policy.
He had made, he was sure, a favorable impression upon the Prince,
and had effectively defended the King and the Tory party. He had
shaken Esther out of her eternal self-possession, if only for a moment.

Yet underneath his efforts to make himself feel triumphant, he
could not repress some nagging doubts. For all his bravado about
trusting the King, he was no longer sure. Suppose he was wrong
about James. Suppose the Frenchmen at the inn were correct. Suppose Esther and the Countess, in their different ways, had spoken
the truth. If so—but he would never believe without absolute proof—
then the man sitting across the room, the somber intense Dutch
prince, would be the King's nemesis. Already the Whigs were beginning to flock round him. The Tories would come flocking too as
soon as they saw the King's intentions. James and his Jesuits would
be swept out of England in a torrent of blood.

Ralph shook his head. No, he would not believe such horror. He
had a more immediate worry. What about Esther? Could he trust
himself to see her again? Watching her now as she talked with the
Prince, he was sure that their encounter was merely part of the day's
work to her. And yet, he remembered with a shiver, she had surrendered for a moment. Was it not possible to entrap her without
entrapping himself? Must he run away from the game because it
was dangerous? Suppose, for instance, she were really in love with
him. Might she not be willing to give up politics and marry him?
Perhaps it was his duty to cultivate her, if only to keep an eye on
her and her family. But more likely this was all nonsense. He had
better get away from her while there was still time—before he was
hopelessly enmeshed. No wise bird tries to charm a snake.

Or was he enmeshed already? He did not think so, in spite of the
empty feeling at the thought of not seeing her again. He was still
his own master. He had defeated her in this campaign and he could

defeat her again. All this cautious self-examination proved in itself that he could not be snared. Why not let the future take care of itself? If the King's cause could be served by seeing her, he would see her. If not, he would keep away from her.

"I am sorry you must go back to England tomorrow," he heard Bentinck say. "You should stay and see more of our country. Although His Highness must go to Dieren within the week, I should be happy to serve you in any way possible."

"You are most kind," James Hemphill said, "but we have urgent business at home."

"But Father, can't we stay long enough to explore The Hague and visit Amsterdam?" There was a trace of petulance in Esther's voice.

James Hemphill frowned. "Certainly not. We have no time for frivolity; our friends expect us in England."

"Very well."

Esther shrugged her shoulders, but the glance she threw at Ralph mirrored his own disappointment. It said more clearly than words that she wished to stay for his sake.

A violent elation swept over him; he felt the insane impulse to laugh. He could feel himself swaying on his chair. If he had been standing, he told himself dizzily, he might have collapsed. Esther was falling in love with him.

But in spite of the breathless fever in his blood, something stirred uneasily, almost audibly, inside him. Anything so violent and over-powering, it seemed to say, must be fatal. He must get away from Esther or be swallowed up. Everything depended upon speed.

"It has been a great privilege to talk with Your Highness," he heard himself say to the Prince, who was also getting up to leave.

"The pleasure has been mine, Mr. Barnard." Ralph felt himself fixed by William's large brown eyes. "Be sure to explain my position to your friends."

Ralph nodded and then bowed. Yes, he thought confusedly, I must warn the King. I must also find out exactly what he intends to do. But first of all, I must get out of here before it is too late.

"Goodbye, Mr. Barnard," Esther was saying as he bent over her hand. "I will see you in London, I hope."

"I hope so too," he said, avoiding her eyes.

CHAPTER

Fourteen

IT WAS DIFFICULT to tell, Sir Ralph Barnard thought as he looked back over the years, whether the Ralph Barnard of 1686–87 was to be pitied or laughed at. Perhaps both. Certainly the man who had tried to make love to Esther Hemphill in the Haagsche Bosch had cut a ridiculous figure—perhaps a pathetic one too, for that matter. The man who had refused to believe the truth about King James was even more ridiculous and pathetic.

Of course, it was easy to excuse young Ralph Barnard for his foolishness. More experienced men than he might have been baffled in his position. Once the error of falling in love with an enemy had been made, the tragi-comic complications were sure to follow. As for his political naïvete, he was only one of millions. More than half of the well intentioned men in England closed their eyes tightly and refused to believe what a child should have seen immediately. And there was something else too. Young Ralph, personally and financially involved in the King's fortunes, had every reason to misinterpret the evidence. When one considered these facts, it was surprising not that young Ralph had failed to admit the truth sooner but that he had admitted the truth at all—and that he had taken such drastic steps to find out the truth for himself.

Yes, Sir Ralph said to himself, putting down his pen, it was almost impossible not to excuse the earnest and confused young agent who had waylaid King Louis' messenger on a hot August night in 1686. Although the intervening years gave a certain unreality to the episode, the scene was still vivid and easy to reproduce.

Standing in the shadow of the warehouse about seventy-five yards from the dock, Ralph was only dimly conscious of the sounds from the river or the night noises from the City. The attention of all his senses was concentrated on the few square yards of space where the man called Denis would appear. The palms of his hands felt

clammy as he rubbed them together, and he could feel drops of
sweat running down his sides under his armpits. His shirt, he knew,
was soaked. He could feel himself shivering a little in spite of the
heat. Still he did not feel fearful. This was nothing like the terror of
Sedgemoor. It was only an intense anxiety that everything should go
right, that there should be no flaw in the proceedings, almost like
the feeling he had experienced waiting for his cue in the play at
Cambridge.

On the barrel in front of him convenient to his hand lay the club
he had fashioned for himself. It was a stout piece of oak about three
feet long and four inches in diameter, with a crude handle. Not an
artistic weapon, he thought grimly, but adequate to the purpose. Unfortunately, there was a strong chance that a blow with the club
would fracture the man's skull; but this could not be helped. Whatever else happened, he repeated to himself for the fiftieth time, he
must not be seen. The man must be flattened with one unexpected
blow. If, by ill luck, the blow failed and the man saw his face, he
would be obliged to kill the fellow outright.

Ralph rubbed his eyes. The strain of trying to pierce the darkness
was beginning to bother them. Perhaps he had been wrong to take
up his post so early. It was now about ten o'clock, and he had been
waiting since nine-thirty. Denis was unlikely to appear for another
half hour. On his three previous visits to King James, the Frenchman
had left his boat and boatman at the dock at eight o'clock, walked
the mile to Whitehall, and returned about a quarter to eleven. It
was almost a crime for an agent to be as methodical as this one. A
man who used the same method four times in a row probably deserved to be knocked on the head, especially when the method was
unnecessarily complex and patently suspicious. Instead of having
himself rowed up to the Whitehall boat-landing in the middle of the
day, along with the swarm of tradesmen and would-be courtiers,
Denis had chosen this deserted dock and a late hour. Very oblig-
ingly he had made himself a perfect target for assault. Now if he
would only hurry.

Without taking his eyes off the patch of gloom in front of him,
Ralph tried to tune his ears to any sound from the dock. One possibility bothered him. If the boatman became bored and began exploring, he would have to be dealt with too; and the boatman was
burly enough to be troublesome. When he was convinced that he
could hear no suspicious sound, Ralph congratulated himself again
on the neatness of his tactics. A long high pile of old timbers and
barrels between the warehouse and the dock screened his position

from the river and formed a long narrow alley down which his man was sure to walk before he turned off to meet the boatman. The position was almost flawless. The question was the proper execution of the attack.

He loosened his sword in its scabbard and fondled the handle of his club. He did not want to start thinking again about the steps by which he had arrived here. To do so would spoil his concentration on the business at hand. His decision had been made; no purpose could be served by reviewing it. He shook his head firmly and rubbed his hands together to warm them. A pox on this waiting anyway. A man could go insane thinking about the number of things that could go wrong, any one of which would be fatal either to his plan or to himself. What if the King sent a guard along with Denis? What if the boatman heard the blow or a scream and came running to the rescue? What if Denis, contrary to all reasonable expectation, made a wide circle around the warehouse and went down to the dock the other way? Worst of all, what if he bungled the attack and was recognized?

Well, whatever the worries, the business had to be done. If one had to go crazy, it was better to go crazy about a simple violent problem like this one than to go crazy worrying about the King's motives. With luck, he could settle the question once for all.

He gritted his teeth as he remembered his conversation with the King after his return from Holland. At first, all had gone well. James had congratulated him on his work. His report on the mail-coach robbery had led to the apprehension and hanging of the rogues who perpetrated it. His reports on Dutch politics had enabled the King to make a correct estimate of the situation in the Netherlands. In short, the King said, he had done more good in the three months he had stayed in Holland than Skelton had done in a year.

But when he related in detail his conversation with the Prince of Orange, the King did not conceal his rage.

"I see," James said. "The Prince undertakes to dictate my policy for me and to stir up my subjects against me."

"Not at all," Ralph said calmly. "His Highness is extremely anxious to cultivate your good will. His first thought is to secure an alliance with you against the French."

James sneered coldly. "Very likely. And to do so he conspires with my subjects. So much the worse for him."

"Perhaps I did not make myself clear, Your Majesty. His Highness tried to avoid all implication of conspiracy by deliberately inviting me to hear his views."

"Not his views, his threats." The King's mouth set itself in a stubborn line. "The Prince of Orange needs to be reminded that I am the King of England, not he. I will decide what alliances are necessary and what internal policies will best serve the Kingdom. If he wishes to gain my good will he must support my policies, not stir up malcontents to oppose me."

"That is true, Your Majesty," Ralph said quietly, fascinated but uneasy at the outburst, "and I am sure the Prince of Orange understands your position. The only policies he warned against were the policies which I am sure Your Majesty has no intention of adopting —attempting to Catholicize England and allying yourself with the French."

The King opened his mouth to reply, and then shut it, as if he had suddenly realized that he was being indiscreet. The self-control obviously cost him an effort, for his face darkened perceptibly; the line of his mouth grew more grim.

"The Prince of Orange assured me," Ralph went on, when it became obvious that the King did not intend to say anything, "that he had every confidence in your wisdom and probity, and I assured him that the liberties of England and the Republic will find in you a firm bulwark."

"You assured him?" James broke out. "Don't presume on your position. You are my agent, not my envoy. When I want messages sent to the Prince, I will send them. Do you understand?"

"Yes, Your Majesty, I understand. When I spoke to the Prince, I spoke not as an official, but as an English gentleman. I voiced my own feelings. The Prince, I am sure, had no notion that I am Your Majesty's agent. And I may add that when the Prince and I expressed confidence in Your Majesty's intentions, the Hemphills were disconcerted. They affect to believe that you have designs against the Kingdom."

"Designs against the Kingdom," the King exploded. "The factious dogs. I will teach them to oppose me. They will see who is King of England."

Ralph was growing increasingly uneasy. There was something wrong with the King's response. Instead of denying the charges and protesting his good intentions, or laughing at the fears of his opponents, he raged. Of course, Ralph conceded, James was under no obligation to discuss policy with a mere agent, and perhaps he had a right to be angry at the presumption of William and the Whigs; but Ralph could not help feeling dissatisfied. He found himself taking advantage of the King's anger to secure information for himself.

"Frankly, Your Majesty," he said, "although the Whigs are factious dogs, as you say, they are not your chief problem at the moment. The problem is maintaining the confidence of the Prince of Orange and of your most devoted supporters, the Tories."

"Let the Prince of Orange and the Tories maintain my confidence," James snapped. "What right have they to meddle in my affairs?"

"Perhaps no right." Ralph spoke very slowly. "But they have very powerful arguments. The Prince has a veteran army and a good navy. The Tories represent the bulk of the gentlemen of England. If they were to engage the support of the Prince, the result might be fatal."

Ralph watched the King digest the information. For an instant James looked like a man who had stumbled on an unexpected step; then his face clouded up again.

"If the gentlemen of England turn from their duty and allegiance, we shall see who has the more powerful arguments. And let the Prince remember what happened to the Duke of Monmouth."

"I am confident that the gentlemen will not turn, Your Majesty," Ralph said as smoothly as he could, "and that the Prince will continue to remain your friend. You will show them that any fears they may have in your conduct are groundless."

"Let them look to their own conduct and obey my commands, or they will have cause to regret it. As for you, Mr. Barnard, don't allow yourself too many liberties or you may have something to regret too. I do not need your advice. I have ministers for that purpose."

"If Your Majesty is displeased with my conduct, I shall be glad to resign." Ralph was beginning to seethe. "As long as I am in your service, however, and charged with protecting you, I must tell you where the danger lies. And the danger lies, Your Majesty, in alienating your friends. I am sure I can protect you against Whig conspiracies, although the Whigs are no mean antagonists. But I am not sure that I can protect you against the whole English nation, aided by the Dutch army."

For perhaps a minute, James said nothing. Ralph, watching his wrathful face, expected to be dismissed upon the spot, but he stood his ground. He would be damned before he would apologize. Let the ministers palter, hedge, and flatter. It was time someone told James a little truth.

"Mr. Barnard." The King had finally gained control of himself. "I do not intend to dispense with your services. They are valuable, in spite of the lectures that go with them. But I warn you again,

THE KING'S AGENT

163

don't presume too much. There is a difference between information and advice."

"Very well, Your Majesty." Ralph could not resist one parting shot. "You will get no advice from me, only this final piece of information. The Whig leaders are waiting for you to ruin yourself by trying to bring in arbitrary government. Your friends need reassurance."

"So much the worse for them," James muttered, as if to himself. "So much the worse for them."

Ralph was startled out of his reverie by a cough. He had seized his club and flattened himself against the wall before he realized that the cough had come from the boatman down at the dock. Trembling all over with shock and surprise, he cursed himself for his inattention, for his wildly beating heart, and for his stupidity. If a cough carried so clearly, what would a sharp blow on the head do? And if he started so violently at trifles, what would he do when he heard Denis's footsteps?

To calm himself, he left his post at the corner of the warehouse and walked the thirty or forty feet to the end of the timbers where he could look down toward the dock. He could see nothing except a few lights on the opposite side of the river, but the activity itself was reassuring. At least, he was not paralyzed with fright. As he turned to go back, he realized something else. The breeze was blowing from the river. That accounted for the sharpness of the sound. His position was not so bad after all.

Quietly he regained the warehouse and took his post. His trembling, he noticed, had subsided, but he could still feel the beating of his heart. He was mad, he told himself, to remain here. He was not fitted to be a footpad. He should have hired some hulking steel-nerved highwayman to waylay Denis. And was not the whole scheme mad? Who but a madman would risk his life to spy on his master—perhaps to learn secrets which it was better not to know. Yes, he must be mad. King Louis' messenger might be carrying innocuous bits of information, not worth the crushing of a fly, let alone a man's skull. Or he might be carrying messages in a cypher impossible to decode. The plan was a fantastic obsession, founded not upon reason but upon a sudden impulse. As soon as he had found out about the messenger, the decision to waylay him had leaped into his mind. Only now, with the club in his hand, did he realize its madness.

But he made no move to go. He merely put the club back on the barrel, shifted his position slightly, and tried harder than ever to pierce the darkness with his eyes. The objections which his mind kept formulating could not communicate themselves to his body, or touch his basic resolution. They were the excuses of a coward, he felt instinctively. If a man listened to them, he was lost. The decision, though hasty, was sound enough. The fact that James and Louis were using a special messenger instead of the usual diplomatic channels proved they had a special need for secrecy. They would not take such elaborate precautions merely to send each other compliments. No, if there was madness in the scheme, Ralph assured himself, it did not lie in the method of finding out the King's intentions—the method was right; it lay in the compulsion to prove the obvious. Ever since his conversation with the King, he had felt an ugly certainty that James was false—that he was conspiring to overturn the religion, the laws, and the liberties of England. Everything pointed that way, once a man opened his eyes. But somehow, he would not let himself believe as long as a hope remained—like a lover, he thought ruefully, who will not believe his love a strumpet until he catches her in the act.

The sound of footsteps came almost as a relief. Someone had entered the alley and was walking steadily toward the ambuscade. Soundlessly Ralph picked up his club and moved closer to the wall. His hands, he noticed, were steady now, although breathing seemed difficult. Ten seconds more would bring the man within his range of vision, he calculated. Once more he measured mentally the distance between himself and the expected position of his target. He would have approximately two seconds, he knew, to recognize his man and strike the blow. He must not miss.

The man passed the corner rapidly, the sleeve of his coat brushing against the wall not more than three feet from where Ralph was standing. Ralph caught one glimpse of the man's profile, white against the darkness; then he took two steps forward and swung. Aside from a slight stinging of his hands, he had no sensation of hitting the man at all. He did not register the sound of the blow or estimate the impact. But the effect was instantaneous. Suddenly the man was lying in a dark heap at his feet as if he had been struck down by a cannonball.

Without waiting to see whether his victim was alive or dead, Ralph seized him under the armpits and dragged him out of the alley, up alongside the warehouse. Halfway to his intended destination, a pile of rubbish, he noticed that the man's hat was missing. Putting down his burden, he returned to get it. He must not leave it where the boatman might stumble on it if he came looking for his employer. After a few moments' search on his hands and knees he found the hat, about ten feet from the spot where the blow had been struck. He hurried back to Denis again, suddenly afraid that the man might have revived and vanished in the dark, but the body was as inert as ever. It seemed to have grown heavier, he thought, as he dragged it behind the rubbish pile.

Once safely sheltered, Ralph began to undress his victim, giving each article of clothing a hasty search before he put it in the bag which he had brought. He hardly expected to find the King's message in a brief inspection, but there was always a chance; he did not relish the prospect of carrying home a bundle of clothes. Now that he was thoroughly engaged in the work, he found himself more irritated than anxious. The clothes seemed specially designed to frustrate him. Only a Frenchman would wear so many belts, buttons, and drawstrings, with knots that could not be untied in the dark. Ralph wondered how the man ever got undressed. The limp body itself irritated him. He was obliged to turn it over six or seven times in order to get the clothes off, and each time the limbs seemed to fall into the worst possible position.

In spite of his irritation and of the sweat which kept pouring into his eyes, Ralph worked steadily and swiftly. Shoes, stockings, breeches, smallclothes, coat, waistcoat, and shirt revealed nothing of interest. Beneath the man's undershirt, however, he found something promising, a small bag hung from a chain around the neck. He rifled it quickly, and swore to himself when he found it full of gold pieces. He stuffed it into the sack with the rest of Denis's property. At least, he consoled himself, the affair would look like an ordinary robbery.

It was not until he had tied the sack and straightened up to go that he stopped to wonder whether or not Denis was dead. Looking down at the huddled form, dimly white in the darkness, he felt a sharp tremor of concern. The Frenchman had not moved a muscle. Now that Ralph thought of it, he remembered no signs of breathing either. With an effort he turned away. Alive or dead, the man was no further concern of his. The important thing was to get away before being discovered.

He had not gone six feet before he turned back again and dropped to his knees beside the body. Denis's hand made no resistance as he picked it up and felt for the pulse. He could not tell whether it was his own hand or Denis's that felt clammy, nor whether the slight movement he seemed to feel was a pulse or his own shaking. As he fumbled for a better grip, a sudden thought struck him. What if he was covered with blood? He dropped the hand abruptly and felt for the man's head. The thick wig was perfectly dry. With an audible sigh of relief he removed the wig and began feeling for the wound. It was not difficult to find. Across the crown of the head under the thin hair was a lump the size of a man's fist. Ralph winced as he probed it with his fingers, trying to find whether the bones underneath it were smashed. He was inclined to think they were not, though he could not be positive. The lump was stretched tight as a drum.

Ralph paused in his work to calm himself and to listen. He had been so absorbed, he realized, that a troop of cavalry could have approached without being heard. The night was perfectly still—almost too still, as if London had died while he was working. He shook his head to remove the thought, then picked up the wig to wipe his hands before feeling for the Frenchman's heartbeat. A letter fell out.

Ralph seized it and examined it quickly. In the dark, he could make out no writing on the outside, but even with unsteady fingers he was able to trace the outlines of the royal seal. It was the King's message; there could be no doubt.

He fought back an almost overwhelming urge to take the letter and run. Resolutely, he stuffed it into his pocket, finished drying off his hands, and began examining the Frenchman's chest. Within a few seconds he convinced himself that he felt a heartbeat, not strong but steady. He put his head down against the man's chest to make sure. Yes, the heart was beating; he could even make out a slight rise and fall of the chest, although he could not hear any breathing. For the present, at least, Denis was alive.

Without waiting a moment longer, Ralph picked up the naked man and carried him back to the alley, putting him down carefully where he would be discovered by the first passer-by. Then, forcing himself to avoid haste, he returned to the rubbish pile, carefully searched the ground to be sure that nothing had been left, and finally, after placing Denis's wig in the sack and re-tying the bundle, moved quietly away from the warehouse.

About three hundred yards downstream from the dock, Ralph picked his way to the water's edge. After listening for a few seconds, he heaved the sack of belongings as far as possible out into the river.

"There," he said to himself when the sound of the splash had died away, "I am safe."

When he reached his apartment, he locked the door and drew the curtains before lighting the candles. He was surprised to find that nothing had changed. He felt as if he had been gone for years.

The familiar furniture and belongings reassured him. His comfortable chair, his books, his table, his bed, his desk with its litter of papers, his washstand with his combs and razor—all helped to restore his sense of identity. He drew his watch from his pocket. It was only eleven-thirty.

For two or three minutes, he stood by the door and listened. No sounds came from the house. He was in no danger of being interrupted. Outside, the night watch went noisily by, one of the men hitting the butt end of his pike against the paving stones. Ralph waited until they had passed before he went over to his desk. His nerves were now firm, he assured himself; otherwise he would have jumped at hearing the watch.

His nerves were not so firm, he quickly admitted, that he wanted to open the letter. There was too much at stake. As long as the wretched thing remained unopened, he was safe. He could go on doing his duty, collecting his rewards, and believing what he wanted to believe. Once the letter was opened, God knew what would happen. If it contained what he feared it contained, nothing in the future was safe or secure.

Finally, he shrugged his shoulders, disgusted with himself for hesitating. Taking a deep breath as if he were about to plunge into cold water, he resolutely broke the seal. The King's handwriting, he recognized immediately. Although at first he had a little difficulty making out the scrawled French, he was soon able to translate it.

YOUR MAJESTY,

Permit me to assure you once again of my complete devotion to you and to our mutual interests. If the work here seems to go slowly, you must remember the difficulties under which I labor—a nation of heretics and a system of government which thwarts me at every turn. Nevertheless, I flatter myself that I am making progress. If I have done nothing for the faith so glorious as your suppression of the Huguenots, I have already taken important steps. My army is in good condition now, and I hope to improve it gradually by introducing more Catholic officers and some regiments of loyal Irish. I have removed the most obdurate judges and will continue to remodel the courts until they are completely tractable. Your Majesty will be pleased to observe that Milord Sunderland, my principal minister, is entirely in our interest. At some opportune time in the future, he will announce his conversion to the True Church.

Within the fortnight I shall announce the appointment of four Catholic noblemen to my Privy Council. Within the next few months I shall dismiss the Earl of Clarendon as Lord Lieutenant of Ireland and the Earl of Rochester as Lord Treasurer. Neither shows any

sign of embracing the faith. Ireland I shall entrust to Milord Tyrconnel, who has, as your know, purged the Protestants from the Irish
army. He will complete the work of establishing the supremacy of
our friends. The treasury, I shall put into commission. I think you
will applaud the wisdom of these dispositions.

As for the Prince of Orange, you may be perfectly assured that
I will never join his league. The negotiations which you have heard
of, and which you will continue to hear of from time to time, are
designed solely to throw dust into the eyes of the prince and of my
subjects. When the time is ripe, I shall enter into a formal alliance
with Your Majesty. To do so now would invite sedition before I am
ready to meet it. Meantime you may trust me implicitly. I have not
forgotten your kindness in the matter of the subsidies, nor have I
forgotten that mutual confidence and entire understanding are vital
to the great work we have in view.

Ever Your Majesty's friend and brother,
JAMES R.

Ralph's first feeling was one of perverse triumph. He had been
right in his suspicions. His assault on Denis was vindicated. He did
not care now if the man died. The King was false beyond the
slightest cavil, as perjured as the vilest informer who ever swore
away a man's life. Everything his enemies had said about him was
true. He was conspiring against the laws and religion of England
and the liberties of Europe. Now he was found out. This was not
the speculation of inveterate plotters or seditious malcontents. It was
documentary proof—the kind of proof for which the Hemphills or
the Prince of Orange would pay five thousand pounds. He, Ralph
Barnard, had uncovered the secrets of two conniving kings. He had
found the truth at last.

But the feeling of triumph soon passed. Ralph, staring blankly at
the candle on his desk, was aware of a vague nausea in the pit of
his stomach.

"Damn his dirty soul," he heard himself say aloud. "Damn his
dirty soul."

He picked up the letter again, glanced at it briefly, and then,
rising wearily, he went over to the bookcase and concealed it in a
volume of Coke's *Commentaries*. Later, he could decide what to do
with it. For the present, he was too numb to think straight.

It was not merely the bloodshed, he thought dimly, although the
bloodshed would be horrible when the redcoats were turned loose
on the population and when the French were turned loose on Europe—or when Prince William came with his bluecoats to sweep
James off the throne. No, it was not merely the bloodshed that was

making him ill. He had seen men killed before. For all he knew, he had killed one not an hour ago himself. It was not even the thought of civil war, with its treachery, its butchery, and its executions—with its heads and quarters.

No, he decided numbly, it was being wrong that made him sick. He had been wrong about everything—blindly, stupidly, and fundamentally wrong. He had listened like an obedient sheep to the parsons, to the professors, to the lawyers, and to the squires—to all the fine, comfortable, respectable men in England. They had all repeated the same phrases. They had all assured him that kings are God's vicegerents, that resistance is heresy, that the safety of Church and state depends upon obedience. Particularly they had extolled the honesty of James. He would protect the Church against its enemies; he would keep the shopkeepers and the rabble in their places and protect the gentlemen. Well, all the gentlemen would soon get a demonstration of the King's honesty and the kind of protection he intended to give them.

Ralph shook his head, trying to clear it of the nightmare. How could he have let himself be so deceived? How could he have ignored the clear evidence of his own senses and let other people do his thinking for him? How could he have been so damned stupid? God's vicegerent indeed. James was too hopelessly dull witted to be the devil's vicegerent. Only bright enough to give England a blood bath and wreck the gentlemen who had trusted him. God damn the timeserving politicians and churchmen who had shuffled off the doctrines of obedience and nonresistance on Englishmen. And God damn Englishmen, and Ralph Barnard in particular, for letting them do it.

There was something worse, something he could hardly make himself formulate. If all the fine respectable gentlemen were wrong, then all the sniveling sneaking fanatics were right. Ralph grated his teeth. Cold, frozen-faced schemers like James Hemphill; slippery, cunning connivers like Esther; half-witted enthusiasts like George; bloody plotters like Ferguson—all of them were right. The notion of divine right was nonsense, and James must be stopped at all costs.

Ralph writhed at the thought. Getting up from the desk again, he went to the window and opened it. Why, if these people were right, he told himself, he had been on the wrong side of the ditch at Sedgemoor. Instead of shooting those poor bastards down with cannon, he should have been dying with them. True the Duke of

Monmouth was an ass—and an illegitimate ass at that—but he was better than James.

No. He would not believe it. He would never admit that all the —what was it that Catherine Sedley had called them?—"jolly gentlemen" were wrong, and all the scum of society right. It was monstrous. There must be a way of escape. Just because the King was a bigoted idiot, his enemies must not be allowed to triumph. He must not be allowed to pull the gentlemen of England down with him—to wreck the fundamental doctrine of their political faith.

The night air was a little cooler now, but not cool enough to stop the sweat from breaking out on his forehead. He mopped his brow with his sleeve and tried to bring his thoughts under control. Another of Catherine Sedley's phrases popped into his mind—something about "loyal gentlemen" and "brains."

Suddenly, on the way back to his desk, he stopped and took a long breath.

"Someone must kill the old son of a bitch," he said aloud.

"I suppose I am the man," he added firmly.

CHAPTER

Fifteen

SIX INCHES of steel. Six inches of steel. The phrase was running
through Ralph's brain when he awoke the next morning. He found
it comforting. It replaced his sick rage of the night before with a
quiet resolve. Yes, there was a way out. If the worst came to the
worst, he could always ram six inches of steel through James's throat.
Six inches of steel would solve everything. The Jesuit cabal would
dissolve overnight and flee the country. Not a dog would bark as
Princess Mary ascended the throne, along with her shrewd competent Prince. England would line up quietly alongside its natural allies, and Louis' ambitions would be thwarted. Six inches of steel.

Ralph rolled over and stared at the ceiling. The dull headache
that had plagued him all night was disappearing. He could make
out the two large dark spots on the ceiling above the bed. They
looked like wine spots, and he wondered idly how they had got
there. His eyes wandered over to the bookcase. Was the letter still
there? Had there ever been a letter? He forced himself to get up
to look, staggering a little as he went over to the bookcase.

The letter was there all right. Not a comma had changed. And
about this time, he reminded himself, someone would be finding
a naked Frenchman down by the docks—if he had not been found
sooner. Perhaps a dead Frenchman. Ralph got the tinderbox from
the mantelpiece and kindled a small fire. Before he could change
his mind, he thrust the letter into it. Whatever else happened, no
one would ever connect him with the assault. Nor would there be
any temptation to sell the incriminating document—to betray the
King to his enemies.

He sat down at the table and put his head in his hands. Sometime today he must face the King, and do it as if nothing had happened. Would the King ask him to investigate the robbery? Would
he admit sending a letter to Louis? Probably not. The King's safest

course was to hope that the robber, an ordinary footpad, had destroyed the letter for fear of being linked with the crime. Ralph smiled ruefully. If the Frenchman were dead, the news might not reach the court for days, not until he was missed at Versailles. Ordinary robberies and murders seldom came to the attention of the court. An unidentified body would cause little commotion.

The maid bringing his breakfast came as a welcome interruption. Even the homeliest housemaid in all London was an improvement over his thoughts.

"A good morning to your worship," she said brightly, putting down the fish and the tea.

"A good morning to you too, Annie. You are looking uncommonly well this morning."

Annie gave him a little curtsy. "Thank you, your worship. I wish I could say the same for you. You look terrible. Did you sleep in your clothes?"

"I feel terrible," he said, "and I did sleep in my clothes."

She looked properly scandalized. "I never thought it of you, Mr. Barnard. I never thought you would come home too drunk to take your clothes off."

"I was not drunk, Annie," he said.

"Not drunk?" Immediately she became all sympathy, screwing her young old-looking face into a contortion of concern. "Ah then your worship is in love. I thought as much when I saw your worship's face all white, and your eyes as big as half crowns."

Ralph could not help smiling. "And what makes you so sure, Annie. Have you ever been in love?"

"Don't laugh, Mr. Barnard," she said. "I an't much to look at, but I know a thing or two."

"I am sure you do, Annie," he said hastily. "I smiled because you are wrong."

"No you didn't, Sir. You smiled because I'm ugly. But I don't mind. I know more about you than you think I do."

"I assure you—" he began.

"Your worship mustn't worry." She reverted to her sympathetic tone. "You'll make yourself ill. Both ladies love you, I'm sure."

Ralph sat up straight. "Both ladies? Both what ladies?"

"Why, the ladies you were worrying about, of course."

"I didn't know I was worried about any ladies."

"Now, Mr. Barnard, you mustn't pretend with me. I have the letters you was expecting right here in my pocket. They came when you was out last night. If I'd known they meant so much, I'd have waited up for you. Then you could have rested easy."

"Very well, Annie," he said, in mock resignation. "You have found out my secrets. Give me the letters. I suppose you have read them."

"I did no such thing." Annie drew herself up with dignity. "I suppose I can tell ladies' writing when I see it. And I suppose I can tell when it an't your sister-in-law's."

"Of course, Annie. You must not take my remarks seriously. Now, will you please let me have the letters?"

"People always think I'm stupid because I'm ugly," she said, keeping her right hand firmly buried in the pocket of her apron. "It an't fair. I can read as well as anyone. I can understand a sermon better than the landlady. And I've been in love too, if you want to know."

Ralph felt ashamed of himself. He had been offensive. "I do not think you stupid, Annie," he said. "I think you could tell me a great many things about myself if you wished to."

"I could tell you one thing," she said. "You are something besides a lawyer."

"What makes you think so, Annie?" he said, interested in spite of his curiosity about the letters.

"For one thing, you don't have any friends; and for another, you don't keep a servant. Of all the legal gentlemen that have lived here for the past seven years, you are the only one that wasn't always talking to someone, and that didn't have a servant to make him look important."

Ralph smiled. "I am not a friendly person, Annie. And I don't need a servant. You take care of me very well."

"Oh no, your worship. I know better than that. You are uncommonly friendly, in spite of your little airs now and then. You could use a man too, to dress you a little better. If you want to know what I think, I think that you are doing something you want kept secret. Maybe in a little while, I'll find out what it is."

"If you find out," he said, "let me know. I suspect I am smuggling rubies."

"I won't give you away, Sir," she said seriously, "but I know it is worse than smuggling rubies—and a fine gentleman like you too."

"I will count upon your secrecy," he said. "And now, may I have the letters?"

"Here they are, Sir." She pulled two letters out of her pocket, but she did not give them to him. "One more word first. If you should get into trouble, let me know. I'll help you in any way I can. You will, won't you?"

"Most certainly," he said. "If I get into trouble, you will be the
first to know."

"Thank you, your worship." She handed him the letters and went
to the door. "Oh, I almost forgot. Both the letters came by men in
liveries. One came all the way from Dublin, the man told me."

Annie was right. The addresses on both letters were written in
unmistakably feminine hands. He could not recognize the handwriting, and the seals were indistinguishable blobs of wax. Neither
was postmarked. After looking at them both for a moment, he
opened the one with the bolder handwriting.

MY DEAR SPY,

I have been thinking about you for a long time now. Ever since
His Lovable but Laughable Majesty exiled me to Dublin I have wondered how you are getting on and how long it would take you to
agree with me about the King. You will be glad to know (I hope)
that my exile ends next Sunday. I shall be back in London on the
27th of August if all goes well. It occurs to me that you and I can
be of great help to each other. (Please don't put an amorous con-
struction on this.) I have picked up a variety of information in this
Irish-infested rathole, and I am sure that you have been even more
successful in Holland and England. Since the defence of our inde-
fensible positions depends upon having the best possible information,
the least we can do is to help each other.

If this seems reasonable to you, please visit me at my house at
Saint James on the 28th. Don't worry about tripping over the King.
As you know, he sets out on his Western progress soon. Besides, I
am being difficult with him. He will be lucky if he gets to see me by
the 15th of September.

Oh, one thing more. Remember what I told you about Mistress
Hemphill. Save your conversation for honest women like

Your humble and obedient servant
CATHERINE, Countess (by merit) of Dorchester

Reading the letter, Ralph felt as if a weight had been lifted off
his chest. All the time, he saw now, he had needed someone to talk
with—someone who could at least understand the problems he
faced. And who better than Catherine? He heard himself chuckle.
My God, how the tongues would wag when she returned to England. Already couriers must be plying back and forth between Dublin and Whitehall. French agents, Dutch agents, Austrian agents,
Spanish agents, and papal agents must be writing long documents to
their employers. He wondered if the Queen had heard the news.
If so, the tears, expostulations, recriminations, excuses, and prom-

ises must be filling the palace. No wonder the King was setting out for a royal progress. If he were wise, he would never return.

For a moment Ralph almost felt sorry for James. How could he keep a woman like Catherine in exile, even if he wanted to? Nothing short of a prison would hold her. And on what grounds could she be imprisoned? He should feel sorry for the Queen, Ralph told himself. How could she, a foreign woman, weighed down by all the respectabilities of her position and her religion, cope with a rival like Catherine? But he could not feel sorry for her. Women who knowingly marry abandoned lechers must take what they get.

He put down Catherine's letter and opened the other. One look at the salutation was enough to give him a queer empty feeling in the pit of his stomach.

MY DEAR RALPH,

It has been two months now since your return from Holland, and every day I have expected to hear from you. The mails still run, you know, between London and Somersetshire. Any message would have found me. Or did our conversation in Holland frighten you? Did you feel, perhaps, that your pure Tory principles were in danger?

I scorn to hold a gentleman to his promise. If you feel that you are compromising yourself, you are under no obligation to see me. If, however, you have been silent out of doubt about my feelings, this is to inform you that I shall be back in London by the 26th of this month. You may see me any time after that at Hemphill House. My Father and Brother will not be there until after the 5th of September. They wish to make the King's tour as unpleasant as possible.

In the event that you are worried, I promise a truce as far as politics are concerned. I will not bring the subject up unless you want me to. We can find, I am confident, other subjects of discussion.

On rereading what I have written, I find that it sounds very forward and unladylike. It was not so intended, believe me. You know my feelings where such things are concerned. If I have offended you in any way, please pardon me. In any event, come see

Your humble servant,
ESTHER

He put the letter down next to the cold fish and tea. His hands, he noticed, were trembling idiotically. His stomach, empty before, was tied in a knot. God's wounds, would he never be sensible? Why should he let a thing like this unman him? He had promised himself he would never go near her again. Very likely the letter was designed to keep him in London while the King made his progress; yet if this were true, she would not mention the subject in her letter.

Well, he was remaining in London anyway. The Secretary of State handled the precautions for the progress.

The letter stared at him from its position on the table. Don't be a coward, it seemed to say. She has been as bold as a strictly brought-up woman can possibly be. She has told you in so many words that you will be alone in the house, that she will forget political differences. The lady loves you, you fool. Seize your chance; you will never get another.

Ralph got up from the table and walked over to the chest of drawers. Seen from another position, he told himself as he pulled out a clean shirt, it was his duty to go to see her. With the King false as hell and all England about to fall down around his ears, there was more reason than ever to learn Whig secrets. Besides one never knew what might happen. He owed it to himself to stand well with the Whigs. A man desperate enough to kill the King should not fear a woman.

The argument did not convince him, but he felt shaken nevertheless. Under his consciously taken resolve not to get involved with Esther again, a nagging premonition warned him that he would not stay away. He shook his head wearily. He would worry about the whole thing later. It was only nine o'clock, but already he had faced too many problems for any single day.

"There is a gentleman to see you, Sir." Annie's voice broke into his thoughts. She was standing at the door watching him change his shirt.

"What kind of gentleman?" Again, he was glad for the interruption.

"A clerical gentleman," she said, then lowered her voice. "I think he is a papist. I hope you are not trafficking with papists, Mr. Barnard."

"Certainly not," he said solemnly. "Send him in."

"I think you know me," the little man said after he had taken the chair offered him.

"I think so too." Ralph closed the door carefully, making sure that Annie had gone downstairs. "If I am not mistaken, you are Monsignor Adda."

"That is correct, except for the title. I am not a bishop." The little man smiled pleasantly, letting his Italian-accented English flow effortlessly off his tongue. "Unless, of course, you call all Italians Monsignor."

"I shall be happy to call you anything you wish," Ralph said, fencing a little and trying to guess why Adda had come.

"Why don't you call me Father? That is easy for Englishmen to say. But let us not waste time on titles. You also know, I think, that I am the Nuncio for His Holiness the Pope."

"I have heard it said," Ralph admitted evasively.

"You may be direct with me, Mr. Barnard." Another smile lit up the smooth, almost translucent features. "You see, I know who you are too. Father Mansuete has informed me."

"I see," Ralph said. He made his voice sound noncommittal, but he wanted to strangle Mansuete. How many others had he told?

"Knowing your occupation," Adda went on, "I knew that my identity was no secret to you."

Ralph could not resist a little malice. "I suppose you also know that you are in England illegally."

"That depends upon one's definition of the law," Adda smiled indulgently. "I know there is an English law which prohibits any official legate from the Pope to the court of England, but whether such a law is null in itself, or whether it applies to a representative like me, I must leave it to you lawyers to decide."

"It isn't and it does," Ralph said quickly, and immediately felt boorish. He wanted to apologize, but he did not know how to begin.

"I accept your rebuke," the little man said quietly. "In view of our mutual problem, the legal question does not seem important."

"Our mutual problem? I am not sure I know what you mean. Perhaps Father Mansuete failed to tell you that I am not a Catholic."

"He told me, Mr. Barnard. He also told me that you are an honest man and a Christian. That is enough for our purposes."

"What are our purposes?" Ralph said, suspicious again.

Adda sighed. "Very simply stated, they are to keep King James from drowning England and Europe in blood. Secondarily to you, but very important to us, is the further purpose of protecting English Catholics against a violent reaction. Do I make myself clear?"

"Not entirely, Father Adda," Ralph said slowly. "I have heard, of course, that the Pope is opposed to some of the King's methods; but to deal candidly with you, I never believed it. Lately, especially, I have been convinced that the Church and the King were working hand in glove together to establish popery in England."

Adda sighed again. "Mr. Barnard, I despair of making you understand our problems unless I can convince you of a few simple facts. The first is this: His Holiness the Pope is a Christian."

"Please go on," Ralph said drily.

"I realize the notion is strange to you Englishmen, but it is true nevertheless. And while, like all good Catholics, His Holiness would like to see Christendom reunited in the true faith, he does not believe this great feat can or should be brought about by unchristian means. In short, he will not murder people to save their souls. He will not employ dragoons as missionaries."

"I must deal candidly with you again," Ralph said. "Considerations of this kind carry little weight with me. I am sure that the Pope would never order a troop of dragoons into the field to suppress Protestants. But he can sit quietly by while King James or King Louis does so. He can weep over the bloodshed and deplore the unchristian violence while he and the Church reap the benefits. Eventually, you may be sure, he will pardon the Kings for their sins."

"You must not believe this, Mr. Barnard. It is not true. No man in Christendom has worked so hard as the Pope to prevent King Louis from dragooning the Huguenots. He has been unsuccessful, to be sure, but he will continue to oppose Louis by every means at his disposal. The Prince of Orange himself is no more bitterly opposed to the King."

Adda had half risen from his chair, a flash of fire in his dark eyes.

"I will tell you another simple fact," he continued, sinking back into his chair. "His Holiness is aligning himself and all his moral authority behind the Prince of Orange's league. You will find, if it comes to the test, that His Holiness will be on the side of Catholic Spain, Catholic Austria, Protestant Holland, and Protestant Prussia against the power and pretensions of King Louis."

"Are you sure of this?" Ralph said doubtfully.

"If you doubt my word, I can show you the correspondence between the Pope and the Prince. But I do not think you will have any difficulty finding out for yourself. It will soon be common knowledge."

"This is encouraging news, even though I find it a little strange."

"Why strange? Look at the situation from our point of view for a moment. Aside from all humane, Christian motives for opposing Louis and his ambition, the Pope has every political motive. Already Louis presumes to dictate to the Church—to make ecclesiastical appointments, to flout the Pope's directives, and to use the Church to further his political ends. If he makes himself master of Europe, the Pope will be his vassal. The Church must not fall into his hands. Is that understandable to you?"

"Perfectly," Ralph said.

"I have faith, Mr. Barnard, that God will not allow His Church to become a political tool for a scheming French villain; but God expects His servants to use all the resources at their command, not to rely upon miracles. This means that we must oppose Louis ourselves."

"I agree," Ralph said.

"That is why we must wake James and his Jesuits from their mad dream of Catholicizing England and align the power of England against Louis."

"You think the dream is mad, then?"

"Most certainly. Would you yourself submit to such a thing, Mr. Barnard?"

Ralph shook his head. "I would oppose it to the last drop of blood."

"Precisely." The little man smiled again. "And you, if you will pardon the compliment, are one of the most loyal men in England. Think of the blood that will be shed when James tries."

"I have already thought of it," Ralph said.

"Very well, then. You understand our point of view. You understand too that if the plot fails, the reprisals against the Catholics will be bloody. The cause of Catholic toleration in England will be set back a hundred years."

"I have thought of that too."

"Good. We are agreed." Adda jumped from his chair with surprising energy and seized Ralph by the hand. "You will help us."

"Help you? I don't understand. I do not wish to appear stupid, Your Eminence, but I fail to see where you need my help. If His Holiness the Pope objects to the activities of James and his Jesuits, surely he can make them stop. If all else fails, he can excommunicate them."

Adda smiled sadly. "I had hoped you understood more about our Church than you do. You must not suppose that His Holiness is the absolute ruler of the Church in the same sense that King Louis is the master of France. The Pope governs as he can, not as he might wish. I will not bore you with the details of the factions within the Church. Two facts are enough for you to know. One is that if the Pope excommunicated everybody who disagreed with him on matters of policy, there would be no Church left. The second is that the King and his French and English Jesuits are true sons of the Church, even though they are tragically mistaken. They are sincerely anxious to promote Catholicism and the greater glory of God. His Holiness, therefore, may counsel them, admonish them, and reprove them, but he can hardly excommunicate them."

"He might excommunicate King James on the grounds of adultery," Ralph said. "Or is that impossible too?"

"I fear so," Adda said, a little acidly, Ralph thought. "His Holiness is Innocent XI, not Macchiavelli."

"You must be patient with me, Father Adda," Ralph said. "I mean no offense."

The little man tugged at his ear, lost in thought. For a moment he reminded Ralph of a Cambridge Don trying to think of a way to explain Greek prosody to a stupid class.

"Let me put the matter in another light," he said finally, his face brightening a little. "If the Pope goes too far in disciplining James, he will drive him irrevocably into the arms of Louis and the Jesuits. If that happens, we are lost. The next Pope will be a Frenchman."

"I do not flatter myself that I understand all the details of this complicated business," Ralph said, "but I see your main point clearly enough. His Holiness the Pope wishes King James stopped before he wrecks England, Europe and the Church. Is that correct?"

"Perfectly." Adda gave him an encouraging smile.

"Good. Now then, there is one more thing that I don't understand. If the Pope himself cannot convince the King that he is wrong, how do you expect me to do it?"

"Ah, now we come to the question. First, let me say this. The King trusts you."

"The King trusts me?" He peered at Adda curiously. When he had assured himself that the man was serious, he allowed himself the luxury of a laugh. "You must be mistaken, Father. You would not think so if you had heard us arguing about the Prince. I was almost dismissed."

"I am not mistaken, Mr. Barnard," the little man said calmly. "I have the information from Father Mansuete. He could not be wrong on a matter like this."

"You mean that my name has occurred in the King's confessions?"

"Father Mansuete did not tell me how he got the information. I assume he did not violate the privacy of confession. Be that as it may, the King trusts you."

"Wait a moment, Your Grace. Don't trust your information too far. It may be true enough that the King has confidence in my ability to get information and to report it accurately, but he has no faith at all in my political judgment. He threatened to dismiss me if I tried to advise him."

"No doubt. No doubt." Adda dismissed the objections with a wave of his hand. "That is unimportant. You may believe me when

I say that he will not dismiss you. He trusts you as a man, almost as a son. That is the vital thing. You are one of three men in England who have any measure of his confidence."

"I am not entirely flattered by the company you put me in, if you mean Milord Sunderland and Father Petre, a knave and a fool."

Adda favored him with a thin smile. "All the more reason why you must spare no efforts to defeat their influence."

"What about Father Mansuete?" Ralph asked. "Certainly the King's confessor should have more influence than a hired spy."

"Father Mansuete's small influence is exhausted already," Adda said, pulling at his ear again. "The Jesuits were too strong for him. He will be dismissed soon. Possibly we should have found a stronger man for the position."

"I am sorry to hear that," Ralph said, captivated by this small glimpse into Church politics and yet depressed at the thought of losing so pleasant a friend.

"Not that Father Mansuete did not try hard. Possibly he did all that could be done. But there is no reasoning with zealots."

"And yet you expect me to try," Ralph said.

"Not exactly." Adda walked over to the bookcase and began examining Ralph's library, as if he had forgotten what he was going to say next.

"Well then?" Ralph asked finally.

"Not reasoning," Adda resumed, taking up the conversation where he left it off. "One might as well reason with a post, as you know."

"Yes."

"The affair is more delicate than expostulation or reasoning."

"You mean you want me to kill him?" The words leaped out just as they flashed into Ralph's mind, the suspicion formulating itself without any conscious control.

Adda's pale face turned paler, the black eyes staring blankly from under the bushy gray eyebrows.

"God have mercy on us," he stammered, crossing himself. "How could you think of such a thing? Surely, you did not think I meant—"

"Forgive me, Your Eminence. I did not know. I spoke before I thought." Ralph paused, watching the effect of his words upon the little churchman. "And yet, I will tell you frankly," he resumed, "the death of the King is our only serious hope. God and His angels, saving your reverence, will never change his mind."

The shock was gradually disappearing from Adda's stricken face, but he had not entirely recovered himself. "Mr. Barnard, I hope for the sake of your soul you do not mean what you say. We must not wish for anyone's death, even the death of our worst enemy."

"I agree, Father," Ralph said placatingly. "You must not think me a monster. But what I said is true, nevertheless. The death of the King is our only serious hope of preventing monstrous calamity."

"I will never admit such a thing," Adda said, "and I do not believe you really think so yourself."

"Perhaps I don't," Ralph said. "But I would be glad to hear of a reasonable alternative."

"You, Mr. Barnard, are one alternative." Adda's color had returned now. "As I said before, you cannot reason with the King. No one can. But you are in an enviable position. By your reports you can show him the seriousness of the opposition, demonstrate the impossibility of his schemes—all this without argument or overt suggestion."

"In other words," Ralph said brutally, "you want me to lie to the King."

Adda blushed faintly. "If necessary, yes; but I don't think it will be necessary. The truth is serious enough."

"You realize, of course, that every time I report opposition, that opposition has an excellent chance of being choked off by the hangman."

"Yes," Adda said quietly. "I trust, however, that you will report opposition beyond the reach of the hangman."

Ralph nodded. "I intend to."

From somewhere under his gown, Adda fished out a handkerchief and mopped his brow. Clearly the interview was a great strain on him. It occurred to Ralph that Adda, like Mansuete, might not be the man for his position. He was too sensitive and decent for intrigue.

"In your reports," Adda said, "you must frequently include the opinion of sane English Catholics—that their salvation lies in placating, not antagonizing, the Church of England and the dissenters. Under no circumstances should Catholics be put in positions of power. The ultimate aim should be toleration for Catholics, not Catholic dominance."

"It is too late for such advice," Ralph said abruptly. "The King has already decided to appoint Catholic ministers, just as he has already appointed Catholic army officers and judges. One of them, Milord Tyrconnel, will be Lord Lieutenant of Ireland."

"Just as I feared," Adda said, half under his breath.

It was clear, for all Adda's knowledge of European affairs, that he did not know everything. He did not know how far James had actually gone with his plans, or how deeply he was engaged with Louis. Ralph was tempted to tell him, but he thought better of it. Adda might be a better representative of the Pope if he did not know how hopeless his task was.

"I have two suggestions," Ralph said, breaking the heavy silence. "The first is that you enlist the help of the Queen. She is an Italian like yourself. Perhaps she will listen to the Pope."

"Impossible." Adda drew in his breath as if he were going to begin a long explanation. Then, apparently, he changed his mind. "The Queen is hopelessly entangled with the Jesuits too," he said simply.

"In that case, why don't you try to enlist the King's mistress, the Countess of Dorchester?"

Adda eyed him suspiciously. "It is too late; the King has sworn to have nothing further to do with her."

"Do you believe he will keep his promise?" Ralph asked.

"I sincerely hope so," said Adda, and Ralph could see that he meant it.

"Believe me, Your Eminence, he won't. I will stake my life on it."

"You may be right," Adda said drily, "but I will leave the Countess to you."

Adda rose. "I shall not intrude further upon your time, Mr. Barnard, if I have your promise that you will do all in your power to dissuade the King from his ruinous policy."

Ralph bowed politely. "No promise is necessary, Your Grace, to induce me to do my obvious duty. There is one more thing, however—"

"Of course," Adda said quickly. "I will see that you are well paid, even though the Papal funds are by no means—"

"No, no." Ralph could feel himself blushing, angry and dismayed. "I meant no such thing."

"I did not mean to insult you," Adda apologized. "A gift is the customary thing."

"Not with me," Ralph said stiffly, feeling more foolish and angry than ever.

"A thousand pardons," Adda said humbly. "I realize now that you were talking about information. It goes without saying that I will furnish you whatever I can. You may expect a weekly report, circumspectly delivered here."

Ralph made an effort to regain his composure before speaking.

"It also goes without saying," Adda continued, "that I shall not mention you in my dispatches or to any of my agents. I shall do nothing to endanger your position. With your permission, however, I shall mention you in my prayers."

"Please do," Ralph said, suddenly touched and restored to good humor by the little man's sincerity. "I shall need them."

Yes, he said to himself, I shall need them. If I am the Pope's last resource in England, things are even more desperate than I thought.

"And I implore you," the little man was saying, "not to lose heart, and by all means not to wish for the King's death."

Ralph smiled. Suddenly he felt a great deal older than the little priest, with his shrewd but fundamentally innocent eyes. He wanted to pat the worried little fellow on the head and reassure him that everything would be all right. Instead, he bowed formally.

"I shall not lose heart," he said, "but you must not expect miracles."

Adda returned the bow without saying a word.

"And if I may offer one suggestion to His Holiness the Pope," Ralph continued, "I suggest that he pray fervently for the Prince of Orange."

Adda put his hand on the doorknob. "Your suggestion is too late, Mr. Barnard," he said quietly. "For months His Holiness has been praying for the Prince of Orange."

CHAPTER

Sixteen

"YOU HAVE NOT changed at all," Catherine Sedley was saying. "You are still the same sweet naïve spy I remember."

"And you, I see, are still the same flatterer," Ralph said, grinning.

"Not at all," Catherine said. "Still a flatterer, but not the same flatterer. I have grown much wiser since we last met. I wish you could say the same."

"I could if I were as unscrupulous as you," Ralph said.

"Ugh," Catherine said. "I wish you would not try to be witty. It spoils your wide-eyed charm. Come over here on the sofa beside me and tell me what you have been doing. On second thought, before you come, go over to the door and tell the butler who is listening behind it to bring us some claret."

Ralph opened the door and found the butler just as she had predicted. The man showed no signs of embarrassment as he took the order and disappeared.

"Don't you think you should discharge that man?" Ralph said as he took his place beside her on the sofa.

"I can't," she explained. "The Secretary of State employs him to spy on me. If I complain too loudly or try to discharge him, they will think I wish to hide something. Besides, LeClerc is easily the best butler in England, and probably the worst agent. Don't worry. As long as we sit together on the sofa, he will not overhear us. He will only appear every few minutes to make sure that we are behaving properly. You will come to like him."

"Doubtlessly. Did he overhear our last conversation?"

"Oh, no, I have had him only since I was sent to Dublin, Mr. Barnard—a special farewell present. But enough about LeClerc, let's talk about me."

"It will be a pleasure," he said. "You know, of course, that I consider you the most fascinating woman in the kingdom."

"Perhaps I am wrong about you," she said. "Perhaps you have been learning things while I was away. But you have at least one more thing to learn. That is, to make your compliments small and specific rather than vague and general. You would have done much better to compliment me on my red dress. I put it on especially for your visit."

Ralph ogled her from head to foot, inspecting every inch with exaggerated concern.

"It is devastating," he said.

"You approve of it then?"

"I don't approve of it, but I like it. I keep wondering how you manage to stay inside it."

"But you don't complain."

"No, I don't complain."

"Good. If you complained, I should worry about both of us."

Catherine put her finger to her lips for caution as the butler opened the door.

"Bring the wine over here, LeClerc." She indicated the small table in front of the sofa. "When you are through pouring it, please ask Natalie to polish the silver in the dining room."

After LeClerc had filled the glasses, bowed and left the room, Catherine handed Ralph a glass, then solemnly raised her own.

"To us," she said.

"To us."

"Spy and whore."

"To us."

"You don't like to admit it, do you, Mr. Barnard?" she said mockingly.

"Not particularly," he conceded.

"But I suppose you will admit that you are in love with me, in your quaint quixotic manner."

"I shall admit nothing of the kind," he said, smiling. "I must keep my burning secrets locked in my heart."

"Good." Catherine tossed her head in a little gesture of approval. "You are a charming gentleman, but a love affair would be impossible. My life is too complicated already. You would not want to make it more complicated, would you?"

"On the contrary, I should like to make it less complicated."

"Perhaps you can, Mr. Barnard." She put down her wineglass. "Perhaps you can make it less complicated by telling me what went on while I was away. Tell me about the women the King slept with. Was there anyone in particular?"

"You probably know more about the subject than I do," Ralph said distastefully. "I don't collect that kind of information."

"Oh come, now. Don't try to play the gentleman with me, Mr. Barnard. Tell me what you know."

"My evidence is all hearsay, but you are welcome to it. If common gossip is right, the King has seen one actress and half a dozen common trollops—no one more than once."

"No one more than once," Catherine said reflectively. "That is encouraging. It must be correct too, since your information agrees with mine. You find it amusing, I suppose, that I should be concerned about possible rivals."

"Not at all," he said honestly.

"Then perhaps I can tell you something that will amuse you, Ralph—your friends do call you Ralph, don't they?"

"Yes," Ralph said, "and I should be pleased if you did."

"I shall, and you must call me Kit. I hate Catherine or Kitty. But as I was saying, you might be amused to know that before I went to Ireland James protested on his knees and with tears in his eyes that he would be faithful to me."

"You didn't believe him, did you?"

"Certainly not, but he did. To hear him talk you would have supposed that I was his first and only love, that exiling me was breaking his heart. What is more, I am sure he thought so at the time, yet within three weeks he was coping that Higgins woman. You don't seem to be amused, Ralph."

"I am afraid I'm not," he said.

"Would you be amused if I told you that when he next sees me he will swear he has been faithful? And that he will convince himself that he has been?"

Ralph shook his head. "I don't know whether it is sad or sickening," he said, "but it is not amusing."

"I am afraid you are a puritan at heart, Ralph," Catherine said. "And I am afraid you have contracted the dangerous habit of feeling sorry for people. For heaven's sake, don't let yourself feel sorry for the King. Remember, he has no notion of how miserable and useless he is. He is perfectly self-satisfied. Let me pity the King. I get paid for doing it."

"You can count upon it," Ralph said. "I shall not pity the King. I should like to ask you a question about him, however. Perhaps this will amuse you."

"What is it?"

"Does the King have the pox?"

The half-smile vanished abruptly from Catherine's face. She studied Ralph as if he had become a complete stranger.

"Are you trying to insult me?"

"Not at all. It is an important question, and I would like to know the answer."

"A gentleman does not ask a lady whether or not she has the pox," she said icily.

"You forget Kit"—Ralph held his ground—"that I am no gentleman. I am a spy."

"And I am no lady. Is that it?"

"So you keep telling me," he said.

"Let me tell you something more then. Don't make the mistake of thinking that a whore can't be a lady. I could name dozens—but why do you want to know about the pox?"

"I am sorry I brought up the subject," Ralph said. "I did not want to insult you. And yet, you should be able to see why I asked. If the King has the pox, there is little danger of a popish heir."

"And you think that because the Queen has had miscarriages, she may be poxed. Is that it?"

"Yes."

Ralph did not try to soften his language. "If the Queen should have a son, the roof would fall in immediately. I hope, for everyone's sake, the King has the pox."

"You are too kind."

"I did not mean you."

"Don't try to be polite."

"Very well, then. I hope the King has the pox, even if he has given it to you."

"You think I deserve the pox, don't you, Ralph?"

"Oddly enough, I don't."

"Do I look as if I had the pox?"

"Certainly not."

"Well, I don't have them. And the King doesn't either, unless he has caught them since I saw him last. Oh, I don't doubt that he has been poxed at one time or another, but not during my regime."

"Then you think his health is good?" Ralph knew the disappointment showed on his face.

"He is healthy as a horse. Be of good cheer, Ralph. Unless something very extraordinary happens, James will live another fifteen or twenty years. You and I will never want for employment."

"Did you ring, Your Grace?"

LeClerc had glided into the room, but not before Ralph had been warned by a quick nod of Catherine's head.

"No, LeClerc," she said pleasantly. "But while you are here, you may fill the glasses again."

"I told you that you would like LeClerc," she said to Ralph. "What do you think of him now? He can hear bells even before they are rung."

"He is magnificent," Ralph agreed.

"Thank you, Sir." LeClerc nodded, apparently unabashed. "I try to give satisfaction."

"From this sudden interest in the King's health," Catherine said when the butler had gone, "I assume that you have changed your views since last time I saw you. Last time, you may remember, you were all zeal and fidelity. You actually turned pale when I told you about James's plans. You should have seen yourself."

"I have learned better since," Ralph said simply, cringing a little to think of the figure he had made.

"In a way, I am sorry. I think I liked you better the other way. Now you will probably do something foolish." Catherine took his hand. "No, I apologize. Truly, I like you this way better. I am glad you have found out what is going on. It is always better to know."

"You are kind to say so, Kit. I feel better now than I have felt since I saw you last."

"That is because I am holding your hand. Don't start. I told you that I don't have the pox."

"Did I start? I did not intend to. Perhaps I need more practice at this sort of thing."

"No, I like you the way you are. Just sit there and tell me what you will do."

"I don't know," Ralph said, relieved to be discussing the problem aloud. "I suppose I should resign immediately. Possibly I should go to Holland and join with the Prince of Orange—or stay here and join the Whigs, for as long as the King would let me remain in the kingdom."

"Don't talk nonsense." Catherine shifted her position on the sofa, drawing herself up abruptly. "What good would that do? The Prince has enough men, and there are too many Whigs already. Take my advice, Ralph. Stay where you are and be sensible."

"You will be amused to know that I was told the same thing by the Pope's Nuncio. He thinks I may be able to change the King's mind."

Catherine received the news with a little toss of her head. "It is

true, then, that the Pope wants to put a bridle on James. How did the
Nuncio find out about you? I certainly did not tell him."

"Mansuete."

"Ah yes. Well, I am surprised to find myself and you on the side of
the Pope, but the advice is good. Take it."

"You think that I can do anything to change the King's mind?"

"Frankly, no. You, the Pope, and the devil himself will not change
the King's mind, but you will have an amusing time trying, and you
will make a few thousand pounds in the process."

"And what about you? Do you think you could do anything?"

Suddenly Catherine laughed again. "What a flatterer. If you and
the Pope and the devil can do nothing, what chance does a poor
countess have? You are more smitten with my charms than I
thought."

"I am smitten, I confess," Ralph said. "And I do not underestimate
their power. They might do much where King James is concerned."

Catherine shook her head. "No, Ralph. Undoubtedly, I could
make the King very miserable, but I could not change his mind.
Furthermore, I refuse to try. As I told you once before, why should I
jeopardize a good pension, give my enemies another club to beat
me with, and spoil the little bedtime pleasure I get, just to irritate
the King?"

With a little gesture of impatience, Ralph disengaged his hand.
"You realize, of course, that if you, or I, fail to do something, James
will be thrown out of this kingdom on his arse and there will be a
bloody war—or worse yet, he will succeed in his schemes, Louis will
dominate Europe, and there will be an even bloodier war."

"Don't excite yourself, Ralph. Certainly I realize it. It was I who
told you in the first place. But the situation isn't my fault. If the
gentlemen of England put themselves in a hopeless position, I can't
help it. If people want to kill each other I am not going to stop them.
Let them look out for themselves. And I will look out for myself."

"You refuse to take any responsibility then?"

"Certainly I refuse. I have no responsibility—and neither do you.
Don't be an ass. It is not your fault that England is populated by
half-wits. It is not your fault that James is a popish fanatic, or that
Louis is a polished, ambitious son of a bitch. For God's sake, Ralph,
use your brain. No one appointed you to save the world. You will be
lucky if you can save yourself."

"What are you going to do?"

"What am I going to do? Nothing. Absolutely nothing. Except, of
course, what I have always done, keep myself and the King amused."

"I am sure that you can do that very well."

"Don't sneer, Ralph. It is a difficult job, and I have a great deal of competition."

"I wasn't sneering."

"Oh yes you were. You don't understand that someone has to look after simpletons. It is not the King's fault that God made him stupid."

"I suppose you think it is God's fault."

"Yes, I guess it is. You must have noticed that He is given to a grim sort of humor."

"You are the second woman to tell me so."

Catherine paused suspiciously. "Who besides me would make a remark like that?"

"Someone you wouldn't like."

"I hate her already. Stay away from her."

"She also said that God cares nothing for Tories, only for change. Do you think so too?"

"Then she is a damned Whig, and shame on you for talking with her. It isn't that frozen-faced Hemphill woman, is it?"

"I don't betray the confidences of ladies."

"No, it couldn't be Mistress Sedition." Catherine checked herself. "How did we start talking on such asinine subjects?"

"You were trying to explain to me why you feel responsible for the King," Ralph said slyly. "You had just established the point that you are not responsible for his foolishness."

"Oh yes," Catherine put out her tongue at him. "Well, Mr. Scruples, I will tell you. I am responsible for the King because I said I would be when I was hired. Does that satisfy you?"

"It helps," Ralph said, half to himself. "The faithful retainer, is that it?"

"If you wish." She pulled a face and then began to laugh. "It sounds ridiculous, doesn't it?"

"A little," Ralph admitted, glad to see her return to her normal mood.

"It also sounds noble, don't you think?"

"At least noble."

"But don't forget that I am being paid for it."

"I won't."

"And don't forget that James treats me as well as his nature allows."

"I will remember."

"And don't forget that you are in exactly the same position."

"I won't. I wish I could."

"Good. We are agreed then. You won't think of doing anything foolish. You will help me to take care of James and let God take care of the kingdom."

"I am not sure," Ralph said soberly. "I wish it were the other way round."

"I do too—the kingdom would be safer. But it isn't. So dismiss it from your mind, and we will have another glass."

As he poured the claret, he heard her begin to giggle softly. "I have just thought of a way to secure the succession," she said. "You could go out and get the pox, then give them to me, and I could give them to the King. What do you think of that?"

"Brilliant," he laughed. "A grateful Prince of Orange will pension us both."

"And as you sit in the powdering tub, you can tell yourself that you gave everything for your country."

"The happy martyr."

"Who knows, our pious Queen might infect the whole court."

"Now, now, we must not be nasty about this."

"Don't tell me that you too feel gallant and protective toward the Queen. It infuriates me. She is a proud, jealous, cold, scheming Italian witch—and I could say more, if I were not a lady."

"We must think very seriously before we start a plague that may spread all over England. I think I like your other plan better."

"What other plan?"

"The one you suggested in our last conversation."

"Did I suggest a plan?"

"How could you forget? You suggested that we find some honorable, patriotic gentleman to assassinate James."

"Oh yes, so I did." Catherine laughed. "I was very brilliant and witty that day, wasn't I?"

"And very penetrating."

"You didn't think I was serious, did you?"

"Only half serious, but you were right nevertheless. It was a capital suggestion."

"It would be capital, all right, if LeClerc happened to hear us discussing it. While you might look a little better without your head, I am sure that I should look very much worse without mine."

Ralph glanced toward the door. It was still tightly closed. He hated to lower his voice. A conspiratorial whisper would ruin the light tone he was trying to maintain.

"All great projects are risky," he said softly. "Do you know where we can find the man to do it?"

"I think I told you before that there is no such man."

In the silence which followed, Ralph could hear the ticking of the clock.

"Let us not despair too easily," he said. "Perhaps we can find him."

"Nonsense," she said. "And even if there were such a man, you and I are not the type to employ him. No, I think that the pox is our only hope."

"Perhaps so," he said. "And yet, as you observed yourself, putting the King out of the way would solve all our problems."

"The nation's problems, Europe's problems, the Pope's problems— not our problems." Catherine shrugged her pretty shoulders. "Let's change the topic. I don't find this very amusing. Tell me more about my rival—the Whig harridan who knows so much about God."

"If I could find the man, would you betray him?"

"I told you I was tired of the subject," she said, reaching for the claret bottle. "Certainly I would betray him. Like a shot. And anyone else who tries to cut off my pension. Now, may we leave this."

"In just a moment," he said, taking the bottle out of her hand and pouring her another drink. "It amuses me. Suppose I were to betray you then. Suppose I were to testify that you suggested the whole plan?"

"I should say 'Have another drink and forget it.'"

"Very well, then. It was just an amusing thought."

"Not very," she said, sipping her wine and regarding him suspiciously, "especially if it occurred to you that you might be the man."

"Me?" He returned her gaze calmly. "Whose humor is distorted now?"

"Not mine. I know when a jest has gone far enough. And remember, just in case you should dally with the idea, I would betray you in a minute."

Ralph laughed—easily, he thought. "No you wouldn't. The judges would be as glad to hang the King's mistress as his spy. A scaffold would not become you. But don't concern yourself, if I were planning to kill the King, I should never discuss it with anyone. Not even you, Kit."

"Oh, all right. I apologize, Ralph." She reached over and pulled his ear. "I must be getting drunk, or I could never have imagined such a thing. Just fancy, you an assassin."

"Yes, just fancy."

"Let's have another toast."

"Propose it."

"To the King's friends."

"To the King's friends."

"May they always take care of him."

Ralph watched her drain her glass; then he drained his own.

"If I were to kiss you now," she said suddenly, "you would not take it personally, would you?"

"Not at all," he said, "but LeClerc might."

"That was the wrong thing to say, but I forgive you. Come here and let me worry about LeClerc."

She put her arms around his neck, kissed him, and then released him.

"There," she said. "That didn't hurt, did it?"

"Not at all."

"Good. And you won't take it personally, will you?"

"Certainly not, Kit."

"That was because we are partners and because I feel a great deal older than you."

"I see."

"Now then, I suppose you had better be off before LeClerc turns in a frightening report to the Secretary of State. You will hear from me sometime soon. I didn't say a word about Ireland. Next time, I will come visit you. It will be safer."

Ralph rose. "You won't take it personally if I kiss you goodbye."

"Not at all."

He pulled her to him and kissed her.

"There," he said. "That is because we can help each other and because really I am a great deal older than you."

The first part of his statement was false, he reflected, as he walked across the park. Catherine could not—or would not—help him. He must do alone whatever had to be done. The second part of the statement was true. He seemed to have aged twenty years in the last twenty days. He wondered if the transformation showed—if casual passers-by noticed the age in his face—if Esther would see the difference. He wondered too at a strange lightness he felt. It was as if his responsibility had made him stronger. For the first time, he felt like his own man, his own master.

It may be the wine, he thought wryly. Or perhaps the kisses. Maybe I did not take them so impersonally as I thought.

Seventeen

"You came," Esther said as he was ushered into the parlor.

She was standing near the fireplace, her green silk dress reflecting the glow of the small coal fire, and her face partially obscured in the uncertain candlelight.

"Yes, I came," he said simply.

"I hoped you would," she said, but she did not move toward him or hold out her hand.

"You knew I would," he said.

"On the contrary." Her voice sounded flat and toneless. "I rather suspected you would not. When we parted, I had a premonition that you were going to stay away from me."

"Well, here I am."

"Yes, here you are."

Again, Ralph felt an odd sense of detachment, almost of anti-climax. After the furious debates with himself, after the anticipation and the agonizing, he was standing here with nothing to say, and feeling nothing in particular.

"Yes," she repeated, "here you are."

"Are you glad to see me?" The words sounded hopelessly stupid, but they were the best he could do.

"Very," she said. "I thought you would never come."

"I got your letter."

"Oh, I thought so. Did you think it brazen?" Esther moved, finally. She walked over to the largest chair and stood behind it, resting her arms on its back.

"No, but I was surprised. I thought our last meeting might have frightened you."

"I was not frightened." A suggestion of a smile passed across her face. "What happened was my fault, you know."

"Not the kiss."

"Perhaps that too. I don't know."

"I don't think so."

"You see," she went on, "I promised my father I would keep you out of the way while he talked with the Prince."

"I know. I still have the horseshoe."

"You knew all the time?"

It all seemed long ago and unimportant now. "Yes," he said. "That is why I was anxious to get back to see what you were hiding, and why I did not kiss you very well."

"I thought you did well," she said thoughtfully, as if trying to remember the exact sensation.

"Thank you."

"I thought I owed you an explanation for what you must have thought very odd behavior," she said. "I am glad you knew."

"There was no need to explain."

"Father and I thought that a stranger might spoil the meeting."

"I understand."

"You didn't spoil it though. Now I am glad you were there. You can see that there was nothing sinister about it."

"I am glad too."

There was a long silence, like that between two strangers who have exhausted all topics of mutual interest. Ralph shifted his weight from his right foot to his left, not particularly uneasy but completely helpless to break through the feeling of constraint. He could only watch her and wait for her to say something more.

"Oh," she said, as if suddenly recollecting herself. "I have not asked you to sit down. Please have a chair."

She nodded toward the chair by which she was standing. As he made his way to it, she turned it to face the chair next to it. He could not help thinking, as they sat down opposite each other, of his tutor at Cambridge and the hours they had spent construing Latin verse.

"You know why I asked you here, I suppose?" she said, with no trace of expression.

"I thought I did," he said, "but now I am not sure."

She lowered her eyes as if she had become intensely interested in her hands, which were fingering the flounces on her skirt.

"It is very simple," she said. "You must have observed that we are in love with each other."

"Yes," he said slowly. "I think I have."

She raised her eyes and looked squarely at him. Aside from a very faint trace of color in her cheeks, she gave no sign of emotion. Her voice still sounded toneless and flat, as if she were discussing the weather.

"This is a miserable state of affairs, I think. Do you agree?"

"I agree," he said, noticing as he did so that his own voice sounded as if it belonged to someone else.

"You remember our conversation in the woods," she went on.

"I think I could repeat every word of it."

"So could I. You understand, then, how impossible this is."

"Yes, I do."

"The last thing I need at this time is to fall in love." There was a note of anger in her voice. "And certainly not with a Tory."

"I am not overcome with joy either," he said drily.

Her tone softened a little. "Exactly," she said. "I thought that perhaps you would have some suggestions."

"Only one," he said, avoiding her eyes, "and that is that we stay as far away from each other as possible. Does that sound reasonable?"

"I have already thought of that," she said patiently, "and I don't think I like it. It is extremely sensible, of course, but I am not sure it is possible."

"To be frank with you, I don't like it either," he said. "I am glad you rejected it."

She looked at him steadily, her brown eyes calm and serious. "You must think of something better."

"Well," he said tentatively, "I suppose under extreme duress we could get married."

Esther made a face. "I said that I was in love with you," she said, "not that I had taken leave of my senses."

"No," he said wryly, "I can see that your senses have not been affected."

"You understand," she went on, like a patient judge instructing a dull jury, "that I want to marry you."

"Yes," he said, "I think I understand that."

She paused judicially. "You also understand that I will not let girlish fancies turn me into a fool."

"Yes," he said, watching the unsteady candlelight flicker across her face, "although I did not know you considered this a girlish fancy."

"Let us not cavil." She dismissed the objection with a shrug. "My position is clear enough, is it not?"

"Very clear indeed," he said. "You will not abandon your father and your plots to marry me."

She made a small gesture of annoyance. "You put the matter very offensively, but you are right. I will not give up the cause and my position in it just because I have the misfortune to love a Tory."

"I see," he said, choosing his words carefully now. "And I agree with you. I will not abandon my career either."

"Just so," she said—the tutor congratulating the student who has finally found the answer. "If you married me, your career as crown lawyer would be over within a week."

"Well then?"

"I think I may have a solution. Listen to this and give me your candid opinion." She spoke gravely and patiently, as if this were a commercial transaction to which she had given hours of thought. "You realize, of course, that you and I have only one real problem."

"I thought we had several," he interrupted.

"No." She corrected him sharply. "We have only one—the King. As long as he retains his power, I cannot marry you without betraying my family and the liberties of England; and you cannot marry me without sacrificing your future and that odd notion of loyalty which seems to mean so much to you. Am I right?"

Ralph stirred uneasily in his chair. Where was this leading? "Yes," he said, "you are."

"Well then," she said triumphantly, "our position is not hopeless. The King, you know, is not immortal."

Ralph heard himself draw in his breath.

"At worst," she went on, "our impasse can only last a few years. And I don't believe it will last more than two or three."

He felt himself relax again. "Do you think the King will die within two or three years?"

"Oh no," she said, "not unless someone kills him. I mean that at the rate he is moving, the crisis will come within that time. He is alienating the nation faster than any of us dared to hope."

"I see." He leaned forward. "And what do you intend to do in the meantime?"

For the first time, Esther showed animation. The color in her face deepened, and her voice lost its cool flatness. "About you?" she said half defiantly. "I intend to see you as often as I can. Is that agreeable?"

"Agreeable, but complicated," he said, letting the first wave of excitement subside. "For me to be seen with you, except very occasionally, would be as damaging to both of us as to be married."

"Never fear," she said, with something like a sigh. "I won't compromise us. With a little practice, I can become as devious as any other woman."

"Your father and brother must know nothing of this."

"I told you before that I have not taken leave of my senses."

"Well," he said, "I guess we will be able to carry it off. At least I am willing to try. There are a few conditions, though."

"Yes?"

"For one thing, I expect you to be true to me and to be honest with me. Does that seem too much to ask?"

"That goes without saying," Esther looked directly into his eyes. "Naturally I expect the same."

"If at any time you should cease to love me, I expect you to tell me so. I don't want to find it out indirectly."

"You have my promise," she said, "but you need not worry; the problem will never arise. Is there anything else?"

"I expect you to be absolutely secret."

"We have already settled that."

"There was something else too, and now I have forgotten it."

"I promise a truce on politics. Was that it?"

"No. I don't care about that. You may discuss politics all you wish, as long as you don't expect me to agree."

"While you try to think of it, I will add some conditions of my own." She spoke slowly now and very deliberately. "First, I expect you to trust me. It will be difficult, I know, because we began under such awkward conditions; but unless we can trust each other the whole thing is impossible. Will you try?"

"Yes, I will," he said, wondering as he spoke if he were telling the truth.

"You will remember too," she went on, "that practically speaking we are entrusting each other with our lives. I expect you to treat mine as if it were your own."

"I will," he said.

"I wish now," she said, "that I had been helpless all my life. I wish I had been a frail little thing, the kind that men want to care for; then you would feel trusting and protective toward me. I know it sounds odd, but I want you to feel so anyway. It is not my fault that I have spent my life in the middle of a battle."

Watching her as she sat opposite him looking cool, competent, and serene, and a little remote in the uncertain light, he could hardly believe what he had heard; but he nodded understandingly. "You may depend upon me," he said.

"And one thing more." She paused, obviously searching for words. "Promise me to be happy, at least part of the time. At this moment you look as if you had been sentenced to a lifetime in the workhouse.

I realize that for two or three years there will be more scheming and sneaking than pleasure, but I hope it won't all be misery for you."

He was about to say "I am happy now," but it was so obviously false that he could not make the words come out of his mouth. Instead he merely nodded and tried to look cheerful.

"I will do my best," he said.

"As you come to know me better," she went on, "I hope you will come to like me as well as to love me. You should try, even though I am not very likable."

"I don't think it will be difficult," he said. "We will come to know each other very well, and I hope you learn to like me too."

"I do already," she said.

"Oh, I remember now what it was I wanted to ask you." Ralph straightened up. "What will we do if things go wrong?"

She raised her eyebrows. "What do you mean?"

"Suppose the King is not restrained or deposed or killed within the next three or four years."

Esther looked at him steadily. There was a touch of ice in her voice. "He will be," she said.

"But suppose he is not. Suppose he succeeds in the plans you fear. Suppose he subjects the country to a popish military autocracy. What then?"

"He won't," she said coldly.

"But suppose he does."

"In that case," she said with a frigid little smile, "my family and I will all be hanged, drawn, and quartered; so you may consider our contract dissolved."

Our contract. Yes, Ralph told himself, that was what it all seemed like—a formal, impersonal agreement, between the parties of the first and second part. Or like a carefully arranged marriage, with no love on either side, but minute attention to the details of dowry and inheritance. And yet in a way, he supposed, this was more flattering and exciting than spontaneous embraces. Behind it lay hours of tossing and turning, of planning and scheming, of rejecting and compromising, of making tortured, inadequate concessions to reason.

"Nothing will dissolve our contract," he was saying, "but the consent of the parties. If things go wrong, I expect you to escape into exile and I will join you."

Yes, he thought, the patient abstract discussion was vital to both of them. It almost succeeded in hiding the monstrous insanity of their falling in love with each other.

"You are sweet to say so, Ralph," he heard her say, "but that won't be necessary. If we fail, everything is finished. But why imagine such horrible things? We will not fail."

No, Ralph said grimly to himself, we will not fail. And suddenly he felt a surge of something like elation. Why worry? He himself could guarantee the future. Tomorrow, if necessary, he could put an end to the whole complicated structure of delay, anxiety, conniving, and duplicity. Within weeks they could be married. Six inches of steel.

"One more promise," he said aloud. "When our problem has been disposed of, I expect you to marry me immediately, with or without the consent of your father. I am sure that he could always find reasons for further delay."

"I was about to make you promise the same thing," she said. "You have my word. And don't fret about my father. He will do what I ask him to when the time comes."

Of course he did not intend to kill the King in the immediate future, he reminded himself. Assassination would be a last resort, after everything else had been tried. Still the knowledge was reassuring. It gave him a steely sense of control.

Esther stood up suddenly and put out both hands to him. "We are agreed then," she said.

He rose and took her hands, soberly and formally. For a moment they stood there looking at each other.

"We are agreed," he said.

For Ralph the kiss began as a ritual—cool, detached, and solemn —the seal on a vow. It ended in a long shuddering sigh. As her arms closed about his neck, his detachment disappeared like a straw in a torrent. In his consciousness there was room only for the warm damp pressure of her lips and the taut urgency of the slim body crushed against him.

From somewhere far away, his voice seemed to be saying, "My God, Esther," but he knew he was not speaking. Nor was she, although her lips were moving against his.

When with a reluctant unspoken consent they drew back to look at each other, he saw her face in a dream-like blur. In the flickering semi-darkness her eyes showed dark and luminous, her face pale, and her lips parted; but the long sigh seemed more vivid than the image. It was as if the drunken, triumphant rush of his sensations prevented him from seeing.

"Ralph," she said, almost inaudibly. "Ralph."

She buried her head against his chest. He could feel her shiver, her shoulders moving like those of a sobbing child. When he bent and kissed her hair, her shoulders, and her neck, she raised her lips again. Again he was submerged in the intensity of the embrace, totally absorbed in lips, arms, and body.

He had no remembrance of pulling her to the sofa, yet suddenly they were there, half sitting, half lying, locked together so tightly that he could feel the pounding of her heart and the labored effort of her breathing. One of his hands, with maddening clumsiness, was fumbling with the fastenings on the back of her bodice; the other was trying to pull her even closer to him.

He had undone the last fastening and was beginning to pull the dress across her shoulders when she released her hold around his neck. He drew back, waiting for her to slip the dress down over her arms; instead she took his hands and pulled them gently away. Then she lay back quietly, looking at him, her eyes soft and smoky.

"There was one condition which I forgot to mention," she said, watching him intently.

He did not reply. He merely disengaged one hand and began to caress her face with it, disturbing the pattern of firelight and candlelight.

"I did not make it clear—" while she paused for words, she kissed the hand caressing her—"that I intend to be your wife, not your mistress."

"It was clear enough," he said, pulling her toward him and kissing her on the mouth. "But you can be both."

She drew away again. "No Ralph," she said thoughtfully. "It is a chance we cannot take. A child would be fatal."

For the space of a heartbeat Ralph felt a flash of cold anger and frustrate suspicion. Could Esther be acting after all? Was this the broken kiss of the Haagsche Bosch all over again? Was she listening for distant hoofbeats? But no, it was impossible. The thought was gone before it could be formulated. Here she was locked in his arms, their limbs pressed together. Her hands were still shaking as they held his; a pulse was throbbing in the base of her neck. If he persisted she could not refuse. She was pleading with him to save them from a disastrous mistake—pleading against all her desires.

"I agree," his voice said, as if from a great distance. "It is a chance we cannot take."

Eighteen

"SIR, SIR, the Duke of Berwick is here."

Sir Ralph was so deep in his thoughts that he barely recognized his son's voice. Almost painfully, he brought himself back to the present, trying to collect himself en route.

"The Duke of Berwick?" he said.

Richard was standing beside him, impatiently waiting for him to take command. The Duke, Sir Ralph knew from long experience, was Richard's special hero. The boy was obviously trying to restrain his excitement, but with little success.

"His coach is outside now." Richard looked like a runner at his mark.

"Very well," Sir Ralph repressed a smile. "You may go and conduct him in here. Mind that you do it properly. If you should see your brother on the way, don't race him for the honor."

He might have spared himself the last two sentences, he knew. They had not been heard, even though Richard had waited politely until he was through speaking. Within five seconds the boy was through the front door, not running, precisely, but not walking either. A moment later there was a loud shout of greeting.

While he was waiting, Sir Ralph carefully gathered up his sheets of manuscript and put them in the drawer of the desk. They were too few, he thought, for the mental labor expended, but he supposed he should not be dissatisfied. The process was fascinating in itself. Perhaps every fifty-year-old should be required to account for his life.

With a final glance around the room to see if everything was in order, he walked toward the door. It was a little odd, he reflected, that Jack, who had been born out of order, so to speak, and had spent all his life in turmoil and chaos should have such a passion for order. It was not merely the man's military training, he was sure,

but something deeper, some original inquietude gradually transformed into a demand that everything should behave properly and
predictably.

Henry burst through the door ahead of the others. "Father," he
shouted, "the Duke says I may ride Hidalgo."

"That is very kind of the Duke, I am sure. Did you thank him?"

"Oh, I forgot." Henry turned on his heel and started back just
in time to run into his brother, who was coming through the door.

Richard looked pained. "Sir," he protested, "Henry has been making a pest of himself again. I was the one assigned to conduct the
Duke. Why does he always interfere?"

Berwick, standing in the doorway, glanced at Ralph over the
heads of the boys. "Richard," he said, "that is what younger
brothers are for, to interfere. I had a younger brother, also named
Henry. He always interfered and I think I was better for it."

"Really Sir?" The hero-worship in the boy's voice almost embarrassed Ralph.

"I think so," Berwick said, as if making a ponderous judgment.
"It taught me patience—a very useful commodity, as your father can
tell you."

"But Father had no younger brother," Henry said. "What taught
him patience?"

Berwick turned toward Henry and winked slyly. "A lady in England, I think. And then there was my father."

"You mean King James?" Henry, who had begun to grin at the
joke, sobered immediately.

"Yes, King James." Berwick, Sir Ralph thought, winced a little at
the question. "I am sure that he tried your father's patience many
times, perhaps more times than he tried mine."

"Gentlemen," Sir Ralph said. "The Duke is very kind to take so
much interest in your improvement, but we can finish the discussion at tea. At present, the Duke and I have much to talk about."

He watched Berwick move instinctively to soften the blow. "Your
father is right, as usual. We must not let pleasure interfere with
business. If you gentlemen wish to go for a ride in my coach, René
will take you. Perhaps he will even let you drive."

"If we go," Richard said, "will you promise to stay for tea?"

"Most certainly." Berwick nodded gravely. "You know I would
not think of leaving before I have a chance to talk with you and
your mother."

As Berwick conducted the two boys back out to the coach, Sir
Ralph stood in the doorway. It was almost indecent, he told him-

self, for a man to be as handsome as Jack. Now, at forty-five, he looked more than ever like his uncle, the Duke of Marlborough—or rather, like the Lord Churchill Ralph had seen at Sedgemoor. He moved with something of the same economical grace and the same easy assurance. Yes, Ralph told himself, watching the boys being handed into the coach, Jack had actually managed to grow more handsome over the years, and in a sense younger. The seventeen-year-old (or was it sixteen-year-old) Berwick he had met in the fall of '86 had seemed incredibly old for his age, already a veteran of a campaign against the Turks, and weighed down with new responsibilities. Yet that prematurely old young man had gradually been transformed into this handsome, smooth-browed marshal of France.

Perhaps the transformation was a matter of training, Ralph speculated, of learning to handle certain types of problems until they became easy, almost second nature. But maybe it was a matter of temperament and luck. From his mother and her Churchill ancestors he had inherited the nerve of a matador; and from his father, the King, he had inherited a set of opportunities and a set of clearly marked duties. He had never been obliged to decide what he was going to defend, only how he was going to defend it. Yes, Ralph decided, smiling to himself as Berwick came back down the path, Jack had been lucky indeed. What if he had inherited his abilities from James II and his problems from Arabella Churchill?

"Well, Jack, did you hear the news, or is this call just a coincidence?" Sir Ralph had taken Berwick's hat and sword belt. He was hanging them on the rack.

Berwick waited until he turned around; then he frowned and stroked his chin. "I heard the news," he said, "but I wanted to see you anyway."

"The news spread rapidly, I see." Ralph motioned toward the sofa.

"Yes." Berwick seated himself. "It was at my door at seven o'clock this morning in the shape of a hot young Jacobite named Randall."

"And what did you think of it?"

"I was a little insulted." Berwick crossed his handsome, silk-stockinged calves. "I had thought that you would consult me before making such an important move."

"I did not want to bother you with it, Jack, until I knew something more definite." Ralph paused to see the effect of his words. "I had a feeling that it would all come to nothing."

"How do you estimate your chances now, after seeing Lord Stair?"

"Oh, I should say that I have something like one chance in three —that is, if there are no further complications."

Berwick leaned forward, with his hands on his knees. "And you really want to go back, Ralph?"

"Yes," Ralph said slowly. "I really do. Does that seem strange to you?"

Berwick brushed an imaginary speck of dust from the gold facing of his blue coat. "I suppose it does," he said. "Yes, I suppose it does. It is hard for me to imagine anyone who knows France going back voluntarily to a country of fogs and Sabbaths, of Whigs and petty shopkeepers."

Ralph laughed. "Spoken like a true Frenchman, Jack."

"Not like a true Frenchman, Ralph." Berwick shook his head. "Spoken like a bastard Englishman."

"Like a true Frenchman," Ralph insisted, still laughing. "I am sure that any Parisian we could bring in off the street would say the same thing."

"Not at all." Berwick continued to shake his head. "No true Parisian would argue the point at all. He would simply think you crazy."

"And don't you think me crazy too, Jack?"

"No," Berwick said thoughtfully, "not crazy. I think you are suffering the common complaint of senile homesickness. I understand it can become rather severe."

"You have not been touched by it, I suppose."

"Senility, yes; homesickness, no." Berwick found another speck of dust to claim his attention. "After all, what should I be homesick for? Certainly not for the grubby little Bourbonnais town where I was born, nor for the Jesuit colleges where Father had me educated. For England? Hardly. I was there less than three years."

"But you did have a pleasant time there, didn't you?"

Berwick smiled. "Yes, I had some pleasant times there, many of them with you, you may remember; but I should hardly call the whole thing pleasant. In England, you know, people are inclined to look down on bastards—even royal bastards."

"It is odd that you should say so," Sir Ralph tried to conjure up a picture of the Berwick he had known. "I always thought you were well treated in England."

"Oh, I was—after a fashion." Obviously Berwick too was trying to recall the texture of those times. "But somehow I was never really comfortable, except with you, of course. Do you remember the first time you ever saw me?"

"Very well. You did not seem unhappy to me, only a little confused by a new situation."

As he spoke, the scene came back, sharp and clear. "I am James Fitzjames," the boy had said, as he stood poised in the doorway of the apartment. "My father tells me that I should make myself acquainted with you. My father is the King, you know."

"Yes, I know," he had said, recovering quickly from his surprise. "I am very pleased to meet you."

"You may call me Jack, if you like." The boy spoke with a slight French accent. "In France I am called Jacques, and I prefer it to James, don't you?"

"I think I do. Please sit down. I have heard a great deal about you, especially about your campaign against the Turks. You were wounded, were you not?"

"Yes, I was wounded, but not seriously." There was no false modesty in the reply. "If my father had not brought me to England, I might have received a regiment in the next campaign."

"Don't be discouraged," he had said. "Your father can give you three regiments if he wishes."

"That is what he told me." The boy patted his obviously new wig. "But my father has no war for me."

"Not at the moment. But don't lose heart. If things continue on their present course he will soon have enough wars for all of us."

Berwick's voice recalled Sir Ralph to the present. "I remember the meeting perfectly," Berwick was saying. "It was sometime in October or November of 1686, a few months before I was given my title. My father had ordered me to see you, and I dreaded the meeting. The King had abominable taste in friends, you know."

"I know."

"I can see you now as you sat there at the table, looking a thousand years old, as if you were carrying all England on your shoulders."

"I was."

"How old were you then? Twenty-five? Twenty-six? At any rate, I liked you at once, I remember."

"Do you remember why?"

"Oh, I don't know. Maybe it was because you were not a courtier. You did not pretend an interest in me for the sake of the King. I remember thinking, in fact, that the King's opinions did not interest you at all."

"I already knew the King's opinions."

"I am sure you did." Berwick smoothed the wrinkles on the side of his breeches. "That was what puzzled me. The King had explained to me what a fine honest gentleman you were and how I should pattern myself on you if I wished to get along in England; yet it seemed obvious to me that you did not care whether the King lived or died."

Sir Ralph shut his eyes a moment. I should have much preferred him dead, he thought.

"What did you think of your father at that time?" he said aloud.

"It is difficult to say." Berwick rubbed his smoothly shaven chin. "I remember being grateful for some of his favors and being a little ashamed of his incompetence, but maybe that came later. When you and I met, I did not know the King nearly so well as you did. I think I was even a little jealous of his high regard for you."

"Had you known your father better, you would have known that his high regard was a very feeble and uncertain commodity."

"So I found out." Berwick gave a sad little smile. "But such as it was, you had it. In fact, I should say we were both lucky in that respect. The King gave you and me as much love and trust as he was capable of, don't you think so?"

"Yes," Ralph said, "I think he did." And perhaps it was that love and trust which saved his life, he thought suddenly. "I except, of course, his feeling for the little Prince. He doted on young James."

Berwick uncrossed his legs and adjusted his left stocking. "That is true—the legitimate heir, naturally. No one else can expect that kind of feeling."

The legitimate heir. Ralph wondered if there was a trace of bitterness in the phrase. He supposed not. In his thirty years of friendship with Jack, he had never seen an overt sign of jealousy. And yet, how could it be otherwise? In his years of struggling to retrieve the errors of his father and his legitimate half-brother, Jack must have been conscious of the irony and injustice of his position.

"At least," Berwick was continuing, "the King liked you and me a great deal more than he liked his daughters."

"Yes, he did. But to be fair, we must remember that his daughters violently opposed his plans."

No, he thought, it was impossible that Jack should be bitter. With his great holdings in Spain, his power and prestige in both France and Spain, he was infinitely better off than the legitimate heir, reduced now to grandiose plans and absurd orders.

"You often criticized his plans too, if you remember," Berwick said.

"That is true enough, God knows; but I did not have a husband with an army, as Princess Mary did, and I did not have your uncle Marlborough to help me, as Princess Anne did."

Berwick shook his head and then resolutely assumed a more cheerful expression. "Well, thank the good God, all that is long past. I would not go back to those days for anything in the world—or to England either."

"I would not go back to those days," Sir Ralph said soberly, "but I will go back to England if I can—Sabbaths, Whigs, and all."

"I suppose you are still planning that trip to Lincolnshire. You never made it, did you?"

"No, I never made it. I was sent into every other part of England, and into Ireland and Scotland, but I never got back to Lincolnshire. Maybe this time I will be luckier."

"Do you ever hear from your brother Walter?"

"Oh yes, at least once a year. He sends me money, you know, for my share in the profits from the estate. I told you, didn't I, that I invested the money your father gave me in land. I helped Walter buy back the old estate my father had frittered away."

"Yes, you told me."

"I have sometimes thought that if I hadn't wanted money so badly, I might have resigned from your father's service before it was too late."

Berwick made an infinitesimal adjustment of his lace collar. "I doubt it," he said.

"You may be right."

Yes, Sir Ralph admitted, Jack was certainly right. Money had been the least of his motives. And yet, who could say for sure? He could still recall the satisfaction of watching the goldsmith count those yellow guineas, and the pleasure of sending those letters of credit to Walter. He had never, before or since, felt so important.

"Didn't Walter have a son killed at Oudenarde?" Berwick was asking.

"Yes, Robert, the youngest."

"I suppose Walter has recovered by now."

"I don't know," Sir Ralph said. "I hope so. He never mentions the subject in his letters."

"It must have been a frightful blow."

"If you don't mind, Jack, I would rather not talk about it."

"I am sorry, Ralph," Berwick said apologetically, "I did not know you took the loss so much to heart."

Sir Ralph immediately regretted having said anything. Jack must think him strangely maudlin for feeling strongly about the loss eight years ago of a nephew he had never seen.

"It is irrational, I know," he said lamely, "but I have always felt that I might have done something to prevent it."

"Nonsense, Ralph," Berwick said. "You were not at Oudenarde."

"No," he said, "I was not at Oudenarde."

To Sir Ralph's relief, Berwick immediately changed the subject. "Do you think that Walter knew what you were doing?" he asked reminiscently.

"Not exactly. But I think he had grave suspicions. When he came to London, he questioned me sharply, and he was a hard man to deceive. I don't believe he was much surprised when I was chased out of the country."

"You will be glad to know that I was completely deceived. I had no idea you were a spy."

"You were not supposed to know."

"And yet I might have deduced it if I had been a little older." Berwick smiled faintly and readjusted his collar. "It never occurred to me to think my father's interest in a young lawyer was strange, or to wonder why you were always taking journeys."

"It occurred to a few other people, however," Ralph said.

"I do recall one thing that seemed strange at the time. That was your taking a commission in my regiment of foot."

"I hoped it would not seem strange. The rolls were full of men who had taken commissions merely as an investment."

"Quite so. The difference was that you actually appeared at the camps, and rather often."

"Not often enough," Sir Ralph said. "I had not had thirty days' exercise in arms when you and I followed the King to Ireland in '89."

"You must have learned a great deal in a short time," Berwick made a little bow.

"You are flattering, Jack, but you know I learned almost nothing. I took a commission to spy on the army, not to become a soldier. Your father and I thought that I could get more information if I wore a uniform. One might say that I became a soldier by accident."

Berwick lifted his shoulders in a gesture of resignation. "You were not the only one. Many of us became many things by accident. I was born because my mother accidentally happened to be an aristocratic whore. I became a French marshal because a Spanish princess thought I would look charming in a marshal's uniform, and I became a Spanish grandee because the Portuguese horse fled from Almanza without striking a blow. General St. Ruth, on the other hand, became a corpse because he accidentally stepped in front of a cannon ball."

In all the years of their friendship, Sir Ralph had never heard Berwick mention his mother before. He would have liked to pursue the subject.

"Let us hear no more about your accidental promotions," he said. "You became a marshal because you were a good man for the position, and you became a grandee because you had trained our horse not to flee. Don't forget, I was at Almanza too."

"Very well, I shall admit my genius." Berwick pulled a solemn face. "And yet I could have sworn that I was exceptionally lucky."

"Only in your choice of friends," Sir Ralph said, imitating Berwick's exaggerated grimace.

"Especially in my choice of friends." This time Ralph could see that he was serious. "I don't want you to go to England, Ralph."

Sir Ralph watched Berwick unbutton the last two buttons on his coat and then refasten them more to his satisfaction. "You are kind, Jack," he said, "but I can be of little use to you now; and I am sure you have other friends who can fill my place."

"It is not merely selfishness on my part, Ralph." Berwick rose to his feet and stood in front of Ralph as if he had rehearsed a speech for formal delivery. "I am thinking of you and your future. Why should you go back to England and put yourself at the mercy of your old enemies? Why should you live in obscurity there when you can live honorably and comfortably here? A new world is opening. Now that Louis is dead and the Regent is in power, a man with your experience and talents could make his way even without powerful connections. And I personally guarantee to get you the position of your choice—in the law, if you like; in the army; or in the administration. You can be the Intendant of Guyenne tomorrow and never leave Paris. I mentioned you to the Regent last week. Or, if you would like to get out of France and away from this nest of Jacobites, I can take you to Spain. You always liked Spain when we were there. The good God knows that Philip could use an honest administrator and an honest general, and I need you there myself to look after my interests."

Berwick stopped for breath. For a moment his handsome face showed as much agitation as Ralph had ever seen on it—more than it had showed in the rout at the Boyne. Almost immediately, he checked himself and sank back to his seat on the sofa. When he resumed, his tone was quieter.

"You must learn to sweep out the rubbish of your past," he said.

"You have already spent much too long trying to retrieve other people's mistakes and to restore things that are dead. Why don't you try now to take the opportunities of the present?"

"I think I have learned the lesson well enough," Ralph said thoughtfully. "It is a matter of deciding which opportunities to take. I like the ones in England."

"Pardon me, Ralph, but I don't think you have learned the lesson well enough. You should have been born illegitimate like me, and it would have been easier. You would have found your past a great inconvenience, not a subject for sentiment."

"You are not precisely the man best qualified to speak on the subject of sentiment, Jack," he retorted smoothly. "It seems to me that I remember seeing you in many places where no sensible man would go, on orders that no sensible man would execute. I cite our journey to England in 1695 as an example."

Berwick shrugged. "I confess it. I have been as stupid as anyone, and more stupid than most. Like you, I tried to carry the King around on my back, and also my half-brother. Maybe I was busier in trying to obliterate my past than you were in trying to salvage yours. Perhaps I was also trying to prove something to the world. I don't know. I only know that I have learned better."

Yes, Ralph thought, Jack had learned better. Like the competent general that he was, he had learned when to cut his losses and retreat. Now he was sitting, cool and resourceful, in an impregnable position awaiting whatever might develop. Ralph felt a great surge of affection for him. Lately people had been saying that the Duke of Berwick had grown cold and calculating, but this was not true. He was as generous and warmhearted as ever. He had merely learned the difference between the possible and the impossible.

"I shall never forget my feeling when my father died," Berwick was saying. "I was sad of course. I think I pitied him more than anyone else did, except possibly you. I almost loved him, in spite of his disposition. And the good God knows I had fought his battles for years. Yet—and I am almost ashamed to say it—I could not help feeling relieved. There he was, dead, and I had no more responsibility for his long train of mistakes and misfortunes. Did you ever feel anything like that?"

"Yes," Ralph said slowly, "I did."

"There was something even worse, something I would not tell to anyone but you. God forgive me, the thought actually crossed my mind that it was a pity he had not died years before—before the Revolution and all the trouble. He would have been spared the disappointment and grief of his last years; and the rest of us would have been spared all those battles, fought in the wrong places at the wrong times against the wrong people."

"The thought crossed my mind too," Ralph said.

"Good," Berwick said. "I feared I was depraved to think such a thing."

"Perhaps we were both depraved."

"Perhaps, but it does not matter now. My point is that with the King's death I began to make my own decisions. Oh, I confess that I felt some responsibility for my half-brother and aided him all I could, but I never deluded myself about his prospects. Do you remember Ramillies?"

"Yes," Ralph said quietly, "I do. I had the misfortune to be there."

"So you did. I had forgotten. Well, one might say that Ramillies helped complete my education. I was down in Spain when I got the news. When I heard how Marlborough had smashed the great French Army, I knew that the Jacobite cause was lost. I knew that my half-brother would never ascend the English throne, unless by some freak of English politics he was invited back."

While Berwick paused and brushed the left sleeve of his coat with his right hand, Sir Ralph allowed himself a brief picture of the retreat from Ramillies. He was trying to get his still unbroken regiment through a row of hedges to protect it from the pursuing cavalry squadrons. He could feel now the sweat break out on his palms as the last man scrambled to safety and the pursuit went roaring off to the right. Yes, he told himself, he too had learned something at Ramillies—but it was something about skill and courage, and not about the Pretender's chances. The slaughter at Blenheim two years before had taught him that the French would not beat the Duke of Marlborough and put Young James on the English throne.

"You see," Berwick continued, "Ramillies completed the work of destroying my past. Since that time I have not been a bastard English Duke trying to regain a throne for the legitimate members of my family; I have been a French marshal trying to save France and Spain from destruction. With the help of the good God I have had some success."

You have indeed, Ralph thought affectionately. The good God, as you call him, may care nothing for Tories, but he must have a sneaking fondness for at least one French marshal.

"You have done well, Jack," he said aloud. "I could wish the rest of the Jacobites had learned so quickly."

"I refuse to concern myself any more about the rest of the Jacobites," Berwick said sharply. "I am concerned about you. You have been wise enough to abandon a hopeless cause, but not wise enough to abandon England."

"Why fret yourself, Jack? There is no very good reason to suppose that they will let me go back anyway."

"I sincerely hope they won't," Berwick said, "but I am afraid they will. I suppose you have heard that Lady Sheldon is coming to Paris. With her to plead your case, you will not be exiled long."

"You think Lady Sheldon will plead my case?" Ralph smiled ruefully. "It might interest you to know that she once tried to have me killed. If I get back to England, it is not likely to be through the good offices of Lady Sheldon."

"Really?" Berwick started. "Did she really try to have you killed?"

"Yes, she did."

"But I thought that you and she were lovers."

"We were." He paused to let the information take hold. "I did not mean to give the impression that she hated me personally."

"Why did she do it then?" Berwick leaned forward, his hands on his knees.

"That is a secret, Jack; and I don't think you would really understand if I told you. You never knew Esther."

Berwick straightened up, smoothing his coat as he did so. "No, I didn't," he said. "Perhaps it is just as well."

"Oh, I no longer bear any ill will against her for making the attempt." Sir Ralph smiled at Berwick's obvious horror. "At the time, I confess, I thought her a monster, but eventually one learns a little tolerance. Still, as I said, I do not expect her to help me get back to England."

Berwick, he could see, was trying to digest the information. He was shaking his head as he attempted to bring the implications under discipline.

"This puts a different face upon affairs," he said finally. "I thought Lady Sheldon was one of the reasons that you wanted to return."

"Your imagination seems to be as vivid as Henriette's," Ralph said, still smiling. "Perhaps, as you keep telling me, I have not learned to forget my past; but I am not so dull that I wish to bring back the most horrible period in my life."

Berwick removed another invisible speck of dust from his coat. "I am glad," he said. "It gives me more hope."

"You have every reason to be hopeful, Jack. My chances, I repeat, are no better than one to three. Nevertheless, I intend to try them."

"I will never understand it," Berwick sighed. "Here you are with a charming wife, fine sons, and excellent prospects; yet you insist on uprooting yourself to return to that land of fog and fanatics, of hot factions and cold women. Can you tell me why?"

Sir Ralph shrugged. "As one of those cold English ladies once told me, no one who asks the question could possibly understand the answer. I suppose it would not help if I told you that I am tired of seeing concierges and wooden shoes, that I am tired of grand monarchs and little lackeys, and that I hate fish soup."

"No," Berwick said, smiling. "It would not help."

"Would it help if I told you that I am sick of Jacobites, that as long as I live on the continent they will be coming around with their absurd plots and their large commissions?"

"Yes, that would help. I am sick of them too. But since I excused myself from the leadership of the Scottish expedition, they have been coming around less frequently; and when they find out that you are through with them they will leave you alone."

"Perhaps," Ralph said, "but I doubt it. Besides, I don't even want to see the poor devils in the streets. I want to see some genuine Englishmen. I should also like to see a real tavern and a real inn. I should even welcome the sight of an English costermonger. Does that make any sense to you?"

"Very little." Berwick shook his head. "It only convinces me of what I said before. You are suffering from senile homesickness, in a virulent form. If you are prevented from doing anything foolish, it will go away. I think I recommend another trip to Spain."

"You are very kind to bother with me, Jack, but my mind is made up."

Berwick adjusted his cuffs. "Don't think you have heard the last of this," he said. "I shall continue to harass you until you get on the ship. In fact, even should you get to England, I shall continue to bombard you with letters, hoping that you will come to your senses. And I tell you frankly, Ralph, that you have upset my plans. Just when I thought I had everything in order, my position well established, I find suddenly that one of my bastions has collapsed and my flank is exposed."

Ralph laughed, trying to conceal the affection that he felt. It was absurd, he supposed, to feel sentimental about the possibility of leaving Jack.

"Nonsense," he said. "Your position will be improved if I go. It will be like losing a regiment of wild Irish infantry. And now, speaking of positions, you and I had better let Henriette and the boys come in for tea, or neither of our positions will be tenable."

"Consider what I have said," Berwick said rising to his feet. "Meantime I shall treat with Henriette. I think I can make her see reason. Her taste in husbands is open to question, but she is a Frenchwoman, thank the good God."

"You have my permission to treat." Sir Ralph raised his voice so that it would be heard in the kitchen. "But I warn you, no one can influence Henriette."

CHAPTER

Nineteen

RALPH CLOSED the window in an attempt to shut out the sound of the bells. For hours now, ever since morning, they had been clanging away, filling all London with their metallic din. Looking through the glass, he could see a small bonfire being kindled in front of a house down the street, and from somewhere far away, probably the Tower, he could hear the boom of a cannon.

Underneath the noise of the bells and the cannon, the official voices of celebration, Ralph could almost feel the sullen silence of the town. Coming home along the Strand, he had noticed that the streets were practically deserted. The few straggling pedestrians and chair men looked as if they were hurrying to shelter; the usual evening cries and shouts were gone as completely as if their owners had been strangled. Only here and there one saw little knots of activity where the servants of some placeholder or the beneficiary of some government contract were shamefacedly piling up materials for bonfires.

He could not help remembering, by contrast, the night of the King's coronation. All London had swarmed in the streets. One could hardly hear the bells and the cannon for the noise of the drunken citizens. Every house had seemed to disgorge thirty people, each one trying to outshout the others. Even the poorest house had been illuminated, and the bonfires had formed solid rows as far as one could see.

Was that only three years ago? It seemed like three hundred. June 10, 1688, an odd date. No one had expected the delivery for another month—three weeks at the earliest. Now here it was and the fat was in the fire. God's wounds, but there would be rejoicing in Paris. Already the news must be on the Channel. What would the Pope say when he heard? Would he give up praying for the Prince of Orange? Would he give up praying entirely and throw in his lot

with the French? Or would he grit his teeth and pray all the harder?
Certainly the last. And yet it must be discouraging to a pope to get
such miserable returns on his prayers. What of the Archbishop of
Canterbury and the rest of the Anglican bishops? Would they order
prayers for the popish heir? They would be obliged to, of course.
What irony.

A popish heir. Ralph drew the curtains and turned from the window, but the sound of the bells followed him. Who would have believed it? After four miscarriages Mary Beatrice had produced a live
son—alive and well, the doctor had said. And now there was no
hope. It must be either assassination or revolution. Patient, faithful
Tories who would endure almost anything from the King as long as
they knew that sometime he would die and leave a Protestant heir
would now sit still no longer. Within two or three weeks a letter
would go out to the Prince of Orange inviting him to bring his army
and rescue England.

Yes, the revolution was at hand. For months now London had
been alive with agents of all sorts: French agents, Dutch agents,
Papal agents, Spanish agents, Whig agents, Tory agents, royal agents,
and lately Austrian agents. The fate of Europe was being decided
here, and the spies were flocking like crows to carrion. One could
almost smell them.

Ralph sat down at the desk and put his head in his hands. Now
that the worst had happened, he felt strangely undisturbed—more
tired than agitated. At least, he consoled himself, he was a better
spy than his competitors. He knew the foreign agents and their missions almost before they got off their ships, or were hired by an
embassy. He knew the contents of the letters that had been sent
between Barillon, the French Ambassador, and the French court.
He could name all the Englishmen who had sent pledges of support
to William in case of revolution. He knew what arms had been collected and where. He had been helped, he admitted, by Adda and
the far-flung system of Papal agents; but mostly the work had been
his own, a matter of getting the right men in the right places, or of
being in the right place himself.

One thing his operations had not been able to predict, he admitted ruefully, was the result of the Queen's pregnancy. When he
had first heard of her expectations, he had not been disturbed. He
had agreed with Catherine Sedley's little sally, "the Italian bitch will
abort again." As the months had gone by, he had expected momentarily to hear of a miscarriage. Even when the Jesuits had boasted
all over Europe that a miracle was taking place—that the Queen

would produce a male child to supersede the Protestant princess and perpetuate the true faith—even then he had not been particularly worried, only concerned at the growing anti-Catholic fury rising in England. The Queen's previous miscarriages had been female; even if a child should be born, he had supposed, it would be female also. Well, he had been wrong, and now the bells were ringing all over London and messages were going out to the ends of the earth. The time for delay and faint hopes had gone and the time for action had come. He had used up the last of his excuses.

Perhaps he had been cowardly to wait so long, he admitted, but he could not honestly blame himself. He had been morally obligated to exhaust every possibility of changing the King's mind before cutting his throat. He had known in advance that the effort would be futile, but he had made it anyway. He had reported the growing opposition to the King's measures, both at home and abroad. The only result had been to make the King more determined and obstinate. "So much the worse for them," James had said at each revelation, and had gone on his stubborn way infuriating the nation. Now, after his attacks upon the universities, the town charters, the laws, and the Church of England, he had convinced even the most rabidly loyal Tory squires that he must be stopped if England was to survive.

Ralph sighed. Perhaps he had not acted sooner because of Esther. Having a personal interest in the King's death complicated the problem. She had promised to marry him as soon as James was out of the way. If he had killed the King earlier, he could never have been sure that he had done the deed for the sake of England and Europe. He would have always retained a sneaking doubt that he had done it for himself. And then again, he admitted, there was the money. In the last two years—since he had discovered the King's treachery—he had made almost twenty-five hundred pounds. Was it possible that he had been content to see England and Europe pushed closer and closer to the brink of disaster because he was being well paid? Was he trading the liberties of England for a small estate? He did not think so. He hoped not.

Whatever the motives, he told himself frankly, he had made the situation more difficult by delay. When the King was assassinated, William and Mary would come as regents, not as king and queen—and regencies were almost always troublesome. In this case, the infant prince would have to be taken away from his mother and raised as a Protestant. England would take no more chances with popish monarchs. Perhaps Mary Beatrice and the Jesuits would try to escape abroad with the child, but this could easily be prevented.

He knew their routes and connections better than they did themselves. If he survived the assassination himself, nothing would go
wrong there.

If he survived the assassination. He smiled grimly to himself.
There was no reason to suppose he would not escape. He had no
accomplices, no one to inform or to turn King's evidence. He had
told no one his intentions. Oh, Catherine Sedley might guess, but
she would have no real evidence, and she would not appear against
him in spite of her threats. He was unlikely to be caught in the act.
In his three years with the King, he had never been interrupted in a
conference; he had been questioned outside by the palace guards
only two or three times. As for Warner, the sly, busy Jesuit who had
replaced Father Mansuete as James's confessor, he must be dis-
patched too; but this would present no great problem. It would also
be a public service, if not a pleasure. No, Ralph told himself as he
half-listened to the insistent bells, there was no reason why he should
not escape.

And suppose he were caught. Well, he would be hanged, drawn,
and quartered certainly. Everyone would pretend to be outraged—
especially the Church of England men, who would be the greatest
gainers by the deed. But secretly everyone would be relieved. More
important, they would be saved. King Louis, with his armies poised
now for an invasion of the Rhine provinces or the Netherlands,
would draw back in horror when he saw his arch rival William of
Orange at the head of the English fleet and army. He would not be
insane enough to attack a coalition of such overwhelming strength.

Ralph got up and began to pace slowly up and down his room.
One good thing, he supposed, about the delay was that it had accustomed him to the idea of killing the King. As far as he could
tell, he no longer had any particular feeling about the matter. Where
at first he had experienced fits of rage and indignation against the
King, periods of horror at his own depravity, and little tremors of
elation at the power in his hands, now he was merely tired of the
problem and anxious to get it over with. Surgeons must feel like
this, he told himself, before they amputate a leg.

"Pardon me, Sir. I heard you walking up and down, and I thought
you might want something."

Annie's ugly face had appeared in the door, and her eyes were
following him with dog-like concern.

Ralph smiled in spite of his pre-occupation. "No, I don't need anything, Annie," he said.

"I thought I would ask. You didn't look good when you came in, your worship."

She stepped inside, closed the door, and stood with her back against it.

"I fear I never look well to you, Annie," he said.

"That an't so, and you know it," she protested. "I know when you look bad and when you look healthy and tonight you look bad."

"You are very kind to concern yourself," he said. "I thought that tonight you would be out celebrating the birth of the crown prince."

"Not likely. Not me." She shook her head violently. "He's a fraud."

"A fraud?"

"Yes, a fraud. Haven't you heard, your worship?"

"Heard what?"

"Where have you been all day that you haven't heard the news?" Annie looked puzzled. "Her Majesty never had a son. The papists brought in that baby in a warming pan and put it in bed with her —that's what they did. The Queen never was even pregnant."

Ralph whistled. "Who told you this?"

"Everybody knows it."

"But who told you?" he repeated.

"Mrs. Hawkins, for one, and Mr. Green the butcher, and the costermonger, and Sammy Stiggins, that's who."

"Who told you first?"

"I'm sure I don't remember rightly unless it was Mr. Harris. You know Mr. Harris. He's a clerk for the India Company."

"Yes, I know Mr. Harris." Ralph remembered the tall, thin, colorless man. "Did he say where he got his information?"

"I didn't ask him, your worship. But what does it matter? Everybody knows it."

Evidently, Annie was dissatisfied with the expression on his face. "You see," she explained, "the King had sent Princess Anne out of town, and the Archbishop was in the Tower. The only witnesses were papists and runagate courtiers. They made sure that no honest Englishmen got to look inside that bedchamber."

Ralph tried to make his face impassive.

"And you really believe that the child is an impostor?"

"There an't a doubt of it," she said sharply. "Them papists are deep ones. Mr. Harris says they've been planning this for months. They even moved the Queen from Whitehall to Saint James so as the priests could sneak through the passages easier with the baby."

"I hate to tell you this," he said, "but your story is not true, Annie.

Unfortunately, the Queen did have a son. There was no warming pan and no fraud."

For a long moment, Annie said nothing. She stood with her back against the door and looked at him, her homely face full of suspicion and concern.

"You must not say things like that, your worship," she said finally. "People will say that you are a papist—or worse, an English traitor. And I know you an't."

Ralph allowed himself to remember the triumphant look on Walgrove's face. "She was bleeding like a stuck pig," the physician had said, "and that fool Heminges wanted to cauterize the rips, can you imagine that? I would not let him deliver my cow. 'You look after the prince,' I said, 'and I'll take care of this.' Well sir, inside of three minutes I had her stopped. I warrant you the King knows now which of us is the better man."

"Thank you for the warning, Annie," he was saying. "I don't want anyone to have ill thoughts about me. If you say that the child is an impostor, it must be true."

"Don't tease me, your worship." She drew herself up. "I can show you something in black and white that will prove what I say."

"Something in black and white?"

"Wait a moment, your worship, and I'll show you."

She disappeared through the door as suddenly as she had come.

It would have been laughable, Ralph thought, this refusal to admit the horrible truth, if it had not been so pathetic and so serious. Faced with the hopeless prospect of a popish heir, good Londoners were obviously trying to convince themselves and each other that no heir had been born. Apparently they were succeeding very well, judging from Annie's attitude.

For weeks before the birth, he had heard rumors around the country that the papists must be watched, that they were capable of producing a ready-made heir; but he had completely underestimated the will of patriotic Englishmen to believe this nonsense. It was almost incredible. Earnest, sober-minded people like Annie had swallowed the story in one gulp.

"Here it is, Sir." Annie was still breathless from running. "I told you I had it in black and white."

She handed him a single sheet of paper, printed on one side with large type. He hardly had to look at it to know what it would say.

POPISH IMPOSTURE

Citizens of London and All Good Englishmen. Be not deceived by the false Jesuitical *Imposture*, the cruel *Practice* and *Deception* perpetrated by the friends of Rome. The newborn child, styled Prince of Wales by the King and his *lewd Hirelings,* is *No Prince,* but the son of a *Labourer,* introduced into the Queen's bedchamber by *Stealth* and *Fraud* in order for to fasten *Popery* and *Slavery* upon Englishmen forever, and to perpetuate the *Tyranny* which we have watched grow daily amongst . . .

Ralph quit reading the words and began inspecting the type.

"Where and when did you get this?" he said.

"It was on the step an hour ago," she said. "I told you I had proof, your worship."

"So you did," he said.

God's wounds but they had worked fast, he said to himself. Within eight hours, they had concocted their story, set it up on their secret press, run it off, and distributed it through the streets of London. Whoever they were, they had the organization of the French Army and the audacity of pirates.

Almost as amazing as their feat of spreading broadsides was their success in spreading word-of-mouth rumors. The story that Annie had picked up from her acquaintances agreed in its essential details with the one related in the sheet. There were differences, of course, and there would undoubtedly be more as the story spread; but the resemblances were close enough to show that both stories had started from the same source.

"You won't repeat what you told me, will you, your worship?"

"What do you mean?"

"You won't say again that the fraud is not a fraud."

"No," he said, "I shall be more careful in the future."

"Thank you, Sir. I don't want to worry about you."

"And I don't want to worry about you, Annie; so please leave the broadside sheet with me. If you were caught with it in your possession, you would certainly lose your ears. The King's officers, you know, would consider it a treasonous libel."

"But I didn't write it," she protested.

"That would make little difference to your ears," he said. "Let me keep it, and I will see that it is safely destroyed."

"I think it's safer with me, Sir," she said stubbornly.

"Why with you?"

A flush spread over her uneven features, giving her a curious, mottled coloring.

"Because, Sir, I can afford to lose my ears more than you can."

"Nonsense, Annie. I would not consider risking your ears."

The devotion was embarrassing. All the more so because it was completely unfeigned.

"That's not the only reason, though, your worship." The blotches began to disappear. "I think you an't to be left with the paper because someone is watching you."

"Watching me?"

Ralph turned quickly to the window, but the curtains were safely drawn.

"I don't mean peeping in on you," she said. "I mean following you around."

He hoped he did not look startled. "Why didn't you tell me this before?" he said as calmly as he could.

"I wasn't sure until today, your worship."

"Are you sure now?"

"I think so, Sir. I don't think I could be wrong. You remember the day you passed by the fruit stalls on Little Sheere Lane, don't you? About two weeks ago Wednesday, it was."

"Yes," he said, "I think I do."

"Well, the landlady sent me there after cherries, and I saw you go by. I was about to call out, but you was walking pretty fast, and then I saw this man right after. He was walking fast too the same way, and it crossed my mind that he might be trying to catch up with you. But when I saw you last, he hadn't caught up at all."

Had someone really followed him to Whitehall that day? It was possible, of course, and yet it was not likely. Years of practice had made precautions against being followed a habit. Perhaps he had been growing careless just at the time when care was more necessary than ever.

"Is that all you saw?" he said.

"It was all I saw that day, your honor," she said. "I didn't think any more about it until this morning. When you left I was out sweeping the steps. Maybe you remember me; you said 'you're looking happy this morning, Annie.'"

"I remember."

"You hadn't been gone but a minute. I had just watched you turn the corner when I saw the same gentleman again. He must have come out of one of the doorways because he hadn't been on the street when I last looked. Anyway, your worship, he went off down the street after you and turned the same corner."

"You are sure it was the same man," he said.

"Positive, Sir." Annie nodded. "He was a big man, about the size of Mr. Smathers the chandler. I could tell he was a gentleman from

his clothes, but he didn't wear a wig and his hair was black. Both
times he was wearing a plain black coat and black breeches, only
it wasn't the same coat. The one today was longer and it had one
of them French collars—you know, with the low cut."

"Was there anything else?" he asked.

"No, your worship." Annie paused for thought. "Oh, he wore plain
shoes with silver buckles and a flat black hat like the one Mr. Sim-
mons wears."

"I see," he said. "Thank you for the information, Annie. You are
very thoughtful to keep such a close watch on me. If you see anything more, let me know at once."

"Do you think it is one of the King's men?" she said. "Do you
think they are trying to catch you?"

"No, Annie," he said reassuringly. "I don't think it is one of the
King's men. You must not worry. I am perfectly safe."

"I wish I could believe that, Sir. You don't know how it troubles
me when I think you're in danger. I wish you would tell me what
it is so as I could help you. I an't much to look at, but I can keep
my eyes open."

"You have helped me already," he said, "and you can help me
more by keeping everything you see and hear a secret between you
and me, and by not asking me questions."

"You may count on me, Sir." Her voice was solemn. "I have never
told anyone about you."

"You are a good girl, Annie," he said. "Now I think that if you
want to help me you should run back to your duties. The landlady
might ask questions if you are gone too long. Meanwhile I shall keep
the broadside and destroy it."

"But don't you want me to bring you a bite to eat, Sir?"

"No thank you, Annie. I am not hungry, and I have work to do."

For a few minutes after Annie had gone back to her work, Ralph
concentrated on the broadside. A cursory inspection was enough to
show that it had not been printed by any of the licensed printers
in London, whose typefaces and idiosyncrasies of setting he knew
by heart. Closer inspection with a magnifying glass showed that the
type, unlike the usual hodge-podge assembled by clandestine printers, was perfectly new. Obviously made in Holland, he thought, and
probably brought over especially for one important printing job. At
this moment, it was probably being broken down and scattered or
destroyed. No printer who valued his head would dare use it again.
Perhaps it was not too late even now to catch one of the distributors
in the act. If they had covered this area an hour or so ago, they

might be no more than a mile farther west. Catching the culprits seemed unlikely, however. No operation as elaborately organized as this was apt to fail for lack of elementary precautions.

And after all, why bother? Let them distribute their broadsides, he thought grimly. Once the King was put out of the way, the warming pan theory with all its absurdities would die overnight. When the danger from James and Louis was removed, people would be glad to admit that the little prince was legitimate. There were more important problems now. Who had been following him? And why? Was it possible that James had come to distrust him and was having him followed? Could it be the French? That sneaking Warner might easily have told his Jesuit friends. Half of them were French and the rest were French sympathizers. The King could have betrayed him inadvertently—to Sunderland, to Petre, to Melfort, to the Queen. Again, the Dutch or the Whigs, now that affairs were rapidly moving to a crisis, might have redoubled their efforts and stumbled upon his trail.

Yes, the possibilities were endless, he admitted. Annie's description was of little help, except in a negative way. It did not fit any of the men he had employed. There was only one sure way of finding out who the man was. He must be caught. And soon. Assassinating the King would be dangerous enough without being followed. Damn those bells. It was impossible to think straight. Perhaps the man was outside now. If one were to blow out the lights and open the curtain slightly, he might see something.

He had risen to his feet, and then rejected the notion as stupid, when he heard a tiny tap on the door. Before he could get to the door, it had opened and Esther had slipped quickly inside.

"I couldn't wait any longer to see you," she said. "What happened today changes everything."

"Yes, it does," he said, "but you should not have come."

She kissed him briefly and then stepped back.

"I know, but don't scold me. I was very careful. Your friendly watch dog didn't see me."

"My friendly watch dog sees everything, I find. She was in here only a few minutes ago."

Now that the surprise was wearing off, he was beginning to feel better.

"Really," she said. "Perhaps I should have come earlier. Sometime I must meet that young lady and find out all she knows about you."

"Why don't we sit down?" he said. "Since you are here, we may as well make the most of it."

He held out his hand, but instead of taking it she reached for the paper on the desk.

"I see you have read the news," she said. "Do you like it?"

He shrugged. "Aside from the fact that it is false, scandalous, libellous, and treasonable, it is excellent."

"You are too hard to please, Ralph. The important thing is that it is timely and effective."

Esther seated herself on the edge of the desk and crossed her knees. As she looked at Ralph, she swung her right foot contemplatively back and forth.

"It is an arrant lie, and you know it," he said, watching her carefully.

"Perhaps; perhaps not," she said. "As long as it helps to drive James out of the kingdom, I shall not enquire too closely. There will be plenty of time for the truth when we are all secure again."

"And you think it will help."

"Everything helps. This, I thought, was especially well calculated, since it will also create a doubt about the succession, and doubts about the succession are invaluable when one wishes to bridle kings."

"Is that why you wrote it?"

Esther laughed. "What makes you think I wrote it?"

"I don't mean that you wrote it with your own hands," he said. "I mean that you employed the man who did it—someone like our friend Mr. Keith, perhaps."

Now that the thought had occurred to him, he had a sudden clear conviction that he had hit upon the truth.

"Why do you say that?" she asked, still smiling.

"Simply because it has all the characteristics of your work," he said. "It is bold, carefully planned, and neatly executed."

"And shameless?"

She had ceased to smile now, and her foot had quit moving.

"If you will," he said.

"Never think it." Her tone was cold. "You know me well enough to know that I have more scruples than most; but where the lives and liberties of Englishmen are concerned, I will never let anything stop me from doing what must be done. And I won't have you calling me shameless."

"I am sorry, Esther," he said.

"You are sorry," she mocked. "Here we are with popery and slavery staring us in the face—with James and his damned army on our necks, with Louis and his cutthroats ready to march—and you are sorry because someone with enough courage to risk his head invents

the lies that may save us. If you feel that way, why aren't you out
on the street lighting a bonfire with the rest of James's pimps and
panders?"

"Please be calm, Esther," he said quietly, "and refrain from twisting my words."

"I am calm," she said icily. "I was never so calm in my life."

He listened a moment before replying. He could hear only the
sound of the bells.

"Don't misunderstand me," he said slowly. "I agree that James
must be stopped, and stopped quickly. I am not sure, however, that
lies about the prince's birth will help."

"Very well," she said. "We will not argue about it."

"I am curious, though. Were you responsible for the broadside?"

"Why are you so anxious to know?" she said. "Do you think I
would tell you if I were?"

"I thought you might," he said. "I don't see why you should not.
We trust each other, don't you remember?"

She put down the paper and turned to face him more squarely.
"Yes," she said, her voice softening a little, "we trust each other, but
we never agreed to tell each other everything. You have your secrets; I have mine. This is one of mine."

"As you wish," he said.

It had been stupid to ask, he supposed, yet the refusal made him
uneasy. Did Esther seriously believe that he might betray her? Had
two years taught her so little about him? Or had he merely angered
her by criticizing the broadside? Once again he felt the little shiver
of estrangement that baffled him from time to time.

"But I will tell you one thing, Ralph." She reached out and took
his hand, almost as if she had read his thoughts. "At this moment,
the printer and the author are on the Thames in a fast ketch bound
for Rotterdam."

"I am not surprised," he said.

"You realize, of course, that I admit nothing."

"Yes," he said. "I realize it."

"Then why don't you kiss me and quit looking as if you were
about to be hanged?"

"Perhaps I am," he said softly, taking her in his arms.

A long minute later, Esther pushed him gently away.

"We won't have long to wait now, darling," she said. "Within a
few months it will be over one way or another."

"Yes," he said, "I think it will. Perhaps even sooner."

"I am glad now that the Queen did not miscarry. I have grown very tired of waiting, haven't you?"

"Very tired."

"Now we will have a brush for it," she said.

"Yes," he said, "I suppose we will."

"I am glad of that too. Fighting is better than waiting."

"I don't know," he said. "It depends upon who does the fighting."

"Not upon who does the fighting, but upon who wins. I think we can win."

"You are not sure, then."

Esther sighed. "Not sure enough. There are too many *ifs* involved. We can win *if* the Dutch are willing to risk an army and a fleet with Prince William, *if* King Louis fails to attack the Dutch borders before the Dutch army is launched, *if* the English will revolt against James, and *if* James's army and navy are seriously weakened by defections. I hope and believe that all these things will happen, but I could wish the complications were fewer."

Ralph admired her crisp summary of the situation.

"Yes," he said, "there are too many *ifs*."

Esther sighed again. "Still, we must take our chances. We must fight for it now or it will be too late. From now on, every moment we delay gives James and Louis more time to enslave us."

"What do you intend to do?"

Still holding his hand, Esther looked at him curiously. "Do you think I should tell you?" she said.

"Yes," he said. "That is, if you trust me and want to marry me."

"You swear that you won't tell anyone?"

"I didn't think it was necessary, but I swear if it will make you feel better."

"It does," she said. "I know it sounds horrible to be so suspicious, but this is a matter of life and death."

"But I have a right to know," he said. "Our future depends upon what happens in the next few weeks—or less."

"Yes," she said, watching him steadily. "It does. That is why Father, George, and I are sailing for Holland next Thursday. We will openly join with the Prince of Orange."

So that was it. The Hemphills were ready to throw off the mask and stake everything on the outcome of the battle.

"I see," he said.

"Are you surprised?"

"Not exactly," he said, "although I had supposed that you might do the revolution more good by staying in Somersetshire to organize the Western counties."

"We can't stay." Her voice sounded as if she were explaining a problem in arithmetic. "At the first sign of trouble we would be arrested. Then we would be of no use to anyone. In Holland, Father's money and reputation may do much good. At this time, an overt gesture is important. Others can take care of the Western counties."

In other words, Ralph said to himself, they are already satisfied with their organization in the West, and content to leave it to their subordinates. Judging from the information he had collected, their estimate was probably right.

"I take it, then, that I won't see you again until after the revolution."

"No, you won't," she said, "unless perhaps you would like to come with us. I think I could persuade Father."

"It is impossible," he said. "I have work to do here."

"What kind of work?"

"I think that I can do more for the nation by staying here than by going to Holland."

"What kind of work?"

"Oh, I think I may be able to sow a little sedition in the army."

"Is that all?" Her expression did not change, but her voice registered disappointment.

"Isn't that enough? You yourself just said that everything depends upon disrupting the King's army."

"It does," she said, "but that is work for generals and not for lieutenants and lawyers."

"There is work for everyone, I should say."

"No doubt," she said slowly, "I hoped, however, that you had thought of something more vital."

"Such as what?"

"Oh, I don't know—just something more vital."

"I can't think of anything more vital," he said. "Can you?"

"I don't know, Ralph," she said. "Probably not. And yet, if no one thinks of something vital, there is a good chance that you and I will never see each other again."

"Don't worry," he said. "We will see each other again—and soon, I hope."

"What makes you so sure?"

"I don't know," he said quietly. "As you said a long time ago, we won't fail."

"I still think so and hope so," she said taking his other hand, "but I hate the thought of leaving you here, and I hate the *ifs*."

"I do too," he said, "but it can't be helped."

Esther slid off the desk suddenly. Momentarily, he thought she was going to kiss him again. Instead she walked over by the bed and sat down in a chair. For a while she sat silent as if listening to the bells and the cannon.

"Wouldn't it be nice," she said finally, "if something were to happen to the King?"

"What do you mean?" he said, feeling his pulses begin to quicken.

"I mean that it would be nice if the King were to meet with an accident—or perhaps a fatal illness—in the near future. Don't you think so?"

"It would be excellent." He kept his tone flat and noncommittal. "But I am surprised to hear you say so. Didn't you tell me long ago that you wanted nothing to happen to the King?"

She leaned back in the chair, resting her head against the top of it and exposing a lovely expanse of white throat.

"Yes, I said so." She seemed to be talking to herself. "And I meant it. Since that time, however, he has done all I expected him to do. He has made popery and absolutism odious; he has made the Tory doctrine of divine right and nonresistance absurd. Having served his purpose admirably, he can be dispensed with."

"I see."

"Oh I confess that I should prefer to see him driven from the throne than removed accidentally. I should like to see you Tories in the field against the King with weapons in your hands, so that you could never lie your way out of your responsibility for getting rid of him. I should also like to see disputes about the succession. But when I consider the hazards that face the revolution, I could be content with something less drastic, and more certain."

"So could I," he said.

"And then," she said, "our troubles would be over, and I would not have to part from you."

It occurred to Ralph suddenly that their voices were unnaturally loud. In spite of the bells, the sound seemed to fill the room. He walked over to the door and opened it. No one was there. He went to the window, cautiously drew back the curtain a little way, and looked out. There were two small bonfires on the street now, each with a tiny knot of people standing around it; but there was no one near the window. When he returned, he seated himself on the bed beside Esther.

"Were you planning an accident for the King?" he said quietly.

Esther looked up at him. "No," she said. "None of my family or friends could ever get the opportunity, or hope to escape. I was only wishing."

"It is odd," he said. "I have been wishing the same thing. And I have a strange premonition that our wish is going to come true."

"You have?"

"Yes."

"Is the premonition strong as well as strange?"

"Very strong."

"Is it this premonition that makes you so confident of our future?"

"Yes."

Esther nodded understandingly. When she spoke her voice was still quiet and cool.

"Do you have any evidence upon which to base your strong premonition?"

"No visible evidence—merely a strong feeling."

"Do you know how the accident is going to happen?"

"Not precisely. If I did, I shouldn't tell you. I should not like you to be implicated, even in a remote way, in any accidents that might befall the King."

"But I suppose you know who will be on the scene of the accident."

"In a general way, perhaps; but again, one can never be sure who will appear at an accident, and I would not wish to speculate."

"I approve your caution, Ralph," she said. "I should not have asked the questions. There is something that concerns me directly —both of us, in fact. Do you think that this mischance will occur before I leave for Holland?"

"Yes," he said. "I think it will. You said you were leaving this week, didn't you?"

"Thursday."

"If my premonition is correct—if the accident happens at all—it will have happened by that time."

"Good. If there is an accident, I shall undoubtedly hear of it. I will send you a message. If there is no accident, you will not see me or hear from me until I return with the Prince."

"Perhaps it would be well if you and your family kept out of town until Thursday. One cannot be too careful where these things are concerned. If you were two or three hours down the river, you could still get any news in plenty of time. It might be well, too, if you were seen constantly. Some Tory friends might be useful."

"I know a place," she said.

"Good."

Esther rose from her chair and seated herself beside him on the bed.

"In case anything should go wrong," she said, "either with the mishap or with the revolution—if I should not see you again—I want you to know I love you. I hope you will remember that."

"I shall remember," he said, "and you must remember too."

"You don't think anything can go wrong with the accident, do you?"

"No," he said. "Nothing will go wrong."

"Are you sure?"

He managed a smile. "Positive."

"In that case," she said, bringing her face up close to his, "let's not wait any longer."

"Do you mean now?" he said. "Here?"

The flush on her face deepened, and he could see the pulse beating at the base of her neck.

"Yes," she said, "I mean now and here."

She began unfastening her bodice, never taking her eyes off him.

"No," she said. "Don't try to help me. I will do this. You make sure the door is locked and then blow out the candles."

CHAPTER

Twenty

THERE WAS A RED blotch on Warner's neck, just above his clerical collar. Looking at it, Ralph was fascinated. He barely listened to what the man was saying. The blotch looked as if it had been put there on purpose to serve as a target, or as if the wound had been prepared in advance. It was an effort for Ralph to keep his hand away from the hilt of his sword in anticipation. He hunched his shoulders forward, forcing them to relax a little, and then shifted the weight of his body in the chair. He did not want to look like a cat about to spring. He must wait calmly until the King arrived and Warner had moved into the outer room. To kill Warner before killing the King would be insane.

"His Majesty will be delayed a few moments," Warner said. "He is conferring with Milord Sunderland."

"Very well," Ralph said. "There is no hurry about my business."

"If you would care to leave any message with me," Warner said smoothly, "I would be glad to give it to His Majesty."

"No, thank you," he said. "My message is confidential."

If Warner grasped the implication that he was not to be trusted, he gave no sign. Probably, Ralph thought, it had never occurred to Warner that he was repulsive, with his dead-halibut face, his officious manner, and his ill-concealed self importance. Or perhaps it had.

"His Majesty is much changed since the birth of the Prince," Warner said. "He is almost transported with joy—as, indeed, we all are."

"So the Countess of Dorchester tells me," Ralph said.

He could not resist the opportunity to deflate Warner. Nothing was so sure to pique him as the reminder that in spite of his efforts the King continued to visit Catherine Sedley.

"Indeed?" Warner was striking back with all the weapons at

his command. "I did not know that you were intimate with the Countess."

"Not intimate," Ralph parried, feeling a little ashamed now for teasing a poor devil who had less than half an hour to live. "Only friendly."

"I must say," Warner said, "that you do not seem particularly happy over the birth of the Prince."

"I am overcome," he said. "It was the most important event in my life."

"It was a blessed miracle," Warner said fervently, as if challenging Ralph to deny it.

Ralph watched Warner's Adam's apple move up and down under the blotch on his throat.

"At least a miracle," he said. "In fact, it may prove to be the salvation of England."

Warner eyed him suspiciously. "I did not think you were a Catholic, Mr. Barnard."

"I am not," Ralph said quietly, "but I know a miracle when I see one. Nothing but a miracle could have changed so many plans so quickly."

"I am afraid you are being merry, Mr. Barnard, and in very poor taste."

"On the contrary," Ralph said, "I am in deadly earnest."

Warner was unconvinced. "Eventually," he said, "you will see the full effects of the miracle."

"I have seen some of them already," Ralph said, "but I doubt that either of us will live to see the full effects."

The trick, he was thinking, is to make the first blow count. If the King cries out before he dies, the affair may get sticky. The stab should be at the base of the throat through the windpipe. After that, a finishing blow through the heart. It should not be difficult. Thank God for heavy drapery and thick walls.

"If only I live to see the little Prince crowned, I shall be satisfied," Warner said.

That will be soon, Ralph thought, but you won't be there to see it.

He had locked the outer door to the apartment as he had come in, and put the key in his pocket. Even if Warner heard suspicious sounds, he would not be able to escape that way. James would lock the inner door when he arrived, making them safe from disturbance from the rest of the palace.

"I did not know that you wanted to outlive His Majesty," he said.

As he had rehearsed the deed in his imagination, he would dispatch James with two quick blows, then call Warner from the outer room and stab him before he could recover from his surprise.

"I meant no disrespect to His Majesty," Warner said stiffly.

"I am sure you did not," Ralph said. "I too believe that you will outlive him."

He did not feel excited, he assured himself—only tensed for action, and uncommonly alert. Last night, of course, it had been difficult to go to sleep, but once asleep he had slept well. Now he felt like a runner about to begin a race.

Warner was hastening to repair the damage.

"I expect His Majesty to live for many years," he said.

"It is possible."

"He is fortunate in choosing his friends and servants."

At any other time, Ralph knew, he would have laughed at such a statement; now he merely shrugged.

"I might add that he is especially fond of you," Warner said.

"Please don't bother with compliments," Ralph said. "I won't tell the King."

"Tell him what?"

"That you are anxious for his death."

Warner's pallid face went a shade whiter. "I said no such thing," he said.

"You said such a thing," Ralph said, "but I am sure you did not mean it. You may rely upon me to keep the little slip secret."

This was cruel, he knew, but perhaps it would shut the man's mouth. He was tired of being told how much James trusted him. Adda, Young Berwick, Kit, Mansuete, and now Warner. It was too much.

"What is the matter with you today?" Warner said, recovering from the blow. "Why are you trying to be unpleasant?"

"I am not trying," he said flatly. "I am unpleasant by nature."

Warner's fish-like face broke into a grimace faintly resembling a smile.

"Now I know you have been making sport of me," he said. "In the year I have known you, I have never seen you unpleasant. I have always considered you my entire friend."

Was it possible? Ralph asked himself. Could this cold, repulsive creature, this conniving knave, seriously believe that he was liked? Could he have taken the small crumbs of politeness that Ralph had thrown him, the normal courtesies, and used them to nourish an affection? Could he have ignored the little gibes or interpreted them as friendly banter?

No. Ralph refused to believe it. He refused to consider this black-frocked zealot a member of the human race. It was much more convenient to consider him a salamander.

Warner continued to smile.

"I think you have been working too hard," he said. "I fear that you have been carrying your devotion to His Majesty beyond reasonable bounds."

"These are not reasonable times," Ralph heard himself say.

He must not clutter his mind with extraneous considerations. He must keep his perspective sharp and clear, or he might bungle his task. For all practical purposes, it made no difference whether Warner was a man or one of the inferior reptiles. He must be cut down. The lives of better men, or reptiles, than he depended upon it. Again Ralph let his eyes wander to the blotch on the man's neck.

"I think I hear the King," Warner said.

Ralph stood up quickly, hitching his sword belt as he did so, then rubbing his hands together to warm them. Warner went to the door.

The King entered rapidly, passed Warner without a word, and threw himself into his customary chair.

"They won't believe it," he said, his voice shaking with agitation.

"Won't believe what, Your Majesty?"

Ralph was surprised but not disconcerted by the unusual turn of events. He quickly made his bow, and then poised himself in front of the King, ready to draw his sword as soon as the moment should arrive. Warner, he noticed, was standing stupidly by the door, staring at James.

"They say the Prince is not my son."

The King was making no effort to control his emotion. There were tears in his eyes, whether of rage or grief Ralph could not tell. They were spilling out from under his heavy eyelids, running down his lank cheeks, and dropping onto his lace collar.

"Did Milord Sunderland give you the news?" Ralph said slowly.

The opportunity was perfect now if Warner would lock the door and get out. James's collar was open exposing his throat; his eyes full of tears.

"Yes," James said. "The dogs, the English curs."

"I am surprised that Milord Sunderland should tell you," Ralph said. "If he has begun telling the truth, he is losing his nerve."

He made a motion with his head, but Warner ignored it. Only the King's command, Ralph saw, would get him away from a conversation like this.

The King wiped his eyes with his cuff.

"But why, Ralph? Why should they believe such a story?"

"What did you expect?" Ralph said brutally. He wished James would not call him by his first name. "Did you think the nation would welcome a Catholic heir?"

James straightened up in the chair. The tears were still flowing, but his voice was steadier.

"You must do something, Ralph. You must find the spreaders of this foul slander and arrest them."

"There are not jails enough in England to hold them, Your Majesty. I can't arrest nine-tenths of the population."

"But you must do something."

"Do something?" Ralph exploded. "God's wounds, Your Majesty, I have done everything possible. For three years I have warned you that you were fatally antagonizing the nation, that you were digging your grave; but you chose to listen to knaves like Sunderland and Petre. Now that it is too late, you ask me to do something."

James's face went white.

"How dare you speak to me like this? How dare you presume on my affection for you? I have thought of you as an elder son, but I warn you, I can think of you as a rebel and a traitor."

The tears were gone now and the mouth was set in its familiar line.

Oh God, Ralph thought wearily, not again—not another expression of affection. Why can't the poor old idiot remain in character? Why must he use up his last moments in calling me his son? Damn his soul anyway.

"I could wish, Your Majesty," he said coldly, "that you had cared for me enough to listen to me; then I would not be obliged to speak to you like this."

The King's mouth worked, but no sound came out.

"You have thrown your chances away." Ralph heard his tone become more violent. "Now it is too late—do you understand—too late."

Warner, he saw, was standing in stunned horror.

"Your subjects have endured all they will take. They have decided to be rid of you."

This was useless and cruel, he was thinking. The King would never understand why he was being executed. Yet for once in his life he deserved to hear the brutal truth, even though it came too late to do any good.

Ralph balanced himself on the balls of his feet, waiting for James to begin blustering again; but James sat as if paralyzed—his arms limp, his eyes blank, and his mouth drooping.

Damn him, Ralph thought. I wish he would quit looking like an old mastiff.

Suddenly the expression came back into the King's face—the look of a man waking from a bad dream.

"You are wrong, Ralph," he said in a voice unexpectedly calm and reasonable. "My subjects love me."

Ralph felt his shoulders sag. He came down hard on his heels.

"They will support me," James went on, "against the few conspirators you have warned me against."

The few conspirators. Ralph wanted to scream. All his work for the last two years had been utterly wasted. James had learned nothing. He still thought that his opposition came from a few malcontents. He refused to admit that he had infuriated all England.

"Besides, I also have a loyal army." James's mouth tightened a little. "If the nation neglects its duty, my army will remind them of it."

What can one expect, Ralph asked himself. If the perverse old dog ever admitted to himself how odious he is, he would cut his own throat.

"And I also have you," James said. "I know that your unseemly words proceed from your love and loyalty. From anyone else they would be treason, but I forgive you."

Ralph looked from James to Warner, who was now beginning to relax, although the sweat was pouring from his forehead.

They were two of a kind, Ralph thought—a pathetic pair of self-deluded bigots.

"As long as the Prince and I have you to help us," James continued, "we need not fear the lies and slanders of our enemies. They will learn who is king of England."

It was maddening, Ralph thought, to stand here bandying words with James while the time for action oozed away. Somehow, he felt, he had been thrown off stride. If he were not careful, he would bungle his mission. He must get rid of Warner immediately.

"You flatter me," he heard himself say.

"Not at all. My only fear is that you have been working too hard, Ralph. You look ill. You must take a few days' rest. Then our enemies will not look so powerful."

"That is what I told him, Your Majesty." Warner finally spoke. "He is killing himself for Your Majesty's service."

James looked around.

"Are you still here? I thought you had gone."

Warner flushed. "I intended to go, Your Majesty. I thought perhaps you might want me."

"No, Father." James softened the blow a little. "I will call you if I need you."

"Very well, Your Majesty."

Warner started toward the outer room.

"Please lock this door before you go," James said. "I have important things to discuss with Mr. Barnard, and I don't want to be interrupted."

At last. Ralph felt his tenseness return with a rush as he watched Warner fumble with the lock. Perhaps now he would lose the nightmarish sensation of being unable to move. As soon as Warner got out of the room, there would be nothing to upset the plan—nothing, that is, unless he were ill. And he was not ill. A little feverish perhaps from the strain, but not ill. All morning he had been clear-headed and alert. On the way to Whitehall he had stopped and doubled back several times to see if he were followed, but he had seen no one. He was inclined to believe that Annie's mysterious spy was a product of her imagination. When he had arrived at Whitehall, he had avoided the guard. No. He was neither ill nor mad. Now that Warner was going, he was ready to strike.

"The Countess of Dorchester and I were talking about you yesterday," James said as Warner left the room.

"Indeed, Your Majesty?" Ralph glanced at the door to make sure that it was tightly closed.

"The Countess convinced me that I have treated you shabbily."

"Shabbily? On the contrary, Your Majesty, you have treated me very generously."

Damn Kit, he thought. Why doesn't she mind her own affairs and leave me alone?

"No, Ralph. She is right." James's face showed unusual animation. "I know now that I have failed in my duty toward you."

"Your duty?"

"Yes, my duty. When you accepted service with me, you had a right to expect advancement and public recognition. I have given you neither. Other men have advanced to fame and wealth."

Indeed they have, Ralph sneered to himself, and they may soon advance to the end of a rope.

"But I intend to make amends for my neglect," James went on. "Within the week, you will be known as Sir Ralph Barnard."

"No, Your Majesty, for God's sake no. You must not say things like that."

"Why not?" James's long face was drawn into a grotesque expression of concern.

"Because you are making my duty impossible."

"Impossible?"

"Yes, impossible."

I must stab him now and get out before he says anything more, Ralph thought. In a moment I shall be screaming.

"No, no, Ralph," James said. "It will not be impossible. The Countess made that clear."

"Made what clear?"

His left hand was clenched around the scabbard of his sword, but his right hand refused to grasp the hilt.

"I can knight you for your legal work without any mention of your more vital services. You can still collect information."

"No, Your Majesty, I must refuse. It is impossible."

He had the impression that he was yelling, although he could hardly hear his voice. If only he could draw his sword, he could put an end to this.

"The Countess warned me that you would be difficult. I insist, however, that you obey me. This is a command."

"Very well, Your Majesty," he said.

I must begin all over again, he thought. I must make myself relax.

"For my work," he said, "the less I am known the better. Still, if Your Majesty commands me to accept a title, I cannot disobey."

James rubbed his right hand across his neck.

"Do I have something on my throat, Ralph?"

"No, Your Majesty."

"I thought there might be some dirt on it. You have been staring at it all the time we have been speaking."

"Have I, Your Majesty? I must have been admiring your collar."

He forced himself to look James squarely in the eyes.

"Having a title may make your work a little more difficult, but it will please me very much to give it to you, and it will be a public recognition of your worth. Later, I intend to appoint you a member of the Prince's household. I want you to be responsible for his safety as you have been for mine."

"I shall be honored," Ralph said slowly.

"You must thank the Countess for this plan," James said. "I might not have thought of it. As soon as she pointed it out, I saw at once how much my future and that of the Prince depend upon you. It is only fair that I should take care of your future too."

Ralph closed his eyes momentarily. Yes, he thought, your future,

such as it is, depends upon me—and the Prince's too. And damn
Kit to hell. Whatever possessed her to put me in this position? Does
she think a knighthood from James is an honor? Or does she want
me publicly branded as a traitor to the nation just as she is publicly
branded a whore?

"What is the matter, Ralph?" James said. "You look terribly ill."

"Ill, Your Majesty?" He passed his hand across his forehead. "No,
I am not ill."

Or was she trying to bind him again to their bargain? What was
it she had said long ago? Something like, "You and I will take care of
the King and let God take care of the Kingdom." Did she suppose
that he could be bribed with titles and positions to remain faithful
to James and betray the nation?

"Please sit down, Ralph," James was saying. "You must not stand
when you are indisposed."

"You must pardon me, Your Majesty," he heard himself say. "I
never sit in Your Majesty's presence. I assure you that I am all right.
I am merely overwhelmed by the sudden honor."

Or did she think that she could arouse his sympathy and pity for
the King? Did she think he was so weak as to let personal gratitude
and pity turn him from his duty?

"You should not be overwhelmed, Ralph." James looked pleased
with himself. "You have deserved the honor."

With an effort, Ralph squared his shoulders and flexed the fingers
of his right hand. They were not paralyzed after all. They could
grasp the sword now, he was sure. The King was sitting straight in
his chair, his red neck framed by the white collar and green coat.

"Pardon me, Your Majesty. What did you say?"

"I said that you have deserved the honor."

Somewhere down the river, Esther would be waiting for the news.
If none came, tomorrow's tide would see her off to Holland. He must
not fail her. She had paid him in advance for the murder.

"Would you care to call Warner and have him bring us some
wine?" James said. "I think some wine would help."

"I can get it, Your Majesty," he said.

Paid in advance, he thought as he went to the cabinet. Yes, Esther
had paid him with the understanding that the King would be killed.
For a moment he let himself think of the payment—the enveloping
warmth, the struggling passion, and finally the delicious languor. He
could still hear her tortured breathing gradually subside into con-
tentment.

Ralph leaned against the cabinet as he opened it and brought out the bottle. Of course, he had not told her that he intended to do the killing himself. She could not blame him personally if the plan miscarried. Or could she?

He poured the wine into the silver goblets. His hand, he noticed, did not shake. It looked resolute and competent as it measured the drinks, as if it were capable of anything and would never again disobey his will. Perhaps it had been right in refusing to act before, in waiting for a better opportunity. James would tip up the goblet and present his throat to his executioner, and the hand would be ready.

"Here it is, Your Majesty," he said, dropping to one knee to present the cup.

"Thank you, Ralph," James said. "Please rise."

As Ralph got to his feet and poised himself again, James raised his glass.

"The wine will make you feel better," he said. "Would you join me in a toast?"

"Yes, Your Majesty. Propose it."

He shifted the goblet from his left hand to his right, ready to shift it back again the moment the King put his goblet to his lips. Meantime, he looked James steadily in the eye, waiting for him to speak.

James's sour face broke into a smile.

"To the King's friends," he said. "May they always protect him."

"To the King's friends," Ralph repeated mechanically. "May they always protect him."

The King put the goblet to his lips, threw back his head, and tossed off the wine. Ralph made no movement. He stood frozen in position while the red neck presented itself to be stabbed; his right hand clutched the goblet and his left hung uselessly at his side. He had not made the slightest attempt to reach for his sword.

"What is the matter now?" he heard James say.

His own voice sounded far away. "Nothing, Your Majesty," it said. He raised the goblet absently to his lips and drank a swallow.

"May they always protect him," he repeated.

"But Ralph, you are weeping."

"You must be mistaken, Your Majesty," he said in a flat, steady voice. "The wine was stronger than I thought."

He had no sensation of weeping and yet he could feel tears run down his cheeks. God's wounds, what ignominy. It was not enough that he had failed like a miserable coward. Now he must weep like a woman.

"Small wonder that you should weep," the King said, his voice hardening. "The way those villainous Whigs slandered the Prince would make anyone weep. I was weeping myself a few minutes ago."

"Yes, Your Majesty."

What had ever given him the notion that he was capable of killing the old dog in cold blood? He knew now that he could never do the deed. Kit was right, he thought wearily. She had known him better than he had known himself. At this moment, standing here snivelling, he was more convinced than ever that the King's death was absolutely necessary, and yet he was powerless.

"But we will have our revenge," James was saying. "You find the wretches and I will have them hanged."

"The printer and the author are already in Holland, Your Majesty." He wiped his eyes with his sleeve.

He refused to make excuses for himself, or to find reasons for his failure. It was enough to know that he had betrayed everyone. Tomorrow Esther would make for Holland. God knew whether he would ever see her again. Probably not. When she found he had been knighted by the King she would consider him a traitor. Within days, the ponderous machinery of war and revolution would begin to move—impossible to stop, once in motion. And here he stood listening to the King making his foolish threats of vengeance against the nation.

"I will have the Prince of Orange send them back," James snapped. "Meantime you must find the rogues who hired them, and you must arrest anyone whom you find repeating the poisonous slander."

"I am afraid, Your Majesty, that the Prince will not send them back. He will bring them back, along with an army. As for the rogues who hired them, if they are not in Holland already, they will be there soon."

No, he thought dully. I may be too cowardly and scrupulous to kill the King, but I am not so base as to hand over the Hemphills or their accomplices. Let them get away and do their worst. Perhaps they can help God save England.

James set his jaw.

"My son-in-law would not dare bring an army against me."

"We have discussed this before, Your Majesty," Ralph said wearily. "And I must tell you again, the Prince of Orange dares to do anything. He will not hesitate to bring his army."

"So much the worse for him. Let him come if he dares. My army is twice as big as his."

"I agree, Your Majesty. But his army is undoubtedly loyal."

Ralph ground his teeth, and cursed himself for his futility. He felt

weak and nauseated. He wanted to get out into the fresh air, away
from these monotonous arguments which always angered the King
and never convinced him. He wanted to go hide somewhere and
forget about everything.

"And you think that my army is not loyal, is that it?" The veins
were beginning to stand out on the King's forehead.

"I am not sure, Your Majesty," Ralph said. "I intend to find out."

"I tell you that they are loyal," James said hotly. "Why shouldn't
they be loyal? They are well clothed, well armed, and well fed. They
will obey their commanders."

There was no use telling James that the commanders were as little
to be trusted as the men. After all, most of the commanders were
Englishmen too. They might fight for James, or they might not.
Lately, Ralph thought, he had detected a great deal of unrest and
dissatisfaction among the troops, but no actual conspiracy.

"I should not like to trust the army too far," he said. "When the
Prince invades us, he will make every attempt to subvert the loyalty
of your troops."

"They will remain loyal," James said stubbornly.

"We shall soon have a chance to see, Your Majesty," Ralph said.

"Nonsense. The Prince will never come."

Ralph did not trust himself to speak. He had endured too much
already. If he opened his mouth, he feared, he would begin to curse
—or possibly to weep again. All he hoped for now was to get through
the rest of the interview.

He noted absently that he was still holding the goblet. With a
sigh he drank the rest of the wine. Then he returned the cups to
the cabinet, conscious all the time that James was watching him
curiously.

"You have not been yourself today, Ralph," James said. "When
we meet next week, you will be Sir Ralph Barnard. Perhaps that
will help. And I shall be more composed. I confess that I was overcome by those ungrateful wretches."

"Yes, Your Majesty," he said weakly. What was it Kit had said?
"Someone must look after simpletons." That was it. Suddenly he felt
a great wave of pity for the King. Poor stubborn old idiot. Poor,
lost, infuriating, impossible son of a whore. It was not James's fault
that he had been born to a position that he was incompetent to
handle—that he was a stubborn fool surrounded by supple knaves.
Even his desire to tyrannize was pathetic, the attempt of an un-
lovable child to gain respect by becoming a bully. As for his bigotry,
what was it but the desperate grasping of a narrow mind for safety

and assurance, in a world beyond its understanding? Most pitiful of all were his transparent, fumbling efforts to buy love and friendship. The poor devil was like the rich boy who is tolerated only because he can furnish the sweetmeats.

"For the present," James was saying, "I should like you to give your attention to the villains responsible for the slander. Later, you may return to your investigation of the fleet and the army."

"Very well, Your Majesty," Ralph said. "I will do what I can."

James rose from his chair and offered his hand to be kissed. There was a self-satisfied smirk upon his face, like the look of an incorrigible child who had once more had his own way. As Ralph bowed and kissed the hand, another brief spasm of anger shook him. Trying to protect the King, he thought, was as futile as trying to manage an artful, determined drunkard who refuses to be diverted from ruining himself.

After the King had left the room, Ralph sank into a chair. For perhaps five minutes, he sat there without moving and without trying to think coherently. It was enough to sit with his eyes closed while he recruited his strength. He felt as if he had absorbed a violent beating. Even his bones felt tired. Finally, he became aware that Warner had entered the room. He refused to give the man the satisfaction of seeing him defeated. He had done more than enough in sparing his life. With a great effort of will, he forced himself to spring to his feet.

"Is anything the matter?" Warner asked.

"Nothing at all," Ralph said peevishly. "I was merely thinking of Father Mansuete. When he had this apartment, it was more comfortable."

"I shall be happy to make any changes you suggest," Warner said.

"I am afraid that you won't have time," Ralph said.

He watched Warner turn pale again.

"The King is not angry with me, is he?"

"Not at all."

Ralph shrugged his shoulders. What was the use of relieving his frustration by baiting Warner?

"I merely meant," he added, "that you will be too busy in the next few months to think of trivial things like comfort."

Warner looked doubtful and a little stricken. Even knaves like Warner, Ralph thought wearily, must have their problems. What hell it must be to live at the whim of authority. Almost as bad as being an unsuccessful assassin.

"Cheer up, Warner," he said. "You have my word that the King will not dismiss you."

"You are very kind to say so," Warner said.

Ralph picked up his hat and squared his shoulders. Some of the color was coming back into Warner's dead countenance.

"No, the King won't dismiss you," he said finally, "but it is only fair to tell you that the nation will."

Ralph had no remembrance of finding his way outside. He became aware of his surroundings only when the door closed behind him. For a moment he stared at the palace grounds as if seeing them for the first time. The next moment both his arms were seized and pinioned by two huge guardsmen and he was thrust back against the door. Within five seconds two officers appeared. One drew his sword and held the point against Ralph's throat.

"Here he is," the other officer said.

"Don't make a move," the man with the sword warned, "or you are a dead man."

"Now then, corporal. Let go his arm and go warn the others. Have them inspect this apartment thoroughly. I fear the worst."

"Murdering swine. We'll teach you a lesson."

Ralph stood perfectly still while one of the men dropped his arm and disappeared. Although he could feel the point of the sword trembling against the base of his neck and see the clenched teeth of the officer who threatened him, he was not alarmed. The surprise had shocked him out of his futile apathetic rage. For the first time in days, he felt as if he were really in command of his senses—as if the violence had brought him back to sanity.

"If you will tell me what you are talking about," he said coolly, "perhaps I can help you."

"Keep your mouth shut," the shorter officer snapped, giving him a tiny jab with the sword.

"You know well enough what we mean," the other said. "We saw you go in."

"Perhaps you would like to see my pass." He spoke slowly and calmly, keeping his eyes fixed on the man with the sword.

"Bugger your pass," the man said. "We want to see what you did."

"Don't waste time talking with him, Jeremy," the other officer said.

The guardsman holding Ralph's arm gave it an additional twist.

"There now, your honor," he said. "Maybe that will stop your tongue."

Ralph waited a moment to get used to the pain.

"The King won't like this," he said through his teeth.

The guardsman started a little and relaxed his hold, but the man with the sword did not waver.

"I don't think the King will ever know," he said. "Get his sword, Thomas."

The taller officer pulled Ralph's sword out of its scabbard and inspected it.

"There is nothing on it," he said. Ralph could sense disappointment in his voice.

"Then he did it with something else," the other said.

Ralph forced himself to smile. "What did you expect?" he said.

He received another little jab for his pains.

"Keep your mouth shut, I tell you," the swordsman said.

"As you wish," Ralph said. "We shall have plenty of time to talk when your men make their report."

He could feel a little trickle of blood from the man's answering jab, but he did not care. The whole thing had become clear to him now, and he was finding a bitter pleasure in his position. For the present he was content to wait.

His reply appeared to have upset the taller officer.

"Why don't you put your sword down, Jeremy," the man said. "He can't get away."

"Not on your life. That is what he wants me to do."

"But suppose we are wrong."

The man called Jeremy kept his sword against Ralph's throat.

"Did you ever know the old man to be wrong?" he said.

"No, I didn't," the tall man admitted.

"Be quiet then and leave me alone."

"Can I let go of his arm, Lieutenant?" the guardsman said.

"Hold it tight," Jeremy ordered.

The guardsman did not increase the pressure again, Ralph noticed. The man must be losing his confidence.

"We might save time," Ralph said finally, "if you gentlemen told me your names while we are waiting."

There was no reply, not even a jab.

"I should like to know whom I must thank for my entertainment."

"You will find out soon enough," Jeremy growled. "Now be quiet."

"Could it be Jeremy Davies and Thomas Wirthin?"

"How did you know?" the tall officer said.

"I sometimes have occasion to study the roster of the royal guards," Ralph said. "Most of the officers I know personally."

"Save your breath," Jeremy said. "You won't get away."

"I would not dream of trying. In fact, I will not go at all until

I have heard some explanations. So make yourselves comfortable, gentlemen."

"I wonder what is keeping them," Thomas said irritably. "They should know by now."

"I don't like it, Lieutenant," the guardsman said.

"Quit worrying, I tell you," Jeremy snarled. "The old man is never wrong."

"If you would care to lay a wager," Ralph said, "I will bet fifty pounds that he is wrong this time."

He watched Jeremy, half expecting another jab, but none came.

"I will go further," he said. "I will wager another fifty that I know who the old man is."

The point of the sword wavered momentarily, sliding down until it was against his breastbone.

"I thought I told you to keep quiet," Jeremy said, but the confidence had gone out of his voice.

"If you are really sporting men," Ralph said, "I have a more interesting proposition. I will wager that tomorrow you will not be officers in the guards."

"We were only doing our duty, Your Honor," the guardsman said plaintively.

"You were, perhaps, but not your officers."

Pressed against the door, Ralph reeled backwards into the apartment as the door was opened from the inside. Only the guardsman holding his arm prevented him from falling on the floor. When he recovered his balance, he recognized Warner, accompanied by a file of guardsmen.

"Now then," Warner said to the two officers. "What is the matter?"

Thomas threw a quick, despairing glance at Jeremy.

"We saw this man sneaking into the palace through your door, Father. We feared some foul play, so we held him here and sent the guard to investigate."

"This man has a perfect right to come see me. Didn't he show you his pass? It is signed by the King himself."

"Passes can be forged," Jeremy muttered.

"These conscientious gentlemen did not bother to look at my pass," Ralph said. "They seem to be convinced that something has happened to His Majesty."

"I assure you that you are mistaken," said Warner. "His Majesty left my apartment only a few minutes ago. He is in excellent health."

"That is right, Sir," the corporal said. "I saw the King myself as I brought the men through the lobby."

A sickly smile came over Jeremy's face. The sword drooped disconsolately in his hand.

"We are glad to hear it," he said. "I hope you understand, Father, and you, Sir"—he nodded at Ralph—"that our zeal for His Majesty's service prompted our actions. We could take no chances where the King's safety was concerned. I trust that you will pardon whatever inconvenience and pain we may have caused you."

"Father Warner understands," Ralph said, taking out his handkerchief ostentatiously and wiping the blood off his neck. "We will not trouble him further. There are a few things, however, that are not clear to me. If you two gentlemen will send your guardsmen back to their duties and remain with me after they leave, I should be glad to hear an explanation."

"Really Sir, we shall be glad to explain and apologize," Thomas said, "but we are needed at our posts."

"If you value your commissions or your heads, you will not stir a step until I am through with you," Ralph said.

"Corporal, return the men to their posts."

The corporal saluted briskly and without waiting for confirmation from his superior officers drew up his men and marched them off.

"Would you like to come inside?" Warner said.

"No thank you, Father Warner," Ralph said. "We will stay here. I shall call you if I need you."

"Well gentlemen," Ralph said after Warner had left, "have you anything to say?"

"Nothing, except that we are sorry for our mistake," Jeremy said sullenly.

"Nothing? I thought you might want to explain why you didn't arrest me when you saw me go into Father Warner's apartment—why you waited until you saw me come out."

The two men looked at each other again, but neither spoke.

"Believe me, gentlemen, I am not angry for myself, but the King might be led to suppose that you did not want to prevent his murder, but only to catch his murderer. The King might want you imprisoned for dereliction or hanged for complicity in what you believed to be his assassination."

"We had to be sure," Thomas mumbled.

"An excellent way to be sure, by being careful not to give His Majesty any warning or making any inquiry in the palace—by giving me a half hour to do the business. You seemed sure enough, I might add, when I came out. Sure, that is, that His Majesty was dead, and that you had caught a Tory to be hanged for the killing."

"I don't know what you mean," Jeremy said weakly.

"Don't bother to lie, gentlemen. It will do no good. All I want to know is one thing. Was Mistress Hemphill with her father when he instructed you how to behave?"

As he watched the two men exchange despairing looks, he allowed himself the faint hope that she might be unaware of the plan to betray him. There was a remote possibility that she had mentioned the assassination to her father and he had set the trap without her knowledge.

"Your reluctance to betray the Hemphills does you credit, gentlemen," he said, "but I assure you that it is useless and unnecessary. I give you my word that I will not have them arrested. I am asking these questions for my personal satisfaction, not to convict your friends. As far as I am concerned, they can sail for Holland, or for China. But I promise you that if you fail to answer my questions you will be in prison by nightfall, with the Hemphills to keep you company."

"I don't know what you mean," Jeremy repeated sullenly.

"What will happen to us if we tell you?" Thomas said. "Do we get off too?"

"If you tell me what I want to know, you can be on the ship for Holland tomorrow with your friends. I am sure that the Prince of Orange will welcome a pair of lieutenants of the guard. I cannot allow you to stay in the country without having you cashiered."

"Don't tell him anything, Thomas," Jeremy said.

"As you wish," Ralph said, folding his arms. "You may consider yourselves under arrest."

"I will tell you," Thomas said. "Only I want your solemn promise that you will keep the bargain you just made."

"You have my word," Ralph said shortly.

"I don't trust him," Jeremy said.

"We don't have any choice."

"Make up your minds, gentlemen," Ralph said. "My time is valuable."

"I have made up my mind," Thomas said. "What do you want to know?"

"As I asked you before, was Mistress Hemphill with her father when he gave you your instructions?"

"Yes, she was."

Ralph took the statement without wincing. In his present state, the death of feeble hope hardly mattered.

"What did she say?"

"She didn't say anything at first. Finally, when I asked the old man if he was sure you would go through with it, she spoke up and said that they were sure. She said she had received convincing proof of your intentions."

"I see," Ralph said. "Did she say anything else?"

"Only one other thing. She said that we shouldn't kill you unless you tried to escape. She said that a public trial and a hanging would do more for the cause than killing you on the spot. She said that you were a gentleman. You would never mention her name in a trial. Her father thought it would be safer if you were killed right away, but she persuaded him."

"She is notoriously sentimental," Ralph heard himself say.

Thomas swallowed hard. He was making a pitiful attempt to retain a little dignity, but his mouth was quivering uncontrollably. Ralph sneered to himself. For all their wiles, the Hemphills sometimes chose very poor instruments.

"Is that all you want to know, Sir?" Thomas said.

"That is all I want to know, but there is something I want you to do for me. When you see the Hemphills this evening, I want you to congratulate them all on their planning. You may congratulate Mr. Keith for following me around and finding out when and where I entered Whitehall. Tell him that I never saw him myself and found out about him only by accident. You may congratulate Mr. Hemphill on his cold calculation and his tireless malevolence. As for Mistress Hemphill, you may congratulate her on her superlative feigning. I could have sworn she loved me. Tell her that she makes love like an angel.

"You must tell them, however, that they made a terrible mistake about me. The next time they choose a prospective murderer, they should do it more carefully. You might ask Mistress Hemphill what gave her the idea that I was an assassin. Can you remember all that?"

"I think so," Thomas said.

"Very well, then, you may go. But remember, if I find you in England after tomorrow, you will have cause to regret it. Do you understand, Jeremy?"

"Yes Sir."

I am not mortally wounded, Ralph thought as he watched the two men go. I shall recover from this. I am only a little sick and dizzy. If I can get home before the real pain starts and if I can only keep from thinking for a little while, I shall be all right in a few days.

He squared his shoulders deliberately, picked up his sword where

Thomas had dropped it, and began to make his way out of the palace grounds.

Yes, I shall be all right, he told himself. But I must not be over-confident. People must feel like this while they are bleeding to death.

CHAPTER

Twenty-one

LOOKING BACK now to the time of the Revolution and the days immediately preceding it, Sir Ralph found that his impressions were an indistinct blur, like the memories of a long illness. Yes a long illness. That was it. From the day of the attempted assassination until long after his escape to France, he had lived in a feverish nightmare, the outcome of which he could sense in advance, but could do nothing to change.

He was not sure, even now, whether his waking delirium had been caused by Esther Hemphill or by his nauseating sense of responsibility for the disasters which followed. At the time, he remembered, he had blamed Esther. She had tortured his waking thoughts and distorted his dreams. She had lurked at the edges of his consciousness, ready to appear at any time. In his more lucid intervals, he had sometimes convinced himself that he was forgetting her, only to find her returning more violently than ever. But even as he blamed her, he had been uneasily aware that his sickness was caused by something more complicated than betrayed love.

One day in London, Sir Ralph remembered, he had seen a large music box made by an ingenious Dresden artificer. When the mechanism was wound up and the key removed, the little soldiers on top of the box levelled their pikes and muskets and marched around after each other while the music played. He had admired the work immensely until he had been struck by its unfortunate resemblance to his own situation. He too had been for a time in control of a complicated mechanism, but he had relinquished the key, and now the redcoats, the bluecoats, the whitecoats, and plaids were moving relentlessly into battle. Nothing could stop them from slaughtering each other.

Sometimes in the night, he remembered, he would wake up shouting denials. No, he was not a coward. No, he was not responsible for sending the poor wretches to their deaths. No, he had not been obligated to commit a murder. No, he had not been appointed to save England or Europe. No, he had not failed in his duty.

At such times, he was actually glad that Esther had tried to have him killed. Somehow the attempt seemed to justify him. It helped a little to know that if he had killed the King he would now be dead himself and the Tories would be saddled with the odium of the murder while the Whigs gloated. He would put himself back to sleep by convincing himself once again that he was right, that he did not have a murder on his conscience, that he was free, and that he would soon get over his childish feelings, or learn to bear them.

Yes, Sir Ralph told himself, those days had been a terrible disease. He did not want to think of them. In retrospect, they were harmless enough, a mere confusion of faded images; but one could not trust them. They were capable of springing suddenly to life—or rather, to a diabolical sort of half life. It was better to leave them alone.

One thing only was worth remembering—Kit. She had probably saved his sanity. As the events of the Revolution moved along, predictably as a bad drama, she had treated the whole affair as a monstrous practical joke. She refused to be concerned about anyone except Ralph and James.

"Everyone must take his own chances," she had said. "As I have told you a thousand times, it is not your fault if people want to kill each other. You will have done enough if you can get yourself and James out of this alive. You must not worry, even about me. I can take care of myself. If all else fails, I can marry some well-connected gentleman and turn respectable."

"You will not follow the King into exile, then?" Ralph had said.

"Certainly not. In exile, I would only be an embarrassment to him. He can find other mistresses for the few short years he will need them."

"I must say, you do not seem much bothered by all this."

"Bothered? Why should I be bothered? I shall miss James a little, of course, and I shall miss you rather a lot; but after all, that can scarcely be fatal. As an adulteress, one learns to become adult."

"I suppose one does."

"In other words, one learns to forget past mistakes and to accept what cannot be changed. As for the Revolution and the wars, we both know that James has handsomely deserved exile, and the people of Europe deserve a bloodletting for allowing themselves to be ruled by malignant idiots."

Sir Ralph took up his pen. He must pick enough details out of the old delirium to satisfy Lord Stair. He could think about Kit some other time. If he ever got back to England again, he would go see her. She was now Lady Portmore, he remembered. She had married David Colyear, later Lord Portmore, and they had produced two sons. It was said that Kit had grown very respectable, but who could believe such an absurdity?

In the summer of 1688 [he wrote] Mr. Barnard (newly created Sir Ralph Barnard) repeatedly warned King James that his policies had led him to disaster, that the whole Kingdom was disaffected, and that the Prince of Orange was coming against him with a strong force. His Majesty, however, refused to believe, much less heed, these warnings. When Mr. Barnard's warnings were finally confirmed by reports from the French agents in Holland, and when the public demonstrations in support of the Bishops against the King had made the temper of the nation evident, His Majesty made a few feeble concessions to allay popular wrath and avert revolution; but these concessions were so obviously extorted from him and so inadequate that they failed of their purpose, it being then much too late to regain the trust of a people too often deceived and affronted.

The King was likewise disappointed in his expectations of help from the French. He did not dare openly announce an alliance with King Louis, fearing that the English Navy and Army would revolt instantly if the French appeared. He hoped, however, that King Louis would maintain such a pressure on the Dutch borders that the Prince would not be able to leave Holland with an army. The event was otherwise. King Louis, foolishly, as it soon appeared, chose to attack the Rhine Provinces of Germany instead of the Netherlands, on the supposition that King James could defeat the Prince, or keep him engaged in a long and bloody English war while the French conquered Europe at their leisure.

Thus His Majesty was forced to rely on the loyalty of his army and fleet, and to hope that the nation would not rise against him in support of the Prince. Here again, his reliance and his hopes were deceived, even more thoroughly than Mr. Barnard had been able to predict. His fleet, buffeted by contrary winds, was unable to oppose the Prince's landing, and his army soon proved untrustworthy, many of the men, including some of the principal officers, going over to the Prince. The people proved even less loyal to His Majesty than the troops. In every area not dominated by the royal army, the population soon declared for the Prince of Orange. Antipopish riots broke out in many sections of the country, and the King's popish officials and his politic abettors began to flee the country as fast as possible. Sunderland and Petre made their escape abroad. Milord Jeffreys was caught and thrown into prison, where he later died.

In view of these reverses, the King decided to send the Queen and the little Prince to France, and to follow them himself. Mr. Barnard tried to dissuade him from this course, but the King was not to be dissuaded. He declared that he would never put himself under the control of the Prince of Orange and an English Parliament, who would undoubtedly insist that his son should be raised a Protestant. He preferred, rather, to join with King Louis and attempt to win back his Kingdom with the aid of French arms. Thus, in December of 1688, the Queen, the little Prince, and the King escaped to France. Mr. Barnard soon joined them there, not only because he had been commanded by the King to do so, but also because he was known to the revolutionists as a royal agent and in imminent danger of being imprisoned, or worse.

Sir Ralph reread what he had written. It seemed accurate enough, but entirely cold, as if the words had killed the memories. Perhaps it was just as well, he thought. Who would wish to re-create on paper the passions of the time? There was his first sight of Saint Germains, for instance, and the demoralizing realization that he was really an exile—that he might never return to England, except as a spy. There was his first Paris rain, his room at the wretched inn, his arguments with the French commissary over supplies for the Irish expedition, his dreary walks along the Seine.

In some ways, he supposed, it was lucky that the whole episode had seemed unreal to him. If he had not been too tired and dispirited to care, he might have drowned himself, in spite of Berwick's attempts to cheer him up. At least he had not waited for letters like most of the exiles. Nor had he indulged in fanciful dreams about a quick return. He had expected nothing and hoped for nothing, except to outlive his pain.

When King James had ordered him to Ireland, along with Berwick and the rest of the expedition, he had not protested. As far as he could remember, it had not even occurred to him that he might resign from the King's service and refuse to involve himself further. He had considered himself committed without hope of reprieve to the King's cause. If the King wanted him to fight, he would fight. If the King wanted him to spy, he would spy. He was sick to the point of exhaustion with trying to guide the course of events. From now on, he would let others bear the responsibility. And if he was fighting on the wrong side, if a victory for King James and the French would be fatal to England and Europe, what then? Certainly his personal efforts would not change the issue one way or another. So far they had merely succeeded in getting him exiled.

No, he had not protested about going to Ireland. Perhaps he had even been relieved to get into action. Almost anything was better than sitting around Paris or Saint Germains watching exiles rub salt into each other's wounds.

If he had been a trifle saner in early 1689, Sir Ralph told himself, he would have been shocked by Ireland. As it was, the country matched his mood perfectly. It was in a state of fantastic confusion. In general, the aim of the Irish Catholics was to drive out their English overlords and, with the aid of the French, help their coreligionist King James recover his throne. But this aim was hopelessly entangled with many competing designs. In fact, there seemed to be as many aims as there were Irishmen.

Some were trying to get the lands of the fleeing English; some were angling for political sinecures in the new establishment; some were intriguing for army commissions; some were defending the interests of their clans; some were actually fighting in the North; some were busy looting the country during the disorders. All were feverishly excited. Dublin, when Ralph entered it, was the maddest city in Christendom. He felt as if he had suddenly entered a party at which everyone had already consumed a quart of wine. Irish recruits, French veterans, English exiles, and an indescribable horde of office seekers, land speculators, peasants, townsmen, sailors, lawyers, and foreign agents—all talked at the top of their lungs, and no one listened.

Ralph found that the interminable hubbub soothed him rather than irritated him. He liked the noisy excitement of Dublin better than the orderly routine of Paris. Seemingly, there was no place in the city where one could think quietly; and the last thing he wished to do was to think. It was better to lose oneself in the crowd at Dublin Castle and listen to the odd cadences of excited Irish voices, or to elbow one's way through the streets and hear the incredible rumors that were being shouted back and forth. Instinctively, Ralph liked the Irish—their warmth, their spontaneity, their recklessness. In his normal frame of mind, he would have made a number of friendships. As it was, he avoided the acquaintances he had made on his previous visit. He could not make any effort himself. It was enough if he could lose himself occasionally in the random emotions of others.

The army, Ralph soon discovered, was almost as confused as the city. Not one officer in ten, he estimated, had the slightest notion of how to transmit an order; and not one common soldier in ten had the slightest intention of obeying an order unless he liked it personally. When Ralph had been appointed a major in the infantry and given the command of a battalion, he had been embarrassed for fear his ignorance should expose his men to danger and himself to shame; but after seeing his command and his fellow officers, his fears vanished. With his thirty scattered days of training in the English establishment, he found himself a military genius compared with most of the others. At least he knew the basic drill maneuvers. He knew how to load and fire a matchlock, how to manage a pike, and how to dig a simple entrenchment. More impressive, he had actually been in a pitched battle and loaded a cannon.

He threw himself furiously into the work of organizing and disciplining his command. At nights he sought the advice of the few veteran French officers scattered through the Irish regiments; in the daytime he attempted to put the advice into practice. Nothing seemed to work. He tried to have two lieutenants cashiered for drunken disobedience. They appealed to their kinsman, the Earl of Antrim, who got them reinstated. He had three privates whipped within an inch of their lives for pillaging. The next morning fifteen men had deserted. He succeeded in getting one captain removed for general stupidity and incompetence, but the captain who was sent to replace him was just as bad as his predecessor. He inspected equipment every morning, and every morning some was missing or damaged.

Most of the time he felt as if he were fighting his way out of a net, but occasionally he saw a gleam of encouragement. Once a sentry challenged him properly. Shortly afterwards, a platoon went through the firing procedure without a mistake. Then one morning, a sergeant caught one of the worst thieves in the battalion, and the men dealt with him on the spot, so severely that thieving practically ceased. On the long march to Derry, Ralph lost only twenty-three men by desertion—a feat which he considered almost miraculous.

He did not flatter himself into believing that he was a good officer. To the men, he suspected, he was merely an unpleasant foreigner in spite of his efforts to gain their confidence and respect. He knew his immediate subordinates hated him for driving them to take pains they would never have dreamed of taking by themselves. From time to time they complained against him to the Colonel; but that gentleman, a gouty Irish noble, knew of Ralph's influence with the Duke of Berwick and the King. He mentioned the complaints to Ralph without attempting to reprimand him. Occasionally, Ralph got the impression that his efforts to keep his men well clothed and well fed were appreciated. Not that anyone said anything complimentary, but the complaints, he noticed, were fewer and less virulent in his command than in the rest of the regiment.

Luckily, the battalion did not come under fire at the unsuccessful siege of Londonderry. Ralph shuddered to think what might have happened had his recruits been called upon to make or sustain an attack, although he supposed they could not have done much worse than the troops actually engaged.

In thinking back on those days, Sir Ralph realized that the vexations and frustrations of his first command had done much for his state of mind. Where some others had worked themselves from health to nervous exhaustion, he had worked himself from nervous exhaustion to something resembling health. Day after day, night after night, he drove himself to transform his horde of peasants into a battalion, and to turn himself into a competent soldier. Gradually his obsession with his task began to drive back his permanent anxieties. One Sunday in early October while his men were at mass, he awakened to the fact that he had not thought of Esther for three days. The realization was unfortunate, since it threw him into a relapse; but for the moment, at least, it gave him a ray of hope.

When his regiment took up winter quarters at Drogheda and he was recalled to Dublin to collect information for the King, he was sorry to go. This time, the confusion in Dublin irritated him beyond measure. In the intervening months, the disorder had increased rather than diminished. James had been unable to reconcile any of the contending factions or clear the town of any extraneous population. The people were louder, more shrilly optimistic, more gloriously drunken, and more riotous than ever. What the King needed, Ralph complained, was not information but organization. He already knew all he needed to know—that the English and their allies would come against him in the spring. The problem now was to train and equip an army capable of defending itself, and to mobilize the resources of Ireland to support it. But the days slipped by in quarrels, intrigues, and rumors; the nights, in drinking and drabbing. Nothing useful was accomplished. Even when Ralph found, by re-establishing contact with some of his old agents in England, that William himself was going to lead the English forces in the next campaign, no one seemed particularly worried. Ralph begged the King to send all the officers swarming in Dublin back to their regiments, to put Dublin under martial law, to set up a regular system of supply depots, and to dismiss the swarm of landhungry petitioners from the court; but James remained inert. All would be well, he seemed to believe, as soon as the French arms and reinforcements arrived in the spring.

In his anger and frustration, Ralph felt his despondency return as strong as ever. He found it difficult to bear the sight of the King. What a pleasure it would be, he thought wearily, to strangle the old fool. What a craven dolt he had been to let this destroyer of hopes and wrecker of lives survive. It was too late now, of course, for assassination. The King's death would only add to the confusion. But to be constantly reminded of one's mistake, to see another kingdom being thrown away by incompetence and mismanagement, to be showered with personal attentions from a man one despised—all this was unendurable. Worse yet, Ralph found, he could not get over his habit of pitying James, or feeling responsible for him. Even while he wanted to strangle the man, he could not help sympathizing with him. Thrown into a situation that would have taxed the best executive in the world, James could only thresh weakly around, trusting to incompetent subordinates and hoping for the best.

By the time Ralph had obtained the King's permission to return to his battalion, he was completely demoralized again. No matter how hard he worked at his task, no matter how busy he kept himself in drilling his men or supplying them, he could not shake his sense of futility and despair. No matter what he did, he realized, he would never see Esther again. No matter what the outcome of the impending campaign, he would be wrong. If the Irish lost, they would be enslaved for many years to come. If they won, England and her allies would be hopelessly crippled, if not ruined. Meantime, he had a duty to his men. Having already condemned them to death, he must do everything possible to get them reprieved, insofar as training and discipline could save them. But the task seemed impossible. In the three months he had been away, most of his work had been undone. The men still retained some knowledge of the maneuvers, but discipline had decayed beyond belief. He was obliged to begin all over again.

Fortunately, this time he received help. With the French regiments which arrived in the spring came Leroux, a veteran French officer. Through Berwick's influence, he was made lieutenant colonel of Ralph's regiment, effectively taking over command from the decrepit Colonel. Problems that had seemed insurmountable to Ralph seemed routine to Leroux. Within three weeks Leroux had organized an effective system of military police, dismissed four lieutenants, improved the sanitation of the camp, found a new source of beef supply, and shot three deserters.

Illogically, as far as he could tell, Ralph felt his spirits begin to mend. He could not say why. Possibly, he told himself, it was because an island of order was forming in the howling chaos. Possibly, he was becoming inured to his problems. Or possibly, it was merely the work as before—along with the assurance that he was not alone.

In retrospect, Sir Ralph was inclined to attribute some of his amendment to the example of Leroux. The old campaigner seemed impervious to worry, fear, regret, or optimism. He went about his duties with efficient, professional detachment. As far as Ralph could tell, the Frenchman's concern never went beyond his occupation. It was impossible to imagine him as a civilian, or engaged in any of the normal pursuits of love or business. He seemed to have been born in an infantry camp, and to have cut his teeth on the regulations. Men stood a little straighter when he looked at them. When he gave an order, it was obeyed without delay and without question. And somehow, along with his impersonal manner went the ability to inspire trust and confidence. There was an indefinable Gallic gallantry about him that made men try to imitate him.

Although Leroux never showed Ralph any special favors, Ralph got the impression that the veteran liked him. Occasionally Leroux stopped in at nights to discuss plans or to give instructions. On these occasions Ralph felt flattered. For days afterward he would find himself aping Leroux's manner—his stoical calm, his matter of fact way of giving orders, his impersonal method of delivering a reprimand, and his patient attention to detail. None of Leroux's qualities, Ralph feared, were transferable, but he imitated them anyway and felt stronger for doing so.

On the morning of July 1, 1690, Ralph knew that he was going to recover. Standing with Leroux about a hundred yards south of the Boyne river, he was watching William's army forming for the attack; but his mind was not really occupied with the enemy across the river. It was concerned, rather, with a sudden sense of well-being. The sensation reminded him of his childhood experience with pneumonia. He had awakened one morning after a desperate night to find that his fever had broken, and he had known instinctively that the worst was over—that he would certainly mend.

"I don't like that," Leroux was saying.

Ralph followed Leroux's gaze up the river to the left. The last of the French battalions was moving away from the Irish flank now.

Ralph could see the white coats of the infantrymen grow smaller as they faded into the green distance.

"Where do you suppose they are going?" he said.

"Obviously, Monsieur, they are marching to prevent the allies from getting around our left."

"Why don't you like it then?"

"Because, Monsieur, it means that the enemy has forced a bridge up the river and is trying to move troops behind us. Besides, Monsieur"—Leroux smiled faintly, the first suggestion of a smile Ralph had ever seen on his face—"I feel naked when those whitecoated gentlemen are gone."

"It makes me feel a bit naked too," Ralph said.

Leroux subsided into silence. If he felt naked there was no outward sign as he methodically scanned the hostile formations with his perspective glass. Reassured by Leroux's calm, Ralph allowed himself to retreat for a moment in his new-found sense of health and confidence. He did not wish to analyze it or test its boundaries, only to revel in it.

Yes, he told himself again, from now on I shall be all right. I am well at last.

He breathed deeply, allowing himself to savor the texture of the rich Irish air. Then he ran his eye appreciatively across the regiments on the other side of the river as if they were objects in a beautiful landscape painting.

"Look there, Monsieur Barnard," Leroux said, handing him the glass. "There are our men. Those are the gentlemen we must deal with."

"Which men?" Ralph asked. "The Dutchmen in blue?"

"No, Monsieur, I mean the regiment exactly opposite us, your countrymen in the red coats. We must keep them from crossing the river."

Through the glass, Ralph could see the men clearly. He could almost distinguish faces, but he could not make out the device on the standard. The regiment was in position, the men standing at ease awaiting the order to attack.

"Do you think we can stop them?" he said.

Leroux took back the glass. "That depends upon the gentlemen behind us," he said.

Ralph glanced back to where his men were sitting or lying. From looking at them Ralph could tell nothing about their mood. Leroux had posted the regiment well. It now occupied a depression in the ground which rose gradually from the river. As long as the men re-

mained down, they were perfectly screened from observation, as well
as from the cannon balls.

"I am hopeful," Ralph said. "Should I order the men to light the
matches now?"

"No, Monsieur. Our friends across the river cannot begin the
attack for another fifteen minutes. We must not burn down the
matches before the fight begins. Wait ten more minutes. It will be
useful, however, if you will have every man inspect his priming.
One must keep their minds occupied."

Ralph gave the command and returned quickly. As he did so, a
cannon ball went whizzing overhead and landed with a thump about
a hundred yards behind. Ralph ducked instinctively, but Leroux did
not move.

"They are shooting at you, Sir," Ralph said.

"So they are," Leroux said.

"Don't you think you should take cover? The regiment can't afford
to lose you."

"Not at all, Monsieur Barnard. One must do foolish things to inspire raw troops. They must see that their leader is not afraid of
cannon balls. After they have stood fire, it will be a different matter.
And I must beg you, Monsieur, if you wish to stand here with me,
do not flinch when the balls go by. I think I can assure you that to
hit a single man with a cannon ball at half a mile is beyond the skill
of the most capable Dutch gunner."

"I am not afraid for myself," Ralph said truthfully. "I am afraid
for you. As your second in command, I should not like to be left in
charge if you should be wounded. A battalion is quite enough for
me to handle."

Another cannon ball rushed by; this time, ten yards to the right.
Ralph stood motionless.

"Well done, Monsieur," Leroux said. "I think you are a natural
soldier."

Ralph felt himself flush with pleasure. The unexpected compliment from the stoical Frenchman seemed altogether the finest compliment of his entire life.

"Two more campaigns will make you an excellent officer."

"Thank you, Sir," Ralph said. The modification of Leroux's praise
did not lessen the pleasure.

"Why are you smiling?" Leroux asked.

"I was thinking, Sir, that today should be the worst day of my
life. In a few minutes, I am going to see the bloody results of an

old folly. And yet, to tell you the truth, Sir, I feel alive for the first time in two years. Strange, isn't it?"

"Not at all, Monsieur. Battles are much more interesting than women."

Ralph paused while another cannon ball hummed past.

"Possibly," he said, "but what makes you so sure a woman is involved?"

Leroux did not deign to reply. Instead he put the glass to his eye again and swept the Irish positions. He paused for a minute or two with the glass fixed on the huts and stone fences of Oldbridge. Ralph could hear him humming tonelessly.

"You see our position there, Monsieur Barnard?"

"Yes Sir." He followed Leroux's pointing.

"Do you see anything significant about it?"

"It looks very strong."

"I sincerely hope so, Monsieur, since it is the key to the battle. It commands the shallowest ford on the river and anchors our line. If it should be overrun, you and I must disengage our men and, as you English say, march like the very devil for the pass at Duleek. Do you understand?"

"Yes Sir."

"And now, Monsieur Barnard, give the order to light the matches, if you please. Our friends intend to pay us a visit."

A scattering of musketry had broken out on the left where a Huguenot regiment was advancing toward the river. By the time Ralph had given the order and observed its execution, the whole army across the river was in motion. The Huguenots were already up to their knees in the water, and the English regiment opposite was within seventy-five yards of entering it.

Before he could rejoin Leroux, the Frenchman had called the regiment to attention. They were standing in their places now observing the advancing enemy. Leroux stood facing his men, his sword drawn, a calm smile on his face. As Ralph approached, Leroux waved his sword in the air.

"*Alors*, my children," he shouted in a loud voice.

Before he could complete the command, his head was smashed off by a cannon ball. Ralph, within two yards, felt himself splattered with a gust of blood as the headless trunk pitched to the ground beside him.

Even as the body fell, Ralph realized that he was in motion to take Leroux's place. He would not allow himself to register the horror of the spectacle. If he did, he was lost, and the regiment with him. He must get the men moving toward the enemy.

Drawing his sword, he turned to face his command, conscious as he did so of his gruesome appearance.

"Forward. March," he yelled, waving his sword and turning to face the enemy.

The English, he noticed with surprise, had not had time to reach the river. Their first rank was still ten yards away from it, the men holding their muskets and pikes at high port as they prepared to enter the water.

"So far, so good," Ralph heard himself say aloud. "We can catch them in the deep water."

He glanced over his shoulder at the men following him. They were marching like sleepwalkers, leaving a wide interval around the spot where Leroux had fallen, and where now a sergeant and four men were gathering up the body. Quickly he averted his eyes to concentrate on the scene before him. To the left, the river was alive with men; to the right, some cavalry squadrons were plunging into the water; immediately in front, the English were advancing as if on parade, splashing into the stream without breaking their cadence. For a moment, Ralph had the sensation of facing an irresistible phalanx, but in another moment the perfect order disappeared as the front line sank in water up to the waist. Over the musketry from the left, he could hear the yells of the English officers urging on their troops.

His own troops seemed impossibly slow. They followed as if they were marching through mud. As he calculated distance and time, he fought back the urge to order them to double their speed. He must maintain his formation at all costs. If his ranks became disordered, they would never reform in time to deliver an effective volley. Leroux had intended to march the regiment to the brink of the river before opening fire, but Leroux, Ralph thought grimly, had not counted upon being killed and replaced. The slight delay, along with the slowness of the troops, made an adjustment necessary. Now, he must stop the men about thirty yards from the river, have them deliver their volleys from that point, and then charge the English before they could get a solid footing ashore and begin delivering volleys of their own. The firing, if well done, should alone stop the attack.

It seemed an eternity before he reached the spot he had picked out for the halt. Most of the English were still in water up to their armpits, but the front line was approaching the bank, their wet red coats rising gradually out of the water. Ralph halted the regiment, quickly took his position between the two battalions, and gave the command to fire.

He expected three smashing volleys of the kind that Leroux had taught the regiment to deliver. He expected the first two English ranks to disintegrate before his eyes. Instead, he heard three wild, scattered, feeble fusillades. Half of the shots, he was sure, had gone straight up into the air. Not more than ten took effect. There was not even a momentary pause in the English advance.

"Oh God," he said to himself. "What now?"

But he did not allow himself to hesitate. He waved his sword again, gave the command to charge, and began to run toward the enemy, whose first rank was just stepping out of the water. As he ran he picked out an opponent for himself, a tall captain who had been first man on the bank and was now shouting something to his company. It seemed to Ralph that he was upon the man in a second. Swinging his sword, he brought it down on the man's shoulder with all his might. An instant later, he was parrying a pike thrust, and in another instant he was spinning to his knees from a blow of a musket butt against his chest. As he spun around, he caught a glimpse of his regiment, all in full flight about seventy-five yards away. Not a man had followed him in the charge.

Almost before his knees hit the ground, he was scrambling to his feet. Why he was not clubbed again or run through with a pike, he did not know. Perhaps the English were as stunned by a one-man attack as he was. Perhaps from the blood on his white coat they thought him mortally wounded. All he knew was that he was running once more, that his chest hurt horribly, and that he expected to be shot down at any instant. Laboring up the gentle incline away from the river, he fixed his eyes on the spot where Leroux had been killed. Ten yards beyond that, he knew, was the depression which had sheltered the regiment. If he could reach it, he was temporarily saved. Suddenly, he was past the bloody patch of grass and throwing himself to the ground in the hollow.

He let himself lie panting for perhaps fifteen seconds before getting to his hands and knees. He had lost his hat, he noticed, but he still held his sword, caked now with blood and dirt. Taking pains not to make movements which hurt his chest, he returned to the edge of the hollow and looked back toward the enemy. They were all out of the water now, and forming rapidly to continue the attack. The pikemen, Ralph noticed, had been distributed through the front rank and on the flanks against a possible cavalry charge. Small wonder the English officers had not deigned to waste bullets on him. They were too busy consolidating their easy triumph. What did they care about one injured major?

About two hundred yards to his left, an Irish battalion was melting away as a blue-coated regiment—Dutch, Ralph supposed—prepared to fire on them. Men were breaking from the rear ranks, throwing down their matchlocks, and running; while the men in the front ranks were feverishly trying to reload. Ralph turned his eyes away before he heard the crash of the volleys. On his right, he could see no Irish infantry at all. A furious cavalry action was in progress, however, as a squadron of Irish horse threw itself upon a regiment just emerging from the river. Farther down, he could make out a large melee, but he could not tell which cavalry was Irish and which enemy.

Seeing that he was in no danger of being fired upon by the English, he stood up straight and turned around to look after his regiment. About a quarter of a mile south he could see a swarm of fugitives which he believed to be his men, but he could not be sure, since there were other bands of fleeing infantrymen and a great number of individual stragglers. Apparently, half the Irish line was running away. He immediately abandoned the thought of trying to overtake his men. Even if he could run fast enough to catch them —and this seemed hopeless—he could never reform them. Their matchlocks were scattered all over the ground around him.

Deliberately, he began to walk toward Oldbridge, which was obscured now in a pall of smoke and dust. He had a premonition that the battle was lost already, but he remembered Leroux's statement. Oldbridge was the key to the position. If it could be held, perhaps the defeat could be averted, or saved from becoming a disastrous rout. He had no precise idea of what he would do if he got there, or how he would get through the fugitives and their pursuers; but he was determined to make the attempt. A wide circle back from the river seemed the most hopeful tactics.

As he plodded along, keeping a wary eye to his right, and glancing occasionally back over his shoulder, he was aware that he still retained his curious sense of well-being. Though the worst had happened—the forces he had unloosed were killing each other left and right—and though he had undoubtedly bungled his own part in this bizarre, unbelievable battle, still he felt as if he had been relieved from a burden. True, his chest hurt. He suspected that two or three ribs were broken. True also, he was covered from head to foot with Leroux's blood. He refused to consider such things now. It was enough to know that if he lived through the battle, he would recover. When he heard cavalry behind him, he swung around, prepared to be sabered. He saw immediately, however, that the horse were Irish, and a moment later, he recognized Berwick in the lead. Berwick pulled up beside him, bringing the squadron to a halt. Ralph saw Berwick's eyes grow wide.

"*Nom de Dieu,*" he said. "Ralph."

"I am glad to see you," Ralph said.

"What happened to you?"

"I lost my regiment."

"So I see—and a quart of blood too, it appears."

"No, only my regiment. The blood is Leroux's."

"You had better come with us. I have lost men too."

Ralph looked at the troopers. Evidently they had been mauled severely. Some had lost their hats, two or three had epaulettes shorn away, several were obviously wounded, and all were grimed with powder smoke. They were accompanied by half a dozen riderless horses.

"Do you think you can ride?" Jack was saying. "We are going to attack again."

"Certainly," he said. "Give me a horse."

Just what happened after he was mounted, Ralph never remembered clearly. At one time, he seemed to recall, he was riding down on a regiment of blue infantry. At another, he was following Berwick into a knot of Dutch horse, swinging his sword at a big blonde trooper. Later, or perhaps earlier, he saw the infantry fleeing from around Oldbridge, and realized that only the cavalry was still contesting the field. At the time it did not seem important. Vaguely he recalled slashing at some red-coated pikemen and hearing musket balls whistle past. Sometime during the battle, he must have thrown away his bloody coat, because when the remnants of the squadron pulled up beside the retreating French regiments, he was in his shirt-sleeves. Only then did he notice that he was covered with sweat and shivering from the pain of his injury.

Now when he thought of the retreat from the Boyne, Sir Ralph could see himself as if he were a detached observer watching an injured young man make his way across the twenty miles to Dublin. After it became evident that the French were adequately covering the flight of the routed army, Berwick had ordered him to ride ahead.

The young man riding the brown horse through the horde of demoralized fugitives crowding the road to Dublin was bent almost double to keep his chest from hurting. He was allowing the horse to pick its way past the carts and wagons, past the abandoned equipment, and past an occasional cow or pig. He was not thinking of the scene before his eyes, or even of a comfortable bed at Dublin Castle. As he rode through the summer evening, he was telling himself that he had made the first payment on his mistake—if it was a mistake. From now on, if he survived the battles, he would find the payments easier. He would find it harder and harder to believe that he had ever had it within his power to prevent these swarms of men from cutting each other's throats. Even now, with Leroux's blood all over his breeches, and probably on his hands, he felt unusually calm. The confused hurly-burly he had just left did not seem as sickening as the half-dead memory of Sedgemoor or of the Assizes.

When he thought of the Assizes, he thought of Esther; but the picture which flashed to his mind, although as vivid as ever, provoked no emotion. It was almost as neutral as the Irish landscape that was passing before his eyes. A picture—no more. To erase it from his mind, he looked toward Dublin, where lights were beginning to appear. King James, he thought, would be there already. He had been escorted from the field by a troop of cavalry as soon as it had become apparent that the battle was lost—at least, that was what a straggler had said. Ralph felt a sudden surge of pity for the Irish. James could get away. The French could escape, or make advantageous terms. But the Irish were trapped. They must fight out this war to its bitter, inevitable end, and then suffer the far-reaching consequences.

He shook his head to banish the thought. The movement hurt his chest. No, he must not think of such things now. For the present, let each man bear his own burdens.

Contemplating the picture of himself as he had been that evening in Ireland, Sir Ralph smiled a little. Berwick was right, he supposed. He must be getting senile. Otherwise, he could not feel so remote from, and so patronizing toward, that young man with whom he still had so much in common—so much in common that he could feel a reminiscent ache in his chest from the cracked ribs. It was strange too that the ride from the Boyne should remain so clear, in its detached way. Other and later events from his Irish days were almost completely gone. He could scarcely remember anything about that day at the defense of Limerick when his regiment redeemed itself in the action at the breach. He was not sure now whether he had been recalled to France in February or March of 1691. Yet he remembered perfectly riding up to Dublin the night of the battle.

About a mile from town, he had heard the yelling and the wailing.

He had straightened up in his saddle, ignoring the pain in his chest. He was tempted to put his tired horse into a trot, but he was afraid it would fall dead. At all events, he had told himself, he would look like a soldier—as near like Leroux and Berwick as possible. There would be one man in Dublin unshaken by defeat and disaster. And actually, the pose would not be difficult to maintain. Through all the fatigue and soreness, through all the confusion around him, his sense of personal deliverance remained—the sense of having passed the crisis of an illness. However he might relapse in the future, he would never be in real danger again. He could endure whatever happened.

As he rode toward the indescribable din and disorder, his horse almost knocked down a man who was staggering along in the middle of the road. The man began to curse feebly, then stopped.

"Why, it is Sir Ralph Barnard," he said, in a thick brogue.

Ralph peered through the gloom. It was O'Hallahan, one of his lieutenants.

"How are you, Sir?" O'Hallahan said. "I thought you was dead."

"I thought so too at one time," Ralph said, "but I am alive now."

"We left you in a bad spot." There was a sheepish tone in O'Hallahan's voice. "I hope you are not hurt or angry."

"Not at all," Ralph said, almost gaily. "Not at all. I think I shall be perfectly well, O'Hallahan. Yes, I think I shall be perfectly well."

CHAPTER

Twenty-two

IN TWO WEEKS Ralph had learned to think of the garret as a prison cell. He had memorized every crack in the ceiling, every detail of the crumbling brick walls, and every blotch on the oilpapered windows. Newgate, he was sure, would be a pleasure compared to this. There was no help for it, however; he must occupy the wretched place for at least one more week, until he and Jack had collected all the information they had come for. He had not minded staying in the fisherman's hut when they had first landed in England, or in the rooms and cottages provided by Jacobite squires. Hiding had become second nature to him. But he resented this stupid little cubicle. Here he was in London with all London life going on only a few feet away, and yet he was cooped within four sweaty walls. It was like visiting London in a coffin.

In the evenings, of course, things were different. As soon as darkness fell, he could slip out into the streets, see the necessary people, and wander about to his heart's content. Already he had covered most of London in his meanderings. He had even taken the risk of going past his old lodgings, of walking up and down Lincoln Street past Hemphill House, of strolling by the mansions around St. James. Dressed in sober black and wearing a mustache which, he fancied, made him look like Charles II, he felt little anxiety about being recognized as long as he stayed out of notoriously Jacobite taverns, where one patron out of five was a government informer. Seeing London only by night, however, made an eerie impression on him. It made him feel disembodied and depressed.

Lying on his narrow cot now, waiting for night or for Berwick, he put his hands behind his head and stared at the ceiling. Damn this waiting. Why prolong the stay further when it was already obvious that the Jacobites were going to do nothing? They all talked fiercely against William and the government, and all protested their devotion to James. Some of them even collected arms and ammunition or made lists of trusty followers. But nothing would induce them to rise and seize a port into which French reinforcements could be poured. To a man, they were determined to lie low until Louis' legions had actually arrived. Otherwise, they argued, they would be cut down by William's regulars and the militia before help came. Ralph could not much blame them for their caution, nor could he blame Louis for not risking his troops until he saw an English insurrection actually in being. The impasse, however, was hopeless, and the sooner he and Jack got out of England the better. Any one of a thousand improbable accidents could give them away, and while he was accustomed to risks, he did not wish to take them unnecessarily, for a project so clearly abortive.

It was odd, he thought as he listened to a coach rattle by outside, the way things worked out. Here it was January of 1696. The war had been going on for seven years. France and the allies had beaten each other into a bloody stalemate. Now Louis, despairing of a victory on the continent, wished to promote a revolt in England. If William could be dethroned and James restored, England would be knocked out of the war and Louis' dream of dominating Europe could be realized. Well, Ralph thought, the only result of the plan so far had been to give him and Jack a long, unpleasant visit to England. The French transports would be collecting in Normandy now, along with ten or twenty thousand troops. All would be awaiting news of an uprising; but the rising would never take place. Once more he would be able to say that he had done his best—and failed.

On the whole, he supposed, he was relieved that the mission had failed—that there would be no rising and no French invasion. In a way, however, the failure made no difference. As he estimated the chances, the rising and the invasion were very unlikely to succeed, even under the most favorable conditions. The English militia and the few regular regiments now in England could contain their enemies until the rest of the British army was brought back from Flanders. The only practical result, as far as he could see, would be to transfer a portion of the war from the continent to England. He had long since ceased to care, he told himself, where the battles were fought.

Yes, it was odd the way things worked out. Before the Revolution he had found his work absorbing; he now found it routine. This was a sign, he supposed, that he had become professional and disinterested. Like an advocate employed by the guilty party, he was committed to use all his skill, but under no obligation to involve himself emotionally. He liked to believe that he was now a better agent than he had been in the days when he had cared so violently about the results of his missions.

A tap on the door brought him instantly to his feet, his pistol cocked and ready.

"Come in," he said.

"Well, Ralph, you have an odd way of greeting guests."

"Kit," he said stupidly. "What are you doing here?"

"Visiting an old friend," she said. "Aren't you going to kiss me?"

"Certainly not," he said, putting down the weapon. "Not until you tell me how you got here."

"Oh, very well, if you must be stubborn. I saw the Duke of Berwick, and he told me where to find you. He said you needed cheering."

"Where did you see Jack?"

"I must say you are difficult to please, Ralph. Why don't you kiss me and then ask your tiresome questions?"

Ralph caught her up off her feet and kissed her, then put her down.

"Forgive me, Kit," he said. "It is wonderful to see you."

"That is better," she said. "I don't blame you for being surprised, but I would hate to believe that you are more concerned with your head than with my body."

"A habit, Kit," he said. "Only a disgusting habit."

"Break it, by all means," she said. "I will not have my favorite spy and traitor turned into a boor."

Ralph motioned toward the cot. "Please sit down, Kit."

"Do you think I'm safe," she said, "with a man who has been in France and who has been shut up in this room for weeks? How is France, by the way?"

"Miserable," he said. "What did you expect?"

"I expected that you would enjoy yourself thoroughly—with the pretty French ladies. I expected that you would have forgotten me altogether."

"Unfortunately, Kit, the French ladies are not so pretty as you have been led to believe. Even if they were, I have little time for them. In the summers I am kept busy fighting, and in the winters I am sent out to spy."

"I am glad of it," Kit said. "As you know, I am not easily given to fits of jealousy. Still, I look upon you as my special property, and I hate Frenchwomen on principle."

"And what about you, Kit?" he said.

"Me? If you mean my personal life, I am glad to inform you that I am getting along very well. King William, bless him, restored my pension—at least part of it—and I now have a husband in mind. He does not know it yet, but he soon will. I expect to be married within the year. You would like him, I think. His name is Sir David Colyear."

"I am sure I shall like him if I ever get to meet him. I applaud his taste."

"Oh, his tastes have nothing to do with the matter. It is my tastes which count. I find him charming and pleasantly dull. As you must have noticed, I have an affinity for dull men."

Ralph laughed. "Thank you," he said.

"I except you, of course," she said, sticking out her tongue at him. "You are bright enough. Your only trouble is that you never use your brains."

"Please, Kit, no more advice. I should not be skulking here today if I had kept away from you."

"Speaking of dull men," she said, "how is James?"

"About the same as ever," he said, trying to call his last talk with James to mind. "Oh, there is one thing that might amuse you. I think he has finally given up mistresses. For the last six months he has seen no one."

"I think I am sorry to hear that," Kit said. "Much as I used to deplore his stupid philandering, I am a little shocked to know it is over. Do you think he is about to die? If he has given up women, he must be very senile."

"I think he is senile, but I don't think he is about to die. He will be around to haunt us for years, I am afraid."

"Let us not talk about James any more," Kit said. "It does no good, and I still find myself feeling sorry for him. I have much more interesting information. Do you remember our Whig friend Esther Hemphill?"

"I remember her very well," he said.

"Did you know that she is married?"

"I had heard something to that effect, but I did not hear any details."

"Are you interested in the details?" Kit's voice was teasing.

"Not particularly—unless, that is, you are interested in telling them."

Kit gave him a sly, sidelong glance.

"I am not," she said.

"Very well, then, don't bother."

"On second thought, I think I will bother. You don't deceive me, you know. I can see that you are consumed with curiosity."

"You can see more than I can," he said.

"You heard, I suppose, that her father died four years ago."

"Yes. As I remember, I got the news just before Steinkirk."

"They say that just after the Revolution, he contracted some sort of lingering illness which gradually wore him out. But I think that when he and his friends got rid of James he had nothing left to live for, so he died. Having spent all his life plotting and conniving, he did not know what to do after he was successful."

"I should think there was still much to do. The Revolution is not secure even yet."

"Possibly not, but securing it is a task for administrators, not plotters. I still say that James Hemphill died because he had completed his work—like a fish that has laid its eggs."

"Let it be as you will," Ralph said. "I have long since learned better than to argue with you."

"You grow sweeter all the time, Ralph. I wonder now why I bothered with James—why I didn't drop him and trick you into marrying me when I had the chance."

Ralph laughed. "We have both made many mistakes, Kit, but that was not one of them. Each of us is too good for the other."

"Nonsense. We are ideally matched. I should have seen what you would become once you had opened your eyes. Well, we won't cry about that now. I want to tell you about the Hemphills. George was killed at Landen, you know."

"No, I did not know," Ralph said slowly. "No one bothered to tell me."

As he spoke, he pictured George as he had appeared at the Assizes, and as he had appeared in Holland that day when he had ridden up to deliver the Prince's message.

"He was not important," Kit was saying, "but I thought you would be interested."

"I am," Ralph said, trying to shake off the feeling of depression. "George had little to recommend him, but I am sorry that he is dead. After his escape from Lord Jeffreys at Taunton, I thought he was immortal."

"You were at Landen too, weren't you, Ralph?"

"Yes, I was there. For all I know, I may have seen him killed."

It was typical of George, Ralph thought, to cause as much trouble as he could. In life he had gone from one scrape to another; now in death, he had managed to get himself killed in the most annoying way possible—in a way that made one review the carnage at Landen.

Landen. Ralph could still see the corpses stacked chest high around the barricades at Neerwinden where the attack had centered, the windrows of bodies that lined the approaches to the position, the swaths of dead redcoats he had seen when his decimated regiment finally broke through into the village. One of those redcoats, he realized now, was probably George. The thought made the memory of Landen strangely personal, where before it had been impersonal, like the recollection of a general disaster.

"You are not listening to me," he heard Kit say.

"I was thinking about George," he said. "Forgive me."

"I was saying that you would not like Roger Aspley, Lord Sheldon."

"You mean Esther's husband? What is wrong with him?"

"It would take too long to tell all that is wrong with him, but for a brief synopsis we could say he is fat, wooden, rich and loutish."

"How old is he?"

"About your age—about thirty-five, I should say."

"If he is as repulsive as you suggest, why do you suppose Esther married him?"

"Why does Esther do anything? For the party, of course. Sheldon may be an ox personally, but he controls a dozen seats in the House of Commons."

"He is a thorough-paced Whig, I suppose."

"He was not thorough-paced enough before he was married, but he is thorough-paced now, you may be sure."

Ralph frowned reminiscently. "I can imagine."

"It is reported about London that Esther can now command twenty-eight votes on any measure. She is almost a political party in herself."

"I dare say she is," Ralph said. "With the Hemphill and Aspley fortunes at her disposal, she will probably control fifty votes in another ten or fifteen years—unless, of course, King James regains power."

"You don't think he will, do you?"

"No, I don't think he will; but there is always a chance."

"Are you glad to find that Lord Sheldon is fat and loutish?"

"Not particularly," Ralph said. "Why should I be?"

"I think you are lying to me. You know very well that you have been eaten up with jealousy."

"That is absurd," he said.

"I agree that it is absurd," Kit said, "but it is true. Isn't it?"

"If it makes you happy to think so, I will say that it is."

"Don't try to squirm away from me. Answer the question."

"Frankly, I don't know the answer," Ralph heard himself say. "I don't believe I'm jealous, but I may be without knowing it."

"You are getting much too slippery for me," Kit said. "I still think you are lying."

"And I think that you are becoming sentimental and imaginative. Now, what else were you going to tell me about Esther Hemphill and her marriage?"

"Nothing," she said, "absolutely nothing. I have said too much already. But there are some other things that you ought to know. I must warn you, for instance, that you are being hunted here in England."

"Who told you that?"

"Several people—among them the Secretary of State. Your home in Lincolnshire is being watched constantly."

"I had not thought of going there anyway," Ralph said. "It is too dangerous. Do they suspect that I am in London now?"

"They don't know anything definite. One of their spies at Saint Germains somehow picked up the information that you and Jack are in England. I suggest that you get out of the country as soon as possible."

Ralph felt relieved. At least he had not been betrayed by anyone in London. The pursuit was still at a distance, even though it might get close at any moment. Some faithful Jacobite might talk loudly while in his cups, or some hanger-on might turn informer in the hope of a reward.

"None of your friends here know where you are staying," Kit said, as if reading his thoughts.

"Only Jack, and now you."

"I am glad to hear it," she said. "I would hate to think that your life depended on the discretion of any of the Jacobites I know."

"It does in a way," he said. "If someone wants to betray me, the officers can trap me on the way to a meeting."

"I wish you hadn't said that, Ralph. Now I will worry until I know you are out of the country. You should never have been a spy in the first place."

"You are hardly in a position to give me advice," he said. "You were the one who tried to convince me that it was my duty to stand by James against all his enemies."

"It is horrid of you to turn my words against me," she said. "I suppose I did talk a great deal of nonsense, but everyone has a right to a certain amount of nonsense."

"We all talked nonsense in those days, Kit." Ralph shrugged. "And the decisions we made then are irreversible. We must live by our previous nonsense."

Kit laughed suddenly. "You are even more impossible when you try to be profound than when you try to be witty. Being away from me may have improved your manners but it has softened up your brain. Please, Ralph, I am serious. I want you to get out of the business."

"It is too late now," he said soberly. "I am too deeply involved. As things stand, only the English want to hang me, but if I tried to quit, the French and the Jacobites would save the English the trouble."

"Do you think you can ever get out?"

"I don't know. I hope so. If James ever dies, and if the wars between France and England ever end, I have a chance. Who knows, perhaps I may even be allowed to return to England."

"I doubt it. Your old friend and her Whig confederates will never let you back in the country."

"Don't be too sure. They forgave you, you know."

"Naturally, they forgave me. If they started hanging prostitutes and adulteresses, where would it ever end?"

"A good question," Ralph said, "but they can't hang all the spies, informers, turncoats, and Jacobites either."

"I still say that you are deluding yourself. Even if they forgave you for spying, they would hang you anyway for fighting against England."

"Possibly," Ralph said, "but let us not spend our precious time worrying about it now. It will be years before the decision comes up."

"I don't see how you ever became a soldier, Ralph. You have never seemed like the type, somehow."

"I'm not sure that anyone is the type," Ralph said. "Killing people is a trade, much like any other. It is a matter of training. I am only sorry that I did not learn it earlier. I might have done some good."

"Nonsense," Kit said, and Ralph was a little startled to see that she was genuinely shocked. "You will never make me believe—someone is coming."

"Be easy," he said, recognizing Berwick's step on the stair. "It is only Jack—and for the first time I won't be glad to see him."

Kit gave him an appreciative smile. "You are sweet to say so, but I suppose I must be going."

"Don't go, Kit. I want to talk to you."

One look at Berwick's face was enough to convince Ralph that something was wrong. Jack opened his mouth as if to say something, and then, seeing Kit, he closed it again.

"What is the matter, Jack?" Kit said.

"Everything," Berwick said. "So much that I can't tell even you, Countess. I can tell you only this: Ralph and I must get out of England immediately."

"Have we been betrayed?" Ralph said. "Are William's officers closing in?"

"Not exactly. You and I can discuss this later. Right now, I suggest that we collect the few things necessary. In less than an hour it will be dark and we can get horses. With luck we can be at Romney Marsh in the morning and on the seas tomorrow night."

"Gentlemen," Kit said, "I seem to be in the way. I will leave now so that you can speak freely."

"No, don't go," Ralph said. "I can conquer my curiosity for at least an hour. I think it will be safer if you wait until dark also."

"Ralph is right," Berwick said. "Let us not press our luck too far. Did you come in a carriage?"

"No, I came in my chair. I left my chairmen at the Eagle's Head over on Basing Lane. They will stay till I get there."

"Good," Ralph said. "I will pour us a small glass while Jack collects his papers. I am ready to go now."

"Don't be so noble, Ralph. I can see that you are perishing for information. I will step out a moment, to the top of the stairs. When you are ready, you can call me. I will take care that no one sees me."

"That is why I love her," Ralph said. "She is the soul of tact."

Kit stuck out her tongue at him, and then left the room, closing the door carefully behind her.

"Well, Jack, what is it?" Ralph said.

"It is an assassination plot."

"An assassination plot? Who is to be assassinated?"

"William."

"William?"

"Yes, William. Just two hours ago, I saw Sir George Barclay. He said that he had a commission from my father to assassinate William. Twenty other members of my father's guard have slipped across the channel to help with the business."

"Did you see the commission?"

"Yes." Berwick wrinkled his brow. "It was sufficiently vague to authorize anything. I don't flatter myself with the hope that it isn't genuine, or that my father did not intend it to mean murder."

"I see," Ralph said slowly. "Why do you suppose the King did not tell you and me what he was about?"

"It is very simple," Berwick snapped. "You and I are soldiers, not assassins. And that is why we are going to leave right now. I came to recruit an army, not a gang of cutthroats. I refuse to be implicated in a thing like this."

"I assume, then, that you are going to warn William of the danger."

Berwick stared at him. "Nothing of the kind. I cannot countermand the King's orders and betray our friends—such as they are. William must take his own chances."

"Perhaps you are right," Ralph said slowly. "A plot involving twenty men or more has little chance of being kept secret long. When and how do they intend to strike?"

"Within a week or two. As soon as they can recruit twenty more men, they will waylay William's coach on Turnham Green as William returns from his Saturday hunt. With forty men they can overpower the guard and do their business."

"Did you try to dissuade Barclay from undertaking the affair?"

"I told him that he was unlikely to succeed and very likely to be hanged, but that did not discourage him. As I said before, I can't countermand the King's orders."

For the first time since he had known Jack, Ralph felt sorry for him. Clearly, Berwick was trying to suppress the disgust and rage he felt at his father's action, yet the emotions showed on his face. One could almost see him struggling to justify the plot against William's life.

"Don't fret yourself, Jack," he said helpfully. "There is not so much difference as you might think between killing people in hot blood and killing them in cold blood. Had your father's men killed William in battle, you would have praised them."

Again Berwick stared at him. "Don't try to gloss it over," he said. "The good God knows I should like to see William dead and my father restored, but I would not be party to a murder for ten kingdoms."

"But we are parties to a murder already unless we try to stop it," Ralph said.

"I will not believe it." Jack raised his voice. "I wash my hands of the whole affair."

"As you wish," Ralph said. "We will say no more about it."

"All I wish is to get out of this miserable kingdom and back to France where I belong."

"I shall call Kit," Ralph said. "We can leave within the hour."

"Well, gentlemen," Kit said as she re-entered the room, "I hope you have told your little secrets now and can stop behaving like schoolboys."

"We have told our little secrets," Berwick said, "but we can promise nothing about our behaviour."

Berwick busied himself with his papers. Some he burned immediately, others he studied, committing their contents to memory before he burned them, and a few he concealed in the pommel of his sword. Ralph tried to carry on a conversation with Kit, but she seemed almost as preoccupied as he. For the first time since he had known her, they had nothing to say to each other.

"Why don't we quit this," she said at last. "Just hold my hand, Ralph, and go on worrying about the kingdom. I shall drink my wine and worry about you. You know, I have a feeling that we shall never see each other again."

"Don't say such things, Kit." Ralph forced himself to speak cheerfully. "The wars can't last forever."

Kit looked as if she were about to reply, but she said nothing; Ralph too lapsed back into silence, watching her as she drank.

Yes, he told himself, she was only too likely to be right. The chances were heavily against their meeting again. Even if he ever came to England again as a spy, he could never risk seeing her. Already she seemed remote, like someone he had met in another life, but perhaps this was because he could not take his mind off the assassination plot. He shrugged irritably. Why should he concern himself with the plot? As Jack had said, let William take his own chances. Certainly no one was better able to look after himself. And after all, it was highly unlikely that thirty or forty would-be assassins could keep a plan secret long enough to put it into successful execution. One was almost certain to betray the others in hope of reward.

He could not help picturing William as he had been at The Hague years before. Well, the cool, politic, saturnine Dutchman had been successful. He had chased James from the throne and welded together an alliance which had stopped King Louis. Pious Protestants were forever saying that God had raised up William to save Protestantism and the liberties of Europe. Ralph was inclined to doubt this. True, William had saved Europe, but he seemed an unlikely instrument of God, unless God were a convinced Calvinist. An instrument of God, Ralph told himself, would be a little warmer, a little more human—perhaps a little more English.

As for himself, Ralph thought, he was not particularly shocked or surprised that James should wish to have his rival murdered. The plot fitted, somehow, with James's character. Always able to convince himself that anything opposed to him was evil, he would find it as easy to order an assassination as he had once found it to order state executions. No, Ralph repeated to himself, he was not shocked or surprised, only furious. It was not exactly logical, he admitted, that he should be furious with someone else who dabbled in assassination, but he was furious nevertheless. He could feel himself grind his teeth.

"We can go now."

Berwick's voice brought him out of his reverie. He let go of Kit's hand and stood up.

"I will walk with Kit over to Basing Lane," he said. "It will look less suspicious if she is escorted. I will meet you at the ostler's in fifteen minutes."

"I shall have the horses ready," Berwick said. He bowed formally and kissed Kit's hand. "Au revoir, Countess."

Kit laughed and kissed him on the forehead.

"Goodbye, Jack," she said.

When they had moved away from the house, about fifty yards up the dark lane, Ralph tightened the pressure on Kit's arm.

"Listen carefully," he said. "I want you to do something for me."

"Anything within reason," she said.

"Day after tomorrow I want you to deliver a message to Willem Bentinck."

"You mean King William's friend, the Earl of Portland?"

"Yes, he is the man. Do you know him?"

"Certainly I know him, but I did not think you did."

"I met him once, about ten years ago in Holland. I think he will remember me."

"How long have you been sending messages to King William's friends?" There was a note of suspicion in Kit's voice.

"Don't be foolish," he said quickly. "This is the first and last. You are not to deliver it until Thursday. I shall be safely out of the country by that time."

"Go on," she said. "What is the message?"

"Tell Bentinck that there is a plot on foot against William's life. Some of James's agents plan to assassinate William on Turnham Green as he returns from hunting. The trap will be sprung within the next few weeks. Can you remember that?"

Kit stopped walking.

"I can remember it," she said, "but is it true?"

"Of course it is true." Ralph tugged at her arm. "Otherwise I would not send you."

"But will Bentinck, or William, believe it? I don't think they will take my bare word."

"Tell the Earl I sent you. Tell him that if he values his friend's life he will believe what I say."

It was beginning to rain. A few drops were splashing off Kit's upturned face.

"He will want to know names and meeting places," she said.

"Tell him that he must do his own spying. I know only one name and I won't tell him that."

"On Turnham Green, you say?"

"Yes. William crosses it every Saturday when he comes back from Surrey."

He pulled Kit against the wall as three or four figures appeared through the dark and passed on down the lane.

"Will you do it for me?" he said.

"Yes, I suppose I will." They began walking again. "But I don't see why you bother."

"What do you mean?"

"Just what I said. Why should you try to save William's life? He has never done anything for you except keep you in exile."

Ralph guided her past a murky puddle.

"Let us say that I don't want to be an accessory to a murder."

"For a man whose trade is killing people, you have become strangely soft-hearted. It must have occurred to you that your only real chance of getting back to England within the next fifteen or twenty years is for William to be killed."

Ralph stopped as they came to the cross street. He could feel the water trickling down the back of his neck. At a distance he could hear a cart clanking over the cobblestones, but there was no one nearby.

"It occurred to me," he said, "but I don't think I want to return over William's corpse."

Kit looked up again. Her face, framed by a wet wig and splashed with water, looked uncommonly fresh.

"You never learn anything, do you, Ralph? You are still too sentimental for your own good."

"Call me whatever you like," he said, "as long as you see Bentinck."

Kit squeezed his hand. "I think you are a lovable idiot," she said, "but I shall deliver the message. Is there anything else I can do for you?"

"Nothing in particular," he said, "except to take care of yourself."

"I have never done anything else," she said.

Ralph thought her voice sounded unnaturally solemn.

"I hope that you and your Mr. Colyear will be happy."

"I am sure we shall be."

"Good."

Ralph stopped walking. The lights from the Eagle's Head had become visible through the rain. The sounds of drunken laughter were clearly audible.

"I must leave you now, Kit," he said. "Jack will be waiting."

"Before you go," Kit said, "I have a request too. I want you to remember me, and to come back to England if you possibly can."

"You may depend upon it," he said. "If it is possible, I will be back."

"Kiss me then."

Quickly, he took her wet face between his hands and kissed her on the mouth.

"Goodbye Kit," he said.

"Goodbye Ralph," she said softly.

She added something else, but he could not make it out as he turned and began sloshing through the rain toward the stable where Berwick was waiting with the horses.

CHAPTER

Twenty-three

"LORD STAIR IS READING your report now. He will be ready to see you in about fifteen minutes. Please make yourself comfortable."

The young Scots secretary looked less officious now than he had seemed earlier. Obediently, Sir Ralph took the chair that was offered him.

"Very well," he said. "Tell his Lordship that I await his convenience."

The secretary bowed and vanished once more behind the double doors leading to Lord Stair's study.

No, Sir Ralph told himself, glancing idly about the ornate little chamber in which he was seated, there was no reason for haste. Ever since three o'clock, when he had handed over his report, his tension had disappeared. At that point the affair had moved beyond his control and he had refused to worry about it. When he had received the order to return at eight, he had accepted it without surprise and without speculation. For the rest of the afternoon he had amused himself by wandering along the Seine watching the boats, the laundresses, and the small boys. He had caught himself cataloguing the sights in his memory in case he never saw them again. Later, he had taken a light supper in a tiny café, lingering over his coffee until seven-thirty, allowing himself barely enough time to keep the appointment. Not once had he tortured himself by wondering how Lord Stair was responding to his report. Not once had he tried to guess what moves the Jacobites were making. Yes, in some respects, this had been one of the most pleasant afternoons he had ever spent in Paris.

He was glad that he had thought to send a message to Henriette telling her of his appointment. Now she would not expect him until late. She would find the waiting a little more endurable.

Whatever the outcome, the suspense would soon be over. It was almost amusing to think of what must be going on in the other room. The whole report could be read easily in an hour, even though it had taken two days to construct. If Lord Stair had fifteen minutes of reading left, he had already passed the death of James II and William, the accession of Anne, Vienna, Blenheim, Ramillies, and Almanza. He was probably reading about the abortive invasion of Scotland in 1708, or perhaps about Malplaquet. At any rate, he would be covering years at a breakneck speed—about two minutes per year. An odd reduction of a man's life.

He was glad, Sir Ralph told himself, that he had put nothing down about Henriette or the boys. In a sense, he supposed, his family responsibilities were relevant to his case. Lord Stair and the government might find in them the best guarantees for his good conduct in England. On the other hand, neither Henriette nor the boys had exercised the slightest influence on his political and military career. The decisions had been his own. He was morally obligated to account for them without introducing any domestic sentiment.

Perhaps he imagined it—perhaps it was another sign of advancing age—but he could not shake off the impression that the new generation of English politicians was almost without feeling of any kind. God knew that men like Jeffreys and Sunderland, Petre and Tyrconnel, James and Louis had been fools, knaves, or villains; but all of them had been equipped with a complete set of emotions. The present crowd seemed pallid by comparison, faint replicas of James Hemphill—as if they had been framed for niggling calculation and petty perfidy. In his own case, Sir Ralph thought, he was probably lucky to be judged by a calculator like Lord Stair rather than a firebrand like, say, old Jeffreys. And yet there was something to be said for prejudice and passion. At least the older generation had seemed completely alive. In fact, they still seemed alive, even though most of them had been dead for fifteen or twenty years. It was easier, Sir Ralph thought, to remember how the Duke of Monmouth had looked thirty years ago than it was to remember how Stair had looked that afternoon.

Berwick was right, of course; one must not get in the habit of dwelling on his past. To do so ruined all perspective. If the new generation seemed cold, no doubt they had good reason. They had been fighting all their adult lives. Naturally they had developed thick skins.

As for himself, Sir Ralph thought, he must be something of an anachronism—not exactly a relic of the past, and yet not completely acclimated to the present. To men like Lord Stair he must seem a trifle quaint—chivalrous, perhaps, and sentimental; yet James, if he were still alive (and thank heaven he was not), would find his old agent unrecognizably tough and unfeeling. King James would never have asked the Ralph Barnard of 1716 to watch over the eleven-year-old Prince; and the Ralph Barnard of 1716 would never have accepted the responsibility. The Ralph Barnard of 1701, the man who had stood by the bedside of the dying James, had found it impossible to sever all ties with the Jacobites, impossible to leave the young Prince completely at the mercy of the asses who surrounded him. The Ralph Barnard of 1716 could have turned on his heel and walked away. At least, so it seemed now.

"His lordship will receive you, Sir."

The secretary was standing in the doorway. The look on his face was almost pleasant. The omens were favorable, it seemed to say.

Lord Stair rose from his chair beside the escritoire as Sir Ralph entered. He bowed formally and gracefully, but Sir Ralph could see no sign of pleasure or displeasure on his face.

"It was very kind of you to come at this late hour, Sir Ralph. I am sorry to have kept you waiting."

"Not at all, your lordship. I am grateful for your speedy determination of the business."

"Please sit down." Lord Stair indicated a seat beside the fireplace. "The business, unfortunately, cannot be settled without further discussion."

Sir Ralph felt a small surge of excitement. At least his case was not to be dismissed out of hand.

"I understand," he said. "I shall be happy to clear up any ambiguities or omissions."

Lord Stair seated himself carefully, crossed his silk-stockinged ankles, and studied the buckles on his shoes.

"First," he said, "let me congratulate you upon the competence of your report. It is a most fascinating document. From it one might reconstruct a fairly complete history of the Revolution and a reasonable understanding of the campaigns that have been fought since."

Sir Ralph nodded an acknowledgement of the compliment.

"Thank you, your lordship," he said.

"Let me say also," Stair continued, "that you have been admirably frank. So far as I can determine, you have tried to conceal nothing and to extenuate nothing."

"I did my best to record the truth," Sir Ralph said.

"And yet—and I shall be frank too—there is something monstrous about your story." Lord Stair began to lapse into a Scots accent.

"By your own admission, you fought against what you knew to be the best interests of your country. You followed a man whom you despised personally and politically, whose claim of divine right you regarded as fatuous, and whose intentions you regarded as fatal to England."

"That is true, my lord."

"The motives of the ordinary Jacobite I understand perfectly. He is attached to the Stuarts from sentiment, from principle, or from hope of private gain. But your motives, I confess, have baffled me completely."

Sir Ralph allowed himself a mirthless smile.

"I am not surprised, your lordship. They have often baffled me. I do not profess to understand them perfectly myself."

Stair shook his head violently.

"I should have been happier to find that you were a frank opportunist or a devout legitimist."

"I think I should have been happier too," Sir Ralph said.

He watched Lord Stair with something like amusement. That orderly Scots mind must be reeling, he reflected.

Lord Stair was contemplating his fingernails.

"I do not see how I can be expected to disentangle a skein like this," he said slowly, "much less arrive at a reasonable decision. My impulse, I confess, is to dismiss the whole affair and let you remain in France; but on the other hand, I cannot help feeling that you have a better claim to pardon than nine-tenths of the Jacobites whom we have readmitted."

"I am grateful for your consideration," Sir Ralph said.

Lord Stair rose and began to pace around the room. Sir Ralph watched him rub his long hands together.

"And then again," Stair continued as if talking to himself, "I keep returning to the fact that you have sinned against the light. We can excuse ignorance and fanaticism. We expect them. They are the human condition, as the French say. But how can we excuse a man who sees everything clearly and deliberately chooses evil?"

"I am sure I don't know," Sir Ralph said, "although I might suggest that the choices were never so simple as you seem to imply."

"The choice seems perfectly simple to me." Lord Stair stopped pacing and faced Sir Ralph. "From your report, and from what you told me during our last conversation, it was also clear to you."

"You mean, I take it, that I should have killed King James."

"I mean nothing of the kind. I mean that the moment you found

out the King's intentions you should have resigned and joined with
the Prince of Orange."

The old monotony, Sir Ralph thought. It was not bad enough having to make the decisions in the first place. Now the damned things
are frozen in the past and I must keep looking at them.

"I do not have any particular desire to defend my choice, your
lordship," he said aloud, "although I think it only fair to point out
that I did not wish to join a revolution but to prevent one—to make
one unnecessary."

"I see." Lord Stair began to pace again. "A very plausible answer
—plausible, that is if you had any reason to hope that you could
actually do anything effective toward preventing a revolution."

"I had every reason to hope, your lordship," Sir Ralph said calmly.
"I thought that if all else failed I could always assassinate the King.
But we have been over this before."

He leaned back in his chair and watched the firelight make weird
patterns with Lord Stair's shadow as it moved back and forth across
the wall. It would be odd, he said to himself, if his pardon ultimately
depended upon proving his intent to commit murder.

"In a few minutes I shall have further information on that point."
Stair's shadow stopped again. "For the moment I prefer not to discuss it."

"As you wish, my lord."

What did he mean by 'further information'?

"You said in our last meeting that you are willing to renounce
the Pretender." Lord Stair resumed his seat by the fireplace.

"That is true, my lord. I have already resigned from his service.
Whether or not you allow me to return to England, I shall undertake no more missions for young James."

"And yet you say in your report (and my informants corroborate
the statement) that you promised King James to look after the interests of the young prince. Are you revoking that promise now?"

Sir Ralph felt his back stiffen. "I revoked that promise when the
prince came of age, your lordship. I considered then that I had ful-
filled my obligation. One can hardly be guardian to a full grown
man."

"I meant no offense, Sir Ralph." Stair's tone was placating. "I do
not question your honor on that point. I must be sure, however, that
you have no mental reservation. My agents tell me that the Pretender wishes to send you to England. I should hate to help him
do so."

"Have no fear on that point, my lord." Sir Ralph relaxed again, consciously striving to regain his detachment. "I shall undertake no more missions, nor do I feel any obligation toward young James. Unfortunately, I never had any substantial influence with him. His mother and his confessors have dominated his life. I was too busy fighting and spying to offer them serious competition."

Lord Stair's reply was interrupted by a discreet knock at the door.

"Come in, McFee," Stair said.

"The lady is here, your lordship," the secretary said as he stepped inside.

"Very well, McFee. Send her in at once. We are anxious to see her."

Lord Stair turned to Sir Ralph.

"I have a pleasant surprise for you, I think. Perhaps you can guess what it is."

"Yes," he heard himself say as he rose to his feet. "I think I can guess."

So the moment had come, he told himself. He was to see Esther again. Perhaps he was lucky that the event was unexpected. He had no time to set himself for the encounter or to strike an attitude. And after all, he thought, why should he not be calm. After so many years what could be less dramatic—a fifty-five-year-old general and fifty-year-old politician. It reminded him somehow of the surrender of Bouchain. Once again he was arranging terms of capitulation. Only this time, the opposing commander was not so gallant as the Duke of Marlborough. She had tried to kill him in particular rather than in general.

"My lord." McFee appeared at the door again. "I present Lady Sheldon."

"I am pleased to see you again, your lordship," Esther said, holding out her hand.

"And I am pleased to see you again, Ralph." She turned from Lord Stair, who had bowed and kissed her hand. "It has been a long time."

"Yes," he said, bowing formally. "It has been a long time."

From across the room the candlelight and firelight had been kind to Esther. Momentarily framed in the doorway she had looked exactly like the Esther he remembered, the same erect carriage, the same slimness, the same air of command. Her movements too, as she had come toward them, had recalled the Esther of the Haagsche Bosch and Taunton. Now as she approached within arm's length, he could see that the light had deceived him. It was as if the Esther of his memory had been redrawn by an unskillful artist, who had recaptured the general outlines but distorted the details. Two large cords in her neck were clearly visible now, and the hollow at the base of her neck, where once a pulse had beat when she was excited, had deepened. Her face, although remarkably unlined, had somehow hardened and become more angular, giving the impression that all the former softness had been taken off like a mask.

"You are looking very well, Ralph," she was saying.

"And you are looking very well," he said.

Perhaps the lie was not too outrageous, he thought. She did look well if one merely looked into her eyes, which had not changed at all, and if one did not compare her with the girl who had defeated Lord Jeffreys.

"It was very kind of his lordship to invite me to see you." She glanced toward Stair and smiled. "He must have known that I had been thinking about you, even before the little Scots girl gave me your letter."

"I am always glad to bring old friends together," Stair said.

"You will be glad to know, Ralph," she went on, "that I granted your request. I sent a special messenger to Lord Townshend with the demand that he reprieve Lieutenant Maclean."

"Thank you, Esther," he said. "I knew you would see the justice of the claim."

She was looking at him fixedly. "My action had nothing to do with the justice of the claim, only with the name signed at the bottom of the letter."

Abruptly she turned toward Lord Stair. "Sir Ralph," she explained, "has always worried unduly about bloodshed. I indulged one of his whims by pardoning a rebel lieutenant."

"His compassion does him much credit," Lord Stair said.

Esther did not reply. There was an awkward pause in the conversation, as if they were actors who had suddenly run out of lines.

"Please make yourself comfortable," Lord Stair said finally. "You must excuse me for a few moments while I consult my secretary. I trust that you will be glad of the opportunity for a private chat."

"You are very thoughtful, my lord," Esther said.

Ralph wondered whether this move had been prearranged between them. Perhaps he was to be cross-examined by Esther alone. He must be on his guard.

"And now," Esther said, "tell me about yourself."

She had seated herself on a high, straightbacked chair, with her profile toward the firelight. Half shadowed, her face reminded him suddenly of her father.

"There is too much to tell." He tried to erase the picture of James Hemphill. "And none of it is very important. If you are really curious, you can read it at your leisure in the report I gave to Lord Stair. It is lying there on the table."

"Lord Stair was kind enough to let me read your report this afternoon," she said. "I did not mean to ask about your official life. I wanted to know about your unofficial life."

"I am sure that my private life is on file in Lord Stair's dossier," he said slowly. "In December, 1701, shortly after King James died, I married Henriette Picard of Arras. We have two sons, Richard fourteen and Henry twelve. Since 1706 we have lived in Paris. That is to say, Henriette and the lads have lived in Paris, and I have lived there between expeditions. Except for our habit of drinking tea and coffee, we are probably indistinguishable from other Parisian families. Is that what you wanted to know?"

Esther shook her head. "No, Ralph. I already knew that too. I was even so curious as to have one of our female agents at Saint Germains make herself acquainted with your wife."

"And what did your agent say?"

"She said Henriette was entirely charming, entirely non-political, and entirely devoted to you. She also said that no art could induce her to reveal any information of value."

"The last part of the report must have been a great disappointment to you."

"A disappointment, yes," Esther said soberly, "but not a surprise. I hardly expected you to marry a woman incapable of keeping secrets. The first part of the report was a much greater disappointment. I had hoped your wife would be ugly, shrewish, and devious."

Sir Ralph forced a short laugh. "Thank you for your good wishes."

"No, Ralph. When I asked you about your unofficial life, I did not want a copy of the parish register. I wanted to know how you felt."

"How I felt?"

"Yes, how you felt. Did you hate me?"

Ralph feared that he was staring. Was it possible that this (what was it that Kit had once called her?) frozen-faced politician really cared how he had felt? The notion seemed grotesque.

Again he forced himself to smile. "If your question means did I hate you for plotting my death, I suppose the answer is yes. Let me hasten to add, however, that the feeling went away within a couple of years."

"You forgave me, then."

"I don't know whether I forgave you or not—probably not. I merely quit thinking about the subject."

An expression of irritation crossed her face.

"But you do understand my motives. You understand why I was obliged to sacrifice you."

"I understand them. I understood them perfectly at the time. Perhaps I understand them too well."

"If you understood, you must have understood also how difficult it was for me to make the decision."

"Difficult? No, I never believed that you had any trouble arriving at your decision. To tell you the truth, I have always considered that you acted in the only way possible to you."

"You are unfair, Ralph." Her voice was louder now. It reminded him vaguely of their old arguments. "You must have known how much it hurt me to lose you."

"I think I knew exactly how much it hurt you," he said, trying to keep the sarcasm out of his voice.

Esther shrugged. "You seem determined to be unpleasant. I don't see why I bother to explain myself to you."

"I am sorry, Esther," he said. "I really don't mean to be unpleasant. All I wish to do is to keep the past straight. At this late hour, I can see no good in trying to rearrange it. You saw a chance to trade my life for a political advantage and you took it. Let me assure you that I hold no grudge. I don't even presume to judge the deed. Still, I can hardly be expected to feel sorry for you."

He watched Esther draw herself up. The line of her jaw tightened, increasing her resemblance to her father. Her eyes seemed to be boring into him.

"Feel sorry for me?" she said. "Feel sorry for me? Why should you feel sorry for me? I am not asking for sympathy. I only want you to understand that giving you up was the hardest thing I have ever done in my life."

"Very well, Esther," he said. "If you say so, I shall believe you."

"Yes," she said slowly, as if talking to herself, "it was the hardest thing I ever did. And yet, given the circumstances, I still think I was right. Love, after all, is an episode. It is not a life's work."

Ralph turned his eyes away from her. There was something unnatural and embarrassing about hearing this woman, with her annoying resemblance to Esther Hemphill, talk about love.

"I am glad that you are happy with your choice," he said.

"I did not say that I was happy," she said. "People who talk about being happy make me ill. I have done better than that. I have accomplished something."

"Yes," he heard himself say. "I suppose you have."

"Don't sit there looking supercilious and patronizing, as if I were someone's maiden aunt. I assure you that my life has been interesting and exciting."

His laugh, he was convinced, sounded easy and natural, but he could not bring himself to look at her.

"Please don't feel that you must defend yourself to me," he said. "I am not patronizing you. I envy your success."

"No you don't." Her voice was flat and harsh. "I can see it in your face. You never really approved of me, and you don't approve of me now. You think I am a hard-faced harridan. And I tell you again, it is not fair."

No, he told himself, probably it was not fair. No Jesuit had ever devoted himself to his mission more completely than Esther had devoted herself to her cause. God knew that she had schemed, connived, cheated, lied, and betrayed; but she had done it all with a selflessness that would have done credit to a Christian martyr. Now when she wanted praise for her devotion and admiration for her success, she found herself regarded as some sort of monstrosity. Yes, in a way it was unfair, he admitted. And yet he could not help being repelled by her and wishing he had not seen her again.

"You must not put words in my mouth," he was saying smoothly. "I think nothing of the sort. You are a handsome woman. Your father and brother would be proud of you if they could see you."

Esther hesitated. "Then you don't regret having loved me?"

With a great effort Ralph compelled himself to face her and look her squarely in the eye.

"I regret nothing," he said.

The lie, if it was a lie, had cost him nothing. It was the least he could do under the circumstances. And perhaps he had told the exact truth.

"Thank you, Ralph," she was saying. "That was what I really wanted to know."

For a few moments, he listened silently to the crackle of the logs.

"Do you ever think about George and your father?" he said finally.

He saw a little flash of annoyance appear in her eyes. Was she irritated because he had changed the subject? Whatever the impulse had been, she checked it.

"I don't think of George very much," she said. "He has been dead for more than twenty years, you know. Oh, now and then someone does something excessively rash and foolish. Then I think of him."

"I see," he said. He wondered if she remembered anything about the trial at Taunton, but he did not want to bring up the subject.

"With Father it is different, of course. I think of him often. Only today I was wishing he could have lived to see the Revolution finally secure and his enemies completely defeated."

"I suppose you know that you are very much like him. You even look like him."

"Thank you," she said. "I always tried to be like him."

Ralph was glad that she had taken the remark for a compliment.

"I often wonder what happened to our friend Keith," he said. "For a few years after the Revolution I found it useful to keep track of him. Then he dropped completely out of sight."

"Oh yes, Keith. I had almost forgotten him. He was drowned en route to Holland—in '97, if I remember rightly. The packet boat went down in a storm."

"I always considered him a very useful man."

Suddenly he could see himself being followed by Keith on the way to Whitehall. An odd image, he thought. He had never seen Keith following him.

"He was very useful," Esther said. "But no more useful than his successor, a renegade Frenchman named Denis."

"I remember the man."

"I did not think you knew him."

"Oh yes, I met him one night in London two or three years before the Revolution. He was employed by King Louis at the time."

"He never mentioned this," she said thoughtfully. "And that is strange too. At one time I was going to send him to France to collect information about you."

"Perhaps he forgot my name."

Now that he had guided the conversation to impersonal reminiscences, he felt better. The experience was almost pleasant, like the talk between two old campaigners from opposing armies.

"Speaking of former acquaintances," Esther said. "I saw a friend of yours recently. I despise the woman, but she talked of you so prettily that I could hardly hate her as she deserves."

"You must mean the Countess of Dorchester. How is she?"

"Candidly, I must say that she did not look very well. She has aged as rapidly as I could wish. But she still retains the same odious disposition and the same sharp tongue. She should have been hanged at the time of the Revolution, or exiled with James. It infuriates me to see these time-servers turn their coats with every shift in the political wind and still go on to prosper under every regime. I can almost respect a Tory, but I loathe trimmers on principle."

"I am sure you do," Ralph said, smiling a little. "Did you tell Kit so?"

"Not in so many words, but I conveyed the idea. Perhaps you can guess what she said."

"Something like 'prostitution has no politics'?"

"Worse than that. Her exact words were, 'show me a hot politician, and I will show you a cold bedfellow.'"

"But I forgave her." Esther hurried on, as if to dismiss a distasteful subject. "She told me something remarkable about you. You were in England, she said, at the time of the plot against King William. You were the first to warn the Earl of Portland about it. According to her story, she conveyed the warning herself."

"That is true," he said.

"I knew it was true the moment she told me. It was so precisely typical, I almost wept when I heard it. You could always do everything for your cause except the one thing needful. You were clever, devoted, and competent; you could see what was necessary to success. Yet, when the moment arrived, you balked at a little necessary bloodshed."

"Perhaps I have a constitutional distaste for murder," he said drily.

"Don't mouth pious nonsense," she said. "As far as James was concerned, you knew it was never a question of whether or not there would be killing, but only a question of who would be killed. You chose to send thousands of men to their deaths instead of one dull-witted, bigoted old tyrant. And now you sit here mentally accusing me of being a monster."

"To deal plainly with you," he said, "I think that neither of us has much to boast of."

"Please don't misunderstand me, Ralph." Her voice was calm and smooth again. "I don't complain of the results. I am glad that you were never ruthless enough for your work. Had you done your obvious duty, we Whigs could never have triumphed so completely. Perhaps I should have been applying to you for permission to return to England."

"Had I done my obvious duty," he said quietly, "I should have been hanged."

"Oh yes," she said. "I had forgotten that for the moment."

"But I do not wish to cavil about details."

She shrugged. "As I said before, your squeamishness allowed the Revolution to run its course. We beat the French, put down the Irish, secured toleration for dissent, put clogs on kings, and smashed popery and arbitrary power in England. Had you done your duty, the issues might still be doubtful."

It was odd, he reflected, how the firelight seemed to harden on her face, as if the rays were frozen. He wished she would turn her head.

"In other words," he said, "you think I saved the Revolution by default."

She shrugged again. "One might say so, although you deserve no credit."

"I hope you will credit me with saving you from a great blunder."

"You saved me, I confess. It was stupid of me to want James killed. Worse than stupid, it was cowardly. I had lost my nerve. My fear that the Revolution might fail made me willing to compound for something less than complete victory. Yes, I am grateful, even for an unintended favor."

"And you believe that the 'complete victory,' as you call it, was worth all the lives it cost."

For a moment he thought he saw something like a sneer on her face, but perhaps it was merely a slight movement of her jaw muscles, as she turned squarely toward him and fixed him in her gaze.

"Worth the lives?" she said. "Most certainly it was worth the lives. What are two or three hundred thousand lives compared with the success of the Revolution? We were fortunate to attain such great objects so cheaply. Three million lives would have been cheap."

Ralph looked away. "I should like to believe it," he said, "but I was at Malplaquet."

As soon as the words were out of his mouth, he was sorry he had spoken them. They could mean nothing to Esther, and he was no longer sure that they meant anything to him. The frightful slaughter of the blue-coated infantry and the decimation of his brigade now seemed more like a dream than an actual event.

"Had you fought on the right side," Esther was saying, "Malplaquet would now be the memory of a great triumph. You would be boasting at the coffee houses of your share in it."

"I don't think so," he said. "I have always considered Malplaquet a victory for the French, and I was decorated for my share in it; but I have never felt like boasting. To me, Malplaquet was merely thirty thousand more lives thrown away."

Esther stood up suddenly and walked over to the mantelpiece.

Ralph saw her glance into the mirror before she turned to face him again. He wondered whether she liked what she saw in the mirror.

"This sort of nonsense makes me ill," she said. "It is the dreary futility one expects from a Tory. A good Whig knows that liberty and progress are worth whatever they cost."

"A good Whig, I have found, can justify any enormity."

Was it possible, he asked himself, that he had ever loved this woman, with her cold disregard for lives and her fanatical devotion to abstractions?

"You are a hopeless sentimentalist, Ralph." Her voice, he noticed, had softened. "It is an amiable fault, but a fatal one. No great object can be accomplished without hurting people. The principle is everything, the cost is nothing."

"So King James told me," he said.

Her shoulders, as she stood there by the fireplace, still retained some of their former beauty. Although the sleek smoothness was gone, the poise and assurance were intensified, as if the shoulders themselves were accustomed to giving commands. Watching her, as she drew herself up in disdain, he found it difficult to listen to what she was saying.

"Are you comparing me to that popish bigot?"

"Certainly not," he said placatingly. "I merely said that you shared one of his views. James, thank God, was never handsome, never charming, never artful, and never brilliant."

No, he added to himself, the poor old devil never had anything to recommend him.

"I shall never understand you, Ralph." She was watching him incredulously. "I believe you actually feel sorry for the scheming villain."

"If it is possible to despise someone and feel sorry for him at the same time, I suppose I feel sorry for him, although I confess it is easier to pity him now that he is dead."

As he spoke, he pictured the James of Dublin Castle, with his pair of trollops, his swarms of petitioners, and his knot of advisers. At the time, he remembered, he had wanted to strangle the incompetent clod. Now the picture was amusing and just a little pathetic.

"Can you feel sorry for a man who ruined your life?"

Ralph felt himself smiling indulgently.

"I do not consider my life ruined," he said, "although I did once. As I told you a few minutes ago, I regret nothing."

The reply seemed to irritate Esther again. Why, he could not imagine. As Lord Stair re-entered the room, he was thankful for the interruption.

"Please pardon me for not returning sooner," Stair said. "I hope I did not inconvenience you."

"Not at all," Esther said. "Sir Ralph and I have had a most interesting discussion. He barely finished telling me that he regrets nothing."

"Perhaps he means merely that regret is useless," Stair said smoothly. "Is that it, Sir Ralph?"

"I don't think so," Sir Ralph heard himself say. "I think I actually meant that I no longer regret anything."

Esther moved back toward him. She was standing now in front of his chair.

"I hardly need tell you," she said softly, "that your statement is no recommendation for a man who wishes pardon for his crimes against England."

"I am afraid it is a fact, nevertheless," he said.

The statement was stupid, he thought. He was not even sure that it was true. Yet he had felt impelled to make it.

Lord Stair, he noticed, was looking from one of them to the other as if he suspected some kind of personal conflict. He seemed anxious to relieve the tension.

"Sir Ralph is a soldier. One must make allowances."

Esther moved her shoulders again in an almost imperceptible shrug.

"Very well," she said, "I shall not insist upon regret."

"Sir Ralph has presented me with a fascinating story, your ladyship. He excuses—or rather, explains—some of his most vital actions upon the ground that he once intended to assassinate King James. He claims to have intimated his design to you and says that you can corroborate his story. Is it true?"

"Perfectly true," she said without hesitating. "As I told you before, Sir Ralph has always worried unduly about bloodshed."

"You approved of the plan, then?"

Mentally, Sir Ralph congratulated Stair on keeping any trace of shock or disapproval out of his voice. It would never do to antagonize Esther.

"I am sorry to say I did approve," she said, with a glance at Ralph. "At that time the plan seemed to offer an easy salvation for the country and for our party. Fortunately, Sir Ralph's heart failed him."

Lord Stair ran his long Scot's hand along the lapel of his coat.

"I cannot help feeling," he said thoughtfully, "that the intent extenuates his actions, although I cannot say precisely how."

"I disagree," Esther said. "It makes him a coward as well as a traitor. Let me quickly add, however, that I consider the question irrelevant."

Sir Ralph sat back in his chair. He was becoming accustomed to being discussed as if he were not in the room.

"Irrelevant?" Lord Stair's voice sounded strained.

"Yes, your lordship. Obviously, we shall get nowhere if we try to decide this matter on the grounds of moral culpability. On such grounds all Jacobites, including Sir Ralph, deserve to be hanged. The question to be decided is whether there is more to be gained by letting him return to England or leaving him here in France. On this basis, Sir Ralph has a reasonably strong case."

"You believe, I take it, that he can do less damage in England, where we can keep him under surveillance, than in France, where he will always be subject to pressures from the Jacobites."

"Undoubtedly," she said. "Knowing Sir Ralph as I do, I fear he will always be tempted to undertake just one mission more for the Pretender; but in England we shall always have sureties for his good behavior."

"You mean his family, I assume."

"Yes."

The iciness of her voice gave Ralph a little chill. He had not visualized clearly until now, he realized, what was involved in his return to England. Could he really put Henriette, Richard, and Henry at the mercy of Esther and her friends?

"On the other hand," Lord Stair was saying, "we must consider public sentiment in the matter. Pardoning notorious Jacobites is a sticky business. We must not outrage our friends by being too lenient with flagrant offenders. And while personally I consider Sir Ralph's case exceptional, I have little hope of convincing others."

"The point is well taken," Esther said slowly. "Believe me, I have been aware of the problem from the first. No one is more anxious than I to keep our friends in countenance. I consider, however, that public resentment can be disarmed if the affair is handled properly. We can represent his pardon as another signal instance of the government's clemency, of our desire to heal old wounds and move forward into a new era. His defection from the Pretender can be turned into a triumph for our policy."

Lord Stair stroked his chin thoughtfully. "Very likely," he said as if talking to himself, "although this may seem small consolation to the widows his activities have made."

"I repeat, your lordship, what I have often said. One must think of the future and not of the past. The vulgar passions of vindictiveness and revenge must not be indulged more than is absolutely necessary. If exile—or a hanging, for that matter—will advance the cause, I shall be the first to recommend it. If, on the other hand, it will actually damage the cause, I shall never recommend it, no matter how handsomely deserved."

"I quite agree with you, your ladyship," Stair said quickly. "I was merely estimating the strength of public resentment and our ability to appease it."

"We shall have another weapon at our disposal," she said coolly. "We can make much of Sir Ralph's merits in the Fenwick affair. It was he, you remember, who gave the first warning to Portland about the plot against King William's life."

"I remember, your ladyship. It is a strong point in his favor."

"We can also represent his long, faithful service to King James as proof of the value of his promises."

"Yes, your ladyship," Stair said. "We can."

"Very well, then," Esther said, "I suggest that you write out a safe-conduct for Sir Ralph and his family. I shall be glad to witness it and answer for its approval by the government."

Sir Ralph found himself staring at her. She had advocated his cause as skillfully as if it had been her own. Although there had been no trace of sentiment in her argument, her obvious determination to brush aside all objections almost made him suspect that she was conferring a personal favor upon him.

It was strange, he thought, as he watched Lord Stair sit down at the escritoire and begin to write, that she should take the trouble. Perhaps he had misjudged the depth of her feelings after all.

"Here it is, your ladyship. Is this satisfactory?"

Stair handed the paper to Esther, who took it, glanced at it briefly, and then countersigned it.

"Perfectly," she said.

She held the paper out toward Ralph so that he could read it.

This is to certify that the bearer, Sir Ralph Barnard, has given adequate assurances for his conduct and has promised fidelity to His Majesty George I. He is to be passed, therefore, through all English ports and allowed to reside, along with his family and personal servants, in England.

SHELDON   STAIR

As he reached out to take the letter, she drew it back.

"I forgot to mention one small consideration," she said. "It was stupid of me to forget it."

Sir Ralph let his hand fall abruptly to his side and leaned back again in his chair.

"I was sure there would be another consideration," he said slowly.

"Don't take that tone with me, Ralph. After all, for a favor as great as this we have a right to expect something in return."

He glanced at Lord Stair, who was looking at Esther with a puzzled frown.

"Name it," he said.

"It is really very simple," she said. "All we want is a list of the Pretender's agents in England. Of course, a list of the Tories who sent pledges to the Pretender in 1714 would also be useful, but we shall not insist upon that."

"You are too generous," he said.

"Please spare me the irony," she said, "and don't indulge yourself in false heroics. We shall find the agents eventually anyway. You will merely be speeding the process. You have my word that there will be no executions—nothing beyond transportation or a few years in Newgate."

"I thought I made myself clear to his lordship in our first conversation. I do not intend to return to England at the expense of my friends."

Esther favored him with a frigid little smile.

"I fear his lordship has shown more indulgence than the government can afford at this juncture. We cannot neglect so good an opportunity to settle our affairs with the Jacobites. If you co-operate, we can wind up the business in two weeks. Otherwise it may drag on for two or three years."

"And you seriously expect me to co-operate?"

Lord Stair, he noticed, was looking absently into the fireplace and shaking his head slowly back and forth. It was clear, Ralph thought, that he disliked the proceedings.

"I expect," Esther said stonily, "that you will act wisely. It goes without saying that no one will ever know where we received our information. You can count on our discretion."

"And your protection too, I suppose."

She nodded. "It also goes without saying that if you refuse you will never be given another chance to return."

"I understand," he said.

"Here," she said, "hold the passport while you make up your mind. It may help you arrive at a sensible decision."

As he took the paper, he felt a momentary impulse to get up and run away with it. The absurdity of the notion almost made him smile.

"When you have your freedom in your hands," she was saying, "you can see how fatuous you would be to trade it for a useless scruple. What is a short respite for a few deluded rogues compared with the future of your family, to say nothing of your own happiness?"

"What indeed?" he said softly.

He pretended to study the passport, running his eyes along the lines of Stair's neat, economical script and over Esther's bold, decisive signature; but all the time, he was conscious of Esther's eyes boring into him and of Stair's slow pacing. He was conscious too of the random crackling of the logs in the fireplace. As he looked up, a large spark arced from the fire and burned itself out on the hearth.

"Well," Esther said, "what do you say?"

It is too bad, he said to himself, that she did not look like this thirty years ago. I could have saved myself a great deal of trouble.

"I say no, of course." He was glad that his voice sounded so completely unruffled. "I cannot even consider such a proposal."

The expression on Esther's face did not change.

"As you will, Ralph," she said. "But you are being extremely foolish."

"Very likely."

"You will regret your choice."

"Possibly."

"As I told you before, you will never get another chance."

"I know that."

"You will never see England again."

"I shall survive the disappointment," he said. "Somehow England is becoming less attractive minute by minute."

Esther frowned.

"You understand, of course, my position in this matter. As far as I am concerned personally, I would do anything for you, Ralph. Anything. Where England is concerned, however, I cannot let my personal feelings interfere with my duty."

"I think we have been through all this before," he said.

"Please understand, Sir Ralph, that if it were possible we should be glad to let you go." Stair's voice sounded flat and discouraged. "But as her ladyship says, we must insist on payment."

He will never be a minister in the government, Ralph thought.

He is not so cold as I had believed. If the decision were his, he would let me go.

"I am thankful for your good wishes, your lordship," he said aloud, rising from his chair. "I know you would oblige me if you could."

As he walked toward the fireplace, he tore the passport into strips. One by one he put the strips in the fire and watched them burn.

"I must not take up more of your time," he said. "You have wasted too much of it on my case already."

Lord Stair bowed politely.

"I do not consider the time wasted. The case has been most instructive, and meeting you has been a pleasure."

"His lordship is right," Esther said. "The time has not been wasted."

He did not want to look at her. Already the Esther of the present had obliterated the Esther of the past; and although it was probably better to have the old images effaced, he could not help feeling a perverse regret for the change.

"No," he said. "I suppose it was worth while."

"It is not too late even now to change your mind, Ralph. His lordship can easily write a new passport."

"No thank you," he said quietly. "I must go now. Henriette will be worried."

Esther held out her hand.

"Goodbye, Ralph," she said. "Perhaps we shall meet again."

"Perhaps we shall," he said noncommittally.

Her hand felt cold to his lips. He released it as quickly as good manners would allow.

"Goodbye, your lordship, and thank you again for your consideration." He bowed to Stair.

"My secretary will show you out," Stair said, conducting him to the door of the study.

"Don't forget me, Ralph," Esther's voice called after him.

But he pretended not to hear it and did not bother to turn around.

CHAPTER

Twenty-four

As SIR RALPH descended the steps of Lord Stair's house into the street, he was met by a light rain. Coming out of the total blackness of the Parisian night, it pattered against him in tiny gusts, making him pull his hat down farther over his eyes. He reproached himself gently for trusting to the clear skies of the afternoon. To have ventured out without his cape was really inexcusable. Now he would have a wetting for his pains. Two miles home through the rain, with disappointment for company.

He did not move against the wall for what shelter it could afford. Instead he began walking steadily down the middle of the cobblestoned street. After all, he told himself, what did another soaking matter? He would be home within a half hour. Henriette would have a warm fire and a hot cup of tea waiting for him. Lizette would have laid out his dry clothes. And actually, he admitted, the rain itself was not really unpleasant. The cold wetness against the back of his neck seemed to clear his thoughts. Perhaps, after what he had just been through, a bath in rainwater was exactly what he needed.

Yes, it was precisely what he needed, like the rain after Blenheim, to rid his mind of disaster. Or was it disaster? As his thoughts fell into rhythm with the steady beat of his shoes against the wet cobblestones, he tried to examine his feelings. England seemed to have vanished behind him somewhere in the rain, but as far as he could tell he felt no bitterness. Nothing like the overwhelming sense of betrayal and despair he had felt at Whitehall years before. Maybe it is all a matter of age, he told himself. Nothing that happens to a man over thirty is really shattering, only an irritation more or less.

Did he actually feel relieved? He did not think so, and yet, he admitted, it was possible. One line of action was now closed forever. England had become irrelevant. From now on, the life he had led in France and Spain would be the only life that counted. He had been cut off almost as effectively as Berwick from his distant past.

Jack, of course, would be glad about the turn of events. Regardless of all evidence to the contrary, Jack would continue to think of the Good God as a Tory. The first thing tomorrow morning he would send Jack a note. What was it Jack had said about a place in the government? The intendancy of Guyenne? Or was it Dauphiné? Spain, he reflected, could not offer enough to a man with the problem of educating two sons. Henriette would love the Spanish landscape, but living in Spain would never please her long. In spite of its rains and its gardens, Paris had its advantages. At least it was civilized. Good food, good wine, and good conversation.

As he paused a moment at the corner, he thought he heard footsteps behind him, but after listening a moment he decided he must have been mistaken. The only sound he could be sure of was the spatter of rain falling from the eaves of the houses. He relaxed his grip on his sword. If nothing else, he told himself, his new life could provide a certain sort of freedom. He would be able to walk down the street without glancing back over his shoulder. He wondered if he would be able to break the habit. Perhaps not. He could not stop himself now from turning onto the side street and quickening his pace a little.

Yes, this new sort of freedom was worth something. In England, there would always be surveillance. Here, continuous harassment from the Jacobites, but nothing dangerous. Not Esther and her friends. It was better, he supposed, to be a comparatively free man in an autocracy than a paroled criminal in a free country.

He must dismiss England from his mind now. In time, he could see the whole thing in a reasonable perspective. Then, perhaps, Walter, Kit, Esther, James, William—even old Jeffreys—would appear in their true proportions, stripped of hope, pity, hate, or affection. Only a fool could expect to make this transition in a day, but the sooner one started trying the better. Sometime soon he would discuss with Henriette his interview with Esther and Lord Stair. For the present, however, it was probably wisest to let the whole episode lie undisturbed and unordered.

When he stopped this time, the footsteps behind him were unmistakable. They stopped too, almost immediately, but not before he had registered his danger. At least three men—possibly four— were back there in the dark about twenty-five yards away.

Without wasting a moment, he slipped off his shoes and began to run.

The clumsy idiots, he said to himself. They should have marched along loudly and boldly, like drunks returning from a tavern. Trust the Jacobites to botch an assassination.

He did not run fast. The wet cobblestones made unsure and painful footing for his stockinged feet, and the rain made vision impossible beyond three feet. Silence, he knew, was more vital than speed. Without the sound of his footsteps to guide them, his pursuers must proceed slowly for fear of missing him in the dark. With his left hand he secured the scabbard of his sword to keep it from rattling against his leg. His right hand he held out in front of him. The narrow street, as he vaguely remembered it, was anything but straight. He did not want to run into a wall.

That the men were Jacobites he had no doubt. Only Jacobites had any reason to murder him. Evidently Randall's threat had been serious. They were prepared to kill him rather than let him return to England. Like Esther, they had believed that he would betray his friends to pay for his passage. Damn them, he thought; at least they might have made sure of their facts. It would be absurd to be killed by mistake.

He was more irritated than alarmed. He would be unlucky indeed if he were caught in this soupy blackness, but now he would be obliged to get an armed escort before going home. He would not be safe until the Jacobites were convinced that he had no intention of returning to England. Thank God he could count on Jack to help him. Once out of this miserable little street he would head directly for Jack's.

. He had run, he judged, about a hundred yards when he drew himself up short. Ahead, possibly thirty yards, he saw a blob of light. It was not, he saw instantly, the light from an unshuttered window, nor was it high enough to come from one of those newfangled lanterns that the very rich sometimes hung over their entrances. No, it was merely a single unmoving blob of light, as if someone had suspended a lantern in the middle of the street about six feet from the ground.

Drawing his sword from its scabbard, he moved quickly against the left-hand wall and listened. He could hear nothing but the splash of rain from the solid line of eaves. Obviously his pursuers were still far behind. But what was ahead? The cold feeling in the pit of his stomach told him that he was in a trap. He had underestimated his opponents. With only two streets to guard, they had been able to block the exits. Very likely that lantern had been placed so that he could not slip past. Behind it must be a man or two ready with drawn swords.

For a single instant he was tempted to yell to the top of his lungs. Maybe he could rouse the neighborhood before he brought the assassins down on him. But he dismissed the notion with scorn. A yell from the street would only lock the shutters and doors tighter.

Slowly he moved toward the light, mentally calculating distances and time. His best chance, he decided, was to advance as close as he dared and make a dash for it. With luck he could run past the lantern and past the men lying in wait before they could act. They would be listening for footsteps and straining their eyes into the dark. They would not expect their quarry to come running. Once past them, he could take his chances on losing them. If he were twenty years younger, the operation would be simple.

Carefully he slipped off his sword belt and scabbard, putting them down silently beside the wall. His hands, he noticed, were steady. In spite of his exertions from running, he was not panting. Hugging the wall tightly and advancing again with extreme care, he moved to within ten yards of the light.

Yes, he told himself, the light came from a lantern. But what was holding it up? There seemed to be a faint sheen of glass behind it and the vague outline of something large. Then it came to him, even as he heard the faint snort of a horse—a carriage had been placed across the narrow entrance to the street. The lantern was hanging down from the side.

He had been tensed to begin his sprint. Now he turned abruptly and began to work his way back up the street. There was nothing for it but to try breaking through his pursuers or to find some friendly doorway and hope he would be passed by. Speed had become essential, he told himself grimly, listening intently to catch any sound. He must not let his enemies converge on him.

Shifting his sword to his left hand and feeling the wall with his right, he retraced his steps. He had covered perhaps thirty yards when he heard the footsteps. At almost the same moment, he felt a break in the wall. An entranceway. Without a second's hesitation, he stepped inside. The passage, he found, was about four feet wide and ten feet long, ending in a locked door, which he tried briefly before turning to face the street. He had half hoped to find something to hide behind, but the passageway was absolutely bare. So be it, he said to himself. They can come in only one at a time. If worst comes to worst, I can make the entertainment lively.

The footsteps were distinct now—within twenty yards, he judged. They were advancing slowly and carefully, as if his pursuers were not anxious to conceal their whereabouts but intent upon making a

thorough search as they went, like dogs trying to start a fox. Then
the sound stopped suddenly, and all he could hear was the drip of
the rain. Perhaps they were listening too or probing around some
obstacle with their swords.

As he crouched down in the farthest corner he swore silently to
himself. My God, what an ending. After all the battles—to say nothing of the skirmishes, brushes, raids, and retreats—to be trapped in a
dark alley and cut down by a knot of misinformed louts. It fitted
somehow, all of a piece. After a lifetime of mistakes, there was finally
one mistake too many. No doubt he deserved his fate. And yet, who
would have supposed that the silly asses would actually try to kill
him. He wanted to scream in sheer frustration.

Of one thing he was certain. Young James had not ordered his
death. God knew the boy had his faults. He was opinionated, super-
stitious, impulsive, and maladroit. But he was no murderer, and
certainly not a murderer of his friends. If anything, he was undis-
criminatingly loyal. No, this little ambuscade was the work of some
officious subordinate—some zealous underling, anxious to prove his
ability and loyalty. His helpers were probably paid Parisian cutthroats. No ordinary Jacobite gentleman would undertake the job.
Nor could any of them organize a guet apens with such relentless
thoroughness. Had the rain not upset the plans, all would be over
now.

It would be over soon, one way or another, he thought. The footsteps had started up again. Although closer, they were softer, as if
the men had become more cautious now that they were coming
toward the end of their cul-de-sac. He flexed the muscles of his
sword hand.

The darkness in front of him suddenly became a shade darker, and
the footsteps stopped, leaving a hollow reverberation as they echoed
through the passageway. Ralph held his breath. For a moment the
silence was perfect except for the half muffled sound of the rain.
Then he heard the sharp scratching sounds of metal on brick, the
point of a sword methodically exploring the passageway. Before he
could consciously formulate his decision, he lunged.

Instantly he was deafened by a scream. The sword was almost
wrenched from his hand. Only then did he have the delayed sensation that it had found a mark, ending up against bone. With a quick
tug he pulled it free and launched himself toward his assailant. If
he could get past the man and into the street he might escape in the
confusion. The next thing he knew he was staggering back from the
force of the impact, as if he had hit a wall.

"Name of God, I am killed."

The voice was heavy and French, the tone conversational, contrasting strangely with the scream which still seemed to be echoing in the passage. Sir Ralph had the impression that the big hulk had been knocked to its knees just outside the entrance to the passage.

Even as he gathered himself for another rush, he realized he was too late to escape. From the sound of the quick footsteps, he could tell that two other men had moved into position beside the entrance —beside their fallen comrade, who was whimpering like an injured child. Instead of lunging again, Sir Ralph moved to within sword length of the opening, his rapier poised to strike at the first sign of a silhouette. His position gave him a slight advantage in this grim game of blindman's buff and he was determined to use it.

From down the street, he heard more footsteps.

Death and damnation, he said to himself, the scream has brought the reinforcements.

"You are being needlessly difficult, Monsieur Barnard," a voice said. "We mean you no harm. We only wish to talk to you."

I dare say, Sir Ralph thought. If you think I will speak and tell you exactly where I am you are not so professional as I thought.

"Please don't make us come in after you," the voice went on calmly. "If we do, I cannot answer for your safety."

And I won't answer for yours either, you suave cutthroat. I hope you are the first to try.

"Why don't you speak, Monsieur?" The voice sounded aggrieved. "Is it that you do not trust us? I assure you, you have no recourse but to take our word."

The wounded man was still whimpering. Ralph could hear him dragging himself away from the entrance.

"Where is he?" a new voice asked.

"He is in the doorway," the first voice said. "Where is the lantern?"

"I did not know we needed it. Shall I go back and get it?"

"Wait a moment. Perhaps he will listen to reason."

Two more of them, Ralph thought. It might as well be a hundred.

"Monsieur Barnard, you heard what my friend said. If you do not come out now, we shall bring the light, in which case, I promise, our conversation will be very short."

Ralph made a quick pass with his sword at the sound of the voice, but he hit nothing. No doubt the man was hiding around the corner. None of them seemed anxious to attack. Perhaps they were not being paid enough.

"I am waiting," the voice said.

"Why don't you shoot him?" This voice spoke French with an English accent.

"Don't tell us our business, Monsieur," the suave voice replied. "We don't intend to rouse the neighborhood unless it is absolutely necessary."

"I think the scream has roused it already. Let's get the affair over with."

"The gentleman is right," another voice said. "We have no time to lose."

There was a sharp click of a hammer being pulled back.

"Don't be a fool," the first voice said. "Do you think you can hit him in the dark?"

Ralph crouched down again, trying to catch the glint of a pistol.

"Go ahead, fire," the Englishman said. "Aim low. You can hardly miss him in a passage so narrow."

Flattening himself against the cold, damp stones, Ralph waited for the concussion.

They will rush, he thought, as soon as they fire. I must be ready.

In the instant of silence that followed, he could hear the steady beat of the rain, heavier now than it had been before, and the subdued moans of the injured man.

There was another sharp metallic click.

"Name of a dog. It won't fire."

"Certainly not," the suave voice said, "the priming is damp."

Thank God, he said to himself. If I get out of this alive, I shall never malign Paris rain again.

"Now let us be sensible," the suave voice was continuing. "While André primes his pistol, go get the lantern. I don't like this shooting in the dark."

"Why don't you go in after him?" the English voice said.

"Once more, Monsieur, don't tell us our business. We shall do it the safe, easy way, unless perhaps Monsieur would like to go in there himself."

"I do not care how you do it, but do it. We are wasting valuable time."

"Calm yourself, Monsieur Randall; Jean will be back with the lantern in a minute and then you may choose the eye you would like to have shot out."

Randall. Sir Ralph sprang to his feet.

"Randall, you damned fool, listen to me." His voice sounded startlingly loud and hollow in his ears. "You are making a mistake. I am not going back to England."

"You are not going anywhere," Randall said in a high, harsh voice.

"I tell you, I refused Stair's terms. You are murdering me for nothing."

"Save your breath. I saw Lady Sheldon hand you your safe conduct."

"Had you stayed at the window longer, you would have seen me throw it in the fire."

"I don't believe it."

"It is true, I tell you. You won't find it on me."

"That proves nothing. You could pick it up again later. But if you will throw out your sword, we will search you."

"Send your axe men a few paces up the street and I will let you search me yourself."

"Do you think I am a fool?"

"You are if you kill me. The Duke of Berwick will hunt you down and kill you, if Young James doesn't do it himself."

"What is he saying?" a French voice asked.

"I am saying," Ralph translated, "that Monsieur Randall is mistaken. He does not want me killed."

"Mere lies," Randall said in French. "Where is the man with the light?"

"Don't be stupid, gentlemen. You are making a fatal error."

"It makes no difference so long as we are paid."

The click of the hammer and the flash of fire came almost at the same moment. Diving toward the pavement, Ralph felt the explosion crash against his eardrums.

"I hit him," a voice said.

"You hit the door."

Ralph lay on the pavement waiting for the pain to start. I must be shot, he said to himself. It couldn't have missed me.

"Go in and get him," Randall's voice was saying.

"Presently, Monsieur."

They are still afraid, he thought grimly. I must get to my feet before they recover their nerve.

"You should have waited for the light."

Getting to his knees was difficult. His left wrist seemed to be sprained. It would not support him.

"Where is the light? Jean should be here by now."

No, I am not hit, he thought. There is still a chance. From his position on his knees, he jabbed experimentally with his sword. At least I will last till the light comes.

"He is alive. I hear him."

Damn, he thought. Now they won't come in after me. They will wait and shoot me down. Is everyone in the neighborhood dead?

Listening, he could hear nothing except the splash of the rain from the eaves. The wounded man had quit moaning.

"Here comes the light, Monsieur."

Sir Ralph lurched to his feet. No, he would not dash out from the entrance and be stabbed in the back. He would wait for the light. Perhaps he could attack his assailants before they shot him.

"Why doesn't the fool hurry? We don't have all night for this."

It is all too stupid, he said to himself. What a miserable way to die.

"Hurry, you idiot," Randall called.

At the same moment a French voice screamed, "Name of God, the police. Run."

Within an instant, the street was full of sound—running footsteps, yells, and curses. Half a dozen lanterns flashed by the entranceway as they moved down the street. Someone tripped and fell heavily with a clatter of metal not ten feet away. Sir Ralph heard another scream close at hand.

Although his brain registered the sounds and sights clearly, he did not move from his position. He felt as if his body had suddenly gone numb, frozen into its posture of defense.

"There is one here on the ground," a voice said. "I fell over him."

"Is he dead?"

"No. He squealed."

"Keep watch on him."

A lantern had paused momentarily just beyond the entrance, throwing a dim light by which he could see a sword lying on the cobblestones. Then the light moved away. Still he made no sound.

"Ralph, Ralph, where are you?"

He recognized Berwick's voice, yet he could not answer.

"I think he is in there," another voice said.

The light suddenly appearing in the entrance half blinded him. It was a moment before he recognized the familiar form standing behind the lantern.

"So there you are." Berwick's voice was gruff, almost accusing.

"Yes, here I am," he heard himself say—a little surprised and pleased to find his voice.

"I was afraid you were murdered."

"I was afraid too."

"Why don't you put down your sword? D'Argenson is chasing the scoundrels."

"Oh, my sword," he said, lowering the point. "Forgive me. I will be myself again in a minute or two."

"Are you hurt, Ralph?"

"I don't think so," he said. "Nothing more than a sprained wrist."

"Good." Berwick's voice had softened now. "The blood on your clothes startled me. You must have had a brisk battle."

"No. Only one brief skirmish."

He saw Jack's eyes widen. "What is that?"

On looking down, he was astonished to see that his left hand was covered with blood. A red rivulet coursed steadily across his palm, down between his thumb and forefinger.

"It looks as if I have been wounded," he said, half to himself.

Berwick put down the lantern, seized the arm, and rolled back the ripped, blood-soaked sleeve.

"You have been shot," he said, probing with his fingers. "One of the bones in your forearm is smashed."

Sir Ralph said nothing. He stood staring at the wound while Berwick bound it with his handkerchief. In a few minutes, he knew, the shock would wear off and the arm would ache miserably; but for the present there was no sensation.

"My curiosity got the better of me," Jack was saying. "When you did not come home I decided to go meet you at Stair's. On the way over, my coach almost ran down d'Argenson and a half dozen of his police. They were combing the area for Randall and his bully boys. D'Argenson suspected something was in the wind, but he did not know exactly what. As soon as I heard that Randall had employed a gang of cutthroats I knew whose throat he intended to cut. We hurried to Stair's but you had already gone. Since then we have been stumbling around the neighborhood in this cursed rain."

"Don't say anything against the rain. I like it."

"We were half way down this little street when we heard a shot. And here we are. I think d'Argenson has got your men."

Berwick picked up the lantern, and Ralph followed him obediently out into the street. Blobs of light seemed to be everywhere now. Shutters were being thrown open. Voices were yelling out windows. And down the street a short distance a knot of lanterns was approaching.

Trust the Parisians, Sir Ralph thought. Somehow they always know when the police have arrived.

"Ah, here we are, Monsieur."

He recognized d'Argenson's voice before he could make out the man's ugly face.

"We are so glad to see you alive."

"I am glad to be alive," he said. "And grateful to you and your men."

"My apologies, Monsieur, for not getting here sooner."

"Not at all, Monsieur d'Argenson. I consider it a miracle that you arrived when you did."

"You are too kind. Had my information been what it should have been we could have prevented the whole affair."

Sir Ralph hoped he was not swaying. At any moment, he feared, he would begin to shiver.

"I am glad you did not prevent it," he said. "It was very important for Mr. Randall and me to meet again."

"Here he is, Monsieur."

A tall policeman dragged Randall forward by the collar. In the chase Randall had lost his hat. Now the rain was running down his face, making him look like a small, disheveled, tear-streaked boy.

"Well, Randall," Berwick said harshly, "I suppose you know what this means."

The blank expression on Randall's face did not change. He seemed to be looking past Berwick, past d'Argenson and the lanterns, as if he could see gallows in the darkness at the end of the street.

"It means that you will be hanged. Do you understand?"

Randall shifted his weight from his left foot to his right. His left hand absently fumbled with the torn cloth of his coat. Although his Adam's apple moved up and down, no sound came out.

"You must have been insane."

"Not insane," Sir Ralph said. "He was merely trying to save his friends. Isn't that right, Randall?"

There was an almost imperceptible nod of Randall's head.

"But you were mistaken. As I told you before, I am not going back to England."

"That is true," Berwick said. "Lord Stair told me so. But even if he were going back, he would not betray his friends."

"Whatever your motives, Monsieur," d'Argenson said, "I can promise you a speedy and impressive hanging."

"Please, Monsieur d'Argenson." Sir Ralph started to hold up his left hand, but a sharp stab of pain stopped him. "Let us not talk of hanging. If you should wish to send Mr. Randall's friends here to the galleys for a few years I shall not object; but as far as Randall himself is concerned I do not even wish to press charges. I have other plans for him."

D'Argenson's gargoyle countenance broke into a crooked grin.

"Permit me to say, Monsieur Barnard, that you have an odd sense of justice. For me, I am charged with the safety of Paris, and I like to hang assassins."

Sir Ralph looked from d'Argenson to Randall and then to Berwick. He was conscious of the hissing lanterns and of the water trickling down the back of his neck. He wondered whether anyone else had noticed that they were all standing in the rain.

"One must make allowances for special cases, Monsieur," he said. "Not all assassins are alike. Besides, Mr. Randall failed."

"As you will, Monsieur." D'Argenson shrugged. "If you do not wish to accuse Monsieur Randall, I shall not hold him. I must say, however, that if he had tried to kill me, I should have him hanged from the highest steeple in Paris. But then I never expect to understand you English."

"Are you sure you are well, Ralph?" Berwick's voice was troubled. "Perhaps it is the wound."

"Perfectly well," he said, hoping that his teeth would not begin to chatter. "Our friend Randall has done me a favor, and I expect him to do me another."

"A favor?"

"Yes. One might say he has freed me from the Jacobites. Since their agent has tried to kill me, they can hardly have the face to bother me again with their pitiful commissions. This little wound absolves me from any responsibility toward them. I can laugh in their faces if I wish."

He turned to d'Argenson.

"From now on, Monsieur, I am merely a Parisian with an English accent."

"Shall I let the gentleman go now, Monsieur?"

The man holding Randall by the collar moved restlessly forward.

"Wait one moment. I have an errand for him."

Randall's eyes were focussed on him now. Some of the shock had gone out of them.

"Listen carefully, son," Sir Ralph said gently. "I want you to go to Avignon and tell Young James what has happened. He will take the news better from your lips than from an informer. Later, I shall write him a letter to corroborate your account. In all probability he will dismiss you on the spot. At least I hope so. If he does, you will be able to go back to England within two or three years. Do you understand what I am saying?"

He is still dazed, Sir Ralph thought, but I think he comprehends.

"Tell His Majesty that I shall remain in France, but that I want never to see either him or his agents. Do I make myself clear?"

Randall nodded dully.

"You must not despair. Although you don't realize it, you have inadvertently saved yourself from permanent exile. Believe me, the Jacobites will never reconquer England. As for the attempted murder, I hold no grudge. Had I been in your place, at your age, I might have tried the same thing."

"You are shivering, Ralph," Berwick said. "We must be mad too, keeping you out in this drizzle without a cape."

"A thousand pardons, Monsieur. It is inexcusable. You must go in at once. It was the excitement, you understand."

"It is not the rain, Monsieur d'Argenson, but the wound, and perhaps a little horror left over from the ambush. I like the rain. And when I get home I shall be perfectly all right."

"Hurry, gentlemen," he heard d'Argenson say. "Gather up that wounded scoundrel and bring along the others. We cannot stand out here all night. Roger, let Monsieur Randall go. Good night, Your Excellency. Take care of Monsieur Barnard."

Yes, I shall be perfectly all right, he was saying to himself as he allowed Jack to take his arm and guide him down the street toward Jack's carriage. The damned wrist will ache and perhaps be stiff for the rest of my life, maybe I shall have some fever too, but I don't care as long as I get home without fainting.

Voices from the windows were shouting questions at him and Jack and at the police—questions that nobody bothered to answer.

"How do you feel?" Jack said.

"Wet and a little dizzy," he admitted.

"I know that. I mean, how do you feel about staying in France?"

Sir Ralph listened to their footsteps on the cobblestones and the splash of rain from the eaves.

"I am in poor condition to make a judgment," he said finally, "but at the moment I feel optimistic—as if I had won a battle. Tomorrow, I suppose, there will be a reaction."

"Henriette will be glad to stay, I think."

"I think so too, although she would have been glad to go."

"I suppose you will send the boys to school in England."

"Yes, I suppose so, in two or three years. I can't think about it right now."

"You saw Lady Sheldon."

"Yes, I saw her."

"She didn't try to help you?"

"No."

He feared he was leaning heavily on Jack's shoulder. If so, Jack did not seem to notice.

"I think you were wrong about Randall," Jack was saying. "You should have let him be hanged. I have never heard of such cold-blooded villainy."

"I couldn't do it," he said slowly. "You see, I am responsible for him."

"I see that you are getting feverish. Don't try to talk any more. We will reach the coach in a minute."

"You see," he went on, "I once planned an assassination myself."

"You will be all right in a few minutes. Henriette has some soup prepared. I will get you a stiff drink of brandy."

"I have often regretted not going through with my plan; but now, illogically enough, I don't regret anything."

"You are chilled to the bone, Ralph. There are some blankets in the coach."

Sir Ralph smiled to himself. No doubt Jack thought he was raving. And perhaps he was—the old problems all seemed abstract and unreal. But the rain felt cold and refreshing on the back of his neck. He could see now that he would reach the coach without being carried.

"On the contrary, Jack," he said. "I feel better. Take care, when we get home, that you don't alarm Henriette."

"You may rely upon me," Berwick said, opening the coach door. "Be careful of that arm now. At this stage of affairs I can't let anything happen to you. Henriette would never forgive me."